MASTER OF THE WILDERNESS

MOUNTAIN MASTERS & DARK HAVEN BOOK
BOOK 10

CHERISE SINCLAIR

VanScoy Publishing Group

Master of the Wilderness
Copyright © 2023 by Cherise Sinclair
ISBN 978-1-947219-50-2
Published by VanScoy Publishing Group
Cover Design: The Killion Group
Cover photograph of Andrew Flanagan by FuriousFotog
Content editing: I'm No Angel
Line editing: Red Quill

This book is a work of fiction. The names, characters, places, and incidents are products of the writer's imagination or have been used fictitiously and are not to be construed as real. Any resemblance to persons, living or dead, actual events, locales, business establishments, or organizations is entirely coincidental.

All rights reserved. No part of this eBook may be used, including but not limited to the training or or use by artificial intelligence, or reproduced, scanned, or distributed in any manner whatsoever without prior written permission from the author, except in the case of brief quotations embodied in critical articles and reviews.

Warning: This book contains sexually explicit scenes and adult language and may be considered offensive to some readers. This book is for sale to adults only, as defined by the laws of the country in which you made your purchase.

Disclaimer: Please do not try any new sexual practice, without the guidance of an experienced practitioner. Neither the publisher nor the author will be responsible for any loss, harm, injury, or death resulting from use of the information contained in this book.

This book is licensed for your personal enjoyment only. This book may not be re-sold or given away to other people. If you would like to share this book with another person, please purchase an additional copy for each recipient. If you're reading this book and did not purchase it, or it was not purchased for your use only, please purchase your own copy.

Thank you for respecting the hard work of this author.

ACKNOWLEDGMENTS

I have the most fantastic people in my life to help me create these books.

My wonderful writing buddies, Monette Michaels and Fiona Archer, have been here for me through brainstorming to blurbing to critting. (And they patiently listen to my whining).

Leagh Christensen and Lisa Simo-Kinzer and my amazing Shadowkittens on FB offer ideas and input. I hope you know how your enthusiasm keeps me returning to the keyboard each day.

Multi-talented Bianca Sommerland handled the content editing, and JJ Foster did an alpha read. Thank you so much! It's always good when a story makes sense, right?

As for fixing mistakes... I have mega-appreciation for my incredible Red Quill editors—Ekatarina Sayanova, Tracy Damron-Roelle, Rebecca Cartee.

Big squishy hugs go to Barb Jack, Lisa White, and Marian Shulman, my beta readers for their super-keen reading abilities.

Finally, you, my readers—thank you so much for everything you do—your emails, your reviews, the way you recommend my books to your friends, and simply your enthusiasm. It means a lot to me.

I'm so very grateful to each and every one of y'all!

AUTHOR'S NOTE - NEW

To my readers,

I love when my adorable Facebook Shadowkittens discuss my books. I learn a lot...and ran into a couple of concerns which I'd like to tackle before you dive into this story.

Pull up a chair, my dears...

First: There is a gray area of consent in fiction—btw, if it's not fiction, there had better be *no* gray area, got it? There are a lot of us who love a power imbalance fantasy where a Dominant knows what you want and will push you into getting exactly what you need. They will touch without permission, will employ subtle coercion, will go past what is accepted behavior in real life. (I even gave y'all a super-empathic psychologist so I could get away with it. lol).

I know you've seen this in my stories—especially the early ones before I realized some readers new to BDSM might not realize I was crossing lines. I wanted to play in the edgier fantasy yet also provide examples of what honest power exchanges look like.

My darlings, the bad news is that in real life, you *have* to use your words, to negotiate for what you want—and even more, to set out what you don't want. Where are your boundaries? What are your limits? Don't forget that Dominants also have boundaries.

And if you forget to set up a safe word, I'm going to be seriously pissed off.

The negotiations in BDSM are part of building trust and can be a lovely, drawn-out dance—as much fun as foreplay is in making love. Just do it.

Second: let's talk about a Dominant exploring your limits. Since I, personally, love being pushed, you'll find lots of it in my fiction. Many enjoy having their boundaries challenged (by someone they trust) and riding that rush of fearful anticipation. It's a yummy excitement.

However! Not everyone feels this way. If you're someone with hard and fast limits and want them respected—you are absolutely not alone. For people like you, a Dominant who pushes your boundaries will lose your trust. And that's okay.

Just as some submissives want boundaries honored, some Dominants are pleased, even relieved, to know where and when they should stop.

The hard part is knowing yourself (and this is a lifelong process, right?) and communicating it clearly to your partner.

When I was in England, we toured gardens. Some were formal, with perfectly arranged flower beds, paths, and fountains that created a refreshing sense of order. Others were cottage gardens with exuberant flowers spilling over the paths and no clear boundaries. Both styles were equally wonderful. And that is the beauty of BDSM—you choose.

So, be careful out there. Communicate, have your safe word, have a back-up person. While you're doing your negotiating, make sure your consent is clear, explicit, informed, and enthusiastic. And have a lovely, safe time.

All my love,
Cherise

CHAPTER ONE

Today, I'm asking for a divorce. Erin Lockwood Palmer barely managed not to crush the grapes in her hand.

No, Erin, don't think about the divorce right now.

Instead, she smiled at the ten-year-old boy who was sitting on the floor beside her. "Want the ammunition for the catapult?" She handed him some grapes.

Bobby examined the fruit suspiciously. "How's something like this gonna break a castle wall?"

Kids are so fun. She chuckled and looked around the living room. "Hmm. We seem to be lacking a castle to aim at. And, since we're inside the house, if we use big boulders or stones like a war catapult, we'll break the windows. So...grapes."

A huff of agreement came from Delilah who was mopping the marble tiled entry. "Don't you dare go busting up the house, boy." Dressed tidily in dark jeans and a tucked-in shirt, the housekeeper had brassy red hair with matching lipstick. She'd arrived today, full of apologies that her daughter was ill and so Delilah had her grandson with her.

Erin didn't mind at all. Aside from being a fantastic kid, Bobby made the time go faster. She glanced at the clock, feeling

1

dread building inside. Today, when Troy got back from Washington, DC, she'd give him the divorce papers.

Even if he didn't want her, he wouldn't react politely to her being the one to initiate cutting ties. A tremor of worry ran through her, making her shake inside.

With an effort, she turned her attention back to the child and the catapult they'd built with pencils, masking tape, rubber bands, and a bottle cap. "Tell you what, when you play outside, you can use rocks."

Not that playing outside would happen today. She glanced at the rain-streaked windows.

"Cooool." Satisfied with the stone versus grapes compromise, the boy arranged the opposing toy soldiers in a line farther away, set one grape into the bottle cap launcher, and pulled the catapult arm back. He released, and the fruit went flying.

Perfect.

Bobby cheered, fist pumping in the air.

"Very good." Erin tilted her head. "But what were you aiming at?"

"The Greek army."

"It appears you missed. Why would that be?"

He frowned. "Cuz the catapult kinda bounced?"

"Exactly." She tapped the Roman soldier standing next to the catapult. "Your soldier engineer here would be scrounging something to weigh down the base."

As Bobby worked on taping the bottom to a heavy piece of cardboard, Erin grinned. Teaching a child how to build toys and fix ensuing problems until everything worked as designed made her mechanic's heart happy.

A couple of adjustments later, the grape struck the opposing force and knocked down a wide swathe of toy soldiers.

The cheering was loud enough to bring Delilah into the room.

"If you're done, my boy, we must be off. Congressman Palmer is due home today," Delilah said.

Erin suppressed a sigh. Her husband had made it clear to staff that he didn't want to interact with them. "Yes, his flight from Washington should be in anytime now."

He'd be in a foul mood. The flight from the East Coast to Sacramento was a long one.

Bobby scrambled to his feet.

"Here, sweetie, take this with you. Anyone who enjoys history should have his own catapult."

Bobby stared at her with shining eyes. "Thank you, Ms. Palmer."

"You're very welcome."

"Now don't forget to change, Ms. Palmer." Delilah gave a meaningful wave toward Erin's clothing.

"Oh, right." Erin eyed her dirty jeans and T-shirt. She'd spent most of the day at a local auto shop where she was restoring a classic 1970 Chevy Corvette. "Thanks for reminding me."

No need to get Troy huffy before their discussion.

She waved goodbye as Delilah and Bobby hurried out.

After a quick shower and putting on pants and a nice shirt, Erin tucked away the clutter from the catapult build. A glance around showed everything was impeccably clean in the room that was a shining example of...bland.

Off-white walls, cream-colored furniture, beige carpet. Much like the luncheons for politicians' wives, the house was adamantly neutral. Her husband had owned it before they married and wasn't about to change the decorating scheme for her. Not in the almost three years they'd been married.

Now there wouldn't be—

Her phone dinged with an announcement from the airlines. Troy's flight had landed. He'd soon be on his way from the airport.

The countdown had begun.

Oh God, I'm really going to do this. Her breathing sped up until she took control of it with slow, deep inhalations.

After glancing at the clock, she nodded. Just enough time to work on the gardener's daughter's laptop. The girl had been in tears after her beloved laptop died, so her father asked if Erin would take a look. He knew Erin loved fixing things. *All* the things, from cars to high-tech devices.

But not when Troy was home.

He didn't think wives of ultra-conservative politicians should have any profession at all and certainly shouldn't be some grease-covered mechanic. She was supposed to be gracious, supportive, and provide him with a baby or two to complete the image of him as a loving husband dedicated to old-fashioned values.

Politicians' wives had to be the most boring people in the world. Who could be interesting when every word must be examined for possible offense, political correctness, and implications to the husband's status?

When she told Troy it wasn't right to be so artificial, he'd mansplained how politicians serve the country. Since her behavior reflected on him, if she upset people, they wouldn't want to work with him. He went on to add that what he was asking of her was a very small sacrifice to keep the government running smoothly.

She rolled her eyes. What with having a senator mother, she'd learned proper etiquette almost before she could walk. But...there was inoffensive behavior—and there was stifling all individuality. Her husband wanted a Stepford Wife.

Frowning, she set out her smaller toolbox and the laptop. For Troy, she'd given up her job, her goals, even her personality, to help further his career.

It'd taken her nearly two years to realize what was happening. But when she told him she thought they should end their marriage, he'd cried and said he needed her. Begged her to stay.

So she had and then realized why he hadn't wanted her to leave. Because he'd been up for re-election. Because a divorce would ruin his pro-family brand. Because he wanted her mom's influence to help him win.

I've been a fool. But now I'm done.

After a glance at the clock, she plugged in the laptop. No boot up screen. She listened—nothing had come to life.

She tried a different cord. Nothing. So...not the cord. It wasn't powering on at all. No fan noise even. *Maybe the battery.* Erin pulled out a micro screwdriver to open the case, as content as a rabbit in clover.

After a few minutes, she flipped on the television, needing something to combat the silence.

She used to watch the news faithfully. Troy made fun of her if she didn't stay current with what was going on in the world. Seriously, though, who wanted to know? Face it, the news media twisted the headlines to present the most worrisome aspects of anything going on.

"Tell me, oh television, what disaster has occurred today to terrify the masses?" She bent her head and pried open the laptop.

The newscasters blathered away, blackening her mood.

In world news: people killing other people, governments being shaken apart, a tornado here, a hurricane there. US news: shootings, hate crimes, and appallingly ignorant politicians spouting a bunch of fearmongering. It burned how they received more airtime than the intelligent ones.

She grumbled under her breath and kept working.

California news: the dry weather, water shortages, latest wildfires, a corrupt politician. "We have the latest news about Congressman Troy Palmer, who—

Erin snapped her head up in time to see the picture of her husband. *What in the world?*

The male newscaster assumed a concerned expression. "Yes, more questions have been raised regarding how the construction of a private prison near Bear Flat, California, got approved."

Oh, this could get ugly. But was Troy involved? Erin shook her head. Surely Mr. Perfect himself wouldn't have broken the law.

Last year, the prison was in the news when convicts staged a riot and broke out. She'd been shocked, especially since their

5

vacation home was just outside Bear Flat. Further investigations revealed that the private prison shouldn't have been built at all, having failed the environmental impact studies. The facility had been shut down.

Would Troy really have taken bribes to open a prison?

She bit her lip, trying to believe in his integrity. But she couldn't. When it came to getting ahead, he would manipulate people, would do or say anything.

Like how he'd lied to get her to marry him.

She'd been so naïve. After dropping out of college at twenty-one and spending two years caring for her dying grandparents, she was still mourning Grammie and Grampie when she'd met Mr. Charming. She'd fallen hard. He was everything any girl could want. He'd listened to her, acted like she was his whole world, been so loving.

And she'd adored him. Why hadn't she seen he needed her mother's influence to help him climb the political ladder? Mom had been a powerful, popular US Senator, and of course she'd helped her daughter's new husband.

Because Mom loved me.

Tears burned Erin's eyes. "I miss you so much, Mom." Her death three months ago had been unexpected. Erin's flight to Washington, DC had taken too long; the heart attack had been too massive. There'd been no chance to say goodbye.

Although Troy had attended the funeral for the media coverage of him accepting condolences from Washington's movers and shakers, he hadn't returned home afterward. Hadn't been there when she was grieving.

Because I'm not useful to him any longer.

While Mom was alive, he'd gone through the motions of being a loving husband. Since her death, he had become increasingly scornful—or maybe she should say, more blatantly scornful.

"You're worthless. No connections—not anymore."

"You don't have any networking skills. Won't even make speeches."

"What good are you to me anyway?"

At the last fundraising dinner, when she'd met him there, he'd hissed at her under his breath while flashing a smile for everyone around them. *"Jesus, can't you make an effort to at least be pretty? God knows you can't talk to anyone, but if you're going to be quiet, at least be ornamental."*

His contemptuous remarks had hurt...but forced her to see how many times he'd said similar things over the years.

When they'd had sex before he left for DC, she was desperate to see if there was anything left between them. But he was aloof, even cold, during and after. When she tried to talk to him about it, he scoffed. "You're overreacting, as always. Maybe if you were any good in bed, I'd be more engaged."

That...had been the last straw. She'd felt so numb, she hadn't even cried. Because it was over. In truth, she didn't love him any longer—hadn't loved him for a long while. In fact, she was far happier when he was gone.

I deserve better. I do.

She'd filled out the divorce papers the very next day.

Considering the things he'd said—and that her mother couldn't help him any longer—she couldn't imagine he'd be very upset about a divorce. Yet a shiver of worry ran through her.

But her hands continued to work, repairing the laptop for the little girl.

When she saw Troy's car turn into the driveway, she hastily packed everything away in her small toolbox and returned it to her sitting room closet.

Just in time.

The front door opened, and Troy stopped in the doorway, complaining about something. Behind him, a man laughed.

Who was with him?

All her muscles were tight as she stood in the center of the living room. Now she regretted not moving out and hiring a process server to deliver the divorce papers.

No, this way was best. If at all possible, she'd keep this amicable. Reasonable.

Should she ask about the bribery investigation?

Bad idea. Bringing up his misdeeds would make it sound as if she was bailing out for that reason, rather than because she was simply done with him.

He walked in. His brother, Emmett, the CEO of Confinement Corp International came in behind him. Both were mid-thirties, around five-eleven, blond, blue-eyed, and clean-shaven.

Despite the long flight from the other side of the country, Troy's hair was still perfectly styled, and his well-tailored suit unwrinkled. He glanced at her. "Erin."

She pulled in a breath. "Welcome back. How was your flight?"

"As annoying as usual."

Emmett smiled at her, polite as always. "Erin, my dear, how are you?"

She suppressed a sigh. Why'd he have to be here, anyway? "Fine, thank you. And you?"

"Good. I'm sorry to disturb my brother's homecoming." He turned to Troy. "If you'll get those papers, I'll be on my way."

"Of course." Troy headed down the hall to his office at the end.

"Erin, I'm glad you're here for Troy." Emmett shook his head. "Those allegations about Bear Flat are hard on him."

She stiffened. A divorce would look as if she wasn't standing behind him. As if she thought he might be guilty.

Then again, it was what she did think.

Rather than blurting something out, she simply murmured a noncommittal, "He does look tired." Between her mother's career and Troy's, she was well versed in how to say nothing when surrounded by verbal landmines.

Footsteps heralded Troy's return.

"Thank you." Emmett took the manila envelope from him. "I'll call you tomorrow and find out how things are going."

Troy smiled. "I'm sure it'll go well."

Emmett nodded to Erin. "It was good seeing you, Erin."

"Have a nice evening, Emmett."

As the door closed behind his brother, Troy headed back down the hall to his office. "I'll be ready for dinner in an hour."

She stared after him, feeling deflated. Ugly.

Angry.

He couldn't even be polite?

Well then, let's get this over with.

Although California had an annoying, mandatory waiting period of six months before the divorce would be finalized, she was moving out tomorrow.

In her sitting room, she used the bathroom. Splashed cold water on her face. Breathed.

With the divorce papers and checklist in hand, she walked down the hall toward Troy's office. Realizing she was hanging her head like a child, she stopped...and narrowed her eyes. Interesting. The off-white carpet here was almost gray with ground-in dirt.

Amusement tickled her throat. Last year, when Delilah was hired, she'd cleaned his office. Troy had yelled at her, ranting that no one, including Erin, was to enter his office.

From the looks of the dust, the housekeeper had been avoiding even the hallway.

That makes two of us.

The door was closed—as usual—and Erin put her hand on the knob. But she could hear Troy talking. He must be on the phone.

His angry voice grew louder. "Listen here, Senator. Either your committee deals with the problem we spoke about...or the news media will get several nice pictures of you with a thirteen-year-old boy." Troy's tone took on a sneer. "Very *graphic* pictures."

Erin snatched her hand away from the door and took a step back.

"Blackmail? Let's not be harsh, Silas. We'll just say a favor for a favor. You enjoyed the party in New York. And the party *favors*. Now it's time to do some quid pro quo, so to speak."

No. Erin's throat closed. What he was talking about *was* blackmail. Was her husband pandering children? For political favors?

It was all...all illegal. *Horrendous.* Her stomach turned over.

Backing away from the door, she retreated down the hall and into the living room. Grabbing her purse, she jumped in her car and left.

And asked her phone for directions to the nearest FBI office.

CHAPTER TWO

What an awful month. With every mile she drove away from Sacramento, Erin could feel her heart grow lighter. Turning off Highway 120, she headed down smaller roads and onto the narrow Kestrel Mountain Road. The engine's purr deepened as the road grew steeper. Not far after the turnoff to Whiskey Creek Lane, she turned down the small, barely visible dirt road through the trees.

At the end was the vacation home Mom had given her for a wedding present. Mom knew Troy would enjoy it during hunting season but had put it in Erin's name only. Thank goodness. Troy had owned the Sacramento house before they married, and he had sole title.

This place was hers. And she needed it badly since, before he fled the country, Troy had cleaned out their accounts and investments. The annual payment from her mother's trust fund had been in their joint account and was gone too.

The bastard. Somehow, he'd gotten word before the FBI showed up to arrest him. He was probably lounging on a tropical beach without a care in the world.

But her? She'd be lucky to keep her head above water. As her eyes filled with tears, she blinked hard.

The last month had been ghastly.

At least her divorce papers were filed. She'd jumped through all the hoops needed for dumping a missing spouse. It would still be months before finalization.

The police interrogations...uh, *interviews*...were finished along with their searches of the Sacramento house, Troy's condo in DC, his office, and even the vacation home here.

They'd gone through all their financial papers. Her fingers tightened on the steering wheel. An FBI agent—a forensic accountant—had shown her Troy's credit card statements for jewelry and women's clothing. There were hotel receipts for Sacramento as well as at luxury resorts for times he was supposedly at political conventions.

He'd been cheating on her.

Seeing Erin's shock, the female agent had gently suggested she get tested for STDs.

God. The agent's sympathy had helped. Not everyone in the world was vile.

However, the press came close. Thankfully, when her statements to the reporters that she knew nothing and had nothing to say didn't change, their interest in her died down. Maybe there was a benefit to appearing as dull as Troy characterized her.

So...he was gone. And she was starting over. Picking up the life she'd abandoned to keep him happy.

Her chin rose. She would use this time and space to remember who she truly was.

In the clearing before the two-story house, she parked near the front steps. The utility trailer she'd towed behind the SUV wouldn't fit in the garage.

Juggling bags of groceries, she headed inside the house and stopped at the panel inside the door to input the security code.

After dropping her sacks on the kitchen counter, she walked into the great room. One wall was all windows, overlooking the pastoral valley down below and the encircling mountains. Light streamed in like a benediction of peace.

Thank you, Mom, for this sanctuary. For teaching me about love and loyalty.

She lowered the temperature setting in the fridge and put her groceries away, then adjusted the thermostat for the heat pump. In late May, nights in the mountains were still darn cold.

Suitcase by suitcase, box by box, she unloaded her SUV and the small utility trailer. She didn't have enough possessions to require a moving van. Before marrying Troy, she'd only spent a couple of years at college before returning home to care for Grammie and Grampie. She'd always be grateful to have had those last two years with them before they'd died.

All the furniture in the Sacramento house was Troy's. She'd left it there.

Ruthlessly thinning what she did own, she'd donated to charities and made lots of presents to the staff and her mechanic friends. The so-stylish clothing Troy preferred her in went to Delilah's daughter. Bobby got an antique clock Erin had restored for Troy's office and a spare eReader. The large coffee-maker-espresso machine went to Delilah.

She'd packed up the few items her grandparents and mother had left her. She brought those along with the clothing she'd kept, personal belongings, and of course, her hobby stuff and tools. Lots and lots of tools.

She'd sold the black gas-guzzler Troy had insisted she drive for the "right image", along with the two classic cars she hadn't finished restoring. The small, practical SUV she'd bought was capable of handling the mountain roads even if she was only here long enough to sell this house.

Bear Flat was...tiny. What with Mom in DC, her grandparents in San Francisco, and Troy in Sacramento, she'd lived in cities all her life.

She'd only visited here a few times to escape the heat in the valley. Although the forest surrounding the house was beautiful, she hadn't even attempted hiking. Face it, she had no sense of direction, and someone had totally forgotten to put street signs on the evergreens.

Using the vacation home for political networking, Troy had been here much more often with various VIPs. In the fall, he'd hire a guide and take his guests hunting.

She'd come with him the first time and never again. To kill a harmless animal and boast about it? *No. Just no.*

Walking into the bedroom with a suitcase, she frowned at the off-white walls and tan bedspread. Was the beautiful old quilt from Grammie's house still in the storage boxes?

Speaking of bedding, the sheets and blankets were rumpled, half on the floor. Troy had been here last month. *The lazy clod.* Scowling, she yanked the sheets off the bed.

And the distinctive stink of stale perfume and sex wafted to her nose.

He'd brought some woman here. *To my house.* And had sex with her here. In their bed.

God. Erin's stomach turned over, and she barely made it to the bathroom in time to throw up.

Afterward, she wiped her streaming eyes and brushed her teeth. When was the last time she'd vomited? Probably in college when she'd discovered that drinking tequila shots was a stupid idea?

Getting involved with a man was also a stupid idea. Never again.

In the hall closet, she found spare bedding. The storage box yielded Grammie's quilt. After the soiled bedding was in the laundry—on the sanitize setting—she cleaned the house and dumped everything of Troy's in the garbage. Especially the mounted antlers.

So cathartic.

Eventually, the whole house was spotless. The breeze through the wide-open windows had cleared away the musty scents. A citrus-scented candle filled the air with cheer.

Moving room to room, she unpacked Grampie's restored antique clocks. The banjo clock replaced the ugly antlers in the great room. The adorable cuckoo clock he'd used to teach her about restoration went into the kitchen. Her nightstand in the bedroom got the 19th century gilt bronze clock with angels.

She dug into the next storage box. Tiny yellow and pink bud vases she'd bought in college went to the kitchen windowsill. One of Grammie's paintings of sunflowers in front of a weathered barn replaced the photo of Troy with his foot on a dead buck. Bright blue and gold throw pillows and blankets from her grandparents' house brightened the couch.

There were past gifts from her mother too. A quirky, blue-framed mirror to hang over the entryway table. Several rainbow-colored candles for the fireplace mantle.

She turned in satisfaction. *Yes, now, the house feels more like me.*

Moving outside, she pulled the deck furniture out of the storage room, opened the sun umbrella, and filled the hot tub.

Coming back inside, she felt as if someone had attached lead weights to her feet. *Lord, I'm tired.*

Time for a break. She made herself a quick deli ham and cheese sandwich and took it out onto the long deck.

The sun's rays up here, around four thousand feet, could scorch the skin, but the air beneath the shade of the umbrella was the perfect temperature. She sipped her iced tea, nibbled on her sandwich, and considered her dismal prospects.

The small amount of money in her personal savings account —the only account Troy hadn't been able to empty—wouldn't last long.

She sighed at the beautiful view of the valley. The peaceful forest setting was now all hers. But she wasn't a small-town girl, and she needed money.

Tomorrow, I'll go to the real estate company in town. The market in California was good, right? Surely this fabulous vacation home would get snapped right up.

Then she'd select a city and start job hunting.

Sell quickly please.

CHAPTER THREE

Wyatt Masterson eased carefully out of the pickup's passenger seat. The gravel road to the family ranch sure hadn't improved since he left last August, and the rough ride had pulled on the stitches in the bullet gash along his side. The fucking knots caught on everything. DeVries' suture technique could use some work.

My fault, letting a sadist patch up my wounds.

He pulled his duffel bag from the back. "Thanks for the lift, Cliff."

"No problem, Masterson." The gray-haired cop worked with Virgil, Wyatt's older brother, who unfortunately, had already left the police station. But since Cliff was off duty, he'd offered to drop Wyatt at the house. "Good to see you back where you belong."

As the pickup headed back down the drive, Wyatt turned to face the massive two-story log house. Originally, it'd been a regular three-bedroom home. His father had built on when his three sons were young and added another section when Cousin Kallie joined them. As his children reached adulthood, Pa had radically enlarged the place to create apartments for each of them—and himself too.

His scheme of keeping them close had worked, even past his death four years ago. Of course, Kallie moved out when she married. Wyatt, Virgil, and Morgan still lived here.

Maybe because there isn't a prettier place in the world.

To the left, conifers covered the mountain slope and filled the air with a sharp piney fragrance. On the right, cattle and horses grazed wide pastures green with spring growth. Closer in were the traditional red barn, stable, and outbuildings.

Nostalgia caught in his throat at the scent of horses and hay. He could almost hear his mother asking Pa, "*Where have those rascals gotten off to?*" Could feel his brothers shaking with laughter as they hid up in the hay loft. Virgil always caved in first. "*We're here, Mom.*" Because big brother didn't like breaking the rules. Hell, Virg had probably been born holding a badge.

Wyatt shook his head. It was a long time since childhood and a long time since Mom died in a car accident, leaving three boys and a grief-stricken husband. Kallie joined them later—and pulled them closer in a lot of ways.

When Pa died of a heart attack four years back, it helped to think maybe he and Mom met up again in whatever afterlife there was. She would've waited for him; that was who she was.

The Masterson Wilderness Guides business continued with Wyatt, Morgan, and Kallie. Pa had left them the house and a business they all loved.

Closing his eyes, Wyatt breathed in, felt the brisk wind off the high mountains, heard the screech of a hawk hunting mice in the pastures. Something inside him relaxed.

Yeah, he was home.

Now to face his brothers. He snorted. With all the fancy sayings about coming home, no one ever mentioned that home was where you went, knowing your family would give you hell.

Because that was what brothers did. At least in this family.

Admittedly, he probably shouted more than the rest combined. At least, he had in the past. Things changed; people changed.

He'd changed.

But maybe not that much. This place had always been home, and the guide business exactly what he wanted to do with his life. Maybe he'd needed time away, but damn, it was good to be back. Here he'd stay—and with luck, there'd be no more shootings or deaths or violence.

A man could hope.

Wyatt opened the front door into the entry, removed his boots, and strolled across the living room in stocking feet.

From the kitchen came Virgil's deep rumble and his wife Sunny's melodic voice. Morgan was there, too, with a quiet, smooth baritone.

Wyatt paused a moment. Yeah, he'd missed them, especially Morgan. Morgan was a year younger—fuck, were they really in their thirties now?—and they'd been a team for everything all their lives. Well, except for women. They'd tried sharing a woman. Although interesting, a threesome was a tad *too* close.

He'd worried what would happen when his brothers found women to love, but when Virgil married Sunny, she fit into their lives like a puzzle piece they'd been missing. Hopefully, Morgan would have the same good taste.

Me, though, maybe not. He'd hoped to find a woman for himself, someone like his mother had been—practical but so very loving, someone who joyfully embraced life and new experiences. But he'd given up on that hope. It was all right though. Short-term relationships were just fine.

And he unquestionably had the best of families.

Okay, let's do this. To announce himself, he thumped the coffee table on the way past. There were too many weapons in the house, and his carcass sure didn't need another bullet wound.

With a flurry of barking, a small dog shot into the living room and danced around Wyatt in happiness.

"Yo, Patches." He bent and stroked the Cavalier spaniel, all brown floppy ears, soft brown and white fur, and huge brown eyes.

"Who's there?" Virgil was halfway across the kitchen when Wyatt reached the doorway. Apparently, the three had been eating supper at the small kitchen table rather than in the dining room.

Wyatt felt his chest tighten again at the sight of his brothers.

Virgil, the oldest, had inherited Pa's massive frame along with Mom's light brown hair and hazel eyes.

Like Wyatt, Morgan got Pa's dark brown hair but had blue-gray eyes from their grandmother rather than brown. They all had the same build, with Wyatt an inch shorter than Virgil, and Morgan an inch shorter than Wyatt.

They stared at him.

"Fucking-A, bro." Morgan charged. "Where've you been?"

Before Wyatt could dodge, he was grabbed in a hard hug—and he flinched.

Morgan released him immediately and stepped back, eyes narrowed. "You're hurt."

"Nothing serious—just a bit banged up."

Taking Morgan's place, Virgil gripped Wyatt's shoulders, his gaze on the stitches on Wyatt's slashed face and the fading red marks visible above his beard.

"You got burned." Sunny pushed her husband to one side. She was an appealing, little blue-eyed blonde. Her parents had the right idea naming her Summer, and her "Sunny" nickname fit even better. "And the stitches on your face are...from a *knife*?"

"Machete—just the tip, thank fuck." He grinned. "That'll teach me not to mess around with sharp tools."

"What else?" Her gaze swept over him, stopped at his arm where bandages made the sleeve bulge, and her eyes narrowed. She was sweet as pie until she stepped into her RN shoes, which was why he wasn't going to mention bullet wounds. "What's there?"

"My arm got scorched. Mostly second-degree." He moved his shoulders. "Village buildings burn fast."

"Do you need something for pain?" Sunny's big blue eyes filled with worry. "Burns are very painful. You must be hurting."

"Nah, it's all good. It was almost two weeks ago."

She poured him a glass of water and set it on the sturdy, oak kitchen table. "Drink up. You need to keep hydrated. Are you hungry?"

"Not just yet, thank you, blondie."

Virgil's a lucky man.

"This is why you're so late getting home?" Morgan planted his sock-covered foot on a chair, resting his forearms on his thigh. "The burns?"

"First, I'm sorry I was gone so long." He met Morgan's eyes. "I know it left you and Kallie working way too hard. Thank you."

Morgan simply shrugged. "You're back. Now explain the burns."

"So...I'm late because when I was booking a flight home, a different organization asked me to help deliver humanitarian food supplies to other countries. Someone on their team had to cancel."

"How'd they know you were available?" Sunny started picking up the empty plates.

Wyatt snorted. "Apparently, two people having a fun time in San Francisco told deVries when I was leaving Ethiopia."

Joining his wife in cleaning off the table, Virgil glanced at Wyatt and repeated, "A fun time?" To Wyatt's delight, although his big brother chuckled, his ears pinkened slightly.

Sunny flushed so hard her freckles disappeared under an avalanche of red.

Because their *fun* time had been spent at a BDSM club.

Morgan frowned. "DeVries?"

"You've met him," Wyatt said. "Virg and Atticus helped him rescue his woman from bad guys a year or two ago. The shootout."

"Ah, right." Morgan's eyes lit with laughter when he looked at their big brother. The straitlaced cop. "A fun time in San Francisco, hmm?"

Not so straitlaced.

Nothing happened in their small town Morgan and Wyatt didn't hear about eventually, so they knew Virgil and Sunny participated in the Hunt brothers' kinky parties up at Serenity Lodge. It'd been a fucking shock when Cousin Kallie fell for Jake Hunt and joined the BDSM activities.

Of course, Kallie and Virgil didn't have a clue Wyatt—and Morgan—also enjoyed kink.

No need for them to know, although when Virgil added a chase-the-subbie game to one of their Fourth of July parties or when Wyatt guided Serenity Lodge's backcountry BDSM specials, he was sorely tempted to join in.

Still, for the sake of their guide service business, it was best to keep the Dom side of his nature hidden.

And since Virgil didn't have a clue, there would be plenty of opportunities to tease big bro and Sunny. Wyatt smiled. "I think I'll blame you for these burns, what with deVries knowing I would be available."

Morgan stifled a laugh and shot Wyatt a conspirator's wink.

For a moment, it was like Wyatt had never left.

CHAPTER FOUR

Hearing the muffled sound of cars the next morning, Wyatt yawned and sat up in bed. His gritty eyes felt as though he had sandpaper under the lids. He eyed the bedside clock. Seven in the morning.

Right. Where he'd been in Africa was close to twelve hours different; it'd be around six in the evening there. No wonder he felt like hell. *Jet lag, one of hell's tiny gifts.*

With a groan, he hauled his ass out of bed. The next couple of days would be miserable until his body clock adjusted. *Suck it up.*

Last night, they hadn't stayed up too late since Morgan had to pick up a group of fishermen early this morning. Virgil had his cop job, and Sunny was a nurse at the Bear Flat Medical Clinic.

The house would be empty since she'd started taking her dog to work. Patches apparently made an excellent therapy dog, especially for children getting shots. Wyatt scratched his chin. He sure could've used a silky-soft, doggy diversion when deVries stitched up his face and side.

After a quick shower, he cooked up a mess of bacon and eggs and had a satisfying breakfast. Funny how much he'd missed cooking in the kitchen where he'd grown up.

Once the dishes were cleared away, he took a trail up the slope to his private campsite. Years ago, Pa had each kid choose a quiet location, a private place to deal with anger, frustrations, and grief. With four people—later, five with Kallie—under one roof, there were times a person needed somewhere to be alone.

Half covered with pine needles and branches, river rocks marked the turnoff. He stopped to tidy the rocks, then followed the familiar path laterally along the slope until he came to what he considered his very own mountain creek.

It gurgled musically, and the water was so clear he could see every rock in the streambed. Farther down, the creek joined others to make the hefty stream that flowed through the pastures.

The air here was moist, and he breathed deeply as he took a seat on the log bench he'd constructed in his teens. Another sense of homecoming swept through him.

My place. He'd never brought anyone to his sanctuary, not Morgan or Kallie, not even Anastasia, who he'd loved and hoped to marry.

This was where he'd raged against every death to impact his soul, starting with the passing of ranch dogs, cats, and horses. Later, when he was a teen, Mom's death shredded his heart. All their hearts. When Pa died, it felt as if the ground beneath him had cracked.

And far, far too soon after Pa, his bright Anastasia had drowned in San Francisco Bay, so far from him. Leaving him in a darker world.

Since then, he avoided getting involved. Cowardly? Yes, of course it was, and he didn't give a fuck.

Of course, there were also times he himself had caused a death—like the convict he'd killed to save Atticus during the prison breakout. The volunteer work in Ethiopia had been to atone for that death, and yeah, it'd helped. Only...he had to kill again.

Death—whether of loved ones or men he'd killed—left marks on his soul.

Here in this hidden spot, thanks to Pa, he had a place where he could just...feel. Whenever it seemed as if the world was all about mortality, he could come here and watch the water flow. The leaves would turn brown; snow would cover the dying grass, then in the spring, everything would turn green again.

The greatest gift of the universe was hope.

After a few long, slow breaths, he settled into meditating, a skill he'd learned last summer from their neighbor Mallory—the most peaceful person he knew. As time passed, this quiet contemplation had become a familiar ritual.

Who would've thought?

An hour later, he went back down the trail, passing the hen house. Huh. Might as well get back into doing ranch chores. It'd be a day or two before he was up to cleaning out stalls, but he could certainly handle the light stuff.

In the chicken yard, the rooster guarded a mixed flock of Barred Rocks, Rhode Island Reds, and Black Australorps. Wyatt tossed scratch to the happily clucking hens. He filled the basket with brown eggs and ignored the Silkie brooding on a nest of eggs. She'd be guarding some balls of fluff soon.

Yesterday, he'd seen the calves galloping and kicking up their heels in the pastures. Springtime on the ranch was the best time.

Smiling, he headed back to the house.

After cleaning the kitchen—a task he'd previously avoided like the plague—he headed into the office.

Last night, Morgan pointed out he'd been dealing with the paperwork while Wyatt was gone all fall, winter, and spring. And Morgan hated being stuck inside with office work. He'd begged Wyatt to take the job back.

Sucks to be me.

After starting on the financials, he realized Morgan had sneakily hoped the paperwork would bring Wyatt up to date on what had changed while he was gone.

He tapped a finger on a contract for leasing horses from Sawyer Ware, who'd bought the neighboring acreage to the south. Last summer, Sawyer had been in prison and nearly died trying to defend his brother Atticus' woman. The escaping convicts had shot Sawyer and run, taking Gin and another counselor hostage.

Wyatt still had nightmares of the dark, cold night. *Seeing Atticus leap from a boulder onto a convict as another tried to shoot him. The feeling of the trigger under his finger. Aiming, pulling. Watching the convict fall.*

He'd taken a life. Yet... *I saved Atticus. Helped save Gin and the other hostage.*

Balance.

Shaking the memory off, he focused on the paper in the pile.

What the fuck? Morgan and Kallie sold our horses to Sawyer Ware?

Anger rose, fast and hot. Wyatt started to stand. *No.* He sat back down, closed his eyes, and breathed, letting the emotion go. After a couple of minutes, he was steady and in control.

"I owe you one, Mallory. Thanks." When the construction contractor taught him to meditate after the shooting last summer, the sessions not only helped his unsettling guilt, but also the quick temper he'd had all his life.

Go figure.

He turned to studying the numbers. Ware had bought their trail horses—and now was leasing them back to the guide business. And damn, according to the numbers, it was a good decision, saving the family the cost and upkeep of the horses.

The horse drive last spring had also been an excellent innovation. Masterson Wilderness Guides had teamed up with Ware to turn a seasonal horse drive into a tourist event. Looked like they'd be doing a late fall drive, too, taking the horses to a winter range in the foothills.

Wyatt smiled slowly. Sounded like fun.

Paper by paper, he waded through the ranch finances, from equipment maintenance to buying feed to sales of calves.

Damned if he didn't enjoy the work, even though it had annoyed the hell out of him in the past. But now... He'd spent the last year teaching farm and small ranch management to villagers. Learning from them too. There were some sustainable measures he'd like to incorporate here on their small ranch.

Interestingly enough, Morgan and Kallie had implemented changes that—after he pushed aside his automatic territorial reaction—were excellent ideas.

A yawn caught him halfway down a page of purchases, and he laughed. His body was certain it was the middle of the night. *Time to move.* He needed to be out in the sun so his body clock could adjust.

He stopped to grab an apple from the fridge since Morgan hadn't sold their personal riding stock to Sawyer Ware. Good thing for his longevity.

Approaching the closest pasture, Wyatt heard a familiar neigh, and a dark bay quarter horse charged up to the fence. The enthusiastic greeting made his eyes burn.

Hickok remembered him.

"I missed you too, champ." He fed the horse bites of apple— Hickok's favorite treat—and stroked his neck.

Finishing, Hickok snuffled Wyatt's pockets in hopes of more.

"Soon, my friend. I'm looking forward to riding the trails with you." After visiting a while longer, he sighed and went to check on a less pleasant method of transportation.

His pickup started, eventually. Morgan must have run the engine a few times, enough the battery wasn't...*quite*...dead. Hell, sitting for nearly a year wasn't good for vehicles. He'd better take it in for a tune-up. If the auto shop couldn't get to it right away, he'd catch a ride home with Virgil or Sunny.

After grabbing his wallet from the house, he unrolled the sleeves of his old work shirt to cover the burns on his right arm. And noticed his jeans were muddy from his sanctuary. Not that he particularly cared.

On the way down the long private drive toward the road, he

glanced up at the vacation house high on a bluff overlooking the valley. Pa had been annoyed as fuck when a developer built it, but Senator Lockwood had been an okay sort of lady. Unfortunately, she'd gifted the property to a total asshole.

Congressman Troy Palmer.

Wyatt snorted, remembering when Palmer had hired the Masterson Guides to take him and his friends hunting. He had a dick attitude, was a married man who fucked around with the local women—and was a liar about his hunting skills to boot.

Guess the congressman's behavior was irrelevant now. From what Virgil had said, the asshole had left the country in front of a host of corruption charges. Made him into a tolerable neighbor —an absent one.

"I'm sorry, Ms. Palmer."

"Not Palmer," Erin interrupted. "It's Lockwood. Palmer's my ex." Even if the divorce wouldn't be formalized for months, she was done with being associated with Troy and had legally changed her name back. She smiled to make up for the rather rude retort. "Better yet, make it Erin."

"Erin, then. And I'm Janet." Janet Turner, the middle-aged realtor reminded Erin of a fluffy teddy bear—comforting and familiar. "What I wanted to say was... After the prison closed last year, the employees and their families moved away, and there are still many of their houses up for sale and for a fraction of what they're worth. As opposed to the rest of the country, we have a buyer's market here. Vacation houses like yours are selling even more badly—if at all."

Erin felt her heart sink. "But...why??"

Obviously uncomfortable, Janet shifted her weight. "Having the prison here brought in...well, the convicts' associates, so to speak. Like gangs. Our crime rate soared."

Instinctively, Erin glanced out the window. No, there weren't any gangsters on the street.

"It's better now; honestly, it is. Last fall, the townsfolk got together to make the area less appealing to criminals. But...the decrease in crime will take time to show up in the information about the area. Right now, Bear Flat's market isn't doing well at all."

Who would want to buy a vacation home where the crime rate is bad? *I am screwed.* If she couldn't sell the place... She noted the realtor's tight expression. "I'm so sorry. It must be rough being in the real estate business right now."

Janet blinked, then smiled. "It has been, thank you. I'm lucky my husband's job brings in enough to tide us over. However, this is a lovely area with good people, and the market will pick up again. It will, Erin."

"Right. Well." Erin bit her lip. *Now what?* "I guess I'll be one of your new residents, at least until I can sell the house."

"In that case, welcome to Bear Flat."

On the way to the auto shop, Wyatt realized he was passing the Bärchen Bakery. Hell, getting the car serviced could wait a few minutes.

When he strolled in, the bakery smelled like sweet decadence. Donuts and cake and—

"Good morning, Morg—wait, *Wyatt*! You're back?" Sometime in the last year, the plump German owner had colored her gray hair a warm reddish-brown. The lines might have deepened in her face, but her eyes still twinkled with happiness.

"Friede." He hugged her hard enough to get a happy squeal. "I've missed you and your cooking. What's good today?"

"You have a sweet tooth just like your father's." She patted his shoulder. "How about a cookie sandwich to welcome you home?"

If he'd been a dog, there would've been drool pooling on the floor. "Absolutely."

A minute later, he took a big bite. Nothing beat two chocolate chip cookies with cream cheese frosting between them. "Can you give me a boxful of donuts and cinnamon rolls? Virgil and Morgan are still a mite irritated at how long I was gone."

"You boys." She rolled her eyes and started on the order. "I'm glad I wasn't there for the uproar."

There hadn't been much. Guess they were all getting older and less volatile. "Seems they did a fine job without me."

Pride in his family mixed with the disconcerting realization of how well they had managed without him. And wasn't that a fucking conceited notion—thinking he'd been essential to the business? He knew better. He, Kallie, and Morgan were a team.

Leaning against the counter, he asked one of the town's best gossips, "So, sweet lady, what's been going on in Bear Flat while I was gone?"

A few minutes later, up to date on the news, he headed outside with his box of goodies. And was already trying to decide what to enjoy next. A cinnamon roll? Or maybe a glazed donut.

He almost bumped into a pair of women on the boardwalk. "Sorry."

"If it isn't Wyatt Masterson." The tall blonde beautician smiled at him.

"Candy." He gave her a polite, but cool nod. She had a vicious tongue, and Cousin Kallie despised her.

"*Wyatt.*" The curvy brunette next to Candy clasped her hands over her heart. "You're back!"

"Katelyn, it's been a while. Are you here visiting Levi?" Her brother was a patrol officer in the Bear Flat police station where Virgil worked.

"No." She giggled. "I got tired of San Francisco and moved back here last fall."

"I get it. Cities are fun to visit, hell to live in." They'd gone to high school together, and years later, he'd run into her at Dark

Haven, a BDSM club in San Francisco. Surprised the hell out of him. They'd done a scene that night—and a couple more times when he'd seen her at the club.

Moving closer, she gazed up into his face. "I work at Hannah's Hair now. And...I'm not seeing anyone."

At her expectant pause, he stepped far enough back to regain his personal space. "Well, I wish you the best in finding someone. Good to see you again." He touched his hat brim and headed down the boardwalk.

This, right here, was another of the reasons he didn't date locals. She was a pleasant person and a nice enough submissive although too chattery and clingy for him. He thought he'd been clear he wasn't interested in more than an occasional lightweight scene. He'd never called her, never even asked for her number.

"Oooh, look at Miss Snooty Bitch." Candy's snide tone caught his attention, and he glanced back. She and Katelyn were staring at a woman leaving the real estate office.

The target of their interest looked vaguely familiar but wasn't anyone he knew. Her hair was the color of Virgil's, somewhere between blonde and brown, pulled into a tight bun. She had fair skin and big dark-blue eyes. No makeup. An inch or two over average height with what he'd call a sturdy build much like Logan Hunt's Becca.

Considering her silky off-white pants, button-up shirt, and low-heeled sandals, he'd guess she was a tourist. Her attire wasn't small-town, more like the fashionable city crap that managed to turn just about any figure sexless.

It didn't suit her at all.

Damned if he could tell what made him think that.

Now what am I going to do? Dread rose inside Erin as she left the realtor's office. She couldn't sell her house. Her small savings account wouldn't support her for long. Despite the fact she didn't have to pay a mortgage, the real estate taxes were steep.

There were other expenses like food and utilities. And cars didn't run on water.

I need a job. Here.

Who would hire her?

As she walked toward her car, parked a block down from the realty office, she passed by two men. One was tall with graying dark hair, and the lines on his face sagged like Delilah's basset hound. The other was a burly man with a big belly and a receding hairline.

The basset hound of a man eyed her. "I know you. You're Palmer's wife." The loathing in his voice was like a slap in the face.

The potbellied man straightened, his expression darkening. "Congressman Palmer? You're the reason the prison was here. Why my son almost died."

"What?" Shocked, she hastily took a step back as everything inside her cringed. "No."

Would the man attack her? She glanced around for help.

She had a moment's hope at seeing a police officer in a black uniform shirt. Big and brawny with super-short dark hair, he stood without moving and stared at her with...hatred.

The pot-bellied man's voice rose. "You and your bastard of a husband got rich off our misery. Polluted our water, brought gangs to our small town. You should—"

"Hey, Simmons." A tall, muscled man in a black cowboy hat moved in front of her, blocking her from the shouter. His voice was deep and easy. "It's been a while."

To her surprise, Simmons stopped yelling. "Masterson, well, I'll be. Wasn't sure we were ever going to see you again."

"Masterson." The basset hound grinned and shook hands with her rescuer. "Welcome home, man."

Gratitude swept through her at the man's intervention. *Thank you, thank you, thank you.*

While the men were involved in their greetings, Erin silently started backing up. The police officer had already left. He sure wouldn't have been much help if she'd needed him.

Instead, that man—the one named Masterson—had saved her. Did he even realize it? She glanced at him.

He'd turned far enough to look at her. His assessing eyes were a dark brown that matched his thick mustache, short beard, and the wavy brown hair touching his shoulders. Red marks on his right cheek looked almost like burns. Down the same cheek, a long cut with black stitches disappeared into his beard.

Ow, that looked painful.

The shouter Simmons followed his gaze. "Hey, she's the politician's wife. Palmer, the one who took bribes to—"

"Are you sure she had anything to do with the prison?" her rescuer said. "Palmer didn't bring her here whenever he came. From the shit I heard him say about her, they weren't close."

"*From the shit I heard him say.*" Troy must have ridiculed her when he was here. She shouldn't be surprised. He'd mocked her before...but each time, it felt as if she'd been kicked in the stomach.

Tears burned her eyes, but she was in public. People's cold, accusing eyes jabbed at her. She had no friends here.

Pulling in a breath through her nose, she stiffened her spine, turned her back, and strode away. Head high. Jaw firm.

Back when Mom put her into a ritzy private high school, she'd learned that taunting grew worse if she cried. These people wouldn't get the satisfaction of seeing how much their scorn hurt. Or how much they'd scared her.

Thank goodness the tall man in the cowboy hat had interrupted.

Wyatt watched the woman walk away, hands fisted at her sides, like if she relaxed, she'd lose her nerve and flee. Reminded him of when Morgan had popped a balloon. Kallie's cat had jumped a foot and stalked out of the room exuding attitude, like, "*I wasn't scared, no, not me. Nothing scares the fierce Maine Coon.*"

He shot Simmons a hard look. "You frightened her. No matter how much of an asshole her husband is, she's a woman."

Simmons blew up like a puffer fish and deflated just as fast. "You're right. My pa would've tanned my hide."

"Mine as well." Anatole Thibodeaux, the lean owner of the Mother Lode restaurant, heaved a sigh as he studied the retreating woman. "Palmer took off without her, after all. Though it's odd his wife is here at the scene of her husband's crimes, so to speak."

Wyatt frowned. "Yeah. It is odd." Did she know how much of an asshole her husband was? About the women Palmer brought in to entertain himself and his guests?

"So, Masterson, I see you got yourself a nice tan from down there in Africa. Did you also happen to have trouble starting a campfire?" Simmons gestured to the burns on Wyatt's face.

"Hey, fires are tricky." Wyatt gingerly touched the healing skin. "Like women. If you don't pay enough attention or move in too close, you'll get burned."

As the men laughed, Wyatt grinned and headed toward his pickup.

Owned by Anatole's brother, Pierre's Auto and Small Engine Repair sat outside of the small downtown area. Nothing pretentious. Just a big auto shop with three repair bays and the office at one end.

As usual, there was no one in the office, so he started checking the repair bays. Walker, the older mechanic, was working on an aged Yukon in one. In the second, young Marco was doing an oil change.

In the third, Pierre was talking to—*go figure*—the politician's wife.

. . .

Erin felt like an idiot. *Why didn't I take the time to buy jeans and a T-shirt before coming here to ask for a job?*

The owner, Pierre Thibodeaux, was about her height of five-nine but all wiry muscle with short black hair and brown eyes. Years of grease had stained his calluses a shade darker than his skin.

And here she was, in her congressman-approved, up-market clothing. In light colors, no less. "I know I look like I can't figure out which end of a wrench to use, but I do know my way around a car. Can you give me a—"

The owner of the only auto repair shop in town looked past her, and his eyes widened. "Wyatt Masterson. It's about time you got your tail-end home."

Even before turning, Erin knew who she would see. Mr. Tall, Dark, and Rugged. In a cowboy hat. The man looked as if he'd sauntered out of one of the Old West movies her grandfather had loved.

And his name? *Wyatt* Masterson—seriously?

The cowboy held out his hand. "Pierre, good to see you." With a deep, rough voice, he sounded like country-western singer Tim McGraw might after a long night of drinking. Could he be any more of a typical cowboy?

Well, okay, maybe he—and his hat—are totally sexy.

Not that she noticed.

After a manly exchange of handshaking and back-slapping, the two stepped apart. Wyatt glanced at her. "Sorry, miss. I didn't mean to interrupt."

"No, no, you did not interrupt us. We were finished." Pierre shook his head at her. "I hire only certified—"

"I'm an ASE-Certified Master Automobile Technician."

The owner's surprise was quite insulting. On her phone, she pulled up the photo of her certificate.

Pierre studied the cell display, then eyed her. "I don't think—"

Tall, Dark, and Rugged interrupted. "You should give her a

chance, Pierre. Your car lot is full, which means you've got a backlog of work. I know Jonas retired before I left last year. Did you ever replace him?"

Pierre's mouth thinned. "You're as pushy as your father was."

Oh great, now her potential boss was angry. Erin's heart sank. Even though the big guy had spoken up for her, he'd probably done her no favors.

Pierre's gaze went to the parking lot, and he scowled. "You brought in your pickup for work, Masterson?"

"Yep. It sat for almost a year. Needs servicing."

"*Merde*," Pierre said under his breath. He raised his voice. "Then we will do this." He pointed to the empty repair bay where they stood. "Put your pickup there."

Wyatt nodded, his lips tilting up under the dark mustache.

"You, *cher*, will service the vehicle. Here. Now."

Yes! No, wait... "Now?" She gulped.

"Yes. You come to me dressed like this; you work like this—or you do not work at all." The short man's dark eyes snapped with irritation.

"My tools are—"

"I have spares." Arms crossed over his chest, he waited as Wyatt Masterson drove his pickup into the bay.

Masterson jumped out, a box from the bakery in one hand. "Key's in the ignition."

Pierre pointed to the door. "Be off with you and do not come back until I call you."

The big man grinned, totally unfazed. "Got it. Good luck, Ms. Palmer."

"It's *Lockwood*, not Palmer." She winced because she'd totally snapped at a customer.

But did he get upset? Not hardly. His eyes just crinkled like he was trying not to laugh. He touched his fingers to his hat brim and... The way he sauntered out of the repair bay, it was like he was heading for his horse that was tied up in front of a saloon.

Pierre eyed her. Waiting for her to react.

"Looks like I'd better get to work. Tools?" At his gesture, she headed for an ugly tool cabinet and started rolling up her sleeves. After an hour or so, her clothes would be unsalvageable. Ah well. She'd never liked them anyway.

Instead, anticipation rose. There'd been no time to play with tools since the disastrous night when Troy blackmailed a senator. Whether she got the job or not, she was going to enjoy herself today.

She pulled in a breath and braided back her hair. Enjoyment or not, she *needed* this job.

Was the city girl—Palmer's wife—seriously wanting to work as an auto mechanic? Interesting woman, one Wyatt couldn't help thinking about. She'd appeared pretty damned determined.

Hopefully, she wouldn't break his pickup. Back home, he parked Virgil's car in front of the house, grateful his brother could catch a ride home with Sunny.

At home, Wyatt put his hat on the hat rack. Heading for the office, he absently scratched at the itching stitches on his face. And scowled. It'd been long enough. Time for them to go. Detouring, he scavenged a small pair of scissors from Sunny's quilting supplies.

Once in front of his bathroom mirror, he angled his head, used tweezers to grab a stitch, snipped it, and pulled it loose. Stitch by stitch until all were gone.

Sunny would probably scold him for not letting her or the doc remove his stitches. But it wasn't as if he hadn't done this shit before. Snip and pull, easy enough.

Now his face didn't look like he had a big black caterpillar on his jaw, and there wouldn't be as many stares. He hadn't liked the wide eyes from the politician's wife. Ms. Palmer, no, *Lockwood*. She must have kept her birth name...or maybe filed for divorce?

Damned if he knew why he'd stepped in to give Pierre a push to hire her. Maybe it was the tiny tremble of her lower lip. Or the haunted look in her eyes.

Gorgeous eyes, dark as night in the shadows, a clear sapphire blue in the light.

Having met her asshole husband, he felt sorry for the woman. But she might not feel the same. Had she been distressed when the prick politician fled the country without her? Or relieved?

Wyatt shrugged. No matter to him. Society women weren't his type. Never had been. Not since his twenties when he'd done his share of sampling the shallow end of the gene pool.

Finished with his face, he started removing the stitches for the bullet wound along his side.

When it came right down to it, he favored practical women, and his volunteer work in Ethiopia had reinforced his preference. He wanted a woman who was a do-er, not a talker. One like his mother.

When he was a youngster, an old guy told him men tended to marry women like their mothers. He'd been horrified.

Now, the thought was oddly comforting.

After dropping the last thread in the wastebasket, cleaning and returning Sunny's scissors, he trimmed his mustache and shaved off his beard. Felt good to have it gone. But he'd already had a start on a beard before the village fire, and afterward, he sure hadn't wanted a razor anywhere near the stitches.

With a smile, he ran his hand over his jaw, smooth except for the long, raised scar and a few of the nastier burn marks. *Better.*

Back in the office, he took a seat behind the desk. Time for another dive into the financials until Pierre gave him a call.

Would Ms. Lockwood really work on his pickup?

He shook his head. Erin Lockwood wasn't of any interest of his. She was probably only here until things died down, and she could join her asshole husband.

Or not. She'd sure looked eager for Pierre to hire her.

Wyatt concentrated on the job to such good effect he put a hefty dent in the paperwork Morgan had left him.

From the gravel yard in front of the house came the sound of a vehicle. The front door opened.

"Wyatt, are you here?"

Ah, his favorite cousin. He yelled back, "Here, Kallie. In the office."

He'd barely reached the door when she barreled through and wrapped her arms around him for a hard hug. "I missed you."

"Missed you too, cuz." His voice came out a bit tight. The bullet gouge over his ribs was still a tad sore.

He had genuinely missed her. Hugging her back, he lifted her off her feet and whirled her around. Four years younger than him, black hair shorter than his, black eyes, and a tiny frame. Her husband had given her the fitting nickname of *sprite*. "How's Jake? Are you two doing all right?"

Kallie stepped back, laughing. "He's wonderful. You do realize we've been together three years, right?"

"Don't care. Even if he's white-haired and using a walker, I'll beat him up if he doesn't treat you right."

His statement got him another squeeze and another laugh. Apparently, Hunt was a good husband.

"C'mon." Taking Wyatt's hand, she dragged him out of the room. "I saw you have yummies from the bakery, and I missed lunch."

"Can't let you starve." He grinned. The pastries weren't going to last to breakfast...especially since he heard a couple of glazed donuts calling his name.

Sipping more coffee and chowing down on donuts, he answered her questions about his time in Ethiopia. As with his brothers, he avoided the true tale of how he'd gotten burned and shot in a different country. It was over. No need to upset his family with how close he'd come to dying.

In return, she caught him up on what had happened while he was gone. She and his brothers had skipped a whole lot in their occasional emails. Like how violent the Aryan Hammers gang had been and how the bastards had set Roger Simmons' house on fire and tried to kill his family. No wonder Simmons had reacted poorly to seeing Palmer's wife.

And Morgan had shot and killed the leader.

Dammit, bro.

What a brutal fucking year they'd all had.

"On the bright side, the guide business is doing fantastic." She gave him a worried look. "Did Morgan mention we're leasing our horses back from Sawyer Ware."

"He did, and I looked at the profit and loss. It's working well."

When she blinked at him in surprise, he realized she expected him to give her hell.

Last year, he might have. "You did good, cuz. Both of you. I'm sorry I left you in the lurch for so long."

"You needed to get away. We knew that." Her expression turned tender. His spitfire of a cousin had a soft heart. "Even if you look a bit beat up, you seem more whole than when you left."

True enough.

"So... I found a list on the desk with the header, *Ask Wyatt*. At the top was a note about offering wilderness hikes just for women? The next one is investigating taking on interns?"

"Yes, we were—"

"C'mon, let's ride and talk."

While discussing the list, they saddled their horses and rode across the pasture and up his favorite trail.

Fuck, it was good to be on Hickok's back, enjoying the creak of the saddle and clink of the bridle. The dusty fragrance of horse, leather, and evergreens. The shifting muscles of his horse under him.

He couldn't stop smiling.

After the ride, as they brushed down the horses in the stable, Kallie paused. "I almost forgot what I was supposed to ask you."

A couple of twigs from low-hanging branches were stuck in her short hair.

He reached over the stall rails to remove the twigs for her. "Yeah?"

"Morgan called to say his fishing group wants to stay out until next Tuesday. And I have a group of photographers doing an overnight on Thursday. But now a group at Serenity Lodge has asked to do an overnight on Thursday as well. Just to the Maud's Creek meadow camp for the night and back the next afternoon."

Jake and Logan Hunt owned a wilderness B&B lodge and partnered with the Mastersons if their guests wanted a guided wilderness trip. At one time, the lodge had specialized in the kink market, especially BDSM. Now the men were married, their business was more mainstream, but they still occasionally arranged BDSM specialty trips.

"You're blushing, cuz." Wyatt chuckled. "I take it this is one of their *special* groups?"

"It is, but a small one. Logan plans to go. Can you do it?" Her gaze was on his burned face. Undoubtedly, she'd had the whole scoop from Sunny. "I don't want you hurting yourself."

"Sure. It'll be fun."

"Awesome. I'll tell Logan he has a guide."

"Email me the details." He rose and hugged her. "You and Morgan can start unloading some of the work on me."

"I might actually get time off?" She patted her chest. "I might go into shock."

He grinned and tried not to feel guilty.

Later in the afternoon, after a call from Pierre, he dropped Virgil's car behind the police station and strolled to the auto repair shop.

Pierre was in his office for a change, his big desk covered with so much paperwork it looked worse than Wyatt's. A whiteboard on the wall outlined the mechanics' schedules next to a calendar with a picture of a classic Mustang.

Ms. Lockwood stood in front of the desk, no longer a pristine model of fashion. Grease and dirt streaked her clothing, arms, and chin. Her hands and nails were gritty. Hair that had been in a bun was now pulled back in a tight braid and tied with what looked like twine.

She looked at him and blinked in startlement. Her gaze was on his face, the long machete slice. Oh, right. He'd shaved.

"Masterson." Pierre nodded and opened his hand to Ms. Lockwood. "Give him a run-down, please."

"Sure." She glanced at the papers Pierre held, obviously expecting him to hand them over. The owner simply looked at her.

She sighed, pulled out her phone, unlocked it, and swiped. After a glance at what must have been a list, she started. "Mr. Masterson, you received the regular oil change and filter service. I also gave extra attention to areas impacted by extended sitting, like checking your brakes for rust, checking the charging and starting system, including your battery, alternator, et cetera. I also went over the cooling system and the various fluid levels. I changed out your windshield wipers, checked all your belts and hoses and valves. Your tires are in good shape, but I rotated them while I was at it."

Wyatt blinked. "All that? So fast?"

"She's efficient," Pierre said slowly as if reluctant to admit to being impressed. "And thorough." The shop owner valued his rep for being scrupulous and reliable. He'd probably been breathing over her shoulder for the entire job.

"Anything I should be aware of?" Wyatt asked.

"You'll need new tires in about ten thousand miles, a brake job at about the same time, which is a bit sooner than average. Other than tires and brakes, you're on schedule for your vehicle's routine maintenance."

Mountain driving explained the brakes.

And damn, she *was* good. "All right then." He plugged his card into the credit card reader and accepted the papers from Pierre.

She smiled at him—no, she *beamed* at him. "Thank you for your business, Mr. Masterson."

He shot Pierre a look.

"Good to see you again, Masterson, and welcome home." Pierre handed Wyatt his pickup's key and turned to the woman. She might not be what Pierre expected, but the owner had needed another mechanic for a long time. "Ms. Lockwood, let's talk hours."

Her dark blue eyes lit up.

Wyatt had to smother a grin. Because she looked more like a kid offered a trip to Disneyland than someone being offered a mechanic's job.

CHAPTER FIVE

Laden with sacks of food for camping, Wyatt followed Kallie out of the grocery store the next day. Blinded by the mid-day brightness, he slowed—and his foot hit something. He stumbled and almost stepped on the big gray cat that had tripped him.

Retreating to the middle of the boardwalk, the cat turned to stare up at him with wide yellow eyes.

Damn. The long hair couldn't hide that the beast was starvation gaunt.

Noting the cat's tufted ears and full ruff, Wyatt tilted his head. "Hey, fuzzbutt. Would one of your ancestors be a Maine Coon named Mufasa?" Before being neutered, Kallie's cat had made the rounds of the area, and Maine Coon mixes kept turning up in the feline population.

Rather than running, the cat perked its ears.

Farther down the boardwalk, Kallie was watching. "Mufasa probably—"

"Fucking cat. Get out of here!" David Whipple, the stocky owner of the grocery pushed past Wyatt to aim a kick at the cat.

Wyatt blocked his leg and shoved the grocer back. His voice rose. "What the *fuck*?"

"It's a damn stray." Whipple's face darkened. "Hanging around the door, annoying my customers, trying to get inside."

Don't punch the fool. Wyatt reined in his temper and eyed the cat. It was hungry. Wasting away. His chest tightened. He'd seen way too much starvation in the last year.

Another breath and his voice came out pleasant. Even friendly. "I'd take it as a favor if you let me deal with the cat." Without waiting for an answer, he set the grocery bags down, took a knee, and held out a finger.

Tail twitching, the cat hesitated, watching Whipple.

Wyatt narrowed his eyes. *Get the fuck out of here.* He relaxed his jaw. "Thanks, David. I got this."

"Fine. Just get the flea-ridden thing gone." Whipple disappeared back into his store, slamming the door behind him, the dumbass.

Wyatt softened his voice. "C'mere, big kitty. Let's get acquainted."

After a long, long moment without any movement, it stretched out its neck. Advancing one step, then another, it came close enough to touch Wyatt's finger with a pink nose.

Another hesitation. Not fearful, not feral, but cautious.

Wyatt smiled. "Yeah, there you go, young lion. I'm a nice guy."

Coming to a decision, the cat rubbed its cheek against Wyatt's fingers.

Alrighty then. Wyatt scritched its neck and head gently, feeling hard bone under not enough flesh. "Someone's been living rough for a while."

"Oh, hell, don't tell me. You want to bring it home." A way down the boardwalk, Virgil had joined Kallie. "He's at it again, cuz."

Wyatt grinned and told the cat, "Don't mind them. They'll come around."

"Wyatt..." Virgil was shaking his head. "We already have a dog."

"Which means we need a cat for balance. A ranch cat. Trust me." Wyatt dug into the grocery sacks, pulled out a tuna pouch, and ripped it open. He squeezed out a chunk.

A second later, the piece of tuna was gone. Yellow eyes met his expectantly.

Wyatt grinned. "See, he's a fine cat." The cat was gaunt, but also lacking an older adult's wider chest. Probably under three years or so. And male.

As it ate another chunk, he looked over at Kallie. "Sunny keeps a crate for Patches in the clinic. Can you run over and see if we can use it?"

"Sure." Kallie grinned. "It's about time you guys got a cat."

She was right. When she'd gone to live with Jake and taken Mufasa with her, they'd all missed having the giant cat around.

"You, bro, are a magnet for strays." Virgil shook his head and headed for the grocery door. "I'll buy cat food while you load your pet."

Wyatt grinned. It wasn't as if they weren't used to him bringing animals home. Before Mufasa, the ranch had anywhere from one to five cats. And usually a dog or two.

For some reason, the strays always found him first.

A couple of stores down, Erin stood on the boardwalk and watched Wyatt Masterson. Such a big man, but his equally big hands were gentle as he petted the grubby cat and talked to it.

The sound of the man's deep voice, his deliberately slow speech, sent quivers through her stomach.

The gray feline was filthy, emaciated, and looked as if it would rather scratch than purr—but Wyatt was going to take it home without a second thought.

Her vision went blurry. For years, she'd been surrounded by politicians who, while telling their constituents they cared, only worried about appearances, money, and power. They'd say, *I'll fix everything for you* and do nothing.

Or like her husband, take everything they could.

But here was a man who saw a starving cat—and fed it. Offered it a home. She could feel her heart melting.

And a degree of her faith in people being restored.

Wyatt rose, and his gaze met hers. His brows drew together, as if he'd seen her tears.

Turning, she hurried away.

But when she glanced over her shoulder, he was still watching her with narrowed eyes.

He was…an interesting man. Ruggedly masculine. Even shaving off his beard hadn't changed that. Some men with only a mustache looked wimpy, but his was dark and thick and set off the firm line of his mouth. A five o'clock shadow edged the hard angles of his jawline.

The cowboy was dangerously sexy—enough to make a woman's heart speed up.

But not mine. No way. She wasn't vulnerable to that kind of thing any longer. *Uh-uh.*

Maybe, at one time, she might have set her sights on having both a great career and being married.

Been there, done that, ripped up the T-shirt.

Now she simply wanted to be the best mechanic ever. And… maybe to be a crazy cat lady. She'd be eccentric and—*wait for it*—single. Very, very single.

Another glance showed Wyatt carrying the cat to his vehicle —the pickup she'd worked on.

I did a good job on it.

The thought brought her back to why she was here in town. She needed work clothes, and the building she stood in front of housed the only clothing store in town—a touristy-type boutique. It was doubtful she'd find what she needed here, but it seemed disloyal to the locals to shop elsewhere.

Unfortunately, as she stepped in and gazed around the room,

she knew her hopes had failed.

Turning to leave, she almost bumped into a tall, curvy woman who'd just walked in. "Oops, sorry."

The woman pushed a strand of strawberry-blonde hair out of her face. "Not a problem. Didn't you find what you were looking for?"

Erin sighed. "No." How did the woman manage to look both sexy and fashionable in jeans and a casual shirt? "I'm not a tourist. I just started work here, and I need work clothes—rugged ones, and—"

"Oh, hey, the owner has stuff for us locals. Wait." The redhead smiled and raised her voice. "Donna, need a hand here."

From the back bustled a short woman with jaw-length brown hair. "Becca, it's good to see you. What can I do?"

Becca turned. "Whoops, I didn't get your name."

"Erin. Erin...Lockwood." There was a huge satisfaction in being a Lockwood again.

"Erin wants work clothing." Becca turned to Erin. "Donna's the owner."

"I have work clothing. Are you new in town?" Donna led the way to the rear of the store.

"Yes. I'm working for Pierre as a mechanic." Their startled expressions made her laugh. "Unfortunately, when I moved, I tossed my old shop clothes, and now..."

"Of course." Donna frowned. "I don't carry coveralls, and I don't think Pierre provides them."

No, a small-town repair shop wouldn't. "The other mechanics wear jeans and cargo-style work pants."

"Easy enough." Donna pointed to the shelves lining the back wall. "See if something here will do."

This is more like it.

Erin picked out a couple of heavy-duty cargo pants with reinforced knees. *Yes.* She even found sturdy jeans in her size. "These will be perfect. Can I try them on, and do you have tank tops and cotton work shirts?"

"I do." Donna showed her.

Coming out of the dressing room, she saw Becca had found a pair of jeans and changed into them.

Standing in front of the mirror, the redhead was checking the fit by waggling her butt. "I love jeans that cup my ass."

Donna laughed. "So will Logan. Are you going to treat him to seeing you in a new top too? My newest order of low-cut, T-shirt styles just arrived."

"*Reeeally*. Logan loves anything low cut."

Smiling at the delight in Becca's voice, Erin tried to remember if Troy had ever acted pleased with anything she'd worn. Usually, she was lucky to get an, "*It's adequate*."

Sometimes it felt as if he'd squeezed all the color out of her life.

"Erin, girl, are you all right?" Becca touched her shoulder gently.

"I..." Her throat had clogged. She roughly scrubbed the damp from her cheeks. "I'm getting a divorce, and I just realized my husband never encouraged me to wear sexy clothes for him. He just wanted me in neutral colors and conservative styles. I got so...tired...of bland."

"Oh, this story sounds like we need wine and time."

"Sorry, no, I don't mean to get all whiny." Erin half-laughed.

"Girl, a break-up is like a prepaid ticket to indulge in whining." Becca gave her a one-armed squeeze around the shoulders. "And I totally want to hear about it."

The sincerity in her voice made Erin's eyes burn. "You know"—she smiled—"I think I'll buy something red just because now I can."

"You can, and you should. You deserve all the colors." Donna pulled her over to a different rack. "These tops are sexy *and* bright. Here's a red one. No, this is even better." She held up a low-cut, clingy shirt in a deep blue. "The color matches your eyes."

"You have beautiful eyes. You need that shirt." Becca nodded firmly, then eyed Erin's hair that was in a low bun. "If you want more color, you could streak your hair to match. Light blonde and blue are fun together."

My hair? "Coloring it would take a hairdresser forever. It's down almost to my waist." She wrinkled her nose. "Stupid hair."

The shop owner pursed her lips. "You don't sound as if you like it long."

"It's a major pain to wash and dry and pin up. But my hus..." She stopped. What Troy wanted didn't matter any longer. "I can...cut...it," she said slowly.

Becca's lips twitched. "Your life is your own. You can do what you want with it."

Cut my hair. Make it colorful. Take the first step on my crazy cat lady journey.

"Yes!"

After they bought clothes—and Erin was talked into adorable sandals that were fifty percent off—Becca led her to a small salon down the street.

Erin glanced around. The place wasn't as posh as the gleaming but sterile, status-conscious one she'd patronized in Sacramento.

With dark oak flooring, cream-colored walls, wood-framed mirrors, and greenery, this salon resembled the casual, friendly one she'd used when she'd lived with Grammie and Grampie.

"Hey, Rebecca!"

Turning, Becca waved back. "Come, Erin, let me introduce you." She led the way farther in. "Hey, you two, this is Erin Lockwood."

Becca motioned to a woman around thirty who was getting her auburn hair foiled. "Erin, meet Virginia Cunningham, also known as Gin. She's a counselor here in town. Her guy is a Bear Flat police detective."

The freckles on Gin's face crinkled with her smile. "Hi, Erin. Welcome to Bear Flat."

Erin couldn't help but love the warm, southern drawl.

"Thank you."

"And here"—Becca indicated the woman in the next chair who was getting her long hair cut. She was average sized, wearing a tank top that revealed muscular arms. She had sun-streaked brown hair, green eyes, and a strong face. "This is Mallory McCabe who owns a construction company."

Mallory had a warm smile. "Hi, Erin."

Trained from childhood at social courtesies, Erin smiled. "It's very nice to meet you both."

"Erin *Lockwood*?" Arranging a styling stand near the front of the salon was a tall beautician with hair such a light blonde it was almost silver. Her tone sharpened to a razor's edge. "More like *Palmer*. You're Troy's boringly sweet wifey."

The curvy brunette stylist next to her giggled. "Oh, *Candy*."

Erin studied the blonde. "I'm sorry. Have we met?"

"No." The stylist smirked. "Your husband spoke of you a time or two." She glanced at the brunette. "Right, Katelyn?"

"Oh, *did* he." Katelyn's tone held a sneer.

Erin's mind went blank for a moment. Because the blonde was the kind of beautiful, tall, slender woman who Troy looked at...as in *looked* at the way he'd never done with Erin.

The memory of the crusty sheets in her bedroom came back. *Oh god.* She took a step back, then stopped and straightened her spine.

No. Troy is in my past. She'd filed for divorce—and she already knew he'd screwed around while married to her. Knew he'd belittled her, not only to her face, but to other people. This wasn't a surprise.

And still... Meeting a woman who'd probably had sex with Troy sent a wave of pure humiliation through Erin. Her stomach turned over.

"Want your hair done?" Candy asked with a mocking note in her voice. "I have an opening."

Erin's shoulders sagged as her excitement over changing her appearance drained away. Her hair could stay the way it was.

"Troy Palmer is your husband?" Gin's Southern accent had turned colder than a northeast winter. "The congressman who took bribes to start up a corrupt prison? That one?"

"Yes. That one. The one I'm divorcing." She pulled in a breath and told Becca, "I didn't lie. I took my birth name back."

Becca reached out. "Erin—"

Erin took a step back. Although Mallory's expression held kindness, Gin's was set to the hardness of stone. It wouldn't be right for Erin to come between friends. Even if she'd hoped for one whole minute those friends might someday be hers too. "Thanks for your kindness, Becca, but I should be going."

Turning, she walked out, feeling so very alone.

Gin left the salon as soon as she could after the incident with Congressman Palmer's wife.

She felt a moment of pity, remembering the woman's hurt expression when Candy said her husband talked about her, implying he hadn't said anything nice.

But...

No, the woman had been married to a creep who'd enabled the ghastly conditions in the prison where Gin had worked as a counselor and from where she'd been kidnapped.

Tasting the bitterness, feeling panic rising inside, she entered the police station.

Manning the desk, Levi nodded. "Hey, Gin." He waved her toward the office with the nameplate reading: *Detective Atticus Ware.*

My Atticus. Gin walked in.

Behind the desk, Atticus rose, his gray-blue eyes warming. "Li'l magnolia, this is a fine surprise. I thought you had—"

Unable to speak, she wrapped her arms around his waist and burrowed in.

"Whoa, sweetheart." His embrace was warm, his muscular

arms like iron as he pulled her closer. "What's happened? Who do I need to beat up?"

His unconditional support was one of the reasons she loved him so much. She rubbed her cheek against his hard shoulder. "I'm sorry. It's just been..." The words wouldn't come.

He made a soft sound in the back of his throat. "Been difficult? You know, you've been antsy for a week or so."

Had she?

He stepped back, cupping her chin in his hand. "Maybe because it's been a year since we met. Since we got together?"

"Meeting you has been the most wonderful part of my life."

"Of course it has." His teasing smile could still make her heart turn over. "But last summer also held the most traumatic parts of your life."

It had. As if summoned, her brain helpfully provided visual and auditory references. *Slash shouting, "The redheaded bitch is mine to rip up." In the prison yard, Atticus' brother lying in a pool of blood, eyes open. Being tied up, slapped, pinched. At the foot of a boulder, Atticus on the ground, struggling to sit up.*

Was this what her problem was? The smells, the heat, the feeling of summer had resurrected the horrible memories of last year. She knew how PTSD worked. "Maybe. Probably."

She held him tighter, a tremor running up her spine. When the convicts kidnapped her, Atticus had come after her, and if it wasn't for Wyatt's good aim, he would've died. She swallowed hard.

"It's been a tough year. Far more violent and bloody than any town should have to experience." Atticus sighed. "William is quitting."

"What? Why?"

"Last fall, when the Aryan Hammers ambushed and shot him and Levi, he's never gotten past it."

"Oh, poor William." Gin felt Atticus stroke her hair, and she tilted her head. "Karen quit the profession too."

The prison counselor who'd been taken hostage with her

hadn't bounced back from the trauma.

Anger surged through Gin again. The private prison had increased its profits by cutting back on staffing and security. In a facility that should never have been built. But it had, because Congressman Palmer had taken bribes. He'd increased his wealth while people were dying.

"It's discouraging," Atticus murmured.

"I'm still so angry and unsettled, and I don't know what to do about it," Gin whispered. "I was rude to someone today."

"*You* were rude?"

At Atticus' shock, she almost smiled. "Congressman Palmer's wife is here in town. Seeing her brought everything back. I wanted to slap her."

"Mmm, when a southerner goes from *bless your heart* to considering assault, it's time for action. How about we start by getting away?"

She blinked. "What?"

Atticus ran his hands up and down her arms. "Neither of us has had a vacation since the mess last year." He chuckled. "Medical leave doesn't count."

"A vacation?"

"Yes." He sat down in his chair and pulled her onto his lap. "You have a light load right now. Juggle your appointments, and we'll head out this weekend for a couple of weeks away."

Leaning against his firm body, she felt the shakiness inside her begin to relax. "But... Yes, I'd love it. Did you want to go to San Francisco?"

"You know, you said once you've always wanted to be a tourist in New York City. Can't get much more different from here. Museums, Broadway, fancy restaurants..."

New York? Excitement surged through her.

"Yes. Yes, yes, yes." Gin hugged him, kissed him, feeling the overwhelming love—and more, the certainty that together, they were stronger than either one alone. "I love you so much."

Oh my stars, I'll get to enjoy Atticus in a suit.

CHAPTER SIX

Seated on a stump in front of the tiny log cabin, Wyatt breathed in the cool evening air, rich with the fragrance of pine and laced with wood smoke from the fire.

This high valley held a batch of one-room cabins and a roof-only pavilion with a grill and a fire pit. There was nothing finer than a chilly mountain evening spent watching the stars appear in a pitch-black sky.

It was good to be out in the wilderness where he belonged.

His new stray probably felt abandoned, having been left back at the ranch. Still, a new cat did best if confined to a quiet area for a couple of days. Yesterday, after setting up his quarters with cat food, water, and litter, Wyatt had introduced the cat to Sunny and Virgil. And Patches.

Wyatt grinned. Sunny's small spaniel probably weighed the same as the cat, although once the cat put on a few pounds, Patches would be outclassed. Good thing the two had decided they'd get along. Of course, Patches didn't have an aggressive bone in his fluffy body—and the cat seemed damn easygoing. Far more mellow than Kallie's Mufasa.

Virgil and Sunny had promised to babysit the new addition to the family until Wyatt got back tomorrow.

"You look comfortable." In his usual jeans and dark flannel shirt, Logan Hunt strolled over from the pavilion. Tall with military-straight posture, Hunt had dark brown hair, steel blue eyes —and a white scar down his cheek.

Hey, they matched.

"It's good to be back where air is thin and cool. In some places in Africa, it's like trying to breathe in a wet sauna." Wyatt pulled in a contented breath. "Did you need me for something?"

"Maybe." Logan leaned a shoulder against the cabin. "The group I've got with me on this trip would like more mentoring in BDSM while they play."

Wyatt waited for Hunt to come to the point. Unlike Jake, his sociable brother, Logan spoke only when necessary.

"I have four couples. Be nice to have another monitor—and instructor."

Wyatt stiffened. "What makes you think I know anything about BDSM?" He'd never attended the Hunt's kinky parties.

Logan's grin flashed. "You might be discreet, Masterson, but my Becca's the sociable sort. Women talk to her. You have a rep."

What the fuck. He knew some men boasted about their conquests, but—"The *women* talk?" Even so, it wasn't as if he dated locals.

Of course, Becca was buddies with several of the San Francisco BDSM club members, and those women talked about everything. He grunted. "Dark Haven?"

"Oh yeah. And hate to be the one to tell you, when Jake and Kallie were there, your cousin learned you're a member of the club."

"Hell." Wyatt scratched the stubble on his jaw. "Who told her?"

"No one. She was helping Dixon at the receptionist desk and spotted your name when she pulled out another member's card."

"Just my luck. She's probably just waiting her chance to tease the fuck out of me." She must not have found Morgan's card, or his brother would've warned him.

Logan eyed him. "Seems being outed doesn't bother you."

"Not particularly." Wyatt shrugged. He wasn't ashamed of his various kinks, of being a Dominant, or of playing in public. Morgan was the same. Virgil though—he was a more private sort of guy.

"You don't come to our Serenity BDSM parties."

"Nothing to do with you, Hunt. It's more a matter of avoiding entanglements with locals. It's a small town, and relationship shit can get awkward."

Katelyn would be a case in point.

Logan raised an eyebrow. "From what I've seen, social crap doesn't bother you much. There another reason?"

Huh. Hunt's question made Wyatt frown. When it came right down to it, he often dated tourists who were staying in the area for a while, even brought them home to enjoy a night in his bed.

"Maybe." He averted his gaze. With tourists, he didn't risk long-term commitment. Dating a local could lead to being with them long enough to get involved.

Just the thought of loving someone kicked up an ache under his ribs—the feeling he got whenever he remembered Anastasia and how much it'd hurt to lose her.

He rubbed his chest. "You've lost people. I'm not sure I'm up for—" *...for risking that kind of pain again.*

Hunt's sharp gaze softened. "We accept we'll lose a dog or cat after a few years; doesn't stop us from loving them. Why is it different when you're loving a human? There aren't any guarantees."

The man had an interesting way of seeing life and loss. Wyatt tilted his head back, watching the darkening sky. The stars were starting to appear.

He'd had almost a year with Anastasia—at least when they'd managed to be together. Would he rather not have met her?

"If you lost Becca now..." Wyatt stopped, unable to even voice the thought.

But Logan knew where he was going with it. "I'd be fucked-up for a long time—and still, I'd thank whatever deity there is for putting her in my life." The conviction in his rough voice couldn't be doubted.

Wyatt tugged on his mustache as he thought. After losing Anastasia, he avoided getting involved again. Did that mean he regretted loving her? Because he didn't, pain or no pain.

He'd have to think about this.

With a sigh, he rose. "So, Hunt, what do you want me to do tonight?"

Logan let out a raspy laugh. "Basic safety monitoring. Suggestions, especially about D/s. One couple is timid. I'll let you handle them."

Wyatt almost grinned. Hunt had been known to terrify even hard-ass loggers. Those poor newbies.

Part of being a wilderness guide was reassuring clients and getting them past their fears.

And Wyatt was a damn fine guide. "Sounds good to me."

Troy scowled at the burner phone in his hand and waited impatiently for the bastard to pick up. Anonymous calls weren't always answered.

"Who's this?"

Troy breathed a sigh of relief. "It's me."

"Where in the hell are you?"

"Out of the US and safe."

"Okay, good. Where are the drives? I need them."

Right to business. Had he expected anything different? "They're safe enough." He mustn't say where. Not until he had the money. "It was a good thing your Fed contact gave you a heads-up, or I wouldn't have gotten away."

"But the drives? I need them. Now."

Troy scowled. Such a self-centered asshole. "And I need money."

He'd done a good job hiding the drives where no one—not Erin, not the Feds—would ever find them.

"Seriously?" The snort of contempt made Troy flush. "What happened to everything you cleaned out of your and your wife's accounts?"

Guilt was a fleeting sensation. It wasn't as if his boring wife needed it. She could get a job easy enough. Fixing cars. "Do you know how much money it takes to get out of the country and enter a new one without being traced? Get new ID? All within twenty-four hours? It took all the funds I had."

"I see. So you want me to bring you money in exchange for the drives."

"In exchange for the location." Troy scowled, remembering how many times the bastard had taken advantage of him. "The drives are *very* well hidden."

It was wise to be cautious. The asshole had a cruel streak, had even boasted that a high percentage of people at the top were psychopaths.

Sounded about right. But this time, Troy had leverage.

There was silence for a moment. "All right. I'll bring you cash."

Troy exhaled in relief. "Perfect. This is how you find me..."

CHAPTER SEVEN

Pierre's auto shop was a busy place today. From her work area at the end of the building, Erin could see Walker, a gruff, older mechanic in the first bay. He and Pierre took on the difficult repair jobs.

Marco, a lanky, twenty-two-year-old used the second, middle bay. Still learning the trade, he was assigned mostly routine servicing tasks.

Which was what she'd done Wednesday. *Boring.*

On Thursday, while watching her closely, Pierre had doled out vehicles needing basic repairs. Still, it'd been more interesting than changing oil filters, right?

Today, though, she was getting challenging repair jobs. She smiled and opened the hood of the car. Pierre had assigned her a tricky, intermittent-electrical problem to diagnose.

Saying the car had a gremlin wouldn't impress her boss. Grinning, she dug in.

Two hours later, she glowed with a mechanic's ultimate satisfaction as the car owner drove away with the engine purring like a kitty. *Because of me.*

God, I love wrenching.

Still smiling, she started cleaning and putting away her tools into her rolling tool cabinet, the one her grandfather bought her when she started working in his old shop. The crimson metal cabinet made her smile. Her grandparents hadn't thought life had to be colorless.

Setting the last tool away, she spotted the owner.

"You're off now. Go home." Pierre tilted his head in a tiny nod of approval. "Nice work, Sparks."

Shock held her motionless for a moment, before she could say, "Thank you." And her voice cracked.

But he was already walking away.

In the next bay, Marco must have heard the nickname and compliment. He scowled at her, his ginger hair falling into his face. He'd been working here for about a year or so and grumbled about still getting stuck with oil changes. Naturally, he would resent her.

Her happiness faded, but only a drop. It wasn't the first time she'd been disliked for being good at what she did...especially as a mechanic. Men were so stupidly competitive sometimes.

Surely she could win these two over. A shop was far more fun if everyone felt as if they were on the same team. They'd see she was a nice person. Eventually.

As she scrubbed her hands, she heard her name called and looked around.

With Pierre beside her, Becca Hunt waved. "Erin, are you through?"

"Um, yes. I am." Erin dried her hands. Pulling off her dirty work shirt, she tossed it onto her tool cabinet, leaving her in a job-related, black tank top. It'd been a Christmas gift from the shop guys where she'd been restoring classic cars. "Did you bring your car in for servicing?"

"No, I came to get you." The redhead's smile was infectious, and Erin smiled back. Not waiting for a reply, Becca hooked her elbow through Erin's and pulled her away. "Bye, Pierre."

"Tell Logan hello." Pierre disappeared into the shop.

Becca dragged Erin to a small SUV. "I have an appointment

to get my hair done, and I'll hold your hand while you get yours fixed."

"I love that you thought of me but"—Erin shook her head—"is it the same salon? I'm not sure I'm up for more insults."

"There's only one salon in our little town, but Candy and Katelyn have left for the day. Veronica has an opening right now. She's almost as nice as my stylist, Sadie."

Nice sounded good. "An opening for what?"

"I told her you need a cut and foils. You wanted blue, right?" Becca grinned. "I love watching women change on the outside—clothes or hair or whatever—to show who they really are inside."

Huh. "What an interesting way to put it." Erin's feet didn't move for a minute.

Yet... She truly did want exactly what Becca suggested. And she'd have someone with her who wanted to be with her, despite what the spiteful beautician had said. "Yes. I'd like that a lot."

"Perfect."

A couple of hours or so later, over the sound of the hair dryer, Erin heard Becca suck in a breath. "Oh, it looks amazing. No, don't open your eyes. One more minute."

The slight tug of the brush through her hair continued.

Oh, God, I hope I don't look like an idiot.

The chair turned toward the wall mirror, and Veronica said, "Okay, you can look now."

Erin opened her eyes—and gawked. Her hair had been a long length of dark blonde. Now the thick wavy mass was mid-breast length. Rich blue strands streaked through the blonde.

"So much color." And life. Her hair felt...alive.

"The blue totally sets off your eyes," Becca said with satisfaction.

"It does. It's a gorgeous combination. Makes me want to grow my hair and go blonde—and red." Veronica grinned. In her fifties, the brunette stylist wore her hair in a short, very chic style.

Erin tossed her head, enjoying the dancing of the strands on her upper back. Troy had preferred long hair; he hadn't wanted her to cut it ever. "This is great. It's so bouncy."

"The weight from the long length had pulled all the wave out." Veronica smiled. "Now it has...movement."

"And it's long enough to tie back and not get caught in an engine."

"So practical." Becca laughed. "And when it's loose, you'll get stares."

Stares didn't sound so good, not after a month of being harassed by reporters. Who weren't here, she reminded herself.

She beamed at Veronica and Becca. "I love it."

After paying, she followed Becca outside. The long summer days meant it was still light, and the air was starting to cool off. The tourist shops were closed, the boardwalk almost empty.

She realized she was the focus of Becca's assessing gaze. "What?"

"A tank top and jeans. It's a classic look for a reason. With your shorter hair, it's very sexy."

Sexy? Erin shook her head. "I'm not looking to be sexy, Becca. I want to look good, but I'm not in the market for a man. Ever."

"Oh. Should I be looking for women for you?"

"Uh, no." Erin had to laugh. Fair assumption, wasn't it? "No, I'm not in the market for anyone."

"Ever, hmm." Becca pursed her lips. "No matter. Come on."

"Excuse me?"

"We're going to the ClaimJumper. Girl, it's Friday, and we both look fabulous and deserve drinks." Her smile widened. "And food I haven't cooked. *Bar* food."

Erin frowned. Going out wasn't in the budget. But even if she had spent more than she should on her hair, she did have a job now.

Okay then.

"Wait...aren't you married?" Erin caught up to Becca.

"Yes, and have the smartest, cutest toddler in the world. Oddly enough, I still like going to our local bar and drinking beer."

Half a block later, Becca pulled open the door to a rustic downtown tavern.

Erin stepped in.

Interesting place. A set of antlers mounted on the rough log wall next to the door held hats and jackets. Sawdust was scattered over the wood floor. The square wooden tables were obviously not secured, and the bigger groups had pushed several together. The air held the aroma of burgers and fries.

Erin's stomach growled. Lunch had been a long time ago.

"There she is!" A blonde with hair slightly longer than Erin's rose from a table near the far corner. "Becca!"

Next to her, a petite woman with short black hair waved.

Erin stopped dead. "You have friends here. I should go."

"No, you should meet them." Becca gripped her arm and headed across the room.

Erin blinked in surprise. The redhead was not only bigger than Erin, but stronger than she looked. Like one of those tough Irish warriors.

"Hey, people, this is Erin Lockwood who used to be Palmer. Yes, her dickhead husband was Congressman Palmer who took bribes to get the prison here, but she didn't know about it. He cleaned out their accounts when he ran, and their divorce has been filed."

Mouth open, Erin stared at Becca who'd just spilled the whole mess of her life. She felt her face turn red.

"Oh." The blonde narrowed huge blue eyes. "Good grief, Becca, if you dumped my information like that, I'd punch you."

"I'm supposed to be the rude one, not you." The brunette frowned too. "This isn't like you."

Becca pulled out a chair and pushed Erin into it. "She met

Mallory and Gin two days ago, and Gin was rude. I wanted to make it clear Erin isn't her nutsack of a husband."

"Oh." The blonde blinked. "You certainly got the point across. I'm surprised at Gin though."

"I'm not." The brunette told Erin, "Gin's a counselor and worked at the prison. When a bunch of convicts broke out, they took her and a colleague as hostages. It was horrible. When reports broke that the prison shouldn't have been built at all, and they'd cut all sorts of corners when running it, well, everybody was angry."

A hostage? Erin could feel her shoulders sag. *Troy, do you have any idea of all the pain you've caused? Do you even care?* "I can't blame her for being upset."

The blonde reached across the table and squeezed her hand. "She'll come around. I'm Summer Masterson, by the way. Sunny."

The woman totally looked like a warm, summer day. "It's nice to meet you." Masterson? How many Mastersons were there? Would she be related to Wyatt?

There's a question I'm not going to ask.

The brunette picked up her beer. "Kallie Masterson Hunt. Sunny married my cousin Virgil."

"Hunt." Erin eyed Rebecca *Hunt* who laughed.

"My husband's brother is Kallie's husband."

"This is making my head spin."

Kallie grinned. "Obviously, you need a beer."

"You know, I really do." Erin settled back with a happy sigh. *I can be a crazy cat lady with* friends.

Wyatt jumped out of his pickup, spotted Logan in the ClaimJumper parking lot, and held up a hand in greeting. *Right on time.*

Earlier they'd had a pleasant trail ride back from Maud's Creek, ending up at Sawyer Ware's place. As they were tying the horses to the horse hitch, Ware had appeared and shooed them off, taking charge of the stock.

Not at all adverse to being freed up, Wyatt rode Hickok across the valley and home. And had enjoyed a steamy shower far sooner than normal. *Nice.* He loved camping and wood fires and riding, but roughing it made a man grateful for hot water.

As they crossed the parking lot, Wyatt had to grin as he heard the music from inside—Johnny Cash belting out "Ring of Fire." Some things didn't change. Gustaf, the owner, loved Johnny Cash.

Not a fan, Logan grunted in annoyance. "I'm going to shoot his jukebox one of these days."

"Hey, hey, a beer will make it all better." Wyatt clapped him on the shoulder.

"Even beer can't fix that music." Logan glanced at him. "Thanks for your help last night."

"It was fun, actually." Their boots thudded on the boardwalk as they rounded the front of the building.

Logan studied him. "You're more skillful than I figured. We'd be happy to have you participate during the trips—or at the parties."

"Thanks, but—" Wyatt started to automatically refuse, then paused. "Maybe."

Logan raised an eyebrow.

"Last night made me think." Watching the couples enjoying their scenes under the trees by the stream, he'd been envious. BDSM clubs were fun, but being outside and with the right person would be magnificent. "I wouldn't mind finding a woman who enjoys what I do."

As they entered the bar, the music grew louder.

Logan grinned. "Not two women?"

Wyatt had tried threesomes a few times. Laughing, he shook his head. "It was fun when I was younger, but I don't like dividing my attention."

"Same here. And good, we'll expect to see you at the parties."

Stopping inside the door, Logan surveyed the room and smiled. "There's Becca and her troop."

Wyatt turned. Logan's wife was easy to spot with her red hair and big-boned, curvy body. He liked her sturdiness. Kallie, his petite cousin, was like a chihuahua—far too easy to step on, especially when he'd been in his teens and growing faster than his coordination could keep up.

Speak of the devil. His cousin and Virgil's wife, Sunny, were with Becca. The three—no, four—women were attracting a lot of male attention, especially from non-locals who wouldn't know most of them were married.

The fourth woman at the table had her back to him. She had eye-catching hair, thick and wavy and... He narrowed his eyes. Hmm, he'd thought the darker streaks in her blonde hair were brown, but no. The color was blue. Interesting. "Do you want to join them?"

"No." Logan headed for the bar. "Becca loves her female-only evenings. I show up to do overwatch, and she's kind enough to let me."

"Or maybe she just likes having a designated driver." Logan was known for never drinking more than two beers.

"There's that."

They took up station at the bar, far enough away to be unobtrusive but with a good sightline in case of problems.

"Wyatt Masterson. It's good you're home." From behind the bar, the grizzled Swede reached across to shake Wyatt's hand. "What can I get you?"

"Thanks, Gustaf. A Bud draft if you could?"

"Hunt?"

Logan nodded. "Same, please."

Two well-filled beer mugs thumped on the bar top, moisture already condensing on the frosty outside.

A man seated at the bar looked over. "Hey, Logan, good timing. What are you planning to do about the new taxes on B&Bs?"

As the two men talked, Wyatt tuned out the conversation and sipped his beer in pleasure. Cold beer had been sadly lacking in the remote villages where he'd done volunteer work.

Turning to rest his back against the bar, he surveyed the room. It held the usual summer mix of tourists who spilled out from Yosemite park, ranging from senior citizens to scruffy-bearded backpackers. Loggers hung together in a cluster of tables. The ranchers, like him, wore cowboy hats, cotton shirts, jeans, and boots. The townspeople favored T-shirts, baseball caps, and jeans.

"Morgan, I thought you were—" A man approaching from the right stopped and frowned. "Ah, you're not Morgan. Sorry." About Wyatt's height, Sawyer Ware had close-cut, brown hair, sharp blue eyes, and a guarded stance.

"Morgan and I get taken for each other a lot." Wyatt smiled. "I didn't get a chance to talk to you earlier when we dropped off the horses. You're Atticus' brother, aren't you?"

Ware's smile flattened slightly, his gaze wary. What with being newly out of prison last year, the man had probably gotten harassed by the more self-righteous townsfolk.

Wyatt held his hand out. "The lease arrangement looks to be working out well."

Ware's shoulders relaxed as they shook hands. "Good to meet you. And welcome back."

"Sorry, Sawyer." Mallory joined them, smiling up at Ware. "Randy and Russell had questions about our next job."

Wyatt grinned. With braided brown hair and huge green eyes, Mallory was one of his favorite people in the world. "Hey, little bit."

"Wyatt! Welcome home, you." She hugged him hard before stepping back to study him. After frowning at the healing burns and slash on his jaw, she nodded. "A bit beat up, but you look just fine."

Wyatt touched her cheek. "Thanks to you, Mal. Your lessons helped. The work helped." When killing a man last year fucked with his head, she'd not only taught him to meditate but helped him find the volunteer position in Ethiopia.

"I'm glad." Her warm smile was as heartening as sun in winter. "You boys can chat; I'm going to join my girl gang. I see Becca got Erin here."

Wyatt blinked. Had Becca taken Pierre's new mechanic under her wing? Interesting.

"Later, my Captain." Mallory went up on tiptoes and kissed Sawyer before heading across the room.

Wyatt narrowed his eyes. The kiss had been far more than friendly.

After Sawyer got a beer, Wyatt tackled the subject. He wasn't much for pussyfooting around. "In Africa, I was out of touch a lot. Seems I missed some news—like you and Mallory?"

"I don't know why she's with me, but..." Sawyer looked over at the table of women. At Mallory. His expression went soft. "But yeah."

Well fuck. An ex-con sure wasn't the man he would've chosen for the sweet new-ager, but the guy was gone over her. And Kallie and Morgan liked him.

Okay then. "As long as you're here, let's talk horses. Cuz Kallie wants to host a couple of city kid weekends. We might need a couple of ponies."

After practically inhaling the juicy burger, Erin leaned back in her chair and nibbled on a french fry. Crisp and salty, the fries were perfect with the icy-cold beer.

This whole place was perfect, lively with country-western music, laughter, and conversations. And the company was wonderful. Sunny was sweet and fun. Becca had a wicked sense of humor. Kallie was down to earth, and Mallory incredibly kind. They were very different from her husband's politician and business associates. When she lived with her grandparents, she'd had friends like these.

Her sigh was so loud the others looked at her. *Oops.* She'd imbibed more than she usually did. She pushed her beer away. Time to switch to water.

"Are you all right?" Sunny asked.

"I'm fine, honestly. I just realized how nice it is to be around real people and not politicians and lobbyists."

"Ugh. It's bad enough when we have people like that as clients. I can't imagine socializing with them." Kallie made a gagging sound. "It's good you're here instead. Say, do you make house calls?"

"Um, what?" Erin pointed to Sunny. "She's the medical person, not me."

"No, no, I mean mechanic-type house calls." Kallie leaned forward. "We have a John Deere tractor. Uncle Harvey used to keep it serviced, and later, a guy from town managed with Harvey's tools. But he moved away, and Pierre doesn't deal with ranch equipment."

"Your cousins can't?" Becca asked.

"Totally not—they're like me." Kallie laughed. "Our idea of mechanics is fixing a buckle on a saddle. Machines aren't in our skill set."

Erin pressed her lips together to keep from snickering. Was there really a male who'd admit to ignorance about engines? Usually, her male customers would stand behind her, mansplaining, while she fixed their cars. "All you need is servicing? Actual problems would take a repair shop, you know."

"No, no, it's problems we want to avoid. Just maintenance."

Huh. If Pierre didn't handle tractors, he wouldn't care if she did. And small towns were supposed to like bartering things. After listening to what Kallie did for a living, she knew exactly what she wanted. "Can I trade you for one of your weekend trips?"

"Um, sure. Is there anything in particular you'd like?" At

Erin's confused expression, Kallie elaborated. "Fishing, backpacking, photography—those sorts of things."

"Oh. Actually, I kind of wanted to learn to hike in the forest without getting lost."

Kallie laughed and stuck her hand out. "That we can do. You're on."

Their handshake of agreement was rudely interrupted by a man bumping into Erin's chair.

"Hey, blue girl. Want to dance?" The guy had a patchy blond beard, a beer gut, and a 49ers T-shirt.

"No, thank you. I'm with friends." Erin tried to keep the annoyance out of her voice, but honestly, couldn't men read body language? Had she been watching the dance floor? Looking around in hopes of meeting a man?

No, no, she hadn't.

"They won't mind if you let loose and have some fun." He jiggled the backrest of her chair as if to get her moving.

"No." She made her tone even more emphatic. "Sorry, not interested."

Although, now he'd brought it up, she would enjoy dancing. But not with a pushy drunk like him. *Uh-uh.*

When his brows lowered and his jaw set pugnaciously, she tensed. Wasn't it just her luck to get a drunk who wouldn't take no for an answer?

"You know"—he batted at her hair with the back of his hand — "the average guy doesn't like fake colors like this."

"Which means the color is perfect!" She glanced at the other women. "I prefer to eliminate *average* guys right off."

Kallie snorted beer through her nose. Becca and Sunny burst out laughing.

The man's face went red, his expression furious. "You fucking bitch, you think you're so smart?"

Oh, damn. She wasn't smart at all.

His voice rose. "I'm gonna—"

"Gonna leave our ladies alone." A man in a black cowboy hat

interposed his body between the drunk and Erin. Despite the friendly-sounding words, his dark voice held a note of steel. "Good plan, thanks."

The drunk took a quick couple of steps back, obviously intimidated.

He should be. From what Erin could see from the back, the cowboy was one big, muscular man.

"Fine. She's a bitch anyway." The drunk stomped away.

Erin slumped as her tension drained away. "Oh, man." She looked up at her rescuer. "Thank you..."

Her words dried up as her gaze met Wyatt Masterson's dark brown eyes. She couldn't look away, could see only his eyes as the surroundings blurred.

Get a grip, Erin. She swallowed. "Mr. Masterson. Thank you."

"It's Wyatt, and you're welcome. I'd like to say dumbass men are rare, but...this is a bar, and it happens." He tilted his head toward the others at the table. "It's why our women usually have back-up."

A hard-faced man with a white scar marring his tanned cheek stood beside Becca, one hand on her shoulder, and another on Kallie's. Another man with short brown hair and unyielding blue eyes stood between Mallory and Sunny.

"I...see." Erin felt incredibly alone.

"Hey, sugar, don't look like that. If I hadn't stepped in, Logan or Sawyer would have," Wyatt crouched beside her chair.

"Gotta say, you're better than I am at getting your way without starting a fight." Becca's man—would he be Logan?—had a deep, rough voice even harsher than Wyatt's.

"I what?" Wyatt looked perplexed.

The other man grinned. "Masterson, you have a rep for being able to get anyone to see things your way."

"It's all the practice. He has the two most butt-headed brothers in the world," Kallie muttered.

"And Kallie for a cousin." Sunny winked at the black-haired woman.

"Kallie can out stubborn us all." Wyatt grinned at his cousin—and Erin decided his smile should be classified as lethal.

When she got her breath back, she turned to him. "You *were* impressively smooth. Thanks for not starting a brawl." When his attention turned from Kallie to her, she wished she'd kept her mouth shut.

His razor-sharp gaze swept over her, almost like he hadn't seen her before. Of course, last time, she'd been in grease-stained, sexless bland clothing. Now she was in jeans and a tank top with loose hair. "I like the blue streaks."

"Guess you're not average, cuz." Kallie snort-laughed at his puzzled expression. She grinned at Erin. "He also likes to dance, which puts him way above average."

The music had changed from Johnny Cash to a faster country-western song, and a few couples were dancing on an open space near the jukebox.

"Was that a hint, cuz?" His gaze returned to Erin. "Do you know how to swing dance?"

"I..." Her grandparents had belonged to a dance club, and if a good tune came on, Grampie would pull Grammie into a fast swing across the living room. Of course, they'd taught her. "Yes. Yes, I do."

"Well, then." He smiled slowly. The long slice along his strong jaw no longer had stitches, and the red marks were healing on his darkly tanned face. It was a very rugged face, but beneath the chevron-style mustache, laugh lines bracketed his mouth.

He looked as if no matter what disaster might happen, he'd not only handle it but have a good time doing so.

As George Strait's "She Lays It All on the Line" started playing, he offered his hand. Her fingers were dwarfed by his wide palm. Heck, even though he was crouched, he was still a big, brawny man—and made her feel tiny.

Rising, he drew her out of the chair, onto the tiny dance area, and with an easy smile, pulled her close. After letting her catch the beat, he swung her out and pulled her back in.

When her free hand found his, he twirled her in and under his arm, until they were side-by-side, then spun her back out.

He was smiling, openly enjoying himself—and always there, catching her when she returned, their hands perfectly meeting each time as if they'd been dancing together for years.

"You *do* like dancing," she said in wonder.

"Yep." He grinned, lifting her hands over her head and spinning her in place—just enough for fun, not enough to make her dizzy. "As long as it's swing and two-step and waltz."

Another spin, back in, and he dipped her, his hold and stance so strong she had no worry over being dropped.

Okay, admit it, being held like this is incredibly sexy. When he set her upright, she asked, "Why only those?"

He pulled her back beside him. "Once you master the patterns, they're easy—and everything is focused on the woman. Nobody watches the guy."

Oh, he was so wrong. There was nothing more attractive than a man who could dance—and it was even sexier when he was concentrating on his partner. "I see."

As the music changed to a slow song, he pulled her in closer and rubbed his jaw against her hair. "I do like your hair. It's as soft as it is thick."

The top of her head came just to his chin, and she rested her cheek on his very hard, very broad shoulder. Flattening her palm on his chest, she felt solid muscle.

Kallie was right—he wasn't average at all.

The politician's wife could definitely dance. Wyatt had asked her partly to show the asshole drunk how to treat a woman—and partly because of the way her eyes had lit up.

She followed his lead like a dream. And he appreciated how

her arms weren't flaccid but tensed just enough to respond to his guidance.

Wouldn't it be interesting to see how she'd respond to him in bed—or even more appealing—under his hands in a BDSM scene.

Because, unlike with Katelyn, there was chemistry here in spades. Erin was disconcertingly appealing, from how dancing brightened her eyes, to the way she felt against him.

Her body was beautifully feminine with a lush ass. Her black tank top showed off well-toned arms and shoulders. The words: I'M A CAR DOCTOR. WHAT'S YOUR SUPERPOWER? scrawled across the front didn't conceal lovely, full breasts. And damn, he liked that she was proud of what she did.

With his hand behind her back, he guided her to the table and squeezed her shoulder as he held her chair to seat her. "You've got some muscle on you. From working out at a gym or were you a mechanic in Sacramento?"

The others at the table turned to hear her answer—and she flushed at the attention. "In the mornings, I restored classic cars. I repaid the use of the equipment by helping in the repair shop." She looked away as if confessing to something illicit.

Before he could figure out how to ask, Becca did it for him. "Your husband didn't approve, did he?"

Erin bit her lip, then shook her head. "His wife being a mechanic detracted from his image."

"What a dick." Kallie had never been one for pulling her punches, and Wyatt silently laughed. But her comment made Erin's shoulders straighten.

"You're a good mechanic. My pickup and I are appreciative." He squeezed her shoulder. "What do you think of Pierre?"

Her expression brightened. "He's a *fine* mechanic."

Wyatt almost laughed because he could tell it was her ultimate compliment. Whether Pierre realized it yet or not, the two were going to get along great.

But for himself, he needed to step back, much as he'd like to pursue his curiosity about her. Considering her correction about her last name, she might well be getting a divorce. But, even if she was, California didn't do insta-divorces...and he didn't date locals.

He straightened and glanced at the others around the table. "Tomorrow will start early. Best I head home. Night, all."

A chorus of good nights met his ears, including a husky, "Goodnight and thank you," from Erin. He met her big eyes—and unable to help himself—ran his knuckles over one high cheekbone. Such soft, pale skin. "Nice seeing you again, blue girl."

As he walked out to the cool summer night, he had to laugh at himself. A crooked politician's wife—the last person in the world he'd be interested in.

But a curvy mechanic who openly enjoyed following his lead in the dance...

So fucking tempting.

CHAPTER EIGHT

The next morning, Erin pulled out of her drive, turned left onto the road, and left again onto the very next private road. It was marked with a signpost, "MASTERSON WILDERNESS GUIDE SERVICE."

Trees surrounded the narrow gravel and dirt road until it opened into a gorgeous valley. On the left, the forest continued up the steep slope.

Oh, hey, that's my cabin perched on the overlook.

On the right were a massive barn, outbuildings, corrals, and fenced pastures. The drive ended in front of a two-story, log house.

After getting out of her car, she eyed the huge building. The logs in the center were darkened with age. The second story and sections on each side were somewhat newer. How many times had the family added on to the place?

The front had two doors, one with another sign for the Masterson guide service.

Kallie came out of the other door followed by a big gray cat —the stray. "Hey, Erin. You're right on time. Have you had breakfast?"

"I...I'm sorry, what?" Wasn't she here to work?

"Oh, such an expression." Kallie laughed. "Breakfast. It's what people eat in the morning."

"Really? Who would have thought?" Grinning, Erin rolled her eyes.

When the cat tentatively approached, she went down on one knee and held out her hand. "Hey, pretty kitty."

Ears perked, the cat booped her fingers, then head-butted her hand.

Awww. Gently stroking the soft fur, Erin told it solemnly, "You look better, young sir. I'm glad you're in a nicer place than on the street."

"Wyatt is one of those 'see a problem, try to fix the problem' people." Kallie snorted. "He was always rescuing one animal or another. You should've heard Uncle Harvey shout when Wyatt brought home an orphaned bear cub."

"No way." Appalled, Erin stared until the cat nudged her back into her petting duties. "Wasn't that dangerous?"

"Oh yeah. Uncle called Fish and Wildlife to come and get it." Kallie grinned. "Wyatt was hoping to raise it; he sulked all afternoon."

"Not for days?" When annoyed at her, Troy could hold a grudge for a good week or so.

"Hardly. Like Uncle Harvey, he'd shout for a minute, and then it'd be over and done." Kallie snickered. "In high school, when he and Morgan tried to dump their chores on me, I filled the sugar bowl with salt right before they came down for breakfast."

Erin frowned. Kallie was so petite, and even in high school, Wyatt had probably been a big guy. "Is Morgan a lot smaller than his brother?"

"By a whole inch maybe." Kallie smirked. "Their cereal was covered in salt, and they started in—and their faces got all scrunched up." Demonstrating, Kallie wrinkled her nose and pursed her lips. "I got the giggles. Wyatt, oh, he shouted. Called me a little brat, pushed me in the shower, and turned on the cold water. I screeched so loud he let go of me, all worried he hurt me. And I totally sprayed him down."

At Kallie's satisfied expression, Erin couldn't help laughing.

"Anyway, that's Wyatt—all storm and over. Granted, he rarely shouts now. He says dealing with teenaged me taught him better ways of getting his own way."

Erin laughed. "I bet you were impossible."

"*Maaaybe?*" Kallie grinned. "Morgan, though, is more mellow, but if you make him mad, he can and will wait and get revenge."

"So, what did he do after your salt trick?" When Erin paused in her petting to hear the answer, the cat put both paws on her knee and rubbed its cheek against her chin. *Awww.*

"Back then, instead of buying candy with my allowance, I'd get Oreo cookies." Kallie's expression darkened. "The jerk replaced the yummy white center with *toothpaste*."

Wow. Erin blinked. "That's completely evil; death would be too good for such a monster."

"I know, right?"

Erin rubbed the cat's furry gray head. Interesting how the brothers reacted so differently to provocation. She'd far rather deal with Wyatt's reaction—to get shouted at and have everything over and done. Grampie had been the same way. He'd slam his hand on the table, shout, and be laughing a minute later. All flash and fury, Grammie had called it.

"Anyway." Kallie pulled Erin to her feet. "If you're not in a hurry, come and have a pastry. I haven't eaten yet, and Wyatt's been buying goodies from the Bärchen Bakery ever since he got back. He says he missed Friede's baking while he was gone."

Gone, hmm. Everyone in town was delighted to have Wyatt back, but where had he been anyway? Before she could ask, Kallie led the way across a wide, front porch.

There were two front doors. One was marked with "Masterson Guide Service" and "Office."

Kallie chose the other door.

With the cat accompanying her, Erin followed through a

small entry and into a huge living room. The logs making up the walls there had been polished to a beautiful sheen. Comfortable, overstuffed couches and chairs filled the room.

Erin frowned. "Becca said your husband and Logan run Serenity Lodge. Do you two live down here instead of there?"

"No, I moved up to Serenity, but my guide equipment is down here. Wyatt and Morgan live here along with the oldest brother Virgil, who's married to Sunny."

"Ah." Erin nodded. "No wonder your house is so big." Four adults under one roof. Interesting.

Kallie grinned. "My uncle hoped my cousins and I would stay, so whenever one of us hit eighteen, he built another apartment on the second floor. We each have living quarters of our own, complete with mini-kitchens, and everyone shares the downstairs." She waved her hand toward the stairs at one end of the room.

Erin blinked. "That was amazingly far-sighted of him."

"Right? I only use mine for showers now and then. When babies start coming, I'm sure we'll remodel."

"The brothers don't mind living together?"

"No." Kallie grinned. "Unlike some families, the guys get along well. And it means one of them is always here to deal with the guide service, and the livestock and gardens."

She led the way into a big country kitchen with warm, brick-colored walls. Tiny herb plants lined the window. The heavy oak table had a box of pastries in the center. "Coffee?"

"I'd love a cup, thank you."

Kallie filled a gray-green stoneware mug, handed it over, and pointed out the sugar and creamer. "Grab a donut or roll. There are lots."

Erin doctored her coffee and chose a glazed donut. She'd barely taken a bite when there was the sound of footsteps coming down the stairs.

"Little bit, are you scarfing down all the donuts?" Wyatt strolled into the living room in stocking feet. An unbuttoned blue work shirt revealed his tanned, very muscular chest. A sexy amount of dark chest hair covered his pecs and trailed down his abdomen, making her fingers want to touch.

He stopped, obviously surprised at her presence, before looking at Kallie. "I didn't realize we had company. Sorry."

"She's probably seen a guy's chest before," Kallie told him.

As he started buttoning up his shirt, Erin saw a long, pink-red scar crossing his ribs to his side.

"That must have hurt. What happened?" Oh, damn, had she blurted the question out loud? "It looks awful."

He shrugged. "Just a flesh wound."

"Like in *Monty Python and the Holy Grail* when the knight's arms were cut off?" she asked in a dry voice.

"Exactly." He grinned. " '*Tis but a scratch.*' "

"Uh-huh." She snickered. However, his *scratch* had red dots lining the sides—all left from what must have been a ton of stitches.

"Wyatt was doing volunteer work in Africa. So far, he's attributed the wound to a rhinoceros horn. *Or* maybe a pissed-off warrior stabbing him with a spear. *Or* fending off a hyena pack." Kallie glowered at her cousin. "Oh, *or* maybe the Cape buffalo trying to impale him."

Erin started laughing. "I had no idea volunteer work was so dangerous."

A dimple in his cheek appeared with his smile.

Oh. My. Should big cowboys have dimples?

Rather than answering, Wyatt chose a donut and took a bite. His deep, smooth hum of enjoyment made her want to squirm.

"Are you going on the trip with Kallie today?" He eyed her low workman's boots and frowned.

"Not this time, but eventually." She glanced toward the window. "I'm here for tractor maintenance."

In the bar, his eyes had been so dark as to look almost black. Today, in the light from the windows, they were a dark-chocolate color.

At her feet, the cat let out a *mrow* and snaked around her ankles, almost tripping her.

She crouched to pet him. "You are very demanding, Sir Cat."

At a choked sound, she looked up.

Wyatt was watching her. The way his eyes lit with laughter and warmth set up a tingle deep inside.

"What?"

His gaze dropped to watch as she stroked the cat with both hands. "Blue girl, if you fulfill a demand so thoroughly, the normal reaction will be to demand even...more."

"Um..." Was he talking about the cat or something else?

Kallie finished rinsing her cup and set it on the counter. "Cuz, can you show her where Uncle Harvey kept the tractor supplies? I need to pick up my group down at Sawyer's. The women were getting a riding lesson, but class is probably over now, and I want to get them on the trail."

He checked a wall clock and nodded. "Head on out. I've got this."

"We'll talk, Erin," Kallie said and hurried out.

Time to get to work. And away from Mr. Tall, Tanned, and Ripped. Erin gave the cat one last stroke and gulped the last of her coffee. After rinsing the cup, she set it in the sink. "I'm ready."

"All right then." He stopped at the door to pull on his boots and don his hat. Transforming into the cowboy.

Leaving the cat inside, he showed her to the machine shed.

The space inside was well-lit by fluorescents and the light from the wide-open garage door. Wyatt pointed out the tool storage, the supplies, the extra oil and filters. "Can I get you anything else?"

"No, this should be everything I need, thank you."

He touched his fingers to his hat brim and grinned.

Damn the man. His smile was a flash of white teeth below the dark mustache—and so infectious she couldn't help but return it.

What could she say to get him to smile again? As he headed out the door, she gave herself a shake.

Work. Right. She turned to the tractor. "So, my darling, ready to show me all your secrets?"

In pure appreciation, she circled it and patted one of the giant tires. "What woman needs a man with a big, beautiful beast like you to enjoy?"

A stifled laugh made her spin around.

Wyatt stood in the doorway, eyes dancing with laughter. "Not to break up your moment of appreciation, but may I put my phone number in your cell in case you need anything. And for when you're done?"

"I...right. Of course." She could feel the heat in her face. Pulling out her phone, she unlocked it and handed it over.

He plugged in his number, sent a text to himself, and gave it back. "I'll be in the house doing paperwork. Text if you need me."

This time, she watched until he was out of hearing before muttering, "I won't."

He crossed the gravel yard to the house...and she sighed. He had a cowboy saunter that totally made her think of him looking at her with those dark eyes...with a coil of rope in his hands.

Gah, she needed to switch her reading to nice, boring inspirational books.

And to remember the facts.

One, you're not even divorced yet.

Two, you don't want to get involved with another man, remember? Look how wonderful your first real relationship turned out.

She glanced up at the house and shook her head. No wonder women turned into crazy cat ladies.

A while later, she had finished the job. Engine and hydraulic oil changed, filters checked and changed, belts and hoses checked, joints and fittings greased, battery charged, tires inspected. *Done, done, and done.*

The tractor hadn't needed more than routine servicing. Someone had taken good care of the beast.

After washing her hands in the oversized sink, she texted Wyatt. "*All done. Recommend you empty the tank and fill it with fresh gas.*"

"*Thx. Be right out.*"

Darn it, she hadn't wanted to talk with him again. He was totally messing with her *single-forever* endgame.

With a sigh, she stood in the shade of a tall maple tree and watched chickens pecking in their pen. The air was warm and dry, filled with the earthy smell of livestock and hay.

Her phone rang, and she jumped. With a frown, she checked the display. What? Why was the Sacramento police department calling her?

Tension tightened her stomach as she swiped to answer. "Yes?"

"Ms. Erin Palmer?"

She wanted to object, to tell him it was Lockwood, but what would be the point? "Yes. Is there a problem."

"I'm afraid so, Ms. Palmer. The neighbors next door to your house in El Dorado Hills reported an intruder. It appears someone broke in and..." There was a pause. "I'm sorry to report the intruder broke many of your furnishings and slashed the mattresses on the beds as well as the cushions on the upholstered furniture. Oddly enough, it appears the electronics and easily stolen items were not taken."

Her brain stalled out. "Oh. Hmm." What could she say? She'd never liked the house, yet this felt awful, like maybe the house was hurting. Still... "I'm not sure what I can do at this point. You probably know that my husband has fled the country, and no one knows where he is. I've filed for divorce—and as it happens, the house is entirely in his name. The utilities were turned off when I left."

"Ah," he said slowly. "The lack of light was how your neighbors spotted the problem—the intruder used a flashlight."

Dammit, she didn't want to be cleaning up what should be Troy's mess. "Troy has a brother, Emmett Palmer. Let me give you his phone number. He'd be the best person to contact for any further problems and what to do about the house." Checking her contacts, she read off Emmett's number.

"Excellent. I'll call him now."

"Thank you." Ending the call, she stared at the phone in her hand, at a loss for what to do next.

"Your house was broken into?" Wyatt was leaning against the maple, arms crossed over his chest.

She blinked. "When did you get here?"

"Right after your phone rang. The police officer has a loud voice. It sounds like the intruder was searching for something rather than trying to steal from you. Any idea of what they wanted?"

"No," she said reflexively, then paused. She'd heard Troy trying to blackmail a politician. Could Senator Silas Welser have tried to locate the blackmail material? Pretty unlikely. Troy would've taken anything incriminating with him.

"Had you left belongings behind that were damaged?" Wyatt asked.

"No. I brought whatever was totally mine and left the rest. I didn't want anything—"

His eyes softened. "Anything to remind you?"

"Uh-huh."

"Do you know where your husband went?"

"My ex, you mean, and no." Her laugh sounded bitter even to her ears. "I found out he'd left the country from the news like everyone else."

"Why'd you come here?" The man looked so puzzled. "To Bear Flat?"

She couldn't help laughing again. "I'm broke. He cleaned out our accounts. I have enough for a couple of months, and that's it."

Jaw hard, Wyatt set a hand on her shoulder, a steadying hand.

"As you heard, he owns the house in Sacramento. His apartment in Washington, DC was a rental. I told his brother to deal with it." She pulled in a breath. "Mom gave me the cabin here as a wedding present, and it's in my name only."

"Damn." Wyatt tugged on his mustache, then half smiled. "At least you have a place to stay."

"There's that, yes. This month has been awful." Feeling exhausted, she sank down in the grass under the tree. "I feel like such an idiot. How could I not know he was...was taking bribes? Breaking the law?"

Wyatt didn't know about the even more appalling things Troy had been doing—and wouldn't since the FBI had asked her to keep quiet while they were investigating if Senator Welser was the only one being blackmailed.

Troy was a criminal. She couldn't get past what he'd said to the senator, "*...the news media will get some really nice pictures of you with a thirteen-year-old boy. Very graphic pictures.*"

Troy had tried to blackmail a pedophile, but how involved was her husband in providing the child? Were there other politicians? Other minors?

She stared at the ground, her thoughts clogging her brain like dirty fuel.

Wyatt sat down beside her, rested his back against the tree trunk, and extended his jean-clad, long legs. "Were you close?"

"Why would you ask that? We were married." But his question was disconcertingly perceptive. Because they *hadn't* been close.

"Marriages vary. From the outside looking in, seems like a lot of the rich and famous—and politicians—get hitched for reasons other than love."

She flinched at the brutal truth. Poking her finger into the dirt to avoid seeing pity in the cowboy's eyes, she admitted he was right. "I thought he loved me. However, when Mom died, he changed. He didn't need me anymore. He only married me so Mom—Senator Lockwood—would help him get elected to Congress and support him there."

"Hell."

She swallowed hard. "He didn't love me. After he left, I learned he'd been cheating on me. For most of our marriage."

At the silence, she forced herself to look up. It wasn't pity in Wyatt's eyes, but the sympathy almost broke her. "Funny thing is, I'd already planned to divorce him, had the papers filled out, then everything blew up, and he disappeared." She huffed a bitter laugh. "I'm not even sure what to do now."

Wyatt stroked his mustache, gaze on the mountains before returning to her. "Depends. How much loyalty do you feel for him?"

Sympathy tugged at Wyatt's heart as he watched Erin's brows draw together. He liked how she gave his question some consideration before answering.

"That's bothered me. It was bad enough to realize he played me and Mom to get elected. But then..." She shook her head. "Marriage means you're loyal to each other, but I can't defend anyone who'd deliberately lie and steal from innocent people like the people in Bear Flat. He's supposed to care for his constituents, not rip them off."

Wyatt nodded. She had thought about this. "Go on."

Pulling her legs up, she wrapped her arms around her knees like a hurt animal trying to protect its vulnerable center. "If he were a boy making stupid mistakes, it would be different. But he's not a boy, and after cheating and lying, he ran, rather than trying to make things right. So, no, I won't stand behind him, no matter how guilty it makes me feel."

Her shoulders had hunched in, and Wyatt liked her all the

better for her doubts. Loyalty was a trait she obviously prized. So was honesty, it appeared.

I was fucking off base when I first saw her and figured the politician's wife was all about her fancy clothing and her asshole husband.

Here was a thoughtful woman. A practical one who wasn't afraid to get her hands dirty.

"So, that's how I feel." She rested her chin on her knees, shoulders tense as if she was waiting for him to give her grief.

Damn, but he wanted to pull her onto his lap and comfort her. "Your reasoning sounds good. There's not much you can do except wait for time to straighten things out." He frowned. "I'm guessing the FBI interviewed you a time or two?"

Her nose wrinkled. "Oh, yeah."

"If one of them left you a card, you probably should call and let them know about the break-in. The cops and feds don't always communicate."

"Oh. Yes, you're right." She sighed and stood. "I'd better get home and make a few calls."

Rising to his feet, he studied her expression. She looked so much like young Kallie when his cuz had been trying to be strong. "Need a hug?" He held his arms out.

Surprise showed in her eyes. With a tiny nod, she stepped close enough he could pull her into his arms.

Her shoulders were tight, and then with a sad sigh, she wrapped her arms around his waist and let him take some of her weight.

Made him feel...right. Like he'd lightened a bit of her load.

Tough little mechanic. He flattened his palms on her back, feeling the wiry muscles and sturdy bones that sheltered a tender heart.

For a minute, he sheltered it, too.

When she pulled back the tiniest bit, he opened his arms and let her go.

She pulled in a breath. "Thank you."

"My pleasure." He tapped her small, firm chin. "Want me to hold your hand while you call?"

Her eyes filled with tears, but she gave him a trembling smile. "Th-thanks, but no."

And he had a feeling he knew why. Although she'd divorced the bastard, someone who pondered on loyalty and honesty might well be hesitant to move on emotionally, even if her bastard husband had done so years before.

CHAPTER NINE

After spending Sunday and Monday on enjoyable guide trips, Wyatt was back in the office on Tuesday. Doing paperwork.

The cat was curled up and sound asleep in the shallow box on the corner of the desk. Previously, Wyatt had used it as his in-box.

Now it was the Bat Box.

Jerking awake, the cat sat up, ears swiveling toward the front of the house. Tilting his head, Wyatt heard boots thudding on the front porch.

Fur raised, Bat gave a low feline growl.

Wyatt chuckled. *Someone* was territorial. Laughing, he headed to the door into the main house. "C'mon, cat. I bet this is Morgan."

It was. His brother came in the front door with his duffel stuffed full of undoubtedly filthy clothing and stopped short at the sight of the Maine Coon at Wyatt's feet. "Whoa, where'd you come from, cat?"

Wyatt grinned. "Bro, meet Bat, our new ranch cat."

"Is that right?" Morgan eyed the feline, undoubtedly seeing the cat was underweight. "Don't tell me—a stray?"

"Oh yeah. Bat, this is Morgan. He's okay, cat." He grabbed his brother in a hug to show the feline that Morgan was part of the family.

Unimpressed, Bat watched, tail twitching slightly.

"Aside from being gray, he looks like Kallie's cat. He'll be formidable when he reaches fighting weight." Morgan went down on his haunches, offering his fingers. "Where'd you get him?"

"He was hanging around outside the grocery store. Whipple was trying to kick him to drive him away."

Morgan snorted. "Did you punch the only grocer in town?"

"Nope, I just sent him inside and brought Bat home."

"Bat—Bat Masterson?" Morgan rolled his eyes, then concentrated on fulfilling the feline's petting demands, watching the cat's body language for clues. The talent was part of why Morgan was in demand as a Dom. He looked up with a grin. "Thank fuck Pa didn't saddle any of *us* with the name."

"No shit." Wyatt grinned. "Did your fishing group go away happy?"

"Yep. Caught and released plenty of rainbow trout. Had ourselves a mess of catfish one night. Then brown trout a couple of times. I taught them how to soak them in milk overnight for the best flavor."

Sneaky. No backpacker would lug milk for miles. Wyatt chuckled. "And so they learn the joys of camping with pack animals."

"Got to play to our strengths." Morgan rose. "Anything going on here?"

"I caught the paperwork up. We should discuss future changes, but I like everything you two have done." Wyatt could see relief in his brother's eyes. "You weren't worried, were you?"

"Eh, wasn't sure if you'd balk over Sawyer's having been in prison."

"He reminds me of Atticus—only with an edge." And Atticus

was a good man. "It's nice to have someone else stuck with the horses." None of them would give up their own horses, but as the guide business grew, managing the guide stock had become time-consuming.

"When I was dropping off the horses, he said he'd like us to join him for an overnight on the ninth to evaluate a few horses he's thinking of buying." Morgan grinned. "He wants to breed for trail horses."

Meant there'd be foals over at the neighboring pastures. Wyatt smiled. There was nothing cuter in the world. "I'll keep those two days free. How about I toss a couple of steaks on while you clean up?"

Morgan smiled. "It's really good to have you back."

A while later, after a hearty meal of grilled steak, baked potatoes, and a token healthy tossed salad, Wyatt took two beers outside and handed one to Morgan.

"Thanks, bro." Scooting his chair around, Morgan put his bare feet up on the railing. "You look better than you did when you left. Did you get past"—he hesitated—"the killing?"

"Yeah. Volunteering as a way to make reparations, helped." Wyatt angled his chair so he could watch the sunset turn the granite mountain peaks a vivid red. "I still hate that I did something nothing can fix. A man is dead because of me." And at least two more men died at his hands during the disastrous food delivery and torching of the village. "But I'd hate it worse if I had let the bastard murder Atticus or Gin. I'm okay."

"Much how I see it too." Morgan's gaze met his, and he grinned. "But I got to that conclusion without jaunting off to Africa."

"Asshole." There were times he wondered if brothers were blessings from god…or vexations sent by the devil.

"Yep," Morgan said with his usual good cheer. "Kallie said you took a Serenity BDSM group up to Maud's last week. Go okay?"

"Yep. Nice bunch. Oh, Logan said Kallie was in Dark Haven's membership files and spotted my name."

Morgan's dark brows drew together. "If she found your name, you know she'd look for mine."

And it would be there.

Starting in college, they'd both explored kinky dominance informally. Years later, they'd discovered Dark Haven during a San Francisco trip. Who wouldn't love a classy BDSM club?

"We're busted, bro." Wyatt took a long draw of beer, savoring the taste, the night air, the pure enjoyment of being home and hanging out with his brother. "Not that I care. I intend to start going to the Serenity parties and maybe joining in when guiding their special trips."

"Yeah?" Morgan eyed him. "What changed your mind?"

As Wyatt stretched out his legs, the cat took advantage and jumped up onto his lap. Petting the beastie, he considered his brother's question. "I had a few hookups over the winter—vanilla ones."

"And you consider vanilla boring—from ice cream to sex." Morgan toasted him with his beer.

"Look who's talking." Nobody in their household liked vanilla ice cream unless it was dumped over pie or brownies or covered in fudge sauce or chocolate chips and nuts. "Looking forward, I figured I should be open to finding a woman who enjoys kink in the bedroom."

"Logical." Morgan beetled his brows. "It's interesting how you and I are into BDSM—and so is Virgil. Is being a Dom hereditary?" Morgan laughed when Wyatt choked on his drink.

But damn. "Are you saying Pa was? And Mom was his..." No, he couldn't even go there.

"You ever wonder about the placement of those plants hanging from ceiling hooks in their bedroom? I mean, they weren't even close to the window."

"For fuck's sake." Wyatt gave his brother a disgusted glare for bringing up the idea of their parents having sex...let alone kinky sex. "I'm going to have to bleach my brain."

The asshole was laughing his head off.

Wyatt took a hefty gulp of beer. Didn't help. Because now he was considering the interactions between his parents from a Dom's point of view. How Mom had often said *Yes, Sir* to Pa, then paused and laughed. How Pa had wrapped her hair around his fist before kissing her—not knowing anyone was watching.

One day she'd eaten breakfast standing up, saying she'd bruised her butt on something.

Hell. "You're right. They played. In private."

Morgan nodded. "Only in the bedroom. Outside of it, she was an equal partner in making decisions."

"Yeah, she stood beside him in everything. Could do just about anything." She'd been amazing. Soft-hearted, generous with her time for any kid needing her attention, yet with a solid core of common sense. "Pa always said she was one who'd do to ride the river with."

Morgan's hard face turned soft. "Yeah. His finest compliment."

It was a term from historic days when cowhands had to herd cattle across rivers full of erratic, swift currents. On a trail drive, you needed buddies beside you who were tough, trustworthy, and dependable. Someone to rely on when everything fell apart.

Wyatt smiled. "She's the type of woman I hope to find eventually." He'd told his mom more than once how he wanted to find a woman like her. When he was young, she just laughed and said it was a compliment to her.

In his teens, when he was actually looking at girls, he said it again. Putting an arm around him, she'd told him that someday he would find an amazing woman. *"I'll keep an eye out for the right one for you."*

Tipping his head back, he smiled up at the dark heaven stretching from horizon to horizon. *Hey, Mom, I'll take you up on your offer.*

Morgan disappeared into the house and brought back another couple of beers. Their usual limit.

"By the way, I got a text from Kallie saying the tractor got serviced by Erin Lockwood." Sawyer said she's Troy Palmer's wife." Morgan scowled. "What the fuck is she doing here?"

Wyatt tugged on his mustache. If his even-tempered brother was pissed off at Erin's presence, how much worse were the hotheads in town?

He knew, having seen Simmons giving her shit. "She's divorcing Palmer, as it happens. And she's in Bear Flat because he took all their money when he fled, and the house here is the only thing she has to her name."

Morgan sat back, thoughtfully. "Huh. And she worked on our tractor? Who showed her what to do?"

"Good thing Kallie didn't hear you being all sexist, bro." Wyatt grinned. "She's an auto mechanic and a damn fine one. Pierre tested her skills out on my pickup and hired her."

"No shit." Morgan rolled the beer bottle between his palms. "I've probably seen her, but I can't remember what she looks like."

Wyatt thought about how she'd looked when Simmons went at her—shapeless beige clothing, hair in a bun. Like a timid mouse, trying not to be seen.

But at the ClaimJumper, she'd been more vivid than the sunset on the horizon. Blue and blonde hair, a black tank celebrating being a mechanic, tight jeans showing off her fine ass, and the joy in her face as she danced with him. "She doesn't look the same now she's free of Palmer. Look for the blonde with blue in her hair."

Morgan wouldn't forget her if he met her now. The thought was oddly uncomfortable.

"Interesting. What do you think of her?" Morgan asked.

Wyatt hesitated. "She's...not what I expected." Haunting eyes, fragile heart, yet strong enough to bounce back from a ton of shit. "She's working hard to get on her feet."

Morgan nodded approval.

And when she was happy, she glowed. Wyatt glanced down at the cat lying on his feet. "Bat likes her."

Morgan snorted and said with more than a trace of sarcasm, "I guess she *must* be all right."

She was, and that was the problem. *Because I like her too.*

CHAPTER TEN

Erin had just arrived home from a long day at the auto repair shop. The atmosphere was humid, like a storm might be coming, and the temperature well into the eighties. She wandered around the house, opening the windows to let fresh air in. Her footsteps sounded loud in the quiet rooms, and she had a moment of envy for the Mastersons' place where there'd always be someone around.

As a crazy cat lady, I should own a cat or two. I'm letting my team down.

Figuring she'd be moving again, she hadn't wanted to get a pet, but it seemed she'd be here in Bear Flat for...who knew how long?

The thought was oddly appealing.

Because I have a job. Although she'd only been working there since last Wednesday. A whole week now. But for the last three days, Pierre had assigned her the vehicles with problems difficult to diagnose.

Frustrating? Occasionally. But—she grinned—wonderfully challenging.

The mood in the shop was also improving. On Monday, she'd brought in pastries from the German bakery. Over the years, she'd learned sharing food helped build a team—and hey, she enjoyed feeding people.

On Tuesday, Walker had been as gruff as ever but said good morning when she came in. This morning, Marco had asked her to show him how she'd figured out the electrical glitch in a BMW. Of course, she showed him. Teaching was fun and improving everyone's skills only made for a better shop.

And wasn't it nice he was comfortable asking her for help? *Progress.*

It was simply great to be working as a mechanic again. There was nothing like the warm 'n' fuzzies she got when a well-tuned motor simply purred...because she'd fixed it.

In the bedroom after opening the last window, she indulged in a long stretch. Her back hurt, her shoulders ached.

And she stank. Wrinkling her nose, she stripped off her filthy clothes and tossed them straight into the washer on hot.

Her long shower started off nearly scalding and ended with a refreshing cool temperature. Best way in the world to feel invigorated again. She pulled on a clean tank top and denim shorts, ignoring the way her wet hair dampened the fabric.

A glance at Grampie's banjo clock showed she had an hour before she had to change to go out. Sunny had invited her for a women's night at the Mother Lode restaurant. Apparently, the group would order appetizers and desserts and skip the boring main course. It sounded perfect.

Anticipation made Erin smile.

I'm settling in, making friends, creating a home.

After donning sneakers, she watered the tiny rosemary and sage in the deck planters, then went to the entrance facing the drive to water the hanging baskets filled with bright purple petunias.

She really shouldn't have succumbed to the garden store sale a couple of days ago. But who could resist? The hanging flowers made her house feel like a beach cottage—even in the middle of a mountain forest.

Before she'd finished the task, her phone rang.

Oh no, has the women's night been called off? But the display read "Bureau of Con—"

Holding the water hose in one hand, the phone in the other, she swiped ANSWER with her thumb. "Hello?"

"Hello. This is John Madison from the US Embassy in Buenos Aires—the Bureau of Consular Affairs. I'm trying to reach Mrs. Erin Palmer, wife of Troy Palmer."

Oh honestly, was it worth giving the divorce spiel? She held off because...Consular Affairs—they handled problems for Americans abroad. "I'm Erin."

"I have quite bad news to tell you, Mrs. Palmer. It's about your husband."

Her stomach clenched, and she swallowed. "Go ahead."

"Is there someone with you? I can call back once you have someone there."

I have no one anymore. The realization hurt deep inside her. "No, just go ahead."

The man took an audible breath. "I am sorry, Mrs. Palmer, but the police here in Buenos Aires have informed the Embassy that your husband is dead."

Oh no, no, no.

But what else would a call like this be? Hearing the words made it real, stealing all the air from around her. "How? He wasn't ill."

"I regret to tell you the police say he was murdered."

Murdered? Troy? The water hose dropped from her numb fingers.

"The police here will conduct the investigation in conjunction with us. When they are...finished, we can discuss bringing him home."

She found a bit of air and pulled it into her lungs. *Murdered.* "I...right." *Troy is dead.* The divorce wasn't finalized, so she was... was a widow. And responsible for him.

"I believe the police detective wishes to speak with you now. Can I give him to you?"

"Um, yes."

"I understand how distressing this is for you. I'm very sorry, Mrs. Palmer."

A second later, the detective came on the line. Although he spoke English, his heavy accent and phrasing made her struggle to understand what he was staying.

When she did, an icy hand seemed to close on her spine.

Troy had been tortured and murdered. Someone had shot him. In the head. The detective wanted to know if she had any idea of why.

The most likely answer was ugly. "I think you should talk to the FBI agent who was investigating my husband."

After she answered more questions, the detective realized she didn't know very much and took the FBI agent's name and phone number before disconnecting.

An unknowable amount of time later, she realized she was sitting on the front steps outside her house. Staring at the gravel as if it held answers.

There were no answers.

Troy had blackmailed a senator, maybe others. She could understand why a victim might go after him. Might kill him. But *torture*?

She shivered, thinking of the house in Sacramento. How the police officer had said the mattress and furniture cushions had been slashed. Looking for something, maybe?

And how had this person found where Troy was hiding when the FBI hadn't?

Standing, she stared at the forest, unsure what to do next. The sun beat down, hot on her skin. Her face was damp with sweat...and tears.

Troy is dead. She could hear his laugh. Subdued, genteel. He'd been groomed from birth to go into politics, even if his parents hadn't lived to see his victories.

She needed to call his brother. And say...what?

I can't. Not now, not yet. Her feet were moving. The coolness of the forest closed around her. Her eyes blurred with more tears.

Troy hadn't been a good man, but no one should die like... Her stomach turned over as she remembered what the detective had said. *Tortured.* From his unwillingness to share specifics, she knew Troy's death had been horrible.

At the thought, she started running, needing to escape... everything. Troy had died, hurting, maybe screaming. *How alone he must have felt.*

She ran faster, on and on.

Eyes blinded by tears, she tripped, staggered, and her ankle twisted with a stabbing pain. She landed on hands and knees on the soft forest duff.

Her leg ached. Her heart ached. Everything hurt. She cried. And cried even more until her chest was tight and her throat clogged.

"Oh, Troy, I'm sorry." She wiped the tears from her face and pulled in a shaking breath. "May you find the grace of mercy and kindness wherever you are."

Because he wasn't here any longer. He hadn't ever loved her, and it'd been a long while since she loved him, but still, grief flooded her.

She hauled in another breath and gave herself a shake.

Get it together, Erin. You have things to do, and crying in a forest isn't getting them done.

She needed to call Emmett. And decide what to do with Troy's body. She should talk with the FBI and see if they needed anything from her or from Troy's stuff.

With a sigh, she started to stand. Pain stabbed through her left ankle. *Ow, ow, ow!*

What the heck? Dropping back down, she looked at her leg to see her ankle had swollen over the top of her sneaker. And boy, did it hurt.

How far was she from the house? Maybe she could crawl...

She eyed the forest, left, right, ahead, behind. No house, only trees. Trees...everywhere. There were spaces between the trunks, lots of spaces, but no obvious trail. At all.

The sun was in the west, and the trail from the house had started off going west, only it might have curved around and...

Admit it, she had no idea at all the direction of her house.

Now what?

Call for help, yes! Duh. She dug in her pocket, pulled out her phone.

No bars. At all. Because she was in a forest with no cell service.

Erin, you are royally fucked.

When Wyatt knocked on Erin's front door, it swung open. The door hadn't been latched, let alone locked.

Frowning, he took a step inside and called, "Erin, it's Wyatt Masterson. Sunny asked me to check on you. She's been trying to reach you."

A few minutes ago, Sunny had called him from the Mother Lode. Apparently, Erin had promised to join her and her girl gang but hadn't showed or called and wasn't answering her phone.

She was a single woman, living alone. He could understand Sunny's worry. And his own concerns were elevated since he knew her home in Sacramento had been trashed, possibly searched.

From watching her, he figured she had an idea of why her house was searched. She hadn't shared the reason with him, but she barely knew him; they weren't friends.

Nonetheless...

"I'm coming in, Erin. Yell if you're here." Silence was his only answer.

He did a quick search of the house to ensure she wasn't incapacitated and unable to answer. *Nothing.*

Everything looked fine. Her car was in the garage, her purse on a table beside the front door. She hadn't driven away or gone off to town with someone.

Maybe she was outside the house?

Walking out the front door, he spotted water flowing in a slow stream from a hose on the ground.

"Shit." He'd seen Erin working in the garage and on the tractor. The woman was methodical and careful. The tractor supplies had been cleaned and everything put away in a meticulous fashion that would satisfy a surgeon.

After turning off the hose, he walked down the drive, studying the ground. Her car tracks headed into the garage. The only marks overlaying hers were those left by his pickup's wheels. No other vehicle had been here.

"Erin, yell out if you're here," he shouted. "Erin!" His voice echoed off the surrounding mountains.

No response.

Returning to the hose, he studied the area around it. A small running shoe had left hatch marks in the muddy area and across the loose soil toward the forest. There were small clumps of drying mud and then only faint impressions. No other footsteps showed. She hadn't come this way before today. No one had followed her.

He glanced up at the sun and scowled. It'd be getting dark soon.

So he took out his phone, pleased to see he had bars. The house probably had internet with a signal booster.

Virgil answered. "Masterson."

"Bro. Your wife asked me to check on her new buddy, Erin Lockwood—Congressman Palmer's ex-wife. She didn't show up at the Mother Lode where they were to meet."

"And?"

"I'm at her house. She left a water hose running, her door

unlocked, and her tracks lead into the woods. There aren't any other tracks around." In other words, no one chased the woman. "I've yelled, and she's not answering."

"Not good," Virgil said slowly.

"I'm going to head after her. She took an animal trail off to the left of the cabin. I've got pink flagging, and I'll mark as I go."

"It's getting dark." Virgil sounded as if he wanted to protest. Big brother worried about everyone.

However, darkness also meant there'd be no search and rescue units dispatched until morning. "I have my SAR pack. If I need to, I'll just camp wherever for the night."

"All right. Got your sat phone?"

"Sure. I'll try to check in if possible."

Virgil made a grumbling noise, but they both knew satellite phones had areas of no coverage. "I'll have SAR out looking for you in the morning if you're not back."

"Sounds good. Let Sunny know for me—and feed the cat?"

"You bet. Be careful, bro."

"Always."

Virgil snorted and hung up. Because of the three of them, Wyatt was the most spontaneous.

Had the most fun, though.

Since he occasionally helped with the local search and rescue team, his SAR pack was stocked and ready to go. He unplugged the satellite phone from his car charger and clipped it to his holster along with his revolver.

Just in case.

Then he set out to follow a city girl.

An hour later, Wyatt was fucking frustrated.

The old westerns he liked to read called this *the gloaming*, the darker part of twilight. The tops of the trees were outlined against the gray sky, the brighter stars were visible, but the ground was shrouded in darkness.

Using a flashlight as well as his headlamp, he could still follow her tracks—mostly because she'd started using a walking stick that dug holes in the pine-needle covered path.

Poor girl must be miserable. About a quarter of a mile back, there were knee and hand marks indicating she'd taken a spill. Several different holes showed she'd tried a variety of branches before settling on one for a walking stick. She wasn't putting much weight on her left foot now.

He'd guess a twisted ankle, probably not a sprain, or she'd still be sitting. It probably hurt like hell, but she was forging onward.

Unfortunately, she was obviously lost. If she'd headed left, she'd have reached the road. Instead she went to the right around the side of the mountain and was going deeper into the wilderness.

But he was getting close. After knotting more pink flagging on a branch, he shouted, "Erin. Eri—"

A faint response reached his ears. *Fuck, yes.* "Keep calling," he yelled, moving in that direction. As he went downhill, the smaller trees and shrubs beneath the evergreen canopy grew increasingly dense.

There she was, sitting on a downed log. The light from his headlamp swept over her.

Dirt, scratches, and scrapes marked her pale face, bare arms, and legs. Her hair was in tangles, her shirt had a couple of small rips. But her head was up. Her eyes were bright—and so very relieved it made his chest ache.

I'm found.

A couple of minutes ago, a man called Erin's name, and she'd answered. From high on the slope, a light appeared. Bushes shook and rustled as the person made his way down.

In the murky twilight, Wyatt appeared out of the forest, looking simply huge.

And so very strong and competent. "Yo, blue girl."

I'm not lost. Not any longer. She sucked in one breath and another. *Don't cry.*

"I'm so glad you're here." A smile was beyond her capabilities. "I'm l-lost." Her voice quavered on the last word.

"I figured. Sunny called me." Setting his backpack on the ground, he pulled out a glow stick, lit it up, and turned off his headlamp. Going down on his haunches in front of her, he assessed her with narrowed eyes.

Probably seeing the visual evidence of the numerous times she'd fallen. The long, red scratches. The blood dried on her legs. Her knees were scraped raw.

He studied her walking stick for a moment, then her swollen ankle. "Sprained?"

"Just a nasty twist, I think. It's not getting worse." At his skeptical expression, she added reluctantly, "As long as I don't put much weight on it."

A crease appeared in his cheek. "Makes walking difficult, yeah?"

Such an understatement. She snorted. "Yeah."

He glanced around. "You found yourself a nice clearing. It'll do to spend the night."

"To *what*?"

"We're a couple of hours away from your place. On a good day. This isn't a good day—it's dark, and you're not steady on your feet. We'll camp here tonight."

"But..." When the sun went behind the mountains a while ago, the temperature had dropped precipitously. The recent night temperatures had been in the 40s; her tank top and shorts were so not going to keep her warm. She was already shivering from the cold. "Wyatt, I'm not... My clothes aren't—"

He held up his hand to stop her. "Give me a minute." He tied a rope to the glow stick and hung it from a low tree limb, illuminating the area.

After rummaging in his pack, he pulled out a zip-up, fleece hoodie. "Let's get you warmed up." He helped her into it, zipped it, and pulled up the hood as if she were five years old.

Any thought of independence died when she realized her chilled fingers were almost numb. Instead, she wrapped her arms around herself. "That feels so much better."

"I bet. A shame I can't make a big bonfire to warm you up, but we're in 'no campfires' season." He pulled a pair of long johns out of his pack. "Stand up for me now and drop your shorts."

She hesitated a moment—but her legs were freezing. She rose, balancing most of her weight on her uninjured leg, and fumbled with the zipper of her shorts. Her fingers still weren't working well. "Dammit."

"Poor baby." Standing in front of her, he undid her shorts and pulled them down. And, okay, cold or not, she totally felt a zing of sexual interest. Because his hands were big and steady, because he smelled like the forest, because...

Because he was Wyatt.

He grabbed a flannel shirt from his pack and tossed it over the log behind her, obviously to keep her bare legs from being scraped on the bark. "Sit there while I get your shoes off."

Once she was seated, he gently eased her left sneaker and sock off her swollen painful ankle.

"Oh, such a relief."

"Good."

But as he removed her other shoe and sock, she grew way too conscious of her bare legs and how her bikini briefs barely covered her crotch. She was totally alone with him, hardly knew him, and they were awfully far from civilization.

"Erin." His dark, dark eyes held hers. "You're safe with me." His deep, rough voice was painfully blunt. And sincere.

She was safe. Looking into his eyes, she felt safe.

He waited for her nod, then worked the long john legs over her feet and up her legs. "Stand for me again."

Rising, she pulled the long underwear up herself. *Warm. So warm.*

He grinned. "There, you're dressed for a fashionable evening out in the woods. Let's finish it off with this."

His pack yielded a thin sleeping bag. After unzipping it, he wrapped the sleeping bag around her, carefully wrapping the bottom around her bare feet.

Shivering, she pulled it tighter and sighed in relief as the biting cold breeze disappeared. "Thank you. Seriously, thank you."

"All part of the search and rescue service." He unclipped a phone from his belt and dialed. "Yo, Virg."

"Where are you?" The man's voice was even deeper than Wyatt's baritone.

"A couple of hours to the west. Erin's got a banged-up ankle, so we're spending the night here. With luck, her leg will be better in the morning—and we'll have light."

"Need me to send anyone?"

"Nope, we're good. I'll call with a report in the morning. Can you have Sunny reassure the womenfolk so they don't worry?"

Sunny's voice came over the receiver. "I will, Wyatt. Take good care of her."

Erin bit her lip against the wave of emotion. She wasn't as alone as she'd thought. "Tell her"—her voice cracked—"thank you, please?"

Wyatt squeezed her hand gently. "Sunny, Erin says thanks. As for me, I figure you owe me a good dessert." Disconnecting, he put the phone back on his belt.

Again he reached into his pack.

"You're like a magician, pulling all sorts of things out of your hat," she muttered.

"You're going to like this one." He set a Ziploc bag on her lap and even opened it for her. "Trail mix."

"Food! Oh wow." She reached in. Dried fruit, nuts, and... "M&Ms." Popping a few in her mouth, she hummed happily. "I bet you're very popular in search and rescue circles." Yes, wherever someone wanted a strong, competent, rugged-type man, he'd be popular.

Beneath his dark mustache, his teeth flashed in a quick grin. An incredibly compelling grin.

And her estrogen levels red-lined.

He held her gaze for a moment, head tilted slightly, then shook his head. "One more thing." He set a bottled water beside her. "Drink it all. There's a stream nearby, so I can refill it."

"An article I read said no one drinks water out of streams or lakes anymore. Because of parasites or germs..."

"How unsafe it may be is controversial. But my water bottle has a filter."

As she nibbled on the trail mix, Wyatt set up a camp so quickly it was amazing. After raising a small tent, he tossed in two sleeping pads and a second sleeping bag.

After clearing a space and brushing away evergreen needles down to the dirt, he heated a mug of water on top of the tiniest burner she'd ever seen.

"Do you always travel with all this stuff?"

"If it's just me hiking, I carry enough for myself. I bring extra if I'm looking for a person. Everything is ultra-lightweight, so it's not too much trouble." He pulled out a couple of odd-looking packets. "Any food allergies?"

"No, I eat everything."

His chuckle was deep and masculine. "Perfect. You have a choice of chicken ramen or beef stew."

He was offering her warm food. *Oh yes.* "Ramen? But either is fine."

"You're easy to please."

. . .

The city girl was surprising in so many ways, Wyatt thought as he set up a latrine area. He wasn't surprised she'd gotten lost. That, he'd expected.

Her eyes were red, the lids swollen. She'd obviously cried her head off. No surprises there either.

But after years of guiding, he'd come to expect his wealthy or well-connected clients to have rather obnoxious entitlement issues.

But she didn't. She was purely grateful, not just for the rescue, but the clothing too. She openly appreciated the little things—like humming when eating trail mix.

He liked that. A lot.

After showing her how to use the trekking poles he carried, he hung the glowstick around her neck, gave her a tiny tube of antibiotic ointment for her scratches, and left her to use the latrine and clean up before bed.

Meanwhile, he suspended the food—no need to feed the bears—and finished setting up the pads and sleeping bags in the tent.

The very *small* tent. It would be better if he slept under the stars. Unfortunately, tonight was going to be one of May's rare rainy days.

Dammit.

A few minutes later, Erin limped into the clearing. She'd managed to get both shoes on, although her left foot was sockless, and the shoelaces were undone. Even better, she was putting some weight on her injured leg.

Her ankle was improving. Good.

Her smile was wide. "I love these poles."

"They're useful. I like to use them when crossing creeks or areas with loose rocks, but they're great when people get a bit dinged up."

"Dinged up. It's my fault. I wasn't watching where I was going."

Why was that, he had to wonder.

After returning the glow stick, she eyed the tent. "Bedtime?"

"It's getting late, yeah. Sunrise is around 6, and it's tough to sleep in when the side of the tent is bright."

"Okay." No argument, no drama. After handing him the trekking poles, she crawled into the tent. And paused, probably seeing their sleeping bags were unavoidably side-by-side. But after a minute, she sat on the one without his pack on it, removed her shoes, and placed them by the door.

"If you need the latrine during the night, the poles will be just outside." Wyatt laid the poles near the door. "The glow stick will be under a chunk of bark so the light doesn't keep us awake."

"Got it, thank you." She wiggled into her sleeping bag and sighed. "This is more comfortable than I thought it would be."

He chuckled. Exhaustion turned the hardest bed soft. Although he had to admit, the foam pads these days were fairly comfortable.

"I'll be in shortly." He headed off to use the latrine and do a quick cleanup with the handwipes he carried.

Back in camp, he tucked the glow stick under a thick length of tree bark. There were enough cracks to let a small amount of light escape, allowing navigation into the tent—and out, if needed.

For a moment, he hesitated before shucking off his jeans and flannel shirt, leaving on his briefs, T-shirt, and socks. Wearing too many clothes in a sleeping bag gave him claustrophobic nightmares.

Tossing his clothing into the tent, he crawled in. His boots went at the foot of his bed, and his pack in a corner.

"I'm awake. You don't have to try to be quiet." She might be awake, but she sounded rather groggy.

"Sorry. Normally, I'd sleep outside, but the forecast is for rain showers later tonight."

"Definitely stay in here then." She gave a sleepy half-laugh.

He slid into his sleeping bag and wrapped his flannel shirt around his jeans in a token pillow.

"Oh, what a good idea."

In the small amount of yellow light cast into the tent from the glow stick, he could see her pull off the fleece jacket and wad it up for her own pillow.

"Perfect." Her sigh held a contented sound. Easy to please, wasn't she?

He shouldn't have judged her by the asshole she'd married. He grimaced. Just consider some of the women he'd dated—especially when he was newly out of college. Back then, he'd let his dick rule, and his dick was impressed with breasts and beauty. It wasn't called the little brain for nothing. "Night, Erin."

"Good night, Wyatt."

Arms behind his head, he closed his eyes and listened as her breathing slowed and deepened. Smiling slightly, he let himself fall asleep.

Erin woke with a jerk. The air smelled wrong; the bed was wrong. She tried to throw the covers back, but they didn't move. She was trapped.

Gasping for air, she sat straight up, seeing a horrible yellow glow just—

"Whoa, blue girl, relax." A man's voice. It deepened to a rough growl. "Erin, you're safe. You were hiking and hurt your ankle, remember?"

Hiking. Her ankle did throb. Oh...she was in the wilderness. And... "Wyatt?"

A masculine chuckle sounded in the darkness of the tent. "There we go; you got it."

"Ohhh. Sorry, I woke you, didn't I?"

"No problem. I sleep light when I'm camping."

Because there were animals out here. She sucked in a hard breath. "I can't believe I just walked into the forest and didn't even think about bears or cougars or *anything*."

"Mmm." There was a pause and the sound of him moving. In the slight light of the glow stick, she saw him turn over to face her. "When I went to your house to check on you, your hose was running, and your front door was unlocked. Want to tell me why you left in such a rush?"

His question threw her right back to the phone call. "I..." Her eyes started to burn as a sob welled up. *Oh god, no, no, I won't cry.* Her breath hitched as she fought it.

A warm hand closed over hers. "Hey, now, it can't be that bad."

"It *is*." As emotions flooded her, the dam she'd built collapsed. And then she was crying, mourning a husband who hadn't loved her at all. And maybe she was crying about that too.

With a firm arm around her waist, Wyatt drew her down until she was tucked against his side, her cheek pressed against his hard shoulder. His T-shirt was soft against her wet face, and she couldn't stop sobbing.

Troy was gone, and she was a widow, and he'd been tortured, and she didn't know what to do.

As the muscles under her cheek tensed, she realized she'd said everything out loud.

But he didn't push her away. One arm held her against him, and his other hand moved up and down her back in long comforting strokes.

He made a gruff sound, not an irritated or horrified one, but more like what she'd voice when looking at a messed-up engine. The sound of resolve before rolling up sleeves and setting to work. "Let me see if I got this straight. Your husband is dead—and he was tortured before he died?"

She nodded against his shoulder.

He hmphed in acknowledgement. "Is he here in California?"

"An embassy called me. From Argentina—Buenos Aires. And I talked to the police there." She sighed. "I was watering the plants on the porch when I got the call."

"No wonder you headed for the closest escape you could

find." He tugged a lock of her hair. "You were crying, I bet. It's good you didn't walk off a cliff, woman."

Not her finest moment, but unlike Troy's criticisms, Wyatt's statement sounded more worried than disparaging.

He seemed to understand why she reacted as she had.

She relaxed against him, needing to be held, to not feel alone. Was it all right to indulge for a few moments? Stretching her arm over his waist, she held on. "Thank you...for letting me cry all over you."

"No problem." He was still stroking her back and occasionally running his fingers through her hair. So very soothing. "I'm trying to get my head around your husband being tortured. Any idea of why?"

Was there any reason to keep it a secret any longer? Troy was gone. *Dead.* Her chest felt like a boulder lay on it, squeezing her heart.

And she felt so disloyal. If she hadn't talked to the FBI...

No, what was she thinking? He'd used *children* for political gain. Her emotions felt like fraying fan belts, whining and burning. Coming apart. "I'm so mad at him. And so sad."

"Tell me."

"I wasn't supposed to, but I guess there's no reason for secrecy any longer. Not now that he's d-dead." She pulled in a breath. "It was probably for revenge. I heard Troy blackmailing another politician. And I told the FBI."

Wyatt was silent, and the minutes stretched on. Judging her, probably.

"He wasn't who you thought you'd married."

Wyatt hadn't been judging her. Her muscles relaxed again. "No. I had no idea he..." She felt the tears start again and blinked hard. "It sounded like he was hosting parties for powerful men, parties where the men could indulge all their vices—like sex with underage boys and girls."

The growl of disgust told her everything she needed to know about Wyatt.

"I guess the parties were where he got blackmail material. I... I couldn't let him continue." She inhaled through her nose. "He was hurting *children*."

"You did the right thing, Erin. It's not easy though." He tightened his arm around her in a comforting squeeze. "Back when I was a teen, I had some friends who boasted to me how they beat up a drunk. Just because they could. I couldn't figure out what to do; it's against the code to rat out your friends, right?"

Or your spouse. "Did you tell anyone?"

"I asked my father. *'Pa, if you saw a friend do something bad, what would you do?'* I made like it wasn't important, but"—he chuckled—"I'm sure he saw right through me."

Erin looked up, seeing the corded neck, the strong jaw, trying to imagine this so-very-assured man as a confused teen. "Did he have advice?"

"He made it harder, actually. He said each person has an unspoken contract with the world—with humans and animals and the earth—and our contract with the whole world is as valid as the various other obligations we owe to our spouses, family, friends, and even our country. So when deciding what course to follow, you must weigh it all...and sometimes, there's no perfect answer."

"Ouch, I guess. How did you decide what to do?"

"A lot of thinking. First, I decided my—and everyone else's—obligation to civilization was as valid as the one to my friends. Then I had to admit my friends broke their contract with other humans. Taking it a step further, if allowed to continue on such a path, their next actions could be even more damaging." He sighed. "I snitched on them."

That was...an amazing viewpoint. Saying you had an obligation to others, even to the earth? But it made sense. People believing they owed loyalty to only their family, business, or country was what had gotten the planet in such a mess.

But taking the high road could be painful. "How did that work out for you?"

His laugh was rueful. "As you can guess, I lost a lot of friends. Although a couple of years later, two of them thanked me. Getting caught yanked them out from under the influence of the bully who led the group."

"But it was lonely for a while?"

"Oh yeah. Brothers are great, but there's a lot of school time when they're not around."

Sympathizing, she patted his chest, feeling the solid muscles beneath the soft chest hair.

She had a feeling he wasn't the type to talk about his burdens, especially emotional ones. But he had tonight—to ease her conscience. "Thanks for sharing. It helps."

Because if she used his philosophy of values, it said she had a contract with all people, not just her husband. And Troy broke his contract with the world, with the citizens he was supposed to protect, and he had harmed children.

She'd done the right thing. "Thanks."

Hearing the patter of rain on the tent, she snuggled against his warmth, and her eyelids began to droop. How could being with a virtual stranger feel as reassuring as being curled in a blanket pile in front of a fire, with Grammie and Grampie in their chairs, discussing their day? The very essence of home and safety.

Here she was in the wilderness, in a stranger's clothing, with a hurt ankle—yet, somehow, next to Wyatt, she felt wrapped in comfort.

As Wyatt heard Erin's breathing slow and her body go limp with sleep, he kissed the top of her head. Blue girl had been through a hell of a time.

Her husband was even more of an asshole than Wyatt had

realized. Thank fuck she'd had the courage and morals to turn him in.

Even so, she'd cried for the bastard's death.

Wyatt tightened his arm around her, enjoying the feel of her soft body against his, thinking of her loyalty to her husband. Her courage. Pa would have liked the person she was.

With his fingers, Wyatt played with the ends of her hair. She was so very different from the person he'd first thought she was. Not a politician's wife and a society woman, but a mechanic with streaky blue and blonde hair. One who liked ramen, who laughed when she danced.

And one who felt just right in his arms.

CHAPTER ELEVEN

With a cup of coffee, Erin took a seat out on her deck. She and Wyatt had gotten back on the trail so early they'd been back before nine.

Below her spread the lush, green valley, bright in the morning. Realizing she was trying to spot Wyatt on his ranch, she turned her gaze in the other direction.

So pretty. Fuzzy white patches of fog on the mountainsides were slowly rising under the warmth of the sun.

A sip of coffee made her smile. She'd added a hefty squirt of dark chocolate because she darn well deserved it. Leaning back, she rested her aching ankle on another chair.

Before they left, soon after dawn, Wyatt had wrapped her ankle with sure, competent hands. Between the bracing and his trekking poles, she'd done just fine.

She'd dreaded how he might react to her slow pace. Instead, he'd been...wonderful. With no sign of impatience, he'd watched her and adjusted his pace so she never felt strained. He stopped for frequent rest breaks—and shared his trail mix.

Even better, he talked as they walked, openly sharing his love of the wilderness. When the sun lit up the granite cliffs, he told her about the different geologic formations. When they crossed a charming creek, he showed her the tiny plants that thrived in the moist streamside. He'd pointed out a deer with a fawn, a cougar sunning itself high up on a ledge, and a red-tailed hawk.

In fact, he behaved as if he was a hiker having an enjoyable morning, rather than a search and rescue person who'd had to rescue her butt.

He was so comfortable to be with...well, except for the constant simmer of sexual awareness. And she'd tried to ignore it, dammit.

But Wyatt Masterson was far too attractive. Not like a lot of those pretty male TikTok influencers. No, his face was too weather-beaten and rough-hewn to be considered handsome.

And pretty? *Hah.* Despite his easy-going attitude, he was almost aggressively masculine, from his thick mustache and beard-shadowed jaw to his muscular, powerful body, all broad shoulders and long legs.

Larger than life and darned overwhelming.

It was good he'd brought her home and simply accepted her thanks. If he'd pushed at all, invited himself in, she'd have had a difficult time saying no to anything he wanted to do.

What was there about his effortless authority that made her body react to just his voice? To go soft when he looked at her?

No, just stop.

She wasn't going there.

And she had things to do this morning.

"Okay, let's do this." Troy's brother started his days early; he'd be at work. She pulled up her contacts and selected Emmett Palmer.

The detective and consulate would have shared the news. Actually, being male, he'd probably managed to elicit more information from them about Troy's murder.

But he knew she'd filed for divorce. Only now...she was no longer almost divorced but Troy's widow. *How awkward is this?*

Nonetheless, she needed to reach out. As Troy's only family, Emmett might want input into the decisions she made.

"Erin. I'm glad you called." His soft tenor conveyed his sincerity. "How are you doing?"

"All right, I guess." What could she say? "I'm so sorry about Troy, Emmett. Are you all right?"

"This is...hard. Really hard." His voice was quiet. "I know he wasn't the best person in the world, but he was my brother. I still can't believe what happened."

He was suffering; she could hear it. Like her, he must have had no idea what Troy had been doing. She shook her head under the slow slide of guilt. If she hadn't gone to the FBI, Troy would still be alive. Emmett didn't know what she'd done.

The FBI had probably told him only what she'd learned—which was mostly nothing. The blackmailed senator had refused to talk about what Troy wanted from him or anything else.

Focus, Erin. "The Embassy in Buenos Aires left me a message. When the police there release"—*the body*—"Troy, they need to know what to...um, to do. Do you want a funeral in the US or to have him buried there or...?"

"Ah, I see. Do you have a preference, Erin?"

"No, no, I don't." Her feelings were too mixed up to make any decisions like this.

"Hmm." She could hear him tapping his fingers on the desk. "Our parents are gone, and other than me—and you—Troy has no one here."

"You'd rather he be buried in Argentina?"

"It sounds cold, but a funeral here would set off another media storm. They'd bring up everything he did. How he died. I don't want that for him."

"Oh." She hadn't thought about reporters. "Troy would hate being ripped apart by the press again."

"Yes. Definitely. Listen, my dear, why don't you let me handle the arrangements? I can work things out with the consulate."

"That would be very kind of you." She let out a breath. "To

be honest, Emmett, I don't have the money. Troy cleaned out our accounts when he left." Her pride stung as if she'd rubbed alcohol into a cut. But Emmett was a high-paid CEO of a major corporation. He could easily afford whatever needed to be done for Troy's burial.

There was a silence. "I guess I'm not surprised he took what he needed. He was running, after all. Do you need some funds?"

She winced. "No, I'm fine."

"You don't sound fine. I'm sure you're shaken by all this. I've got a couple of days free this week. How about I drive up to the mountains to see you? If you want, I can stop by your house for anything you might have forgotten there?"

"Thank you, but no. I have everything that was just mine."

"All right. I'll come up, we can talk, and maybe make sense of all this. And put it behind us."

She liked the idea of talking over what Troy had done. But with Emmett? Have Troy's brother here in her quiet refuge? The refusal emerged before she even thought it through.

"I appreciate the offer to talk, but I'd rather not think about any of this." Great, now she felt totally rude. Why couldn't she manage to speak about sensitive issues without putting her foot in her mouth?

There was a pause before he said gently, "Of course. Do you have anyone you can speak with?"

She bit her lip. She sure couldn't tell Troy's brother she'd blurted everything out to a virtual stranger. And slept in his arms afterward.

He added quietly, "I would like someone to talk to, also."

Guilt loaded onto her shoulders. How could she refuse to be there for a grieving brother?

But...but she and Emmett weren't close. Weren't even especially friends, just polite in-laws. "I'm sorry, Emmett, but I can't." She felt as if she was kicking a puppy.

"I...see. In that case"—his voice took on an icy note and for a second, she understood how he'd become a CEO—"thank you for calling, Erin. I'll see to Troy's arrangements."

The phone went silent, and she stared at it for a moment, stunned at the abrupt end to the conversation.

"Huh." She sighed and placed a call to the consulate to let them know Emmett would be in touch...and to ask for copies of the death certificate.

Because Emmett's question about belongings reminded her she had to deal with Troy's house. Feeling her eyes start to burn again, she started to make a list of her next steps.

Feet up on his desk, leaning back in his office chair, Wyatt stared at the ceiling as he waited on hold for a friend to answer the phone.

It'd been an interesting twenty-four hours. He never objected to a nice hike—and Erin was a good companion. When he realized the forest was completely foreign to her, he'd enjoyed sharing his world. Her comments and questions showed she listened and thought before responding. Even better, she'd made him think and even stumped him for answers a couple of times. She didn't fill the air with idle chatter either.

He'd take her hiking any day or time.

Over the past week since talking with Logan Hunt, he'd reconsidered his stance on dating locals. Logan had made a valid point. It wasn't the locals Wyatt was avoiding as much as it was the possibility of getting involved. Perhaps it was time he stopped being a coward.

And, he had to admit, a woman with big blue eyes, a courageous heart, who liked to cuddle was proving difficult to resist.

As if hearing his thoughts, the cat jumped up and stared down into Wyatt's face.

"Yes, Bat, I know you like to cuddle too." Chuckling, Wyatt petted the cat until he curled into a purring ball of fluff on his chest. "Hate to say it, but you're not as snugglesome as a pretty mechanic."

Then again, holding Erin had ensured he had a hard-on for the remainder of the night. He'd probably have been awake anyway, mulling over what her ex-husband might have been up to—and how it would impact her.

Thus, the reason he was stuck on hold this morning.

Jameson Stanfeld was a Special Agent with Homeland Security. DeVries had introduced them soon after Wyatt became a member of Dark Haven in San Francisco, and they'd all hit the shooting range a couple of times. The agent was a stand-up guy.

"Wyatt? Are you back at last?" Stan's strong voice held enough of a Texas accent the word "last" was drawn out.

"Yep, home in Bear Flat. How are you doing? And how's Dixon?"

"I'm good—and Dixon is just fine." The contentment in the statement made Wyatt smile. He figured Dixon's firecracker nature kept Stan's seriousness from turning stodgy. And, as his Master, Stan kept Dixon corralled...somewhat. "Are you plannin' to visit San Francisco?"

"Not anytime soon—it's our busy season. But I hear a bunch of your Dark Haven crowd is coming to the Serenity party at the end of July. I'll be going this year."

"Dix and I might make it. Gotta say, it's about time you attended the Serenity events." Stan paused. "What's on your mind then?"

Wyatt tugged on his mustache, hoping he wasn't overstepping his bounds. "There's a young woman here who I'm concerned about. Her name is Erin Lockwood—previously Palmer. Troy Palmer's wife, and she..."

As he talked about Palmer's torture and death, he heard scratching noises. The agent was taking notes.

"A blackmailer whose house is broken into, and he's tortured to death." Stan summed it up. "Could be a victim wants revenge. Or maybe to get whatever damaging evidence he had on them."

"Kinda what I figured." Wyatt dropped his feet from the desk and set Bat on the floor, getting an annoyed *mrow* in response. "I know this isn't your area. I'm mostly trying to get a handle on if Erin's in danger."

Stan was silent for a minute. "From the way Palmer abandoned her and what she's doing now, she's a victim, not a conspirator in the blackmail scheme. Not a beloved wife, either. Whoever killed Palmer will probably be satisfied with his death. It's interesting the murderer found him when the FBI couldn't. I wonder how he gave himself away."

"Maybe he tried for more money and wasn't careful enough to cover his tracks. Or spilled his secrets to the wrong woman." It wasn't likely the asshole would go long without finding a woman to fuck.

"It's sad to say about a person who passed, but the world is better without him in it."

Wyatt nodded. Anyone who preyed on children needed to be taken out of play. Jail would've been fine, but dead... Maybe justice had been served in this case. "Agreed. Thanks for confirming what I was thinking about Erin."

"Not a problem. But, Wyatt..." Stan paused. "Just in case, keep an eye on her."

"Yeah. Thanks for letting me run this past you." The agent had confirmed what Wyatt had thought. As well as confirming there was still a risk.

She'd already captured his interest. But add in possible danger? "She'll get both eyes as often as I can."

Yesterday, Erin had cried after hearing about Troy's death. And again when she hurt her ankle. And in the tent last night, she cried all over Wyatt. Add in crying this morning after talking to Emmett.

Honestly, Erin, you were divorcing the man. Only she'd loved him once, had lived with him, and he'd died in a horrible way. It was okay to cry for him.

And she had. Which was why, despite the cold compresses, her eyelids were puffy and her eyes red. Her emotions felt as fragile as one of her antique clocks.

Using a cane she'd picked up at the second-hand store, she limped into "her" bay in the auto repair shop only two hours late.

"Hey, Erin, the boss was looking for you," Marco yelled from under an SUV.

"Okay, thanks." She'd left a rather vague message on the shop's voice mail to say she'd be late getting in this morning. Pierre probably wanted to know why.

In fact, the Cajun shop owner was already heading toward her, a glare quite evident in his gaze. Until he spotted her cane. He frowned. "You have yourself a bad leg, *cher?*"

"I took a spill yesterday." As his frown deepened, she added hastily, "I can still work. It's not like there's a lot of walking to do here."

"No." But his gaze was on her face and her swollen eyes. "If your ankle hurts so badly to make you cry, you should not be here."

"It's not that."

He waited, reminding her of Wyatt and his patient silences.

"My husband... I got a call yesterday telling me he's dead."

Pierre shook his head and put his hand on her arm. "Come and you will tell Pierre all about it. Then we will decide if you will work."

His sympathy made her swallow hard and just nod, unable to speak.

As she followed Pierre to the office, Marco yelled from under the SUV, "Hey, Sparks, I brought donuts. They're in the break room."

He'd called her Sparks. Was sharing goodies. Before she could react, they walked through the first bay. Walker turned, and his eyes narrowed as he saw her face. With a concerned expression, the older mechanic tilted his head as if to ask if she was all right.

She nodded, blinking back tears.

Because she'd become part of the crew.

CHAPTER TWELVE

After work the following Monday, Erin walked down a side street off Main. Gold Dust Avenue led past the Methodist Church and a small B&B, and there she found her destination.

The white-sided, one-story house with a red-brick foundation boasted a sign in front: BEAR FLAT LIBRARY. The yard was well-tended and charming with indigo benches next to the sidewalk. Maybe in case someone couldn't wait to get home before starting their book?

Stepping inside, Erin drew in a blissful breath at the lovely smell of books, books, and more books. The scent ranked right up there with the fragrance of bread baking and freshly laundered clothes dried outside on a sunny day.

Also the aroma of bacon in the morning. Maybe because Grampie would make breakfast for Grammie and Erin on Sundays.

Moving past the aching homesickness, Erin looked around.

To make the house into a library, many walls had been removed, creating an open, friendly atmosphere—especially in the colorful children's section to the right.

Several preschoolers sat at the small tables. With her brown hair up in cute space buns, a freckled high-school girl was reading them a story.

The tiny, gray-haired librarian behind the checkout desk had a nametag of MRS. GANNING. Her brown eyes, a shade darker than her skin, were welcoming. "Come on in, we don't bite."

"That's good to hear." Erin smiled. "What do I need to do to check out books?"

"Show me a driver's license and anything to prove your current place of residence."

"Perfect." She showed her ID and the last Bear Flat utility bill. Having gotten library cards in the past, she remembered what was usually needed.

The librarian worked at the computer for a minute, moved to the printer and laminator, then handed over a plastic card with Erin's name and a barcode at the bottom. "Here you go, Ms. Lockwood. Would you like directions or—"

"Make it Erin, please, and I'm fine just wandering around." Erin almost wiggled in happiness. "Libraries are the best places."

"I feel exactly the same way"—Mrs. Ganning cast a fond look at the children—"Especially during story time." Then she frowned, probably because it was clear the children had lost interest in the story being read to them.

Unsurprising. The teen was simply reading.

"She needs to show them the pictures," Erin murmured. "Preschoolers are all about visuals."

"Are you volunteering?" Mrs. Ganning asked.

"Uh, but—"

"Very good." The petite woman marched out from behind the counter, shooing Erin in front of her like a herd dog with a stray lamb.

But, but, but...

With two sharp claps, Mrs. Ganning commanded the attention of the small group. "Camila, I need your help behind the desk."

The girl's relieved smile seemed familiar. Was she the real estate agent's daughter?

"Children, Ms. Erin will finish reading you the book." Mrs. Ganning took the book from Camila and handed it over.

Everyone looked at Erin.

Oh, boy. This felt like an auto mechanic's challenge—get it running or else. Erin focused on the group. Only five children. They could all see the pictures if...

Holding the oversized book, she sat on the floor and leaned against a low bookcase. "Join me here so you can see the pictures."

That worked. With the shortest child between her legs, she had two on each side. "So what has happened so far?"

As they took turns catching her up on the story, she mentally constructed voices for the various animal heroes. The story sounded fun.

She started reading, adding drama to...everything. "With a screech, the hawk swooped out of the sky." She used her hand to show the hawk diving down and landing—on one child's chubby little hand.

The adorable boy let out a participatory shriek—and they all burst into giggles, Erin laughing as hard as they were.

Catching her breath, she continued, stopping occasionally to ask questions like "What should he do now?" before turning the page.

When the mean hedgehog showed up, Erin's "Uh-oh," was echoed by five high voices.

The last page arrived, and she uttered the closing, "The End," to a gratifying chorus of: *Can we read another one?*

But when she looked up, she saw Mrs. Ganning as well as the parents at the edge of the section. They were all obviously listening. She could feel her face get hot. "Sorry, kids. I think your parents are here to get you."

"Awww," one sweet-faced girl mourned. "Can you come back again, Ms. Erin?"

"That was great," a tall mother was saying to Mrs. Ganning. "I've totally missed the boat with my reading skills. Is she a new librarian?"

"I'm afraid I drafted her with no warning." Mrs. Ganning had an approving smile for Erin. "However, I'll do my best to get her back for more."

The reader group gave Erin heartwarming hugs, then ran to their parents and the counter to check out their book choices.

After straightening up the area—because Grammie would've tanned her hide if she hadn't—Erin headed into the stacks to find her own reading material. Thinking of a certain big cowboy, she picked up a couple of western romances and a contemporary suspense. Unfortunately, the library didn't have any truly kinky novels. Not that she'd have checked one out anyway. She wasn't about to set a BDSM book on the counter.

At the desk, she handed over her books and brand-new card. While Mrs. Ganning went through the check-out ritual, Erin waited and simply savored being in a library.

"Can I convince you to volunteer for more storytelling sessions this summer?" Mrs. Ganning smiled and pushed a sheet of paper forward. "You can pick and choose your times."

Erin studied the paper. There were slots for reading to various ages, slots for helping people with their reading skills, slots for working with children on kid projects.

"You totally should volunteer. You're good." Kallie stepped up to the counter. "I was with a group in the magazine section, and we all ended up listening to your story instead of working."

Erin choked on a laugh. "Sorry?"

"No, you're not." Kallie grinned, then studied Erin. "Being a mechanic, are you any good with craft projects? I'm leading a kid's STEM group, doing hands-on stuff."

"*Stem*—as in plants?"

Kallie laughed. "STEM like the acronym for science, technology, engineering, and mathematics. Our task today is supposed to be making battery-driven toy cars."

Erin eyed her. *Supposed to be?*

A girl, maybe around eight years old, ran up. "We have the cardboard all cut out."

"I'll be right there." As the child trotted back to her group, Kallie sighed. "I do *not* know what I'm doing. I'm good with horses, not mechanical stuff. Please help?"

Laughing, Erin told Mrs. Ganning, "I'll be back for my books." She hooked an arm with Kallie. "I'm great with cars—even toy ones."

A few minutes later, she saw the picture of what was supposed to be the finished project. *Piece of cake.*

"This will be fun." She waggled her eyebrows at the six children, all around seven or eight. "When you're done, we can race them."

The far-too-loud-for-a-library cheering made her laugh...and wince at the *shhhs* from a couple of people. Was she going to get the group thrown out?

But an unexpected smile from Mrs. Ganning let her know all was forgiven.

"Hey, Mr. Masterson, did you see? I won!" Roger Simmons' boy, Heath, jumped up from the sidewalk in front of the library.

"I saw. Your machine was definitely the fastest." Wyatt squatted down to examine the odd-looking device. The slab of cardboard had four tiny wheels. Wires from a battery case with two AA batteries led to a cardboard platform supporting a mini-DC motor that turned a propeller. "That's very cool, kid."

"I know!" Heath's chest puffed out proudly. "She helped us make them." He pointed to...damned if the woman wasn't *Erin*.

She was kneeling with a glue gun, helping a young girl fix where the axle of her tires had come loose.

Wyatt strolled up behind her and said in a stern voice, "Ms. Lockwood, Pierre's going to fire you for moonlighting."

She jumped a foot and turned.

Her narrow-eyed glare made him laugh.

"You are so mean." Her dark blue eyes sparkled with laughter in the sunlight. "And sneaky."

"Looks like the kids had fun." The sound of their giggling and enthusiastic voices made his heart warm.

"I had fun too." She turned and bumped the woman who'd sat down beside her. "In fact, I think I had more fun than Kallie."

"You did." Kallie bumped her back in a way that indicated his favorite cousin had a new bestie. "Horses are easier."

"You speak the truth. Speaking of horses..." He stuck his thumbs under his belt. "Are you an experienced rider, Erin?"

She snorted. "Not even close. Back when I was in college, I rode a horse. Twice."

"You're a perfect choice." This actually might work. She'd be safer in the wilderness than in her home—and he'd get to spend time with her. "This weekend, we're evaluating horses to see which ones work best for trail rides. We need another beginning rider."

Her blue eyes widened. "Me?"

The Dom in him wanted to see all the ways he could make those beautiful eyes go big.

Behave, Masterson.

"Yes, you. You'll get a free overnight trail ride into really gorgeous country. I'll have a chance to teach you survival skills for the next time you wander into the forest."

"I don't know..."

"You have to come." Kallie slapped Erin's shoulder. "Jake and I are going, and so are Sawyer and Mallory. We'll have a great time."

At Kallie's eager invitation, Erin relaxed, and her wary expression turned to interest. "Well. Okay, yes. Thank you."

Huh. Upstaged by my own cousin. Not that Erin appeared to be interested in other women.

Her caution was understandable, especially considering the asshole she'd married. And honestly, he liked her for it.

He reached down and pulled Kallie to her feet. "I walked over with Jake, by the way. He's inside talking to Mrs. Ganning."

"Ah, is it seven o'clock already?" Kallie raised her voice. "Clean-up time, kids. We leave the place better than we found it, right?"

Wyatt chuckled—because it was the mantra of hikers everywhere. *Leave no trace.* Joining her, he started gathering scraps of cardboard and wires.

"So what are you doing here, cuz?" Kallie asked...and he realized his attention had strayed. Because Erin had bent to pick up some batteries. She had a gorgeous ass; yeah, his thoughts had gone there.

Kallie snickered and dug an elbow into his side. "Men."

"Guilty." He rubbed his ribs, watching as a girl asked Erin a question, and she knelt to answer. She couldn't have been more serious or attentive if the question had come from the president.

"I like her," Kallie said. "You be nice to her."

Family. Wyatt ruffled his cousin's hair in the way she'd hated since she came to live with them as a teen. Still worked. He sidestepped the gut-punch she attempted. "Jake's hoping to talk you into a beer at the ClaimJumper and invited me along."

"After the trauma of dealing with mini cars, a beer sounds great." She turned. "Hey, Erin, want to join me, Jake, and Wyatt for a beer at the ClaimJumper?"

Erin glanced at Wyatt, hesitated, and shook her head. "Thank you, but no. I have a bunch of stuff to get done at home."

"Well, damn." Kallie sighed, then smiled at Wyatt. "Grab Jake and I'll meet you guys there. I need to hand the kids off to their parents."

"All right." He smiled at Erin and touched his fingers to his hat brim. "See you this weekend, blue girl."

. . .

Hands filled with cardboard scraps, Erin watched him walk away, and okay, she totally sighed inside. That cowboy walk of his. It wasn't a swagger, more like a saunter, and incredibly masculine... it got her every time.

But...

In cities, most people only knew the media stars, politicians, and influencers in their own small areas of interest. Small towns were different, maybe because the entire town could be an area of interest. Within it, certain people attracted more interest—and gossip—than others.

In the stores, in the auto shop, at the library, Erin kept her ears open. Gossip was so fun. Who wouldn't love it? What was more interesting than hearing about other people?

Wyatt was a popular man—and a popular topic of conversation in town. So she knew he was fun and amazing and hot—and he didn't date locals. Apparently, he averaged around three dates—with out-of-towners—before moving on.

Grinning, Kallie bumped her shoulder into Erin's and made her jump. "Sure you don't want to join us for a beer?"

"I honestly do have stuff to do." Sure, she could put laundry and cleaning off for a night, but it would be wise to keep her distance from the sexy beast. Like a magnet, he pulled her in more and more the closer he got. But considering what she knew, any involvement at all with him would be crazy.

"Wyatt's single. In case you were wondering. Oh, but...maybe you're missing your husband?" Kallie flushed. "Okay, that was insensitive. Sorry."

During a quiet moment with her, Erin had shared about Troy's death. "No, it's all right. Troy did just die, but our marriage had been over and done for quite a while. And he'd been cheating on me a lot longer than that. I don't miss him." She shook her head. "I'm just sorry he never got a chance to make things right with the world."

In all reality, he probably wouldn't have even tried.

The cynical look in Kallie's eyes indicated she held the same opinion. But she stayed silent as they finished the clean-up and went inside.

"Mrs. Ganning, here's your volunteer back." Kallie took the scheduling paper from the librarian and handed Erin a pen. "Sign yourself up to keep reading to munchkins...and afterward, you can stay on, like today, to help with my group." She put a finger on a date, then another. "Here and here."

With an amused huff, Erin put her name in the slots. "You're short and totally cute, like you should be dancing in the flowers —not bossing people around."

Laughing, the librarian handed over Erin's stack of books. "She got the skill from the guide business she and her cousins run. Keeping fools from killing themselves in the wilderness isn't for the faint-hearted."

"There is that." Kallie grinned at Mrs. Ganning. "See you next week."

Carrying her books, Erin walked out with Kallie. "You didn't check anything out?" Was the woman not into books?

"I read—not as much as Becca or Mallory—but I use an eReader so no one gets to see what I read." Kallie waggled her eyebrows. "I like erotic romance where the bedroom door is *wide* open."

Erin snickered. "EReaders—winning the gratitude of kinky bookworms everywhere."

"See, you get it." Kallie stopped on the sidewalk. "So, what kink do you prefer?"

Erin's mouth dropped open. Did the brunette have no filters at all? "Um."

"Hell, I stepped in it again, didn't I?" Kallie shrugged, totally unconcerned. "I'll start. I like mostly BDSM, especially Dom-sub, with maybe some sadism tossed in for fun."

No, there were no filters there. None at all.

"Your turn," Kallie prompted.

Erin could feel her face heating up. "About the same. Male Dominant, not female."

"See? I knew I liked you." Kallie bounced up and down on her toes. "I've got to go, but we are *so* going to talk. About the ride—and about books."

Watching the short brunette jog down the sidewalk toward Main Street, Erin could only shake her head. There was no way she'd be lured into talking about her fantasies, even under the guise of books.

Not a chance.

CHAPTER THIRTEEN

This wasn't going to work. Erin scowled at the clothes she'd tossed onto the bed. Jeans and tank top, hoodie, down jacket. Those were all good. But weren't riders supposed to wear special boots or something? Aside from business and formal shoes, all she had were sneakers and her low work boots—which essentially looked like sneakers but with all the safety features for mechanics, like a composite toe, slip resistant, and protection from electrical hazards.

Maybe she should call and cancel.

Only it sounded as if they needed a beginner to evaluate their horses. She was definitely a beginner.

And face it, she kinda—really—wanted to spend time with Wyatt.

She shook her head. *Right, Erin. That right there is why you should cancel.*

Turning, she reached for her phone. But right then, her playlist brought up Gloria Gaynor's "I Will Survive". Her hips started to sway even as her back straightened as she raised her hands over her head and belted out the song with Gloria.

She *did* have her life to live, dammit. She wasn't going to let her lack of clothes—or her fears of moving on—make her lie down to die.

Pounding on the door made her jump. Hastily turning the music down, she hurried across the house and flung open the door.

"Rebecca?"

"Erin." The redhead's arms were full of bags. "Sorry about pounding. I started off knocking, but I heard your music out here and figured you couldn't hear me."

"Uh, no, I couldn't." Erin stepped back and motioned. "Come on in." Why was Becca here? They didn't have anything planned, right?

"Wyatt called me. Kallie was supposed to get you fixed up with the right gear, but her women's group stayed out an extra day, and she won't be back until later tonight." Becca set all the bags on the floor with a sigh of relief. "Anyway, I grabbed what she'd started putting together for you and added more. We keep a bunch of used clothes and footwear at the lodge for people who need stuff."

Erin dropped down on the couch. "I was just trying to figure out what I needed and realized I'm in trouble. I don't have riding boots or whatever it is you're supposed to wear."

"I got you covered." Becca grinned and pulled two pair of boots from a sack. "I remembered the sandals you bought when we were shopping were size eight, the same as me. One of these should fit you."

"You're amazing."

Becca laughed. "I know. But honestly, it was Wyatt and Kallie who remembered you might not have everything you need."

Wyatt. Why did just the mention of his name send tingles through her? *Dammit, don't go there.*

As Erin pulled on tall socks and boots, Becca started unloading other stuff. "Here are a couple of riding helmets to try on. I know you have jeans. Even though it'll be warm, wear those. Add a long-sleeve shirt over those tank tops you love, and a jacket for when it chills off at night."

Shirt, right. She had the jacket. "What about camping things—a sleeping bag or a tent??"

"All provided by the trail outfitters. You just need clothes to wear there and back."

As Becca took a chair, obviously to supervise, Erin grinned. "Where's your adorable boy?"

"You mean Logan or Ansel?"

"Girl, in no stretch of the imagination would anyone consider your man to be an adorable boy."

Laughter lit Becca's face. "Good point. You know, the first time I met him, he scared me spitless. After I talked to him, he scared me even more."

"I can actually imagine it; however, the way he looks at you now is..." Erin fanned herself. "It's a wonder it doesn't steam up the air."

Becca just grinned, then motioned to the boots. "Do those work?"

"They're surprisingly comfortable."

"Good. Let's see what else you're planning to take." Becca rose. "Besides, I'd love to check out your house. I'm snoopy."

Erin laughed. "I'm the same way. Let me show you around."

The kitchen got Becca's nod of approval. "I love the clocks."

"Those were my grandfather's. I kept a few to remember him." Erin smiled. "He was the one who got me into mechanics and into restoring clocks."

"You loved him a lot; I can see it." In the bedroom, Becca smiled at Grammie's colorful quilt. "That looks like you, even if the rest of the room doesn't."

"Eh, Troy insisted on neutrals. I'm slowly adding colors." Erin nodded at the back wall. "When I get some money ahead, I might paint an accent wall. Maybe a color to coordinate with the quilt."

"It's a great idea." Becca gave her a sympathetic smile.

"Moving on and letting go of the past is tough. But you're doing it."

After Becca left and Erin had everything packed and ready for the next day, she sank down on her chair on the deck and looked out at the valley. At the mountains. And the wide sky. A land as big as she wanted to be. As joyful. *I love this place. It's my new beginning.*

"Yes, Becca. I'm doing it."

CHAPTER FOURTEEN

Erin grinned as her horse splashed through a small creek that flowed over a stretch of granite. The flying drops of water sparkled in the sun.

The afternoon sun scorched her shoulders and denim-covered thighs, but soon the trail would be back under the trees. Shade had become sparse as the elevation rose, and despite the air vents in the riding helmet, her head felt hot.

Holding the reins in one hand, she let herself sway with the slow gait of her sweet brown mare, Daisy.

The trail was wider here in the meadow, and people were riding in pairs. Kallie and Jake at the front, followed by Sawyer and Mallory. Since she was still a novice, Sawyer had put her in the middle of the group with Wyatt beside her. Morgan and short, red-haired Alexia, his date for the trip, brought up the rear at this time.

Jake and Kallie called frequent breaks, partly for novice riders like her and Alexia, and so Sawyer could collect people's impressions of the horses. After each stop, everyone would switch mounts, and he'd rearrange the line.

So far, only one horse had given her trouble, unwilling to follow any of her directions.

Another horse—thankfully not hers—had shied when Sawyer whooped and tossed his hat in the air. Heck, she'd probably jumped more than her horse had. She'd noticed Wyatt had been ready to grab her horse's reins.

"So what kind of a camp are we going to?" Jake's deep smooth voice drifted back to Erin. "Do we get cabins?"

"Sorry, but no," Kallie answered. "We'll be setting up tents and making lots of noise to see how the horses do. And because it's fun."

Kallie had said on normal guide trips, Wyatt would usually lead the way. But as the line was formed today, he arranged to ride beside Erin to start her lessons.

Before they'd started, he gave her a small backpack with what he'd called the essentials. A knife, a headlamp, sunscreen, Stuff to make a fire and filter water, an emergency shelter, warm spare clothes, water, and food. Even a tiny first aid kit.

He'd given her a stern look. *"I expect you to keep this and use it whenever you're out hiking—no matter how close to the cabin you stay."*

The thoughtfulness of the gift left her speechless.

At lunch, he'd opened a map, put a compass on a rope around her neck, and worked on teaching how not to get lost. And what to do if she did—showing her the attached whistle, how to signal for help.

Admittedly, after hearing about Troy's death, she hadn't been thinking about safety at all. She hadn't even taken her house keys with the mini-multitool on the keychain. Although the knife on it was so small, maybe she could have cut a piece of firewood in a week or so.

"Tell me, what are you going to do if you meet a bear on the trail?" Wyatt asked her. "When you're on foot?"

"Run. Absolutely run."

His deep laugh was so very infectious.

She grinned reluctantly. "Why do I get the impression I gave the wrong answer?"

His white teeth flashed under the dark mustache. "Because you're smart that way?"

She sighed. Who would have thought there was so much to know? "Okay, tell me. Or, better yet, how can I avoid them?"

"Sorry, city girl. The good news is we don't have any grizzlies in California, but we *do* have an abundance of the black ones."

"The blacks are nicer, right?" She grinned. "Horror movies always use grizzlies, not black bears."

He grinned and said so softly she barely heard, "So cute." In his normal voice, he explained, "Grizzlies are bigger and more aggressive. Unfortunately, the multitude of clueless tourists have taught our local bears that campsites have food. The beasties can get forward."

Oh great. "What do I do?"

"If you meet one while you're out walking, back away slowly while talking. If it keeps coming, wave your arms, yell, throw things at it. Use bear spray. Fight as a last resort. Running is never a good choice."

Fight a bear, oh sure. She frowned. "What about mountain lions?"

"Use the same method. Always do everything you can to look bigger too. Open your jacket, raise your arms."

"Got it."

"The main rule for hiking safety is basic." The way Wyatt stroked his hand over his horse's neck in an affectionate gesture reminded her of how he'd touched her when she'd cried on his shoulder. His sleeves were rolled up, showing muscular forearms and a dark tan. "Always let someone know you're out hiking, where you're going, and when you're expected back."

"Right." Sadness was a heavy boulder just under her sternum. She had no family left. The people here were all...beginning... friends. Not ones she'd feel right imposing on. She tried to smile but couldn't meet his gaze. "Got it."

"Erin." The silence made her look at him. His eyes were kind. "Just a text works. Just say, 'I'm hiking the trails to the west of my house for a couple of hours. I'll text when I return.' If they don't answer—because us guides are often out of cell range—you text the next person on your list. And you can put me first on your list, sugar."

The understanding in his voice, the open offer made her eyes fill with tears.

Just in front of them, Mallory turned. "Since I work in town, I'm rarely out of cell phone coverage. Text me if you're hiking."

Oh God, she was going to cry, dammit.

Mallory gave her a sympathetic smile and turned back around.

As Erin tried to wipe her eyes without looking like she was, Wyatt winked at her and started talking about games he and his brothers played as children. How they'd learned to track their father who would give them clues like pieces of string from a fraying shirt or digging his heel into a muddy spot, breaking branches, even leaving strands of his hair dangling on a branch.

Then he'd take them back over the trail and show them everything they'd missed.

"It was damn embarrassing," Morgan called from behind. "But we got better, and he stopped leaving deliberate clues." Morgan was like a quieter version of Wyatt, and when the two of them had been organizing the group, they'd almost seemed to read each other's mind.

Wyatt snorted. "After we got good, he started hiding his trail, teaching us how people can hide from a tracker. Eventually, it was a game where one of us was prey, and the others would track him."

Erin stared at him. "Wow, you took hide 'n' seek to a whole new level."

Kallie called back. "Morgan and Wyatt are scary good. Virgil and I never win against them, whether we're the prey or the trackers."

"It's because you don't have a sneaky bone in your body, little bit." Grinning, Wyatt glanced back at his brother. "As opposed to Morgan, who's purely devious."

"He is." Looking over her shoulder, Kallie grinned at Erin. "But Wyatt's a natural at tracking. He always finds Morgan."

Erin frowned. "I've seen movies where the fugitive walks in a stream to hide their tracks. What else do you do?"

"Tie a cloth over your hair so it doesn't get caught on anything—especially you long-haired types," Morgan said.

"Watch your footing. Choose rocky areas or places with thick pine needles. Loose dirt and mud will hold a track."

"Avoid grass and low brush where your weight will break stems," Kallie said as if reciting from memory. "Especially in damp areas."

"Wrap your shoes if they're the kind with a tread." Wyatt grinned at her. "Running shoes like yours leave great tracks."

"Well, I'm so glad my shoes were helpful when I got lost." Her tone might have been light, but she was so, so grateful he'd found her.

He must have understood, because he murmured soft enough that only she could hear, "If you get lost, blue girl, I *will* find you."

She met his gaze, seeing the steadfast commitment in the dark brown eyes.

As the sun rose higher, all of them except Alexia continued instructing Erin in wilderness and tracking education until her head was crammed full.

Their games sounded like a lot of fun. Once she mastered hiking, she was totally going to try tracking.

"When we get to camp, you can practice what you learned," Wyatt said. "First, you'll try leaving a good trail."

"Ooookay, and second?"

"Second, you'll hide your trail. From me."

"And you'll try to find me?"

"Oh yeah." Wyatt's lips tilted up slightly. "There'll be a

penalty if I catch you too quickly." The dark promise in his voice made her tingle.

She wet her lips. "A penalty. I see." Maybe a kiss or... As her longing for him to touch her, kiss her, rose like a warm wave, she looked away from his perceptive gaze.

No, Erin. You're going to be a crazy cat lady. No more men.

And the small voice inside her whispered, *maybe just for a short time...for fun?*

The camp was set up, and the group had dispersed to various areas. Morgan took Alexia and Jake to check out the fishing. Mallory and Sawyer were grooming the horses.

Wyatt was doing his usual perimeter check, circling wide around the camp in search of potential dangers. *So far, so good.* They were the only people in the area. No sign of cougar or bear. No poison oak—which was rare at this elevation.

He stopped at the sound of splashing, then grinned. The camp was a short distance from a clear mountain stream, and apparently the women had found it.

"Oh, my aching butt." Erin's voice drifted upward. "And my legs—how can my *legs* hurt? The horses did all the walking."

"It takes work to stay in the saddle," Kallie told her. "Sit here. The water's cold enough it'll be like using an ice pack."

Erin's squeak had Wyatt covering his mouth to stifle a laugh. Fuck, she sounded cute. And made the Dom in him want to see what he could do to make her squeak again.

"Sheesh. Now I know why a friend complained about their long beach ride during their Caribbean honeymoon."

Snickering giggles came from Kallie. "Was her hootch a smidge tender?"

"Considering the way mine feels, I'm guessing yes."

Shame on you, Masterson. Eavesdropping is rude. Grinning, Wyatt leaned against a tree.

"The first day of riding is the worst for soreness," Kallie said. "Of course, there are some women who might enjoy a bit of pain down there. Right?"

"Kallie!"

"You've read BDSM books, I know. Oh, don't even try with that innocent face."

"*Maaaybe*."

Wyatt tilted his head. Really? Blue girl enjoyed BDSM stories?

"Thought so. Have you read Sinclair or Blake or maybe Cartwright? So hot."

"Yes to all, however, *you* need to cool down." There were splashing sounds.

Kallie eeped, then laughed. "As it happens, I got lucky and found a man who makes the books look tame."

"You...you what? Jake?"

"Mmmhmm." Kallie sounded damn smug.

No matter how old he got, he'd probably always have difficulty hearing his cousin talk about kinky sex. Considering how many randy young men he'd punched when she was a vulnerable teenager, he might never break out of that mindset.

Shaking his head, Wyatt escaped the area.

As he strolled the perimeter path, he considered. Erin was interested in him and more than in a friendly way. He'd been a Dom long enough to be able to read the signals of sexual attraction. Each time they'd met and on the long ride here, the chemistry between them grew stronger.

The attraction went both ways.

Back when she was lost in the forest, he'd been careful. Hadn't even flirted. He wouldn't take advantage of a vulnerable person, one who'd been lost, one who was mourning. Although it sounded as if her love for her husband had died quite a while ago.

She wasn't lost now.

She was interested.

And damn, she liked kink.

Let's see where this goes, little mechanic.

Hiding behind a cluster of bushes, Erin tried to not to pant—and failed. Sheesh, her heart was pounding, and she was totally out of breath. *Girl, you're out of shape.* Time to start running again along with practicing the self-defense moves she'd pulled together into her own customized routine.

But right now... Even if she was panting, she could do it silently.

A minute later, she heard the crunch of boots on dry pine needles. He'd found her *already*?

The footsteps went past where she'd turned off the trail. A minute later, they returned, slower. Paused. She heard a huff of satisfaction.

A second later, the damn cowboy walked right over to where she was hiding. He bent, extending his hand.

Taking it, she let him pull her to her feet. "You found me awfully fast."

"Mmmhmm. Too fast." With a wicked smile, he pulled her closer. "Penalty's a kiss."

The cowboy hat shadowed his face, but she could see the focused look in his eyes as he watched her, maybe to see if she agreed.

Could he also see the way her insides were melting at the thought of kissing him?

"Ah, a willing victim," he murmured. Bracketing her face with his hands, he held her still. His lips were firm and warm, lazily moving over hers. When she opened her mouth, his tongue slipped inside to tease and tantalize.

Without thinking, wanting more, she reached up for him, wanting to pull him against her.

Still kissing her, he molded her against him, one hand behind her head, the other cupping her ass. He was all steely muscle—and a very thick erection pressed against her pelvis.

Heat flared until her whole body felt alight.

"Yo, Wyatt, Erin, suppertime!" The yell came from where Kallie and Jake had been fixing food.

"Damn." Wyatt let her go with obvious reluctance. "I can think of something I'd rather eat."

What did he mean?

Oh.

He chuckled, running a finger down her undoubtedly red cheek. "I'd like to penalize you a whole lot more...but we'd better join the others."

The next couple of hours was totally fun. Since the summer was starting to get dry, rather than a forbidden campfire, the food was prepared on a couple of portable stoves they'd set up in a fire ring. Afterward, Jake angled red, orange, and yellow glow sticks in a tepee shape to simulate a fire, and people sat in a circle around it on logs and pads.

On a log, Wyatt sat beside her, close enough his thigh and arm rubbed against hers—and left her constantly aware of him, of his size, his warmth. He'd been eating grapes with his meal, had fed some to her, and run his thumb across her bottom lip each time.

Everything he did made her skin more sensitive. Made her want him more.

Dammit.

Instead, she tried to concentrate on the others around her. It wasn't too difficult; this was a great group.

After getting everyone's opinions on the horses, Sawyer mentioned he'd ridden rodeo when younger and shared the fiascos that could—and did—happen.

Then Kallie, Morgan, and Wyatt tried to one-up each other with trail guide disasters.

Erin had laughed so hard her stomach hurt.

Now, naturally, she needed to visit the facilities. Rising, she quietly headed for the latrine area, waiting until she was out of sight to rub her sore butt. Even with the pad, the log was like rock.

A few minutes later, after cleaning up, she made her way back, following the ribbons someone had used to mark the path. An owl, disturbed by her passage, hooted and took off with a whup-whup-whup of huge wings.

Once back in the clearing, she saw Wyatt was straddling the log, still part of the group, but turned slightly. So he could keep an eye out for her?

He spotted her immediately.

Yes, he'd been watching for her.

When she reached the group, he held out his hand to steady her as she sat down beside him. His thumb glided over the back of her hand, and he frowned. "You're cold, sugar." Pulling off his jacket, he wrapped it around her.

It was heavenly warm from his body heat...and carried his masculine scent along with the fragrance of the peppermint soap he used. "But...now you'll be cold."

"I'm good. Here, this should help warm you up." He handed her a cup of hot chocolate.

Taking a sip, she tasted the chocolate, accompanied by the almondy flavor of Amaretto and the richness of Baileys Irish Cream liqueur. Just inhaling the fumes gave her a buzz. "Oh wow."

He grinned and pulled her against his side.

Being cared for like this...she wasn't used to it. And it was heady stuff.

Don't get used to it, Erin. But for now, she'd simply enjoy being coddled.

As the group enfolded her back into their conversations, contentment hummed inside her. Friends, a night under the stars, and chocolate.

"The good news is no one will be driving home tonight,"

Morgan said a while later. "Unfortunately, *some* people's tents are at a distance. If you get lost, bro, you're on your own."

Wyatt's laugh made her insides quiver. "I think we'll manage." Taking Erin's empty cup from her and setting it aside, he tucked her hair out of her face. "Ready to call it a night?"

"I am." She huffed a laugh. "This log is getting harder the longer I sit on it."

Everyone laughed.

"I hear you," Alexia called. "Me too."

Wyatt grinned. "We're out of here. Night, everyone."

There were a chorus of good nights as the rest also started for their tents.

Rising, Wyatt pulled Erin to her feet.

Every single muscle in her lower half set up a chorus of aches. "Ow, ow, ow," she said under her breath.

He grinned, not releasing her hand. "I have something for your sore muscles. But first, you have to make it to our campsite." Hand on his hat, he flicked on the headlamp and tucked the sleeping pad they'd been sitting on under his arm.

Holding his hand, she walked just behind him on a narrow animal track, going steadily upward.

At an opening in the trees, she glanced down to where they'd been. The bear-proofed food and firepit area was empty. In the dark night, Jake and Kallie's tent at the edge of the forest glowed with light. There was another glow close to the horses where Sawyer and Mallory had set up. Morgan and Alexia's glowing tent was on the other side of the clearing. "Why is everyone so far apart—and we're even farther away?"

"When we have clients, we keep everyone together to ride herd on them. Otherwise, privacy can be nice."

"Oh." All the rest were couples. *Duh, Erin.* "Of course. Right."

The trail ended on a high bluff where he'd set up two tents bigger than the one he'd used during her rescue. The benefits of having pack animals, he said.

He laid the sleeping pad on the ground several feet from the tents and put the second one from the tent beside it. "Let me show you why I picked this spot. Sit, little mechanic."

She frowned. "I'm not actually all that short."

"True enough." His gaze swept over her in almost a caress, and his expression warmed. "You're taller than average and stronger. I like it. But you're still enough smaller than me that I can feel protective." His voice lowered, even as his eyes danced with humor. "It's good for my manly ego, you know?"

"Oh, in that case, okay." She laughed and gingerly lowered herself to the side-by-side pads. *My poor butt.*

"Lay back." He turned off his headlamp and set his hat in his tent.

Bossy man. But she did.

Once on her back, she looked up, and as her eyes adjusted to the lack of light, the entire dark sky seemed to open overhead. Slowly, star after star appeared, then like magic, the beauty of the Milky Way. "Ooooh, it's beautiful. The stars are so big."

He laid down beside her, one forearm behind his head. "Mmmhmm. The sky looks different when there are no competing lights."

And it was so quiet. She could hear a hint of the others. Jake's laugh. The soft gurgling of the stream. Wind through the trees farther down.

This spot, though, had no trees—the entire nightscape was theirs.

After a while, she whispered, "Thank you. I've never seen anything so beautiful." And he'd shared it with her.

"You're welcome." He rose up on an elbow to look at her. Picking up her hand, he pressed a kiss into her palm, his lips warm. "I'd like very much to kiss you—and see where it goes—but if you're not of the same mind, it's time for you to say good night."

The low hum of attraction had been increasing all day. And

every time he'd looked at her in that way he had, with banked desire in his gaze, her heart had sped up.

Yes. Every hormone in her body sizzled in agreement. Tugging her hand from his grasp, she touched his face. And waited.

His smile was slow and dangerous. Tangling his fingers in her hair, he lowered his head. His lips brushed hers—but he didn't go right for the deep and wet but gave her soft kisses with teasing nibbles on her lower lip. After a small bite along her jaw, he went back for a slower kiss, enticing her to open her mouth.

When she did, his hand in her hair tightened, and he possessed her mouth so completely her head spun. By the time he returned to teasing, nipping her chin, and sucking on her lower lip, her entire body had roused to an unsettling heat. Her skin felt sensitive—everywhere.

He took her mouth again, tempting her tongue until she gave back as good as she took. A rumbling sound was his approval.

She edged closer—and winced as her thigh muscle spasmed.

He made a tsking sound. "You need a rubdown and stretching, or you won't be moving tomorrow."

A rubdown—like a massage? It sounded awesome.

"I wouldn't mind having my hands on your bare skin...all over." He traced a finger from her chin, down her neck, between her breasts, waking every single nerve. "But, again, not without your consent."

She tried to catch her breath. *Yes. Yes, touch me all over* sounded like the right answer.

He lifted a dark eyebrow. "Want a naked massage, blue girl? And possibly more?" The heat in his gaze showed exactly what he was promising.

I can do this without going off the deep end. And hey, it should get him out of my system, right? Wasn't that what other people said?

"Yes. And more."

His lips curved. "We'll see if you're still of the same mind in a few minutes. Because I'm going to make you whimper...and I'll enjoy it."

What? When he moved away, she sat up to watch.

"Boots and socks off, Erin." He gathered some things from inside his tent and returned.

She set her boots off to one side.

"Let's get the rest off too." He laid whatever he'd picked up at the edge of one pad, knelt beside her, and pulled her shirt up over her head. A cool breeze swept over her skin, making her shiver.

"This goes too." He ran a finger along her bra, and her nipples tightened until they ached. Reaching around her, he unfastened the clasp and slid the bra down her arms. His gaze dropped, and his expression grew dark and appreciative. "Oh, now there's pretty."

His hand cupped one breast, his palm rough with calluses, making her shiver at the carnal abrasiveness on her tender skin.

"Hell, I'm supposed to be giving you a rubdown." His grin flashed. "Sorry, I got distracted." He dropped a kiss on her lips. "Belly down, sugar."

God, how could she want a massage so much and sex even more? It was worse when he reached beneath her, unzipped her, and dragged off her jeans and briefs.

She was...naked. Out in the open.

But although the starlight was bright enough to make shadows, the dark enfolded her like a blanket.

Picking up a tube from the side of the pad, Wyatt squirted lotion from it onto his palm. He straddled her hips without resting his weight on her. Slowly, he ran his hands up and down her back. The lotion was cool, his hands firm.

"Oooh, that feels good."

"It will...and then it won't."

What did he mean? But she didn't care, not as long as he kept going.

He did—with long, smooth strokes, up and down her aching

back. So relaxing. Then, the massage changed. The heels of his hands made firm circles on each side of her spine, working upward to her neck. Back down. His thumbs edged upward beside her vertebrae, digging into the long muscle until the tightness gave way with a painfully glorious release.

Moving higher, he kneaded her knotted shoulder muscles until she could feel the heavenly warmth of her circulation flowing unhindered again.

He moved off her.

"Oh, heavens, the massage was wonderful. Thank—" She started to sit up and was stopped by his hand in the middle of her back.

"Stay put, sugar. We're just getting started." He pulled her legs apart and knelt between them.

"But—"

He leaned forward, and the heels of his hands pressed down on her bottom. Her very sore bottom.

"Eeek!"

"Fuck, you have a cute squeak." He was laughing—and not letting up as his powerful fingers forcefully kneaded her glutes.

"Ow!" She tried to look over her shoulder at him and saw only an ominous shadow. "That hurts."

"That's the point. If I don't do this, it'll hurt a lot more tomorrow." His thumbs dug into a tight area, and she squeaked again. But she could feel the rewarding warmth as the knot released.

Slowly, he worked his way from her butt down her legs, which also hurt.

"I still can't believe sitting in a saddle could make my legs so sore."

"Takes work to stay balanced on top of moving objects." He knelt to one side and slapped her bottom with a stinging spank. "Roll over now."

Lifting up onto an elbow, she rubbed her stinging ass with

her other hand. "You're enjoying this too much. Should I have asked if you're a sadist?"

The thin edge of a waning moon over the trees showed the way his brows rose—and a dimple creased his cheek. "As it happens, I don't mind handing out a mite of pain for a good cause."

As he firmly rolled her onto her back, she managed to close her mouth. "A good cause?" Why was her voice coming out so husky? Because she was lying naked, breasts and pussy exposed, and he was talking about pain?

"Like now, when pain is required to feel better." He ran his hands up her legs, massaging the fronts of her thighs before straddling her hips again. Leaning forward, he massaged around her collarbones. Digging in enough to make his point.

Because when he was finished, her muscles felt as if they were doing a happy dance.

"For some people, pain can enhance sex."

"What?" She blinked in shock at the easy way he'd said such a thing.

"Sugar, I'm sure you've heard of BDSM." He kneaded her pectoral muscles, then took possession of her breasts, his hands shockingly warm. Gently, he caressed them, plumping them, stroking, cupping.

When he concentrated on her nipples, capturing each, circling and tugging, the zings of excitement shot straight south. He pinched the tips, rolled them between his fingers, and her back arched up, pressing her even more into his control.

"Gorgeous." His lips tilted up as he fondled her now-swollen breasts. When he returned to her nipples, the peaks were throbbing.

The bluff had grown lighter with the rising moon. His gaze was intent on her face as he increased the pressure on her nipples. His pinch grew tighter, and even as she gasped, the pain blossomed into a heavy, warm pool of need.

She made a sound, almost a moan, and saw the crease in his cheek as he smiled.

He knelt beside her hip. Gripping her left calf, he set the other hand on her knee to keep it straight as he lifted her leg up. The muscles down the back of her leg stretched almost painfully. He did the same to her right.

"Tomorrow, stretch out—your legs especially—before you get back on a horse."

"Ugh, it'll feel worse tomorrow, won't it?"

"Sure will." He chuckled. "Now for something you won't enjoy. Bend your knees."

When she did, he set the bottoms of each foot against the other, splaying her open.

Exposing her completely. What kind of position was this? She wiggled, trying to get away. "Wyatt..."

"This is going to hurt, baby." His legs kept her feet from moving as he pressed her knees out and down.

Her very, very sore inner thigh muscles set up a shriek only she could hear. "Ow, *nooo*."

He brought her knees up—*thank you, god*—chuckled and pressed down again, his grip inescapable.

"Ow, ow, ow, stop."

"No, you can take more and be the better for it." His grip didn't loosen, but he was watching her carefully enough he let up before the pressure hurt too bad.

He'd forced her to take that pain. Why did that realization send warmth straight to her core?

He pressed down again.

Owwww. "You truly are a sadist."

"Not especially. I only hand out pain if it accomplishes a goal, like ensuring you'll be able to function tomorrow. One more now." He brought her knees up again, then down, stretching her sore muscles and ligaments, and finally back up.

Her legs quivered, but the ache was a warm one rather than

the jangling pain of before. The cruel massage had definitely helped.

"Thank you...but I still hate you," she muttered.

"Now, what is left?" The laughter underlying his dark, rough voice made her wary. "Hmm."

Kneeling between her knees, he ran his hands up her inner thighs and stopped at her groin. His thumbs stroked over the crease between her thighs and mound.

Her breathing stopped as every nerve down there wakened. "Wyatt?"

"Saddles are hard on tender bits. This part needs a massage, too, don't you think?" His low voice held amusement as he opened her...and exposed her clit.

There, right there, was where everything wanted his touch—only no, she didn't. Not really...did she?

Slowly, he traced a finger down one side to her entrance.

The burst of pleasure was so shocking her whole body halted, even her breathing. "Wait."

He stopped, still touching her, but unmoving. His gaze held hers. "You have the choices here, sweetheart." His lips quirked. "At least as far as stop and go."

Oh, that reservation in his purely confident voice made her shake inside. And she wanted so very badly for him to continue. Her mouth formed the word. "Go."

"Good girl. You know, it'd be a right shame to neglect certain parts." His big fingers closed around her outer labia, massaging slowly and firmly.

She sucked in a breath at the deep, sliding pain in the tissues. She was genuinely sore. Yet the discomfort beneath his ruthless attentions only increased her growing pleasure.

She could see the flash of white when he grinned and went down on one elbow, still between her legs. He turned his head to nuzzle her inner thigh. "So soft."

His other hand was still on her pussy, and he drew his fingers down, pressing against her entrance.

She could feel her own wetness.

"Very nice." His chuckle was totally male. "Perhaps it'd be best to massage this part from the inside." Slowly, he slid two fingers inside her. "Yes?"

Oh god, it felt so good. "Yes. More. Please." But she wanted —"Your..."

"You'll get all of me, blue girl, don't worry." He leaned forward, and she felt the warm puff of his breath. "But not just yet."

Then he licked over her clit.

The way she squirmed was fucking adorable, Wyatt thought. To keep her in place, he braced himself with a forearm across her pelvis.

Little subbies didn't get to dictate during sex.

She tangled her fingers in his hair; yeah, he liked that.

When he ran his tongue around her clit, her breathing changed, and her fingernails dug into his scalp. Damn, she was going to come too easily.

Well, she *was* tired and tender. He wouldn't play with edging...this time. Instead, he closed his lips over the bundle of nerves, savoring the fine taste and scent of her arousal. Pumping his fingers in and out, he sucked and tongued her clit until she came like a rocket.

Way too easy.

Way too quiet, actually.

He lifted his head to see she'd pressed her hands over her mouth to silence herself. Modest? Totally fucking endearing.

Now he had an urge to go somewhere he could truly play with her, somewhere she wouldn't be inhibited about screaming when she came.

Maybe at a Serenity party. He'd seen her reaction to sensual pain, the way her pupils dilated, darkening her blue eyes.

How interested was she in truly *experiencing* rather than reading about BDSM?

Right here, perhaps he could try verbal restraint? No, take it a step further. Let her offer herself and see what happened.

He gathered her hands and held her wrists in his left hand. Slowly, he reinserted two fingers to use as a pussy monitor. The moonlight was enough to show her full breasts, how her chest rose and fell.

Now, let's see how you react to orders.

"You've been a good girl, Erin." He could feel a shiver running through her. "Do more for me, little bit. I want your legs farther apart now."

Her eyes opened fully, and she stared up at him. Her breathing paused...but her pussy clenched. Had grown even wetter.

"I want to see you, all of you."

But, but, but... In the dim light, Erin could see the harsh angles of Wyatt's face, the strong jawline. His eyes were shadowed, yet the feeling of his intent gaze on her naked body was like a slow hand caressing her.

His voice had deepened, taken on more of a growl, and her willpower simply drained away. Her legs parted without any input from her. Wider and wider until she saw him nod.

He was looking at her, down there. It was humiliating and, somehow, erotic as hell.

And even more so when he wiggled his fingers inside her, making her clench. "Very nice, sweetheart."

She tried to move her arms, to do...she had no idea what, but his hand tightened around her wrists. Holding her. Restraining her. Keeping her under his control.

The ground beneath her seemed to soften, dropping her lower on the earth.

She swallowed. "Wyatt..."

"Shh." His head tilted slightly. "I'd be pleased if you spread yourself for me." He set her palms over her outer labia and repositioned her hands farther apart to fully expose her clit and entrance. "Just like that."

When he lifted his hands, she started to let go, and he made a sound of disapproval deep in his throat.

She froze.

"Exactly so, Erin. Keep yourself open for me."

She couldn't look away from his dark eyes, even as he slid his fingers back in and pumped slowly, sending pleasure soaring through her.

Pulling out, he brushed his slick fingers over her fully unhooded clit.

The light touch made her gasp, and his teeth flashed white in a smile. "Keep your hands in place, sugar." He lowered himself down to rest on his elbows, his wide shoulders rubbing on her bare thighs.

She was trembling inside, her whole lower half aching with need. With anticipation.

Leaning on one elbow, he set his other hand between her hands, pressing down on her inner folds. Two fingers trapped her clit between them like scissors.

The squeezing pressure at the base of the swollen ball of nerves sent a deep thrum through her, and the need to come coiled tighter and tighter.

Bending his head, he licked over her clit that was pinned in the most intimate of traps. His tongue was wet, hot, pulsating on her, driving her mercilessly up and up, until the sensations engulfed her in flaming pleasure, and another orgasm ripped through her.

"Oh, oh, oh." Her fingers dug into her own flesh as he sucked mercilessly on her clit and sent her over again.

She was gasping for air, her heart hammering as if it wanted to jump right out of her chest.

There were the sounds of a zipper and a condom wrapper

being torn. Still dressed, he settled his body over her. His jeans were unzipped, lowered, and his shaft pressed between her legs.

"Erin, look at me." His voice was rough.

She opened her eyes. He rubbed his scratchy cheek against hers, and a smile played at the corners of his mouth. "I love watching you get off."

Maybe she'd have answered him if she could've thought of an answer. "Um..."

He chuckled and kissed her, slowly, deliberately, before looking at her again. "You okay to take me? No is a permitted response."

No was the furthest thing from her mind. "Yes. I want you inside me. All of you."

An approving sound was his only response before he was pushing inside her. She was swollen, and he felt huge as he entered her. She stretched around his thick girth, the hot pressure intensely pleasurable.

Her neck arched, and she moaned as the slow penetration continued and continued...until he was fully sheathed.

"Mmm." Wyatt held still for a moment, letting her adjust—and letting himself regain control. Because she felt like heaven. Every inch of his dick was surrounded by her tight heat.

Her eyes were half-lidded, her lips parted as she took shallow breaths that showed she was savoring his possession as much as he was.

He teased them both, gliding in and out, escalating slowly, before moving to powerful thrusting. Claiming her in the most physical of ways.

Her arms wrapped around his neck, and her fingers squeezed his shoulders, making him smile. One of his favorite kinds of pain.

But a minute later, her breathing slowed, and she started lifting her hips to meet him. At times, he enjoyed cooperative action, but tonight, he wanted to know how she responded to domination.

Because the way she got off was what Doms like him dreamed of.

He hooked his arm under her left knee, pulling her leg up, doing the same on the right. Spreading her wide, removing her ability to control...anything.

Her eyes darkened again; her cunt clenched around him, and he had his answer. "Now, sweetheart, I'm going to take you hard," he whispered.

Her legs jerked slightly and got nowhere. She was realizing she was vulnerable to whatever he wanted to do. Rather than fight, she melted beneath him.

He thrust into her slick heat, over and over with full penetration each time, and felt the pressure building up. For him—and for her. Her cunt tightened around him, and he angled so as to rub over her clit with each stroke.

Her neck arched, and with a gasp, she went over again, battering around his cock in convulsive spasms.

Sending him into his own climax. His balls drew up tight, and his dick felt almost white hot before the lightning coursed through him, upward and out, searing his world with pleasure.

Pulling in a deep breath, he opened his eyes and smiled down at Erin.

Her eyes were closed, she was still panting through lips swollen from kisses. Her arms were around his neck, and when he moved, she clung harder—like she didn't want to let him go.

And he liked that. A lot.

A little while later, clothes in hand, still naked in the faint moonlight, Erin stood in front of the two tents. *Am I supposed to sleep in mine—or with him?*

What did she want to do?

They'd had sex. Amazing, intense sex, and it seemed as if tremors still shook her world. Her emotions.

Holding the pads they'd used, Wyatt joined her and set a warm hand on her bare back. "Erin, it's your choice."

How did he know what she was worrying about? Then again, she *was* just standing here.

"If you prefer to sleep alone, I understand. If you'd rather sleep with me"—he kissed the top of her head—"I very much enjoyed holding you last time we shared a tent."

She swallowed. Decided. "With you." She pulled in a breath and tried to say lightly, "Hey, there might be bears."

"I'll protect you from any and all beasties." He tossed in the sleeping pads, then patted her butt. "In with you. I'll grab your sleeping bag."

By the time he returned, she'd set out the pads, side-by-side. He opened the sleeping bags so one would be under them and the other would be a blanket.

Placing her boots inside the door, he tucked a flashlight in one. "In case you have to get up."

As she got under the top sleeping bag, he went outside to strip off his clothes, completely unselfconscious as she watched. How come men never seemed to feel inadequate?

Of course, he sure didn't have anything to worry about. The moonlight on his powerful body showed solidly packed muscles. His cock, even flaccid, was impressively large, thick, and symmetrical, resting on heavy testicles.

Crawling inside, he set his jeans next to his boots and rolled up his shirt for a pillow.

Oh, right. She could do that too. Sitting up, she found her clothes and pulled out the shirt.

Sliding under the sleeping bag, Wyatt sat beside her. Bracing her with an arm behind her back, he used his free hand to fondle her breasts.

When she jumped, he chuckled. "Sorry, blue girl. Would you prefer I keep my hands off you tonight?"

She'd often wished Troy would ask her questions like this—and hadn't realized how difficult it was to answer honestly. "I...I like being touched, actually. At least in private."

"Noted." He squeezed lightly, nipped her neck, and pulled her down to lie beside him. "Snuggle up, pretty girl, we have a full day tomorrow."

She breathed in his clean pepperminty scent as she lay her head on his shoulder. Her breasts pressed against his side, and she curled one leg over his.

Pulling her closer, he rubbed his chin on the top of her head. Night, sweetheart."

"Good night." Unsettled, she was wide awake. She could feel the slow rise and fall of his chest, the heat of his body. Outside the tent, an owl hooted a few times, but otherwise, the world was quiet.

Leaving her to her thoughts. To wondering how she'd come to be here, in the arms of a man who wasn't Troy. The first man since Troy. And...the fourth man she'd ever had sex with.

Troy had certainly been no virgin, but after the honeymoon was over, he'd lost any interest in pleasing her. All too often, she'd felt like one of those—what were they called? Fleshlights?—a way for him to get off without exerting any effort.

Reading hot romances had taught her she might be missing a lot, but she'd figured the writers were exaggerating. Of course, they'd make all the sex scenes sound fantastic.

But tonight... She hadn't known sex could be *like* that. After making sure she was on board, Wyatt had simply taken over. Just thinking of how he'd directed her, how he'd taken what he wanted, how he'd driven her past what she'd ever thought she'd do... Oh, it made her want to start it all over again.

The BDSM books would label her as a submissive, wouldn't they? Because when he told her what to do, she wanted to obey. Wanted to hear him say *good girl*.

God, this was confusing. She hadn't felt such an intense need to please anyone before, not even Troy. Why now?

"Your brain is going to get all worn out," Wyatt murmured, pulling her closer. "Want to talk about what's keeping you awake?"

Absolutely not. "I'm sorry." She rubbed her cheek against his chest, feeling how his velvety skin stretched over hard, underlying muscles. He was all rough, tough cowboy and so very considerate.

Be careful, Erin. You're not prepared for anyone like him. "I'm ready to sleep. Honest."

"Mmmhmm." His amused chuckle showed he'd let her get away with the lie. But the slow stroking of his hand up and down her back had her boneless within a minute.

And asleep within the next.

CHAPTER FIFTEEN

As the walls of the tent brightened to gold with sunrise, Erin woke. Sometime during the night, she'd turned over, and now they were spooning. Wyatt's heavy arm lay over her waist, and she was hugging his forearm and hand between her breasts. His chest pressed against her back and shifted with his breathing.

Closing her eyes, she savored the feeling of being held against his strong body. Of his biceps under her head, his knees behind hers.

Don't get used to it, Erin. Just don't. Remember—he doesn't date locals and moves on after a few dates.

She'd been fully aware before coming on the trail ride and had accepted his invitation for sex with her eyes wide open. *This isn't even a date, just a hookup.*

She breathed out past the ache deep in her chest.

Because she might have wanted more.

He was so different from Troy. Oh, they both possessed gregarious natures, far more than her. But when Troy was talking to other people, it was like Erin didn't even exist, even if she was standing next to him. Wyatt, though, held her hand or put an arm over her shoulders or behind her waist and would include her in every conversation.

When she wasn't with him, he still kept track of her. Not in a stalkery way, but just keeping an eye out. Last night, he'd been talking to Jake while she was passing out food. When she'd stumbled, he appeared immediately to see if she was all right and hadn't burned her hand.

His attention made her feel noticed. Valued.

Heady stuff.

Don't let it go to your head, girl.

The man wasn't looking for a relationship.

Neither am I.

She'd already proven her inability to choose a good man. And having barely escaped the wreckage of her marriage, jumping into a love affair would be incredibly foolish. *Cat lady, remember?*

She'd save her pride and her heart if she politely backed away.

The decision seemed to turn the bright daylight to a bleak morning. But such was life.

She sighed, and the arm around her tightened.

"Awake, my girl?" His voice was as rough as a gravel road and so masculine it made her senses sing.

"Mmmhmm. I guess it's time to get up."

"You think?" The arm over her lifted, and he stroked his fingertips along the undersides of her breasts.

Everything inside her was rousing. Heating.

And she panicked. Making love—*no, having sex*—again would probably rip her heart right out of her body. Because she wanted him with every cell of her being. Wanted him to take her...and far, far worse, wanted him, *all* of him.

Wanted to hear his voice, to make him laugh, to touch him and—

I need to get out of here.

"Um, sorry, cowboy. I need to...ah, use the facilities." Pushing back the top sleeping bag, she sat up.

"When nature calls, it calls." He ran his hand down her bare stomach and propped himself up on an elbow. "Are you going to come back and join me for another hour or two?"

Yes, yes, yes. She looked over her shoulder.

His eyes were heavy-lidded from sleep, and his thick hair was tousled, making her want to finger comb it to neatness. Stubble darkened his jaw. His bare chest had a scattering of dark hair across the pecs and a thick red scar along his ribs.

"You look like a ruffian." One who'd been in more than his share of battles.

"In that case, I should steal a kiss." Wicked humor lit his eyes. He flattened her onto her back beneath his heavy body and kissed her, long and slow.

When he lifted his head, she could only stare at him as heat raged through her body.

He kissed her nose and sat her back up. His gaze ran over her, snagging on her breasts. Smiling, he ran a fingertip around her nipples that were still reddened from last night. "What else can I steal?"

Me, you can steal me. She clamped her jaw shut on the words. Because if she gave in now, he would steal her heart as well.

"Behave yourself, cowboy." Moving out of reach, she started putting on her clothes.

He heaved a loud, pitiful sigh even as he watched her with open male appreciation. "Are you going to come back for a...nap?"

"Wyatt." She hesitated. "This was... I don't think..." She swallowed and shook her head. "No."

"No." He said it softly as if trying it on for size. After a moment, he tilted his head in understanding and acceptance. "As you wish. If you help Kallie make breakfast, I'll pack up the gear."

"Yes. Thank you." Her words were only a whisper past the thickness in her throat. And then, she escaped out into the bright morning light.

• • •

As Wyatt disassembled their camping spot, he considered what had happened.

From his side of the river, it'd been a great night. On the trail ride and at supper, she'd been a delight to talk with.

Even as a novice camper, she'd turned her hand to helping set up, to cooking and cleanup, taking on her fair share and more.

With tracking and survival lessons, she had a mind like a sharp trap—he only had to tell her anything once. And she went all-out when playing.

During sex, she was honest about what she wanted. Her husky words, "*Yes. More. Please,*" echoed in his head.

Great. Now he had a fucking uncomfortable hard-on.

The sex had been fantastic. She was a giving partner and openly responsive. Those squeaks...

He grinned and shook his head. She'd been just as easy to read this morning. Her body wanted him, but her emotions and her head had put up a big red NO.

Served him right, now didn't it? It was usually him pulling back after a fun night of sexual escapades or a good scene.

Erin's rejection would ensure his head didn't get too big for his hat.

Stacking the gear near the horses, he nodded at Morgan and Kallie, who were leading the horses to water. At the cooking area, Mallory, Erin, and Alexia were working on breakfast.

Erin had her hair pulled up into a messy bun on top of her head and was laughing at something Alexia said. The white streak on her chin was probably flour. Was Mallory teaching her how to make camp stove biscuits?

His stomach growled.

Chores accomplished, he put a foot up on a log, crossed his arms over his thigh, and simply enjoyed the sight of an enchanting blonde with blue streaks in her hair.

Mallory saw him and said something.

Erin looked over her shoulder and met his gaze. Her color went an enticing pink before she turned away.

Yeah, he wanted this woman. Just how serious was she about those second thoughts of hers?

Gin breathed in the fragrance of pine needles, leather, and horses. The air in the Sierra mountain range was so different from the humid green smells of the deep south where she'd grown up.

Last year, when Atticus told her he loved the smell of a clean stable and how horses had their own perfume, she thought he was crazy.

But she'd come to love the ranch smells too. And the horses, bless their big hearts.

She patted Molly's neck, grateful for her gentle mount. She'd never be as crazy about riding as Atticus and Sawyer were. Or the Mastersons and Kallie, for that matter. But being fond of horses and loving afternoon trail excursions?

You bet.

Especially with scenery like this in front of her. She smiled at the rider in front of her. Atticus. Her broad-shouldered cowboy probably had the finest butt in all the world.

Although she couldn't decide if he looked better in jeans or a suit. Atticus in a suit was mouthwateringly impressive, and she'd indulged herself during their two weeks in New York.

Once back home, Atticus decided their horses needed a trail ride, which was why they were riding out to meet his brother Sawyer, who was returning with the Masterson group.

Riding behind Gin were Levi, another cop Atticus had invited, and Katelyn, Levi's sister, who had invited herself after she learned Wyatt was with Sawyer's group.

On the ride, Katelyn tried to pump Gin and Atticus for information about Wyatt. She seemed more than a bit infatuated. Even now, talking to Levi, she was going on and on about Wyatt.

Gin shook her head. The woman was a real chatterbox.

Katelyn never stopped for a breath. "And when I saw him in San Francisco, he showed how much he liked me. He listened to me, I mean, really listened, and we connected so well. I know if I get a chance, he'll remember how much he liked me."

Levi cleared his throat. "Katelyn, if he hasn't called—"

"No, no, it's only because of that woman, Erin Palmer. He was dancing with her at the ClaimJumper, and now, she probably has her hooks in him. After all, she managed to catch Troy Palmer, and with his money and status, he could have had any woman he wanted."

Gin grimaced. Katelyn did have a point about the politician's wife.

"Wait, what do you know about Palmer?" Levi's voice was as flat as if he were interrogating a felon rather than his sister.

"Oh...well. Um, not much." Katelyn's voice was hesitant. "Candy and I met Troy and his brother last fall when they were here on vacation. They were both so nice. I didn't know he was a bad congressman."

"*Nice*. Right." Levi made a disgusted sound, and Gin grinned. It must be difficult to be a law enforcement officer and have a clueless sister.

Katelyn kept going. "Anyway, that Erin Palmer is why Wyatt hasn't called me. I'm sure she's a real drama queen, and she's using him to make herself feel better."

Gin frowned. She didn't know if anything was going on between Wyatt and Erin Palmer, but when it came to Katelyn, everyone in town knew Wyatt Masterson avoided local entanglements.

On second thought, a determined woman might well change his mind, and Katelyn seemed very determined.

As they went around the next shady curve, Molly let out a loud whinny echoed by Atticus' horse, Festus.

Atticus called, "I see Sawyer's group ahead."

"Right on schedule," Levi said from the rear.

They'd been riding next to a forested stream area. As the trail opened up into scrub trees and granite outcroppings, she saw there was a line of horses. Sawyer and Mallory were in front, followed by Jake and Kallie, Morgan and a woman.

Bringing up the rear were Wyatt and...oh, spit, speak of the devil. The sight of the corrupt politician's wife, Erin Palmer, stuck in Gin's throat like a hair in a biscuit.

The woman was attractive enough. Despite being half a foot taller than Gin and far more muscular, she had man-pleasing curves. But her attempt to get attention by putting in blue streaks was awfully common.

Gin winced at her own thoughts. *Running down a woman based on her appearance. That's shameful, Virginia Cunningham.*

Nonetheless, it was just wrong Palmer's wife had manipulated her way into Gin's circle of friends.

What if Wyatt was serious about her? After profiting from all the lies, Erin Palmer thought she'd come here and ruin more lives? Break Wyatt's heart?

Wyatt was a wonderful man. He and Morgan had helped Atticus track the convicts who'd used Gin as a hostage. He'd killed one of those convicts, and the death had hurt the big-hearted cowboy. He deserved someone wonderful, not a self-serving politician's wife.

Leaning forward, Gin studied Wyatt and the woman.

The two were riding, side by side, and at a casual glance were merely talking. Only...Gin was well trained in the nuances of body language. His body was angled toward Erin Palmer. Their bodies and gestures mirrored each other's. He held her gaze too long, listened too intently. His crooked smile was quick and often.

Gin's heart sank. *Wyatt wants her.*

From behind her, Katelyn raised her voice. "Hello, fellow riders."

Oh, well now. Gin smiled slowly. Maybe all was not lost. Erin Palmer had competition—a pretty brunette who really, really wanted Wyatt Masterson for her own.

Despite her aching butt and legs, Erin was enjoying the ride. To her surprise—and relief—Wyatt wasn't annoyed she had essentially turned him down for both sex and anything in the future.

And he'd let her keep her distance. Troy would have pursued her, tried to put his arm around her, done all sorts of possessive stuff. Not Wyatt. Instead, he'd buried his intense sexuality and was simply...friendly.

In the morning, he'd pulled Jake off to ride with him and, at the next break, had done the same with Sawyer.

Erin had enjoyed getting to pair off with her women friends. During their ride, Kallie told her more about the Mastersons' guide service and mentioned how popular Wyatt was. Morgan handled the fishermen; Kallie took the women and family groups, especially ones with small children. Wyatt did everything though, especially macho hunting groups. Kallie wouldn't take them, and Morgan hated guiding shooting expeditions. Wyatt, though, got along with everyone—and managed to keep even macho hunters in line.

Having experienced the power of that commanding voice of his, she totally got it.

After the last break, he'd paired back up with her and resumed her wilderness survival lessons. He didn't flirt, had acted so very casual, as if he hadn't been inside her, hadn't licked her—or made her hold herself open or...

She growled under her breath because he was doing just what she wanted...right? Only, dammit, she missed the flirting, the touching, the look in his eyes that showed he wanted her.

Erin frowned, realizing Wyatt had gone silent. "Um, what?"

In the sunlight, his gaze held a dark amusement. "You're growling at me, blue girl."

"I'm what?" Oh, hell, she had been. Like a teenaged groupie angsting over a rock star. Her face heated with her embarrassment. This would never do.

She narrowed her eyes. "It's because you have food caught in your mustache."

"Ah, do I now." He ran his hand over his perfectly clean mustache, past his mouth, and over the dark stubble on his chin. "Better?"

That smirk.

"If I hit you, your horse would buck and set mine off, and I'd end up on my butt in the dirt." Still, it was so very tempting.

"Mmm. Not a good plan"—laughter lit his dark eyes like moonlight on a quiet lake—"since your ass is already sore."

When he busted out laughing, she realized she had growled at him.

Heavens she loved his laugh. Not the quiet, subdued sounds made by way-too-civilized people, but just plain open and hearty.

She couldn't help grinning back at him.

Shaking his head, he reached for her hand.

"Hey, Wyatt!" It was a woman's voice.

Erin looked toward the front of the line and saw another line of riders approaching.

She cringed at the sight of the brunette beautician from Hannah's Salon, Katelyn, who was friends with sarcastic Candy. The two women who'd probably been to bed with Troy and his brother.

The beautician was riding beside Becca's friend, Gin—the one who hated Erin for being Troy's wife. The two were headed straight for Wyatt.

Upon receiving a narrow-eyed stare from Gin, Erin felt an icy wind sweeping away her afternoon's contentment.

She managed to smile at Wyatt. "Looks as if you have friends wanting to talk." Ignoring his low-voiced, "Erin," she gently steered her horse into a wide detour away from the two women.

Glancing over her shoulder, she saw the curvy beautician

advance on Wyatt, going stirrup-to-stirrup. Taking his hand, she made a happy giggling sound and rubbed his knuckles against her face in an intimate action. One that showed they were more than just friends.

Well.

The slice across her heart was unexpected. And disturbing.

Honestly, Erin, you already knew he has lots of women. The beautician's reminder should hurt your pride—not your heart.

It should; it didn't. Her pride was barely ruffled, but her chest ached.

I don't believe this. She'd backed off—because she knew she'd get too invested.

Way to go, Erin. And now it hurt.

Dammit.

As she rode farther away, she saw Gin giving her a smug smile.

Yes, yes, your friend succeeded in driving me away from the man. Good job.

Just as well. Seriously.

Erin bent to stroke her horse's neck. "Thanks for getting me out of there and giving me time to get my head on straight."

So who should she ride with now?

Two men had arrived with the women. One had a short beard and a black cowboy hat. He regarded her with an unreadable expression.

The other, maybe in his twenties, with super-short hair, she'd seen before in a police uniform shirt. He gave her a scathing look.

Ooookay, then. She needed to avoid all four of them.

And Wyatt too. Like she knew she should have from the beginning. She had her friends, her house, a great job. After Troy, she sure didn't need a man.

Note to self: Get a cat. Maybe four or five.

CHAPTER SIXTEEN

"Oh, hey, I should get munchies for the road." Erin picked up her purse as she, Sunny, and Becca got ready to leave the Bärchen Bakery where they'd had lunch. Sweets would make the long drive to Sacramento much nicer.

"Excellent idea. I'll get *streuselkuchen* to take back to the lodge," Becca said, "I didn't have time to make my usual assortment of sweets for the lodgers."

"You spoil your guests—and your man." Sunny pursed her lips. "Come to think of it, if I take the doc Danishes, he'll be in a good mood all afternoon. And I can save some for Virgil."

Erin smiled. The way Sunny talked about her husband, he sounded like a human Superman—the yummy Henry Cavill version. No wonder Sunny liked pampering him.

They lined up at the counter and to Friede's amusement, Becca and Sunny debated the merits of strawberry *plunder* vs raspberry-cheese-and-almond *plunder*.

Which meant Erin had to add two each of the fruit-filled puffy pastries to her order. It was such a hardship.

Nom, nom, nom.

"I'm so glad we got together before you left," Sunny gave Erin a squeeze as Friede started filling their orders.

"Me too." Erin thought of what was ahead of her—cleaning out Troy's house—and her throat tightened. "It helps, knowing I'm coming back here. After."

The consulate had expedited the death certificates, and under her mother's oversight, she and Troy had made out wills soon after they married, simply leaving everything to each other. After years as a lawyer, Mom had been a stickler for having one's legal ducks in a row.

Thanks, Mom. You made this a lot easier.

This trip was to put Troy's—*her*—house up for sale. Not that she'd get much considering it was still mortgaged.

She had an appointment with a realtor this evening followed by difficult days in front of her. Although Emmett had sent in a cleaning crew after the house was searched, she needed to dispose of personal stuff.

As soon as the place sold and she had money again, she could reimburse Emmett for the cleaning.

Wasn't it odd she'd come here thinking to sell this house and go back to the city? Instead, she was selling the city house...and returning here. The thought made her surprisingly happy. This was where her life had started afresh, letting her remember how good life could be.

Aside from feeling unhappy every time she thought of a certain wilderness guide.

As if summoned, the door of the bakery opened, admitting the two mean beauticians from Hannah's Salon. Candy *and* Katelyn.

Oh joy. Erin turned her back.

The women lined up in front of the glass-fronted counter, discussing what they wanted to get.

"Sacramento is a long way to be running back and forth, Erin." Becca frowned. "Can't you hire someone to deal with emptying out the house?"

"I can't afford it, and I'd still have to be involved. After the realtor decides how much furniture to leave for showing, I hope an auction house will take the rest." They should. Troy's taste in furniture had been *very* expensive. "The personal stuff and whatever they don't take will have to be donated or dumped." And she'd have to make those decisions.

"Sounds like a lot of work. When will you be back?" Sunny asked.

"On Sunday. I asked Pierre for the rest of this week off." He'd patted her hand and told her to call him if she needed anything. She had a great boss.

"We'll get together when you're back and have a Mother Lode dinner," Becca said as she paid for her order. "And hey, I forgot to ask you about Wyatt. I heard you two got real *cozy* last weekend." She waggled her eyebrows suggestively.

Erin tried not to flinch. She'd been the one to push him away, and it was totally unreasonable to hope he wouldn't give up, yet for the last two days, her breathing had stopped each time her phone rang.

None of the calls were from Wyatt. Her heart felt like it'd cracked a gasket, letting sadness leak out.

Pushing the feeling away, she grinned at Becca. "You're so snoopy. Is 'cozy' a special Serenity Lodge word for sex?"

"Hey, snoopiness about everyone's love lives is a small-town obligation."

"Absolutely." Sunny nodded with a solemn face, despite the laughter in her eyes.

"You two. Someone needs to throttle your engines." Now what would be the best way to—

"Here's yours, Ms. Erin." Stepping up to the counter, Friede's teenaged grandson carefully opened Erin's box to show he'd gotten everything she'd ordered.

He was so cute. Erin smiled at him. "Everything looks fantastic."

Sunny pointed to the cookie sandwich and the cinnamon rolls in the box. "Those are Wyatt's favorites. It seems you two have the same taste in pastries. This is an excellent start."

Off to the right, the beautician named Katelyn made a disgusted sound—and glared.

Erin's smile slipped slightly. On Sunday, she'd be returning to this small town and her new friends. Which was wonderful.

But it hurt to realize the only thing she would ever share with Wyatt would be a taste in pastries.

The contented conversations of their clients made Wyatt smile as he finished cleaning up after supper on Tuesday. It'd been a hot day, typical for mid-June, but up this high, when the sun went behind the mountains, the air cooled quickly.

After an early start Monday morning, they'd ridden for a long day, camped one night, and rode higher today to reach one of his favorite areas.

One he would've loved to share with Erin after seeing how much she enjoyed the wilderness.

"Yo, bro. Brought you a drink." Morgan walked up with a couple of beers that had been chilling in the icy water of the stream. He glanced at the small groups, five men with two women, all resting comfortably and chatting. "This is a good group."

"Photographers are great. Far better than hunters. Whole different mentality." Wyatt shook his head, remembering one group of entitled assholes.

"You thinking of Erin's husband?"

"Oh yeah. Strutting around like he owned the world, lying about his hunting skills—of which he had none."

"She's well rid of him." Morgan handed over a beer. "You two seemed damn tight last weekend. And then not."

"And then not. True enough." After making love with her, it'd been difficult to keep his interactions with her non-sexual, because he wanted to touch her, hold her. During the return trip on Sunday, he'd backed away to give her space.

Later, when he'd resumed her survival lessons, she'd seen he wasn't going to press her and had relaxed. Even without sex in the mixture, he enjoyed being with her. But...he still had hopes for more.

Unfortunately, Katelyn had driven Erin off. And when he escaped the beautician to ride with Erin again, she'd been distant.

Dammit.

"She backed away from me the next morning." Wyatt sat down on a log where he and Morgan could talk and still keep an eye on their group. "I'm not sure why. It might be too soon for her after Palmer."

"Mmm." Morgan eyed him. "Did you play vanilla—or did you scare her with your pussy play? No, you must not have; she was able to sit on a horse on the ride out."

Wyatt laughed. He and Morgan had visited Dark Haven together enough to know each other's kink styles. "She's new to everything. I gave her a taste of pain, not much. She enjoyed it, and she's also submissive. But...she might well have had second thoughts afterward."

She wasn't the first vanilla he'd schooled in submission and pain. Some women dove right in. Others—even the ones who loved it all—backed away like he was a dealer handing out drugs. They didn't want to think of themselves as people who were submissive or who liked pain with sex.

"At least she enjoyed what you did—even your wimpy torture."

Wyatt grinned. A woman's fun bits were wired directly to the pleasure centers, and carefully administered pain could take some women far higher. With them, every hurt turned into added sensation and overwhelming pleasure. He fucking loved those scenes.

But Morgan was a Dominant and an all-round sexual sadist, handing out a river of pain and turning it into a flood of pleasure. Floggers, whips, canes were his favorite tools.

Already guessing the answer, Wyatt asked, "Did you have a good time with Alexia?"

"She's a generous woman in bed"—Morgan grimaced—"but hates pain."

"Damn." Women who enjoyed kinky sex were few and far between. Submissives who liked pain? Even rarer.

"Yeah. At least I can visit Dark Haven when I get antsy."

"There is that." Wyatt glanced over at the clients who were vehemently arguing about the best lens to use for mountain sunrises. *Photographers*. Shaking his head, he grinned at Morgan. "I've noticed you have your pick of any of the masochists at the club."

In fact, one had thrown herself on her knees and begged—which annoyed the owner, Xavier, who disliked pushy behavior in the club submissives.

"Because I'm just that amazing." Morgan's grin flashed. "What are you going to do about Erin?"

"When we get back, I'll give her a call." He smiled slowly, thinking about the delightful mechanic. "I don't think she had much experience before marrying the asshole. She's the type to need time to think. And to be honest about what she wants."

"Honesty is rare." Morgan smiled. "Good luck, bro."

CHAPTER SEVENTEEN

A *green tunnel* is what Grampie would've called this narrow road with towering evergreens on each side. With her car windows down, the dry pine fragrance filled the air. No air-conditioning needed.

She smiled at the feeling of coming home.

The Sacramento place had never felt like this—and it would be gone soon. The realtor was sure the house would sell quickly. Unlike here, the Sacramento housing market was booming—especially in such an exclusive neighborhood.

It had been a productive, exhausting four days of legal business and preparation. After advising on a few pieces of furniture to leave for staging, the realtor had recommended an auction house for the rest.

Erin had packed up the pantry, a few kitchen items, lamps, and bedding into the back of her SUV. Troy's clothing and the rest of the usable items went to various charities. Family items and photos went to Emmet. A cleaning service would visit tomorrow to put a final shine on the place. After paying the mortgage and utility bills, she was flat broke again.

And exhausted. She'd only slept a few hours each night and spent the rest of the time cleaning out room after room. But hey, by finishing early, she'd have the rest of today and all day Sunday to relax.

She turned into the tiny dirt road and backed up to the door to make it easier to haul in boxes. With her duffel bag and purse slung over her shoulder, she ran up the steps and unlocked the door. Inside, she set her bags down, started to punch in the security code but...it wasn't beeping. Hadn't she set the alarm when she left?

Yes, yes, I did.

A sound from behind made her spin.

A huge, bald man with tats on his neck stood in the doorway of her bedroom. "What the fuck. You're not supposed to be back yet, cunt."

Fear froze her. "Wh-what... Who are you?" Such a stupid question. Her mind went frantic.

Scream? No one around.

Run? He'd catch me.

Could she move far enough to hit the alarm button?

"Now, you've seen me." He pulled a knife and looked her up and down. His lips twisted into a lust filled smile. "Might as well have some fun first, yeah."

Oh God.

He lunged toward her, and all she could see was the knife, the sharp edge. Her body reacted automatically. She slapped his arm away, and he dropped the knife.

Twisting her hips to add power, she punched his nose with all her might and felt things crack.

He reeled back—far enough she could hit the red ALARM button on the security panel.

The high-pitched klaxon was deafening.

"Fucking bitch!"

She couldn't block his next blow, and her head exploded with pain. Falling sideways, she hit the floor hard. Before she could get away, he kicked her in the stomach.

Oh *god*. Gasping for air, she curled around the horrendous pain.

Swearing, he took a few steps away to pick up his knife.

Move! She shoved up and lunged toward the umbrella stand. Grabbing the cold metal bar beside the umbrellas, she swung it as forcefully as she could.

It hit the side of his head. She felt the impact all the way up her arm—and he roared louder than the ear-splitting alarm siren.

Holding his head, he staggered out the door.

She grabbed the door frame to hold herself up...and fell backward.

Ow.

Her head was... No, that was her phone ringing.

Answer it. Answer it, Erin.

Why was her brain so fuzzy? She dragged her cell out of her pocket, got it unlocked. "H-hello."

"Ms. Palmer, this is your security. Your alarm went off. Do you have your password?"

"Call the police." She pulled in a breath. "*Call* them."

The phone fell. She tried to pick it up but ended up lying next to it instead.

Silence worked its way into her ears. The alarm had stopped. *Right.* It was supposed to quit eventually.

Must move. Sit up, Erin.

Don't want to. Her head was pounding so hard it might split open.

What if he comes back? The thought had her pushing against the floor.

Ow, ow, ow. Her belly felt as if the man had shoved a knife in it.

One more time. She managed to sit. Had the alarm gone off again?

No, the wailing sound was different—and getting louder. *Oh.* It was a police siren. The red and blue lights strobed against her windows as car doors slammed.

"Ms. Palmer? Bear Flat Police." A uniformed officer appeared in the door. Clean shaven, graying hair. He spotted her where she sat on the floor. "Ma'am, are you hurt?"

"I—"

Another officer came in. Levi had been part of Katelyn's group last Sunday. He scowled at her and glanced around the room. "Nothing's out of place. Did you set the alarm off by accident?"

"I—what?" She blinked, trying to get her eyes to focus. "No, no, it was... A man broke in. Attacked me. I pushed the alarm."

"Yeah, right." Levi's laugh was jeering. "Isn't your car in the driveway? The SUV?"

"Yes."

"So someone broke in with your car sitting right there in the open? *Riiight.*"

Why did it feel as if she was having to defend herself? Wasn't she the victim? "He was already inside. When I came in, he rushed me." Good, her words were coming clearer.

"Uh-huh. We always have burglars in the middle of the day." Levi shook his head. "You had a fight with a boyfriend, I bet."

"Levi." The gray-haired man stepped between them. "That's enough."

"What's the story?" Another cop walked in, a huge one.

"Lieutenant." The gray-haired cop motioned to her. "She says she got home, a man was here inside, and she pushed the—"

"Bullshit," Levi interrupted. "She's just a drama queen who—"

"Levi." The big lieutenant's warning was unmistakable. Odd how his voice sounded almost familiar. She hadn't met him before.

"Come, ma'am, let's get you off the floor." The gray-haired officer knelt beside her and with a hand under her arm, tried to help her up.

She got halfway, when the world went fuzzy, and her knees buckled.

The giant lieutenant caught her around the waist. She let out a horrible yelp as pain flared across her abdomen. Changing his hold, he guided her to the couch.

Pressing an arm against her aching belly, she managed to sit. And had the most futile yearning for Wyatt to hold her again. Tears blurred her vision.

"See? Drama queen?" Levi stood in the front doorway.

The lieutenant glanced over his shoulder. "Wait outside, Officer Kranz. Now."

Levi shot her another glare and stomped out.

"Ms. Palmer, I'm Lieutenant Masterson, and this is Officer Lambert." Masterson went down on his haunches in front of her. "Can you tell me how you got hurt?"

Masterson? "How many Mastersons are there?" She realized she'd spoken aloud when the gray-haired cop snorted.

"Sorry, sorry." She shook her head, and everything in her brain flared with pain. *Owwww.* "Um, I got home and came inside. The door was locked, but when I went to put the password into the alarm, it wasn't blinking. A man was in here. He was huge. And bald, and he had a knife and attacked me."

I could have died. He'd planned to kill her. She started shaking so violently her bones hurt.

"Easy there, you're safe." The lieutenant patted her hand. His voice was a deep croon, so much like someone else's.

Wyatt. He sounded like Wyatt—his voice slightly deeper and not as rough, but so similar just hearing him made her feel better.

"Did you try to run?" Officer Lambert asked.

"He was too close. I wanted to hit the alarm, but he was almost on me, so I...I hit him. I think I broke his nose."

Masterson made a sound almost like a laugh. "Did you now?"

When he said it, she realized her hand hurt. Turning it over, she looked down. The knuckles were red and purple and swollen.

"Ah, so you did." Officer Lambert sounded impressed. "What happened?"

"It...it gave me enough space to push the alarm button, only then he hit me." She gingerly touched her scalp and winced.

The lieutenant gently turned her head, moving her hair. "Yeah, you're bleeding. Looks like you get a trip to the clinic." His voice turned grim. "What else?"

"He knocked me down and kicked me. When he went to get his knife, I made it to the umbrella stand and...I hit him." She pointed to the two-foot-long breaker bar lying on the floor.

"Jesus, Mary, and Joseph, you hit him with that?" The lieutenant eyed the heavy, steel bar often used to remove lug nuts. He grinned.

She nodded carefully. "He ran—and he was holding his head." Which seemed only fair since *her* head seriously hurt.

Officer Lambert walked to the door. Crouched. Walked outside. "Yeah, he's leaving a blood trail."

"You and Levi follow it," the lieutenant ordered before turning his attention back to her. "Were you unconscious?"

"No, I... Just mostly dizzy?"

"Yeah, let's get you to the doc."

No, no, a clinic would cost money she didn't have. "I don't need a clinic."

His eyes glinted. "Guess I can call an ambulance and—"

"Wait, I can ask Sunny—she's a nurse—maybe she can—"

"Sorry." His lips twitched as if he was suppressing a smile. "Sunny will be at the clinic. Ambulance?"

"No. The clinic," she said hastily. "The Bear Flat clinic's fine."

In his pickup, Wyatt scratched his cheek—and the six-day beard.

It'd been a great group he and Morgan had guided into the back country. The photographers handled horse camping with virtually no complaining—and lots of enthusiasm about the scenery. Snowmelt kept the creeks and waterfalls rushing. The wildflowers were in full bloom. The happy group had taken shots of plenty of wildlife, including deer grazing in vividly green meadows and black bear cubs playing.

They'd gotten back earlier, but when unpacking the leftover food, he discovered a client's prescription medicine. So he ran it up to Serenity where the man was staying. Another hour disappeared while talking to Logan about doing trail repairs.

Now he was headed back down the mountain, and a big meal was at the top of his to-do list.

Slowing for the corner, he glanced at Erin's drive, even though Kallie said she was in Sacramento this week.

There were a couple of cars parked in front of the house. One was a cop car.

What the fuck?

Jamming on the brakes, he barely made the turn onto the tiny dirt road. After parking next to the cop car, he eyed the other one. Atticus Ware's car—the detective drove an unmarked vehicle.

Wyatt climbed the steps and, ignoring the front door being ajar, he knocked. Only a fool wanted to surprise armed and possibly jumpy cops. "Hey, Erin, Atticus. It's Wyatt."

"Come on in, Masterson." Atticus appeared in a doorway off to the right.

Wyatt looked around. "Where's Erin?" Worry was a nasty coil in his gut. "Is she okay?"

"I got here after Virgil took her to the medical clinic, but he called to say she'll be fine."

A simple accident wouldn't bring the police detective out here. "What happened?"

"She surprised a burglar and caught a couple of hits." Atticus' frown turned to a smile. "She nailed him with a breaker bar. Gutsy woman."

Wyatt stiffened at the thought of anyone hurting her. *I'll kill him.* He fought the fury down and gritted out, "I thought crime had gone down after the town drove the gangs out." Although the vigilante-intense monitoring of criminals had stopped, the residents were extremely proactive about their neighborhood watches.

"Crime *is* down. I don't think this was a typical burglary."

Wyatt recognized the voice coming from the bedroom. In his late fifties, Officer Cliff Lambert was the oldest cop at the station. According to Virg, the gray-haired, cynical man wasn't interested in advancing. He liked being a patrol officer.

As Atticus stepped out of the doorway, Wyatt walked into the bedroom and stopped short. Nothing looked out of place except for the shattered glass and metal fragments from a broken clock. "Was he looking for cash, maybe?"

"Probably." Atticus scowled.

"She interrupted him," Officer Lambert said. "I'm not sure if her timing was good or bad."

"It's damn isolated. Made it easy to break in, I'd guess." Wyatt's hands fisted. Erin could have been badly hurt.

"Not especially easy. She has a security system, and he didn't set it off." Atticus shook his head. "I'm going to have to figure out how he got around it."

The sound of a car came from outside. Wyatt followed Atticus to the front door.

Virgil was helping Erin out of the car.

Jumping down the steps, Wyatt strode over. Her face was pale, and she moved like she hurt.

She looked up at him. "Wyatt." Her voice cracked.

The tone in her voice was familiar. As a teen, his sturdy cousin had tried just as hard to hide her distress whenever she reached the limit of her endurance.

"Sugar, you sound like you need a hug." Very, very gently, he pulled her into his arms—and she started to cry.

She wasn't small. She was above average height with lean muscles and sturdy bones. But right now, she felt...frail.

He wanted—needed—to beat the fuck out of the bastard who'd hurt her.

Instead, all he could do was hold her. Stroke her back. Rock her slightly. Support her in whatever way she needed.

Well, he was good at providing an anchor. Over the years, a lot of submissives had cried on his shoulder—hell, some of them begged for that kind of release. Anastasia had been a weeper. Occasionally, the weeper was a client he'd guided into the wilderness. For a few women, the relief of escaping their usual responsibilities meant anything set them off.

And he'd hold them.

Near the house, his brother was waiting, eyes narrowed as he watched Erin. Virg was a typical cop—suspicious of every-fucking-body.

Wyatt wouldn't take a law enforcement job in a million years. As Erin's tears dampened his shirt, he jerked his chin toward the house. *I got this, bro. Leave.*

After a stubborn pause, Virgil headed away. His phone rang, and he pulled it out as he walked inside.

A while later, Erin's crying turned into hitched breathing, and she lifted her head. "I'm so s-sorry. I—"

"Shh, you're fine." He kissed the top of her head. Stepping back, he cupped her face and used his thumbs to wipe away the tears. "Atticus said the intruder hit you. Anything busted?"

Her lips quirked up slightly. "You're so practical. No, I just have a headache and sore stomach. Sunny was there." Her voice dropped. "She's married to that lieutenant. Did you know?"

Wyatt smothered a laugh. "Yes, I know."

"Anyway, she made sure I saw the doctor quickly. He said I'll be fine." Her gaze went to the open front door. "Did they catch the guy?"

"I haven't checked." He frowned at her. "You look rough. How about I take you to the ranch, and you rest. We can deal with this tomorrow."

Her eyes filled, but her chin came up. "I can do it. I need to do it. To see what he did."

So stubborn. "All right, slugger." He put his arm around her and hooked his finger in her jeans belt loop.

Rather than heading for the sound of voices, she went through the small house, living and dining area, kitchen, laundry. Nothing appeared to have been taken.

Finally, they entered the bedroom where the three cops were talking.

As she looked around, the pained sound she made was like a person who'd been gutted. She was staring at the fragments on the carpet. Her lower lip trembled. "He broke the antique clock my grandfather gave me."

Yeah, the clock was toast. Wyatt noticed the paint on one wall had scrape marks. The asshole had probably thrown the clock against it. He pulled her closer to remind her she wasn't alone.

"Officer Lambert." Virgil checked his watch. "Your shift is long over. Thank you for staying with the detective."

"No problem, Lieutenant." Lambert offered a nod of sympathy to Erin and headed out.

"Ms. Palmer, this is Detective Ware." Virgil nodded at Atticus.

Her not correcting them about her name showed just how shaken she was. "It's Lockwood, not Palmer." Wyatt got a nod from his brother in acknowledgment.

Atticus smiled at Erin. "Ms. Lockwood."

Virgil motioned toward the door. "Let's sit in the living room and talk."

As Wyatt moved her forward, Erin asked Atticus, "How did the man get inside?"

"Through the sliding glass door to the deck." Atticus followed them into the living room.

"Oh."

With her leaning on him, Wyatt could feel the tremor run through her.

"Nothing appears broken except in your bedroom," Atticus said. "Did you have any cash or valuables in there?"

Her laugh held tears. "I wish I *had* cash for a burglar to take. No. Nothing like that."

Anger roused inside Wyatt. She'd been trying so hard to get back on her feet.

In the living room, she looked up at him. "Thank you. For the hug and the help, but this isn't your problem. You don't have to—"

"Erin." Wyatt's reproving tone silenced her. Irritation vied with amusement in the big cowboy's expression. And then, as if she hadn't spoken, he helped her sit and joined her on the couch.

He wasn't leaving. The relief almost sent her back to crying. As the cops sat down across the coffee table, she put her hands in her lap, trying to sit straight despite the pain in her stomach. Trying to show she could handle whatever happened.

"So tough." Wyatt took her hand in his warm one. His weight on the couch tipped her toward him until their shoulders rubbed together.

And oh, she needed him here.

Her sanctuary had been...invaded. The burglar had been in her bedroom, where she slept. Going through her belongings. Her breathing went ragged again. All she'd wanted was to start her life over, to live joyously and now...

"Hey, hey." With a hand on her cheek, Wyatt turned her head so she had to meet his dark eyes. His thumb rubbed her chin. "You're banged up, but you're not alone. I got your back, and we'll figure this out."

He kept her gaze trapped until she nodded.

She was so, so grateful he was there. "Thank you." She put her hand on her stomach, trying to make the shaking inside stop, then pulled in a fortifying breath. "I'm good."

"You're so full of it." He tilted her chin up, planted a quick kiss on her lips, and released her, still keeping his grip on her hand.

And...with him there, she could face whatever the police needed to ask.

"Ms. Lockwood." The detective had blue eyes and a level gaze. "First—"

"Before you start"—Wyatt interrupted—"Erin, the detective —Atticus—is Sawyer's brother."

"Oh." The stiffness in her spine eased slightly as she saw the resemblance. The two did look a lot alike.

Wyatt chuckled. "And, if you haven't figured it out, the lieutenant—Virgil—is my brother."

The lieutenant was clean-shaven with short hair, his body slightly bigger than Wyatt's, his eyes hazel rather than brown. But...yes, they had the same rugged, weather-beaten faces, with lines at the corners of their eyes from squinting into the sun. Laugh lines. Strong, angular jaws.

He had honest eyes...like Wyatt's.

It helped to know the detective and lieutenant weren't as much strangers as she'd thought. She glanced at Wyatt and whispered, "Thank you."

He winked.

She turned to the two law enforcement officers. "If it doesn't break your rules, please call me Erin."

"Erin it is." Atticus smiled at her before turning serious. "I noticed you looked around. Was anything taken?"

"No, not that I could see. I don't understand."

"He attacked you. Did he come here for that?" Wyatt was scowling.

"No, he seemed surprised I was here. He was going to k-kill me because I saw his face." The shudders were getting worse.

Wyatt put his arm around her, carefully pulling her close. Close enough the heat from his body seeped into her. "Maybe discuss this later, Virg. I take it the bastard got away?"

"The burglar was heavily bleeding," Atticus said. "Levi

followed his blood trail down the road to a turnout. He'd probably parked his car there."

Her heart rate picked up. "He got away." He might come after her.

"No, he didn't." The lieutenant rubbed his face. "The station called me a few minutes ago. He was found. He'd veered off the road and crashed into a tree."

"They caught him?" Wyatt asked.

"Not exactly." Lieutenant Masterson shook his head. "He was pronounced dead on the scene."

"He...he's dead?" Nausea vied with relief. "But—"

"At a guess, he probably had a concussion, was speeding, and lost control of the vehicle," Atticus said.

"I..." Guilt was an uncomfortable lump in her belly. She'd hit him so hard. The concussion was her fault; his *death* was her fault.

"Hell." Wyatt gripped her shoulder and gave her a gentle shake. "I can see what you're thinking, but you're wrong. The man brought it all on himself. Breaking into a house, attacking the owner, driving when he wasn't capable. Speeding. Actions have consequences. You're not to blame for any of it."

His words helped. A lot. And, if she had it to do over, she couldn't see anything else she might have done. Not if she wanted to live. With a sigh, she met Wyatt's gaze and nodded.

A corner of his mouth tipped up. "There we go."

"Not to be cold-hearted, but I'm not unhappy he can't come back. I'd rather you be safe." Atticus tilted his head. "I learned last year how doggedly some criminals pursue revenge."

What an ugly thought. "Um, can you give me a recommendation of who to call to get the lock fixed so I can sleep tonight? Or maybe there's a way to jam the door so it—"

"Uh-uh." Wyatt squeezed her hand. "You'll spend tonight down at our ranch."

"I can't do that."

"Sure you can. Tomorrow, we'll come back and clean up. Get the lock fixed."

She stared at him. He'd been like this on the trail ride. Smoothly in charge without raising his voice and as impossible to stop as an 18-wheeler with a stuck gas pedal.

He rubbed her arm. The heat of his hand on her bare skin made her realize how cold she was. Chilled from fear. "But—"

"No buts." He turned to the police. "We done here for now?"

"There are a lot of questions unanswered, but we may never get answers. We're done for now." Wyatt's brother smiled at her. "Go rest. If I have more questions, I'll ask them tonight at supper or at breakfast tomorrow."

"Sounds like a plan." Wyatt carefully helped her to her feet. "It's late, sweetheart. Let's find what you need for an overnight and head for the ranch."

Her protest died on her lips. She *didn't* want to stay here where she'd been attacked. Just the thought made her shiver in fear. For tonight, she wanted nothing more than to stay right beside Wyatt. Where she felt safe.

Tomorrow, she'd be braver.

CHAPTER EIGHTEEN

A few minutes later, at the Masterson ranch, Erin felt as if adrenaline had burned up the last of her body's reserves. As she followed Wyatt down a hallway on the ground floor, her legs didn't want to move.

With her duffel bag over his shoulder, he opened the door into what looked like a big apartment. "This is our guest apartment. There's—" Stopping, he studied her.

She realized she'd taken a step back. Had started to shake. *Don't be a wuss, Erin.* She took a step into the big...empty...room. So very empty.

"Whoa there, li'l dogie. What's wrong?"

"Nothing. It...it looks very nice, thank you."

"Bullshit." He studied her face, then the room, then her face again. "I'm a guy, not a woman. You and me, we had different childhoods, upbringings. Means you won't react the same way I do when you run up against bad shit."

She stared at him. Where was he going with this?

His lips twitched. "What I'm saying is you have to use your words, little bit. Do you hate the rooms?"

"No, no, they're fine," she whispered and couldn't go on. Dammit, what was wrong with her? She couldn't stop shaking.

"Easy there." He ran his hands up and down her upper arms. And, oh, she just wanted him to hold her again. God, she was weak.

"Erin, would you rather spend the night with me? You can have the bed. Or even the couch. Sleep with me or sleep alone."

Oh, please, yes. "Yes. I-I just don't want to be alone. Not tonight." Maybe she could have stayed with one of her new women friends...only they all had partners. Here was better. With Wyatt.

"In that case, let me show you my place." He led her back through the house toward the stairway and next to it, opened an elevator only big enough to hold, at most, three people.

"Your house has an elevator?"

He chuckled and ushered her in. "Yeah, Pa installed it one summer after Virgil broke a leg and Morgan sprained an ankle. Stairs are a pain in the ass when you're busted up."

As the elevator rose, she tilted her head. "You have a beard now."

He rubbed it thoughtfully. "Shaving in the back country is just asking to get cut up. I'll deal with it tomorrow."

The elevator opened onto a wide landing with two doors on each side. Wyatt opened one and waved her into a cozy living room. "This is my place."

Creamy white walls set off an oversized leather couch in a rich cranberry color. On each side were indigo, denim-covered armchairs—and fluffy gray Bat was curled up on one cushion.

The cat blinked green-gold eyes, jumped off the chair, and came to greet her.

Pressing a hand to her belly, she started to bend.

"Uh-uh, wait." Wyatt scooped up the cat. "She's hurt, Bat. Say hello from here."

Carefully, she offered a finger, was accepted with a quick cheek rub, and petted the cat for a minute. "Why is hearing a purr so comforting?"

Wyatt smiled and touched Erin's cheek. "Means there's no

enemies in sight. Right now, you're probably seeing bad guys everywhere. You're safe here, sweetheart."

She blinked at the blunt statement and saw the grim determination in his expression—nothing would get to her without going through him.

And something inside her relaxed. She was safe here. She'd never realized how amazing the feeling was until it was gone—and then restored. "Thank you. Seriously, thank you."

The sunlines beside his eyes deepened. As he set the cat down, she finished looking around.

One wall held mounted antique rifles amidst photos of men in fringed leather outfits. Above a white stone fireplace, carved horses pranced across the mantel. To the left of the fireplace was a flat screen TV, on the right a well-filled bookcase.

A glowing chandelier made from antlers drew her gaze up to the sloped ceiling with exposed dark wood beams. "You have a beautiful place."

"Thanks, I like it. Want to eat first or clean up?"

"Clean up, please." Her skin felt...itchy. Covered in fear, sweat, and pain. Dirty.

He led the way to his bedroom and flipped on the light. Blue and red curtains in a subtle plaid framed floor-to-ceiling windows that showcased the surrounding mountains. A king-size, wrought-iron bed had red and white blankets—and was tidily made. Another western-style rug like the one in the living room pulled all the colors together.

"Bathroom's in here."

The bathroom was a lovely decadence with glossy wood cabinetry and a green-and-brown tile floor. An accent wall of deep green made her smile. "I love accent walls."

He tilted his head. "Your house doesn't have any though."

She shrugged. "Troy."

"Ah. Want a shower or bath?" He set her duffel bag down on the long counter.

She turned her attention from the massive tub with jets to a big shower enclosure. Much as she'd love a long soak in the tub, getting in and out would be too painful. "A shower."

"Shower it is. Towels and washcloths are in here." He opened a cabinet door showing shelves with stacked emerald-green towels. "Use whatever you need. I'll be in the living room."

This was just what she wanted. An interval of solitude without being completely alone. And a chance to cleanse the feel of violence from her skin.

Water poured down from the showerhead, steam rising. Stepping under the flow, she let the water wash away everything—including a few more tears.

On the living room couch, Wyatt was reading through the latest farm and ranch magazine and trying not to worry when Erin came out of his bedroom. Tossing the magazine aside, he rose and looked her over.

Wet-haired, she was barefoot and flushed pink from the shower. Her eyes were bright again, the strain gone from her face.

"You look better."

She smiled. "I feel so much better. Thank you."

"Just so you know, Becca, Mallory, and Kallie all called to check on you. They said you could stay with any of them or just call and talk."

"They did?" Her surprised, pleased expression melted his heart. She obviously hadn't realized she'd found a place in Becca's crew.

"You probably have messages on your phone."

"Oh." She frowned. "The battery was low; it's probably gone dead."

"We'll get charged up. Are you hungry?"

"Very. If it isn't too much trouble?"

"None at all." He walked over, and damn, she smelled as sweet as one of Friede's pastries. Like coconut and vanilla.

Slowly, he put his arms around her and pulled her close. She was still toasty warm from the shower, her skin damp...and she tipped her head up. Wanting his kiss.

Her lips were so fucking soft.

Enough, Masterson. He'd just meant to be comforting, not turn it into something more. With a sigh, he released her.

But damn, she didn't let him go. Her arms stayed around his waist.

So he hugged her against him, stroking her shoulders. Avoiding temptation like the desire to curl his fingers under the curve of her perfect ass.

Focus, Masterson. He cleared his throat. "I don't keep much food up here, but we can make sandwiches and heat a can of soup. Or if you want company, today is pizza and movie day, and we can join Morgan, Sunny, and Virgil downstairs. It's Sunny's choice of movies today, and she wants *Men in Black*."

"This isn't in the dining room?"

"Nope." Wyatt grinned. "We normally eat there, but if we're home on Friday nights, we go the lazy slob route."

"Lazy slob. That's you all right. You better be careful, or your beer gut will stretch your shirt." Laughing, she patted his abs.

"Brat." He lifted her hand and nipped the fleshy area at the base of her thumb. A palmist had told him it was called the mount of Venus.

Her color heightened, so maybe the palmist had the right idea. He nibbled it again before kissing her wrist. Her fast pulse beat against his lips.

Nice.

"Um." She shook her head as if to remember what they'd been talking about.

Damn, she was fun. "Decision?"

"They won't mind us joining them? Me joining them?"

"No, we'll just bake an extra pizza for the two of us."

"In that case, pizza and movie and company sounds wonderful." She bit her lip. "I kind of don't want to think about anything until tomorrow."

Violence up close and personal could twist a person up. He'd been there. It made sense to step back for some time and distance. "Sounds like a plan."

Considering the amount of seating in the huge living room, Erin decided the Mastersons must be used to having guests. Virgil and Sunny shared a couch with Patches, the small spaniel, curled up beside them. Morgan took a big easy chair.

On another couch, Wyatt had sat down right beside Erin—and the rub of his hip and hard thigh against hers was an unsettling comfort. Her inner self seemed to think if she was touching him, she was safe.

The room itself was made to be used. The furniture was soft and roomy. There were plenty of end tables and coffee tables for drinks and food.

And boy, they did have food. Coke and pizzas with a variety of toppings—mostly meat. A side of chicken wings. And potato salad because Morgan apparently loved the stuff.

Her, too, actually.

This was so nice. She was in a warm living room with an even warmer body beside her and Bat purring on her lap. Sunny's *Men in Black*, an older action-adventure movie, was more comedy than serious.

The Mastersons weren't a silent audience when it came to movies. Erin joined in, talking back to the movie, laughing at the jokes, cheering when the hero got in a good zinger.

It was the perfect distraction from her life.

Virgil and Sunny were adorable together. Morgan was quieter but with a great sense of humor.

When the movie was over, Sunny brought out dessert—vanilla ice cream smothered in fudge syrup on top of brownies.

"Oh, yum." Erin put her hands together in a begging gesture.

"Ha." Sunny grinned. "When Virgil called to say Wyatt was dragging you here for tonight, I knew just what to make." During their meal at the Gold Dust, everyone had discussed favorite desserts.

Erin raised her eyebrows at Wyatt. "You *dragged* me here?"

Smirking, he pumped up his biceps. "It's good to have muscles."

With an effort, she yanked her gaze away—because O-M-G, the man had muscles.

"If he oversteps, Erin, let me know," Virgil said in his deep voice. "I'll shove him in a cell and throw away the key."

"Pfft, Bat would defend me," Wyatt said.

Recognizing his name, Bat perked up his ears and rubbed Erin's hand for more pets.

Virgil grinned. "He's turning into a fine ranch cat. You did good, bro."

With a twitch of his tail, Bat lay his head back down, his chin resting on Erin's thigh. And she knew just how he felt.

This was a warm and happy place.

And had wonderful desserts. Finishing the last bite, she sighed. "This was amazing, Sunny. Thank you."

Sunny smiled. "Chocolate never fails to make me feel better."

"So, Ms. Lockwood, tomorrow, we'll get your security password changed, and the locks rekeyed—just in case. And do clean-up." Wyatt stroked her shoulder, looking down at her. "How's your gut feeling? And your headache?"

"How did you know?" The movie and food had been great, but her head still hurt.

"I've gotten thumped a time or two." His smile was wry. "And everything hurts more in the evening."

"No shit." Morgan smiled at her. "Want Tylenol or ibuprofen?"

"I would die for ibuprofen."

He gave her an easy grin and went through the entry and a door on the other side.

She lined up her memory of the building from the outside. There should be an additional door on the outside with the "Masterson Wilderness Guides" company name. "Your office?"

Wyatt nodded. "We all have the usual over-the-counter meds in our apartments but keep more extensive first aid supplies down here."

Wilderness guides, horses, ranching. Yes, she bet they had plenty of injuries.

"Here you go." Morgan handed her a couple of pills.

She washed them down with the last of her Coke. "Thank you."

Rising, Wyatt helped her to her feet. "Let's get you to bed before I have to carry you up there."

"She doesn't look that heavy." Back in his chair, Morgan grinned. "It'd be my pleasure to help you upstairs, Erin."

She gaped at him. Was he flirting?

Wyatt growled under his breath, put an arm around her waist—and kicked his brother's leg as they walked past.

Morgan yelped and then was laughing as hard as Virgil.

When Erin glanced at Sunny, the blonde rolled her eyes and mouthed, "Brothers."

Brothers, indeed. The way they teased each other had driven away her sadness and fear.

In the elevator, with Wyatt's arm around her and Bat weaving between their feet, she realized she was smiling.

Wyatt stepped out of the bathroom, wearing a pair of cut-off sweats, and smiled at the sight of Erin in his bed. She had on one of his old T-shirts, worn to softness. Her hair spilled over the pillow in a way that made his fingers want to touch, to tangle in the strands, to grip and...

He sighed. He was male, there was a woman—one he desired—in his bed. Of course his mind would go there.

Didn't mean he was going to act on it. This wasn't the time. She needed safety and gentleness and care, all things he could give.

Erin opened her eyes. "Wyatt?"

He sat on the side of the bed and brushed her hair from her face. "I'm going to sack out on the couch. Do you want the bedside light left on or off?"

"I... You have a giant bed and... Can you sleep in here?" Color crept into her face. "Or will it, I mean, having someone in your bed, um, bother you?"

It wouldn't be the first time he'd gone to sleep with a halfie. "No, I can sleep with you in my bed. Want a giant teddy bear, do you?" More like she didn't want to be alone after being attacked. After being threatened.

"Yes?"

"Then that's what will happen." After opening the bedroom door for the cat, he piled a couple of pillows against the headboard and picked up his eReader from the nightstand. "Go to sleep. I'm going to read for a while."

"Oh, okay." The way she blinked, she was exhausted. "What time do we need to get up in the morning?"

This conversation sounded as if they were an old married couple, and the idea was oddly appealing. "No particular time. We're all off tomorrow." He had a thought and frowned.

"What's wrong?"

"Not wrong exactly, but... I think you should share how your husband died with Virgil. Just in case Palmer's problems end up in your lap, I'd like the law enforcement here to know to keep an eye out for you."

"You think the burglar had something to do with Troy?"

Wyatt reached over and took her hand. "Probably not, but there's no way of telling. I don't like how your other house was trashed. Let's be cautious, yeah?"

" 'K." She yawned. "It's not a secret. You can tell him, or I will."

"Good girl."

Hell, what was it about her that brought out the Dominant in him? The way her gaze dropped and pink colored her cheeks pointed to a submissive nature. She liked being called a good girl. No, this wasn't the time. He needed to monitor his words more closely.

"Sleep, Erin."

An hour later, he set his eReader on the nightstand.

Erin was curled up against his side, sound asleep. She'd started off on one side of the bed, watching him as he settled back to read for a while. She'd barely fallen asleep before a nightmare had hit—and he'd woken her enough to rouse her out of it.

Fuck, he knew far too well how violent experiences bled into dreams. His jaw tightened at the thought he'd let her down, hadn't been there to protect her from the intruder. His guilt wasn't logical, but his instincts didn't care about logic.

Everything in him wanted to protect her from anything and everything that might harm her.

She'd tried so determinedly to keep it together today. And had trusted him with her tears, her emotions, even asked him to stay with her now... Her trust was an honor—a gift—that shook him.

One he'd do his best to deserve.

He smiled down at her, moving a strand of hair out of her face. After her nightmare, she ended up plastered against him.

There'd be no complaints from him. She was soft and snuggly.

Bat obviously agreed since the cat was sound asleep against the curve of her legs.

Turning off the bedside lamp, Wyatt dislodged Erin far enough he could slide down in bed and tuck her against his side again. Rubbing his cheek against the top of her head, he breathed in the fragrance of vanilla and coconut.

Damn, she sure smelled edible.

A weight on Erin's side roused her from sleep, and it moved down over her hip and leg. She froze at the rush of fear. A dim light showed she wasn't at home.

Where am I? What was—*oh*. She breathed out slowly. This was Wyatt's house.

And his cat had just walked down her body as if she was a lumpy sidewalk. No wonder she woke up.

Heart still hammering, she tilted her head to scan the room. Just to—*you know*—make sure it was empty of intruders and all.

It was.

At the foot of the bed, Bat perched with his tail curled around his paws. Looking smug.

The bedside clock showed it was the middle of the night, and she was dying of thirst—stupid pizza. Besides, after the scare she had in waking up, all her muscles felt twitchy. She needed to walk around and shake it off. Slowly, she edged out of the bed.

Cold water, she decided a few minutes later, was one of the finest things in the world. Thirst sated and having moved enough to relax, she tried to crawl back into bed as quietly as she'd gotten out.

With a rumbling sound in the back of his throat, Wyatt wrapped an arm around her waist, pulling her closer. Her back was against his chest. Her butt nestled against his groin—and a solid erection. His arm lay over her waist, elbow bent, so his hand cupped her breast. Squeezing gently, caressing.

Heat flared through her body along with a whole different kind of heart hammering. Because he made her feel alive. Made her grateful for being alive.

Just then, his hand on her breast stopped, and she felt him freeze. Heard him say, "Fuck, sorry," under his breath as he shifted his hand away.

He'd totally been asleep.

She sat up, turned, and laid on top of him, propping herself up with her forearms on his chest.

His eyes looked almost black in the low light. "Sorry, sweetheart. I didn't mean—"

"I know. It's okay."

He cupped her cheek, his thumb brushing over her chin. "How do you feel?"

"Um..." She wiggled slightly. "My stomach is okay. No headache either now."

"Good to hear." His expression was easy to read. *Relief.* He'd been worried about her.

A small hollow in her heart filled. With her grandparents, Mom, and even Troy gone, it had felt as if she could disappear, and no one in the world would notice. Or care.

He would. And...what about those messages from the women? It seemed she wasn't as alone as she'd felt.

I'm not alone. And I'm alive. She bent her head and kissed him—and blinked at the unexpected feeling of his beard on her skin. It was long enough to be soft, and his lips were firm.

He let her have her way as she kissed him and sucked on his lower lip. His mouth opened to let her tongue fence with his.

So nice.

Maybe too nice. Heat radiated from his body, and under her forearms, his broad chest was distractingly muscular.

His powerful hands stroked her back, detonating unexpected sparks of desire. Heat bloomed low in her pelvis. She lifted her head to get a breath...and heard a thud as the cat jumped off the bed and padded out of the room.

Wyatt curved his hand around the side of her neck. "Exactly how far are you planning to go with this, sugar?"

"I..." She swallowed and met his gaze. "I'm alive—and I want to celebrate." She hesitated. Had she made a wrong assumption, thinking he'd want to have sex? "All the way? If you... You don't have to, if you—"

"Sweetheart, I can't think of anything I'd rather do than celebrate you being alive and victorious."

Alive. And...victorious. She heard the respect in his voice.

She *had* won. *I'm stronger than I give myself credit for.*

A moment later, she realized he was waiting for her to finish thinking. His smile deepened. His hand on her neck slid up, fingers tangling in, then gripping her hair. He pulled her head down—and claimed her lips. Ravaged her mouth.

The gentle heat of arousal blazed into a terrifying inferno.

He rolled, putting her on her back, and flattening her beneath him. Pausing, he studied her face. "Pain? Your stomach?"

"No, no, I'm good."

"All right then." He kissed her some more, holding her in place with his hand in her hair and his solid weight on her body. As he leisurely took what he wanted from the kiss, the sensation of being overpowered made her head spin.

Sitting back, he pulled her T-shirt up and over her head, then kissed his way down to her chest. His beard skimmed teasingly against her bare skin.

"You, sweetheart, have gorgeous breasts."

What could she say? "Um, thank you?"

He chuckled, then made her gasp when he took a breast in each callused hand and started kneading them. Squeezing and plumping and playing until they swelled and throbbed.

Wetting a finger, he circled each areola, the moisture cool against the hot tissue. He watched her nipples pucker into sharp points before tugging on each and pinching the tips until they were almost, almost painful. Until she quivered inside.

Bending, he closed his mouth over one, sucking, running his tongue around it before sucking insistently until it swelled to a pulsing distention.

He switched to the other side. Teasing and torturing her breasts until the sensations turned into a swirling, aching arousal nothing would fix.

She felt incredibly alive.

When he laughed, she realized she was pulling his hair with one hand and pushing on his shoulder with the other.

Sitting up, he looked down at her and rubbed his knuckles over one distended peak and the other, even as his gaze focused on her face.

Her nipples were so sensitive, each light brush made her squirm.

"I'm going to make your clit look and feel just like these, swollen and tender." His lips curved up. "And then I'm going to take you so we can *celebrate* together."

Her mouth went dry at the promise in his voice.

A while later, Wyatt smiled at Erin's low moan and flicked his tongue over her engorged clit again. Because that was a sound to warm a Dom's heart.

She'd come twice already, and as he'd promised, her clit—her pussy, actually—was puffy and nicely sensitive.

Be fun to see what suction would do. And clamps. And—

No, Masterson. This time needs to be sweet and slow.

She didn't need anything close to violence today. This was a celebration of life—and, to him, a celebration of how fucking amazing she was.

"*Wyaaaaatt.*"

He grinned at her husky whine. "Yes, sweetheart?"

"Please, I want you inside me. I can't come, not again."

Oh, she could. Women never realized how many times they could get off. But if she wanted his dick, he'd cooperate. Hard as it was to remember, he wasn't her Dom. He shouldn't push her boundaries. Well, not *too* far anyway. "All right. Over you go."

He rolled her onto her belly and set her onto her hands and knees. "Stay right there like the good girl you are."

The quiver running through her was palpable under his palm. So beautifully submissive.

Moving over to his nightstand, he stripped off his sweats and sheathed himself in a condom. His toy bag was beside the bed, so he reached in for the portable wand and sheathed it.

It'd be a shame not to give her one last climax, now wouldn't it?

Erin felt him behind her, pushing her lower legs out so he could kneel between them. God, she couldn't believe she'd gotten off twice already, and the feel of him still sent up an ache of need inside her.

His shaft pressed flat against her buttocks as he leaned over, balancing on one arm while his free hand played with her still swollen breasts, bringing all the sensations back. When he squeezed her nipples, hot electricity shot straight to her lower parts.

He ran his hand down over her stomach and mound, then slid his fingers along her pussy. Leaning forward, he kissed her cheek, and his voice was a rough whisper. "I like how wet you are. I'm going to enjoy taking you."

His erection pressed against her entrance. Slid in an inch. Two. The deliberately slow penetration, his hand on her pelvis holding her still, made her feel...taken.

Possessed.

Controlled.

A tremor ran through her, and she whimpered.

He paused until she had her breath back, then whispered in her ear, "You can take me, Erin."

She could; she had before, and she could feel his concentrated regard, how closely he was monitoring her as he pressed in again. His confidence that she'd give him what he wanted along with his concern for her welfare...the combination plunged her even deeper into surrender. Her insides involuntarily clenched around him, the sensation of tightness and fullness almost unbearable. Eyes closed, she panted.

His pelvis pressed against her buttocks. "There we go. Look

how brave you were. You did good, sweetheart. And you feel like heaven, all around me."

This cowboy, who could be so bluntly honest, had just given her the sweetest of compliments.

In a slow, sensuous glide, he withdrew, and sank back in. Rhythmic—and way too slow. Around his shaft, her body hummed with desire. She needed—*needed*—to move, only she could do nothing, pinned between his hand and his hips. He was in total control of *everything*.

In and out, retreat and advance, each penetration ruthlessly slow and deep.

Her clit, her whole pussy felt swollen, making him seem even larger. "Please..."

He chuckled. "I love it when you ask so politely." His speed picked up with head-spinning friction.

She heard a loud hum from beneath her.

Before she could react, he pressed a wand vibrator against her clit.

"Aaah!" Pleasure soared through her.

His thrusts changed to deep and hard and fast. Added to the vibrations on her clit, the forceful sensations were overwhelming. Pressure in her lower half built rapidly, inside and out.

And then, pleasure exploded inside her in intense toe-curling waves and engulfed her body until even her fingertips and toes were tingling.

His arm tightened around her as he came right after her. His shaft thick, intimately deep.

And she wanted him there. Wanted him.

After he cleaned up, Wyatt slid back into bed, thoroughly enjoying how well Erin fit into his arms. Soft and warm and fragrant. With her head on his shoulder, she had an arm over his chest and a leg flung over his thigh.

"Thank you for the celebration." Her voice was still husky,

her eyes heavy-lidded. So lovely.

"Anytime you feel like celebrating, you come to me." He frowned slightly, hearing how what he intended to be a teasing response had come out more like an order.

Looking down at her face, he saw her brows draw together. "When we were camping, you talked about BDSM and giving pain with pleasure. And you're very…"

Looked like her courage had given out, although he was impressed she'd brought the subject up already. "I'm very into being in charge in the bedroom—or tents? I'm what's known as a sexual Dominant. From the way you respond to being under command, I'd say you have a submissive nature, at least when it comes to sex." A crease appeared in one cheek with his smile. "Not especially at other times."

Her mouth opened. Closed. All the protests he'd expected weren't forthcoming. Because she was thinking it over.

And how rare was that?

Dammit, he genuinely liked her. Could easily fall in love with her, no less.

A chill washed over him, like he'd swallowed ice water. Loving…left a person open to loss. His mother hadn't been that old when she died. Anastasia had been even younger. Life didn't offer any fucking guarantees, now did it?

With his friends who'd ended up single, the loss had been due to betrayal or growing apart. *Death* had taken his woman.

He sighed, thinking of the time after Anastasia's death, the grief he'd gone through. About the sadness Pa had carried after they lost Mom.

Yet, he wouldn't have given up his time with Anastasia, even if he'd known the ending would be too soon and too painful.

Nothing ever stayed the same; no one lives forever. And love —it was what living was all about.

He looked down at Erin and smiled.

She'd fallen asleep in the middle of her thinking.

Yes, he could love this one.

CHAPTER NINETEEN

Erin opened the door to her house and heard the distinctive sound of the vacuum cleaner. She frowned at Wyatt. "I thought Morgan was just here to let the repairmen in."

Wyatt had left her in bed this morning, telling her to sleep in, since he had errands to run, and Morgan had volunteered to deal with the locksmith.

They were so nice to her.

But was Morgan...cleaning?

"Why don't you go check what he's up to," Wyatt said. "I forgot something in the car. I'll be right in."

"Okay." She followed the noise to her bedroom where Wyatt's brother was vacuuming the carpet. "Morgan."

He looked up and grinned. "Hey, Erin, you're here." After one last pass, he turned the vacuum off. "Your new house keys are right there. The one for the sliding glass door matches the front door."

"Wonderful. Thank you." She picked up her keyring and replaced the old house keys with the new ones.

"Sure. Hopefully, I got all the broken stuff and glass up."

"I appreciate it, but you didn't—"

"It's good you're still here, bro." Wyatt walked in and set down two big sacks. "And looking so energetic and all."

"Why is energetic a good thing?" Morgan gave his brother a wary look.

The mischief in Wyatt's eyes would give anyone pause. "We're painting a wall."

"Are we now."

"You're what?" Erin turned to Wyatt. "What wall?"

"In here. You need an accent wall." He pointed. "This one is scraped up."

She flinched. Because the intruder had thrown her antique clock against it. *The bastard.* Pulling in a breath, she shook her head. Grampie wouldn't want her crying over something he'd given her. He'd say it was just a thing.

Okay. Okay, Grampie.

"You like accent walls." Wyatt pulled out a bright quilt. Grammie's quilt. She turned to look; how had she not realized it wasn't on the bed? "Becca helped me pick out a good color to coordinate with this."

"Going to an artist for help. Smart, bro." Morgan squatted and pulled a paint can from the other sack.

Erin bent to look. The lovely teal color on the lid matched one of the primary shades in the quilt. "I love it."

The feeling inside her was odd. Warm and happy and...and cherished. Wyatt had been listening when she talked about loving his bathroom's accent wall. No, he'd *heard* her. And he'd put in time and effort to get the perfect color.

He was different from Troy. So very different.

"It's not a big wall, won't take long. I'll get started taping around it." Morgan picked up the sack filled with paint brushes, masking tape, and plastic to cover the floor and headed out.

Wrapping her arms around Wyatt, Erin rose on her tiptoes to kiss him. "Thank you."

His arms tightened, and he deepened the kiss, turning it far,

far hotter. When he let her go, her blood was simmering...and her stomach rubbed against a very thick erection.

"Fuck," he muttered. "Now I need a cold shower."

She sputtered a laugh. "It's your own fault."

"So it is, little mechanic. Speaking of which, Pierre said to call if you need anything." Wyatt tucked a strand of hair behind her ear. "Marco and Walker said the same."

"They did?" Happiness swept through her. The other mechanics *were* beginning to like her.

A few minutes later, Erin sat on the plastic-covered carpet, wielding a smaller brush near the baseboard. Wyatt had hooked his phone up to her small bedroom speakers, and music filled the room.

Country, of course.

When "Cowboy Casanova" came on, Morgan turned, jerked his chin at Wyatt, and winked at her.

She sputtered a laugh, making Wyatt turn. He looked from her to Morgan. "Causing trouble again, bro?" He flicked a drop of paint at his brother.

"Now, now, no paint fights." She wagged a reprimanding finger at him. "This is my bedroom."

"Yes, *ma'am*," Wyatt said, and she snickered. The obedient words were totally contradicted by the self-assured stance, the rough, deep voice, and the laughter in his gaze.

Morgan grinned at his brother, and they both returned to painting.

As the bouncy song music drove away the toxic spirit left by the intruder, her spirits lifted. The wall was almost covered now with the gorgeous blue, one that made her smile.

Wyatt was singing along, painting in time with the beat. His western shirt clung to his broad shoulders, showing the flex of ripped muscles beneath the fabric. Really, men should always tuck their shirts in. At least if they had such gorgeous, tight butts.

After a moment, she realized he'd stopped singing...and was looking over his shoulder at her.

At her staring at his ass.

Oops. "Um..."

He simply grinned at her. She'd noticed how a lot of stuff she'd find embarrassing or upsetting just rolled right off his big shoulders. And how cool was that?

But... She eyed him. "Kallie told me you used to get grumbly and yell. But I've never even seen you raise your voice."

He and Morgan exchanged a glance, then Wyatt crouched down beside her. "When Kallie came to us, she was...like fourteen and a total mouse. She hadn't been subdued as a kid, but after her parents died, I swear, she got quieter and quieter. We didn't know why—and hell, I was eighteen, Morgan seventeen. Stupid about how people work, right?"

Teenaged boys becoming men. Erin nodded.

"Virg took on being the nice big brother, Morgan was the quiet, supportive one. I was the cousin who teased her, trying to get her to let loose. So she'd know it was fine with us if she did." He shook his head. "Not the smartest way to counsel a wounded spirit."

"It worked though," Morgan offered. "He'd act like a stompy bull to make her laugh or shout, and she learned to give him hell back. She's so cute when she loses her temper. But afterward, she'd go back to being so fucking careful around us that it hurt."

"Eventually, thanks to Jake, we found out why she felt so insecure. And we did family counseling." Wyatt chuckled. "As for my temper, it's a lot easier to talk my way out of problems than shouting at someone."

A stompy bull. Erin tried to visualize Wyatt at eighteen, being all grumpy, and she grinned. "I bet you were totally cute."

Morgan huffed. "That's your take-away? I tell you he'd shout at Kallie, and you think he was cute?" He shook his head, muttered, "Hopeless," and went back to painting.

Leaning forward, Wyatt whispered in her ear, "I'm still cute."

When she snorted, he grinned and kissed her brief and hard. "And you're adorable."

He returned to his section to paint, leaving her feeling like she'd melted into a puddle of happiness.

A while later, she realized Wyatt had asked her something. "I'm sorry, what?"

Wall finished, he'd closed the paint can. "What shall we make for supper tonight? It's my turn to cook, which means you're drafted to help."

"I..." She looked around at the house. "At your house?"

His eyes darkened, his brows drawing together, and he went down on his haunches in front of her. "Erin, unless you have a good reason, you'll spend at least one more night with me. Just so I know you're all right."

"I..." There was nothing she wanted more. "Yes."

Beneath the dark mustache, his teeth flashed in a devastatingly sexy grin. "Exactly the right answer, my girl. Very good."

The way her heart rolled inside her chest at his simple words of approval was going to be a problem.

A big problem.

CHAPTER TWENTY

As the coffeemaker chugged, Wyatt flipped the sausage patties over. Beside him, Erin stirred shredded cheddar cheese into the scrambled eggs.

He smiled down, enjoying her company, despite his lack of caffeine. His family would usually pour him coffee and wait for him to finish before expecting any coherent conversation.

But Erin was a peaceful companion. And, as it happened, morning sex—at least with her—worked as well as caffeine.

It was only the two of them for breakfast this Monday morning with Patches and Bat supervising. Sunny and Virgil had already left for work. Morgan was gone to guide a group of older fishing enthusiasts up to one of the mountain lakes for a few days.

Pierre had told Erin she could work, but to come in late and have a short day.

"It's nice to have a quiet morning for a change." He set the two patties she'd requested on a plate for her and served himself the other four.

She snickered. "You really do have a crazy household. What will it be like when you're all married with children running everywhere?"

"Fuck, it'll be chaos." *All of them married. With children? Him* married? At one time, he'd have immediately dismissed the idea, but as Pa predicted would happen, his view had changed.

Pa had been full of advice on relationships. "*Sow your wild oats, boys. Don't be in a hurry to settle down. Not until you find someone who'll fill a place in your heart, the one you can't imagine living without. Someone you know you'll want even when you're both old and gray.*" Pa's voice had turned rough with the last words. Mom had died the previous year. And they all knew he'd've given anything to have grown old with her.

When Wyatt was dating Anastasia, he'd been in love; yeah, he didn't question his feelings for her. Yet he'd never envisioned being at her side through all the years to come. His focus had been on the present, on missing her when she wasn't around.

Why hadn't he wondered about their children? Imagined grandchildren? Or growing old with her?

"Here you go, my furry friend." Erin tossed Patches a piece of toast the spaniel caught with a snap. "Ooooh, excellent catch."

Patches wagged his silky tail at the compliment.

Great. Now Wyatt was imagining a couple of toddlers at her feet, glowing when their mama told them they'd done good. She'd be an amazing mother. And grandmother.

And yes, he'd still want her when her hair was gray, and she needed a cane. Hell, she'd undoubtedly smack him with her cane if he got pushy.

Because she was a woman who'd do to ride the river with.

Erin looked around the kitchen in satisfaction. All clean. Wyatt was putting the last of the dishes in the dishwasher. "You're awfully good at cleaning up."

"Didn't used to be. Morgan and I did our outside chores without complaining too much, but cleaning inside? Hell, we were escape artists." His smile was rueful. "I figured out years later Kallie'd taken on a lot of our chores, because she wasn't comfortable standing up for herself." He smiled slightly. "I bought her a bunch of fancy woods and specialized carving tools to go with my apology."

What a perfect apology. "Did Kallie make the carved figures I've been seeing in the house?"

"Yeah. She has a talent." He grinned. "She got mad at Jake once and left a carving of him—naked—on the coffee table. Tiniest dick and balls I've ever seen."

Erin snorted. Talk about an excellent revenge. Bracing her hip against the table, she studied Wyatt as he swiped the dish sponge over the counter. "So you're doing a lot of the inside cleaning these days. What changed?"

"Virgil married Sunny, and she's... Eh, *nurses*. They see dirt and germs everywhere. She gets antsy if the place isn't clean, and she works full-time. No one wants to turn her into a maid. She suggested Morgan and I hire someone if we didn't want to clean."

Erin bent and petted Patches, then Bat, who acted as if the dog was infringing on *his* person. "I guess you didn't?"

"Sure we did. A housecleaning crew comes every couple of weeks and deep cleans the place. But Morgan and I also got better at the basic tidy-up-after-ourselves shit."

Erin had to laugh at his long-suffering sigh.

Then his jaw went tight. "What drove it home was seeing a few of the less enlightened countries in Africa. Not all of them, of course, but there are areas where women work way too fucking hard, and the men expect to be treated special because they have testicles. I don't want to be that kind of dick."

His words made her heart turn all soft and mushy. Because he meant them. And showed it.

"So does Virgil treat his wife right, or are you having to be a good example?"

Wyatt laughed. "He told me if he pulls his weight—or more

—she has energy for fun times. And you know how us over-testosteroned idiots are about our fun times."

"Oh yes, I know." She snickered, bent, and whispered to Patches, "Be grateful you got rid of those hanging balls. They reduce your intelligence by half, at least."

The dog perked up his ears and wagged his tail at Wyatt as if to say he knew which of them had all the brains.

"Blue girl, you're a brat." Wyatt hooked an arm around her and pulled her close. "Cleaning, jobs, cooking—I'm all about equality. In bed, though, I'll assign the workloads. If you're not... satisfied...afterward, you can complain."

His hand on her ass pressed her pelvis against a rock-hard shaft. When he fisted her hair and angled her head to take her lips, every brain cell in her head blanked out. Bubbles of desire fizzed in her blood like champagne.

She drew in a shaky breath. "Um, right. Sounds like a fine plan."

He chuckled and nibbled on her jaw. "Mmmhmm. We'll divide it this way until we're old, and your hair is gray, and I've gone bald." He squeezed her bottom, sending a tremor through her. "Then, if you bop me over the head with your cane for getting too frisky, we might renegotiate."

"Okay, I... What?" The meaning of what he'd said made her straighten and step back. Hadn't she'd just moved out of Troy's house? Yet here she was, being all domestic in Wyatt's house.

"No, it's just...*no*." He talked about the future, like assuming they'd be *married*. She retreated another foot, and his arms dropped.

"Erin?"

"No. No, I'm not"—she shook her head—"I'm not doing serious. I don't want to be in a committed relationship. Not now, maybe not ever."

His expression turned puzzled. "Sweetheart, why—"

"No, just no." Her anxiety broke free like fire whipped by a windstorm. Her last relationship had her losing *everything*. What had she been thinking, getting all comfortable with Wyatt. Cooking breakfast with him. She was supposed to be a crazy cat lady, not getting all dependent on a man. Another man.

I have such a great track record of choosing men.

"Erin." Wyatt reached out his hand. "Let's talk about—"

"No, no talking. This...I'm sorry if you thought I wanted..." She shook her head, her panic increasing. What could she say to get out of here? "I'm thinking of moving back to the city. And I need to go, or I'll be late to work. Thanks for...thank you. It's been fun."

Thank goodness she'd driven her car here last night. She hurried out of the house, feeling his eyes on her.

CHAPTER TWENTY-ONE

As Rascal Flatt's mournful breakup song of "What Hurts the Most" came on, Wyatt covered up his wince with a long drink of his beer. Didn't it just figure Gustaf wasn't playing his usual Johnny Cash tonight?

The ClaimJumper was, as usual, raucous on a Saturday night. Tourist season was in full swing, and the place was packed. He and his brothers had been lucky to snag a table.

It was rare the three of them managed to go out for a beer together during the summer. As a lieutenant, Virgil worked a Monday through Friday schedule. However, Wyatt and Morgan were usually off on guiding trips, especially on weekends. Today, though, he and Morgan had just returned after co-leading a big group. They wouldn't leave again until after their party on the Fourth.

A shame he wasn't in the mood to be sociable. He winced as the tune's refrain played, saying how after the woman walked away, the man mourned for what might have been.

Yeah, I feel your pain, buddy.

It'd been twelve days since he'd seen Erin. Since he stood in the kitchen and rambled on about growing old together, and she looked at him like he'd drowned her favorite dog. She hadn't been able to get out of the house fast enough.

Maybe it was for the best. He'd sure read her wrong, thinking she wasn't truly a city girl. She'd seemed so fucking happy here in Bear Flat. If she was serious about returning to Sacramento, they had no future at all.

He'd learned his lesson with Anastasia, who was all about culture and entertainment—theaters, art galleries, music, fancy dining—and thought nature should be confined to a city park. Love couldn't overcome everything.

A loud voice from near the bar caught his attention.

"...seems all sweet and humble, but hell, it's the same smarmy bullshit her douchebag husband pulled to get elected as a congressman. Afterward, the bastard accepted every bribe coming his way, screwing over his own people."

Wyatt glanced over. It was Levi Kranz, one of Virgil's patrol officers, doing the ranting.

"Let it go, Kranz," one of the guys at the bar said. "The prison was closed down."

"And my fucking shoulder still hurts. Those Aryan Hammer bastards wouldn't've ever been here without the damn prison. Simmons' kids still have nightmares."

Wyatt saw Morgan's mouth flatten, his muscles tensing at the reminder.

While Wyatt had been gone, violence from the gangs in town had culminated in arson. Morgan killed the gangbanger who'd held a gun to young Heath's head.

"Heath was lucky you were there, bro," Wyatt murmured. "You did good."

Virgil smiled slightly. "The patrol officers were lucky too."

Morgan's shoulders relaxed, and he nodded.

At the bar, the argument was still going.

"Doesn't matter that it was her husband who took the bribes," Levi was almost shouting. "She profited too. The bitch was living high on the hog."

For fuck's sake. Wyatt stood and placed his hands flat on the table. "Officer Kranz, we don't talk about women that way."

Levi's face flushed. "She is a—"

"And I could be wrong, but I've heard it's difficult to live high on the hog when your husband cleans out all your bank accounts as he's running from the law."

"Yeah, well, she still—"

"While running, Palmer might have been a tad upset, considering *she* was the one who turned him in to the FBI after hearing him blackmailing another politician."

The entire bar had gone silent at this point, and Wyatt winced. Although she'd told Virg about her husband's murder, she might not have shared about the FBI. But damn, it riled him up to hear her reputation trashed—and by a cop, no less.

"You...you—"

"*Levi.*" Virgil didn't stand. Just gave his officer a frown that any individual with an eye to his future employment would understand.

Levi's face flushed, then paled. He turned to face the bar, concentrating on his bottle of beer.

Virgil eyed Wyatt. "You getting serious about Erin?"

His hand tightened on his glass. The question ripped through his defenses like barbwire punched through skin. "Might've been but she's planning to go home to the city."

"Damn," Morgan muttered. "Sorry, bro."

"Yeah," he sighed. Nothing else he could say.

"You know, I wasn't sure about her at first." Virgil leaned back. "The way she looked when she got here put me off. And her husband... But Sunny likes her and"—his eyes unfocused, as if he was seeing her in front of him—"she reminds me of Patches as a pup. All ears and fat paws."

"You're saying Erin has fat feet?" Morgan gave their brother a stare, then pulled Virgil's beer away from him. "Time to switch to water, buddy."

"Ha." Virgil grinned. "No, I mean the way Patches was always tripping over his big paws and long ears while he tried to grow into the dog he was meant to be. I get the impression Erin got shut down by her asshole husband before she had a chance to grow into her paws."

Virgil's thought patterns were a wonder. Wyatt half-smiled but nodded. "Sounds about right. Before the asshole, she spent a couple of years caring for dying grandparents. Her life got put on hold."

"Bummer for sure." Morgan pushed Virgil's drink back to him. "Here, bro. I won't tell her you said she has fat feet."

Virgil laughed and turned to Wyatt. "Sunny hasn't said anything about Erin leaving Bear Flat."

Interesting. "Yeah?"

"Give her time, Wyatt." Virgil pulled his beer closer, shooting a look at Morgan.

Time. Right. "I'm not a city man. And she said she'd be moving back."

"Was she calm when she said that?" Virgil asked. "When Sunny gets het up, she says shit she doesn't mean—a way of putting up fences. Barricading her soft spots, right?"

"Hell, we all hand out bullshit when it comes to guarding our wounds," Morgan murmured and grinned at Wyatt. "You do it too, bro."

"Point." Wyatt sat back, running his fingers through the condensation on his glass.

Erin had been upset that morning. True enough. And she actually hadn't said she was moving—just how she was thinking of it. Yeah, raising a barrier between them.

Question was...why did she feel the need to go to such an extreme? She could've just told him to back off. Was it him she didn't trust—or herself?

He tapped his finger on the glass, thinking of how she looked in his bed. Of her laughter. The way she concentrated so fiercely when she was working in the auto shop. The way she smiled when she petted Bat.

The way her lips felt under his.

Looks like I should figure out if she really wants to back off. She was worth taking the time to be sure.

CHAPTER TWENTY-TWO

When her text message alert went off, Erin felt her heart leap—and fall like a rock.

No, Ms. Optimist. Wyatt is not texting you.

God, she missed him, and wasn't that just crazy? How could she have grown so attached to a man she just met? She'd probably latched onto him because he was the direct opposite of Troy. A rebound kind of thing. It wasn't real—and she sure wasn't ready for anything real.

It was good she had backed away if she was thinking "fling", and he was thinking "serious". Only an insensitive jerk would lead on a wonderful man.

I'm better than that.

She rubbed her chest. Shouldn't she be getting over him by now? If there was nothing substantial there? It'd been two weeks.

Shaking her head, she checked her text message. *Right, the children.*

She cleaned and stored her tools away and locked the cabinet. Pierre was in the second bay, talking to Marco.

When the boss noticed her, she motioned toward the exit in an unspoken, *I'm leaving now.*

He nodded, glanced at the parking area, and laughed.

She turned.

The children had arrived, and Kallie was herding them off to one side. They were carrying the various parts needed for their newest project—wheels, plywood, chains.

Oh, the kids were all so cute. Such enthusiasm and energy. She had a moment's pang, regretting she'd never have any baby mechanics of her own.

It could be worse. At least before marrying Troy, she'd gotten an IUD for birth control; he hadn't left her with a baby as well as a financial mess.

"I left the motors and batteries locked in the metal bin beside the building. Have fun." Pierre handed her a key, then his lips quirked. "I might come out and help. Building a go-kart started me on the downward slope to being a mechanic."

She laughed. "I started with automobiles, but oddly enough, the Department of Motor Vehicles won't give ten-year-olds a license—even if they put together the engine. I had to build a go-kart to be able to actually steer what I worked on."

The men grinned.

"Thanks for donating, Pierre." She headed off to get the project started.

And tried not to think how nice it would be if she could share the day's fun with Wyatt later.

The first step to understanding what a person wanted was to talk to them. So Wyatt was on a search for the person in question.

The STEM group of kids weren't outside the library, so he strolled inside, holding his Stetson in one hand. A quick search revealed no Kallie, no children of the right age, no appealing blonde with blue streaks in her hair.

Hmm. Despite being the soul of discretion, Maud Ganning usually knew everything about everyone. Stopping at the checkout counter, he smiled at the tiny, brown-skinned woman. Last year, she'd cut her white hair short, letting it go natural. It looked great.

"How are you doing, Maud?" When he'd reached his twenties, changing to calling all the Missuses and Misters by their first names had been a rite of passage. In the case of Mrs. Ganning, it'd taken him a few extra years.

"Quite nicely, thank you, Wyatt." Interest sparkled in her dark brown eyes. "What brings you into the library today?"

"Would you happen to know where Kallie and her class have wandered off to?"

She tilted her head in consideration. "Are you looking for your cousin or for Erin Lockwood?"

Caught. "Erin, of course."

His smile died as he considered the elderly woman who was one of the smartest people he knew. Motherless in high school, he'd run into boy-girl relationships problems. Mrs. Ganning had been kind enough, wise enough, to set him straight on how women felt about things. Maybe she could help him out again.

"Maud, she told me she wasn't interested in a relationship and was considering heading back to the city. Damned if I want to act like a stalker, but...she's important. Got any advice? Should I back off or keep trying?"

"Back to the city? Unlikely. Not when she's wrapping our town around herself like a warm blanket on winter's night." Maud pursed her lips. "However, my boy, I can't tell you if she fibbed because she's not interested or because you pushed too hard and too fast."

The city part was a lie.

Hearing Maud confirm his opinion let his ribs expand and his lungs fill nicely with air.

So...was Erin not interested in him? Considering her enthusiasm right up until he talked about growing old, he doubted that was the problem.

The back half of Maud's statement made him frown. "Are you saying I'm pushy?"

"Wyatt Masterson, when you want something, you're as impossible to stop as a stampeding herd. Of buffalo."

He winced at the accuracy of the statement. Even worse, "want" was far too mild a word for what he felt for Erin. *Fuck.* "Got it. I'll rein it in."

"If you truly care for the woman, she'll be worth all the patience you can summon up." Maud patted his hand. "She and Kallie took their class to the auto shop to finish building those go-karts."

Wyatt blinked. "Damn, where was Erin when *I* was a kid?"

"From what I understand, she was rebuilding cars at about the same age you started solo camping." Maud nodded toward the door. "Off you go..."

"Yes, ma'am. Wish me luck."

Her gaze was beneficent. "I do. I like the thought of you two together."

Outside, adjusting his hat on his head, he realized he was smiling. *Best blessing ever.*

A few minutes later, he stood in the auto shop's shadow and watched Erin working with the students. Building go-karts looked like hella-fun.

And she was...amazing. Patient, letting them do the work— no, even more. She was letting them figure things out for themselves. She only stepped in when they got stuck or to demonstrate a more efficient or safer way to work.

Dammit, there he went again, envisioning her with a flock of children around her. *His* children—as well as a batch of nieces and nephews.

He shook his head. *No stampeding the woman, Masterson.*

Turning, he headed back for town. This wasn't the time to interrupt her. The children were her focus—as they should be. He'd find her when there was time to talk.

And he'd listen with all his senses.

Erin breathed in the satisfying fragrance of metal and sawdust and a hint of gasoline from the lawnmower motor used for one of the karts. The group had scavenged enough donations to patch together two motors, one gas-powered and one battery-driven. There was still a lot of work to do, though.

A while ago, Pierre appeared, unable to resist lending a hand with the small engines, and a bit later, Walker brought out a coping saw to use on the trickier plywood parts and stayed to help.

The next time she turned around, Marco was on his knees, assisting Heath in assembling the axle and wheels on one kart body.

"This was so cool!" Nevaeh ran back from the metal storage bin. "Can we come back tomorrow?"

When all the children looked eager, Kallie laughed. "No, we'll stay with the scheduled classes."

"Awww."

Heath nudged the brown-eyed girl. "It'll give us time to find more stuff. Dad has an old lawnmower in the shed."

"Oh, you're right." Nevaeh bounced on her toes. "We need paint. Mommy has some in the garage. Can we paint flames on the side, Ms. Erin?"

"If you all agree, absolutely."

"I bet we'll end up needing sunglasses to look at the karts." Laughing, Kallie glanced at Erin. "I'll herd them back if you finish locking the parts up."

"Deal. See you next Monday."

Kallie paused. "Aren't you coming out for the Fourth of July party at the ranch?"

"Ah, I'm not much for parties. But have a great time." *Don't ask any more questions, please.*

"I've spent most of the last couple of weeks out on guide trips, so we haven't had a chance to catch up. But you were looking forward to the party the last time we talked." Kallie's black brows drew together making her look like a pissed-off Tinker Bell. "Did you and Wyatt have a fight?"

Erin tried to keep any expression from showing, but she must have failed.

Kallie took a step forward. "What happened?"

"Nothing. I just...I'm not interested in dating right now." Erin saw an escape and took it. "Kallie, you're supposed to be walking with the kids." With Heath leading, the bunch was half a block away.

"Oh, hell. We're going to talk, woman. Count on it." Kallie sprinted after the group.

Talk with Wyatt's cousin? Not going to happen.

Once she finished locking up the parts and picking up any stray pieces of scrap the children had missed, she grabbed her small backpack out of her car and headed downtown, leaving her car at the shop. She only needed a few groceries, and it was a wonderful evening for a stroll.

Farther down the street, a petite woman with red hair was on the sidewalk.

Behind her were two college-aged men talking in loud voices. The tallest walked with a strut—reminding Erin of a customer who'd bought a big Hummer to look macho. Next to him, the blond with a faux hawk was built like a football lineman. With a beer gut.

As they came closer, Erin stiffened. The woman was Gin, Atticus' girlfriend who blamed Troy and Erin for the prison and the ensuing troubles because of it being here. Having dropped off her car for servicing this morning, she was probably on her way to pick it up.

Perhaps it'd be smart to cross the street to avoid an awkward encounter.

Erin frowned at the way Gin was walking. Back stiff, hands fisted—and fast. Was she trying to get away from the men behind her?

Just as Erin wondered that, the linebacker behind Gin got

close enough to grab her shoulder. "Hey, hey, don't be so snooty. We're talking to you."

Spinning around, Gin hit at his hand. "Let go!"

He laughed. "C'mon, we just want to be friends. *Good* friends." He yanked her toward him.

Oh honestly. "Hands off, asshole," Erin rushed forward.

Rather than backing off, Linebacker laughed. "Look, Gator, you're getting a girl too. A blonde, no less."

Oh hell, the men had obviously been drinking.

Gin had gone dead white and was panicking. Fighting, but not in a smart way.

What to do, what to do? Erin yanked her ballpoint pen from her shirt pocket. It made a nice pointy weapon. And, because reinforcements would be nice, she shouted at the top of her voice, "Help! Fire! Help!"

Eyes widening, Gator took a step back.

Yes, yes, please just leave. Her heart was already pounding as fear swept over her.

But Linebacker didn't release Gin. "Shut her up, Ga—"

Targeting him, Erin stabbed his arm with the sharp pen.

"Shit!" As his grip loosened, Gin yanked her shoulder out of his hold. Even better, she scrambled for the raised garden in front of the realty office and picked up a hefty, decorative rock.

Furious, Linebacker swung at Erin.

Damn, he's big. She dodged—grateful the alcohol had slowed him down. Spinning, she shoved his shoulder and kicked his leg out from under him as he stumbled sideways.

Even as he fell, a thrown rock smacked him in the head. Then another. He landed hard on the concrete sidewalk.

From a house across the street, a woman yelled, "I'm calling the police!"

"Fuck this." Frantically, Gator yanked his friend to his feet. "Let's get out of here."

Backing away, Gin had a rock in each hand.

Good thinking. Erin grabbed a rock in her free hand and joined her.

But the two assholes were heading back toward downtown. Gator had to steady a cursing Linebacker who wasn't walking too well.

With a relieved breath, Erin turned.

Frickity-frick-frick-frick. Gin's eyes were still wide, her breathing way too fast. She was in a panicked, meltdown state. Not a surprise, considering what Becca had said about her being abducted by convicts. This must have hit too close to what she'd been through.

Erin sighed. No matter how rude the woman had been, she needed help now. Erin tossed her rock back into the mulch.

"Hey, Gin. How about we walk over there?" She pointed to the tidy church across the street. "It'll get us farther away from the assholes."

Gin was still pure white, but her eyes were starting to focus. "Yes," she whispered. "Please don't—"

Don't leave, Erin filled in.

"I'm here. Don't worry." Erin stayed just slightly ahead, leading the way to the church's front lawn. With a sigh, she simply sat right down in the grass. "I swear, my legs are still shaking."

Gin stood a moment, then dropped next to Erin. Legs bent, she rested her forehead on her knees—and trembled.

"Hey, hey, it's over. We're safe." Unsure what to do, Erin rested her hand on Gin's shoulder and realized she was silently crying. "Can I call someone for you?"

With a shuddering breath, Gin shook her head. After another minute, she straightened, wiped her face, and smiled at Erin. It was a shaky smile, but to manage one at all after a damn panic attack, well...respect!

Pulling out her phone, Gin read the display, texted a reply, and turned to Erin. "I let Atticus, which means the police department, know I'm all right. They were already on their way.

Now they'll look for the men and probably give them a very rude escort out of town."

"Perfect."

Gin shoved her phone back in her pocket. "I want to thank you, Erin. I was... What did you do to make him let go of me?"

"Oh." Erin glanced at the ball point pen in her fist. Blood streaked the silvery metal. *Ugh.* "I stabbed him with this."

Gin blinked. "A pen?"

"Useful things." Erin moved her shoulders in a shrug. "I was barely a teen when I started working in auto shops—surrounded by men. My grandfather made me take self-defense lessons—ones taught by women for women. I practiced with him or whoever he could recruit. They taught me to use whatever is at hand—like you did with the rocks. Good job there."

Gin stared at her, then her lips tilted up in a real smile. "A ballpoint pen. Rocks. And they left."

"We did good, yep."

"Thank you." Gin shook her head. "It's been a while since I lost it so completely."

"You had good cause. Are you feeling better now?" Erin eyed the redhead, seeing her color had come back, and only a few trembles showed in her fingers.

"I'm good." Gin sighed. "I had a lot of panic attacks after being kidnapped last year. You've probably heard about it by now. But it means I also had lots of practice in recovering and shaking the attacks off."

"It sucks you had such an ugly experience," Erin muttered. And Troy had been very much part of the reason.

"Erin." Gin shook her head. "I've been horrid to you, and you jumped right into the fight anyway. I...I am very grateful." Her soft southern drawl had grown even slower.

Erin held onto her resentment for a few seconds before letting it go. "I've heard a lot about how disastrous it was to have the prison here." And the consequences were still going on, considering the real estate market. "I get why everyone's so angry; you're not the only one."

"No, I over-reacted. Atticus says your husband screwed you over as badly as he did our town. I truly am sorry and hope you can forgive me." The eyes that met Erin's were a soft green-brown and sincere.

"Forgiven. I've put my foot into it enough times I know how it can happen."

Gin half-grinned. "Oh, my stars, Atticus and I have had some horrendous miscommunications."

"Apparently, you two have managed to work through your fights." Erin ran her hand over the cool grass. The blades felt silky under her palm. "From what everyone says, the man adores you."

"I have to say, it still leaves me amazed." When Gin stretched out her legs, Erin knew the redhead was getting back to normal. "From what I hear, you've captured your own cowboy's heart."

"No." Erin shook her head. "Just no."

The hazel eyes narrowed slightly. "So you haven't captured him...or maybe you don't want to have captured him?"

Damn her for asking such a question. "I..." Erin swallowed against a dry throat.

"No, putting you on the spot isn't fair." Gin rubbed her hands on her pants. "On the ride, I could see Wyatt was totally attracted to you. And from what Kallie says, he cares about you."

Her words set up a warm glow. He cared.

No, no, not good. "He shouldn't. He mustn't."

"I'm not sure I understand." Gin's puzzled expression shifted to compassionate. "Oh. Atticus told me your husband has passed. Are you...do you still have feelings for him?"

"No, no, not for a long time." And didn't she sound cold-hearted. "I'm sorry he didn't get a chance for repentance, for making things right." Erin shook her head. "Unfortunately, I'm not sure he ever would have."

"Is the problem with Wyatt? You don't like him that way?"

My god, the questions. Even worse, Erin could see that Gin wasn't simply being nosy—she appeared to care about the answers.

Of course she cared; Wyatt was her friend. Because Wyatt seemed to be friends with every damn person in this whole damn town.

"Maybe you prefer a different sort of man?"

Erin snorted. "I don't know how any woman with a functioning set of ovaries wouldn't fall for him. He's smart and protective of everyone around, and it seems like whatever he does he's awesome at it." Her lips tipped up. "Nothing gets him upset. I mean, have you noticed how easily he laughs? Like the whole world makes him happy."

Gin's eyes had widened. "Oh, honey, you've got it bad."

Erin froze. "No, no, I don't."

"Bless your heart, girl, make all the protests you want. My hearing isn't broken...and I was listening."

Listening and asking questions. In fact... Erin bit her lip. When they were introduced, Rebecca mentioned Gin being— "You're a counselor, aren't you?"

Gin had a merry laugh. "I *am*. At least, you're not completely disgusted about my job the way Atticus was."

Erin blinked. "Ah, sounds a bit awkward."

"Oh my stars, it so was. It was the first of those just-shoot-me-now miscommunications we blundered into—and backed out of, thank heavens." Gin folded her hands in her lap and gave Erin a compellingly sympathetic smile. "Wyatt cares for you. You care for him—but you don't want to. Why is that?"

Erin tried to hold out. But oh, she'd wanted someone to talk with for so long. The words spilled out of her mouth like she'd stomped on the gas pedal. "It's too soon. It must be. And when I fell for Troy, I thought he was simply amazing, and I believed he loved me, but I was so wrong. I had no idea who he really was."

Gin made a comforting sound, like a verbal nudge to continue.

"I shouldn't get involved, not with anyone. I'm going to be a crazy cat lady"—Erin ignored the snort of laughter—"and maybe someday, I'll be smart enough to pick out a good man."

The counselor was openly grinning. "First, considering how many people I see making bad choices, whether they're young or old, first or second marriages, I'd say making a mistake in love is just par for the course. Heaven knows I did. I was engaged and caught my fiancé cheating on me."

"Ohh, that's horrible. I'm sorry." Erin frowned. Troy had been a horrible person, but he was also an excellent liar. She'd made a mistake, but should she be so hard on herself for falling for a con man? She wasn't the first or last person to be wrong about a lover.

Gin leaned forward.

"Second, about your *someday* stuff. I do understand. I met Atticus far too soon after I ended my engagement. Like you, I wasn't ready to jump into anything new. But I don't think you can stick a pin in a timeline and say, 'this is when I'll find love'."

Erin winced.

Gin added, "And, to be honest, it doesn't seem like wonderful guys are thick on the ground."

"Isn't that the truth," Erin muttered.

"But if you're truly not ready, fair enough."

Erin ruffled the grass under her fingers. So soft and so resilient. Dying back over the winter, shooting up when the weather warmed. Growing lush and green as if it'd never been buried in snow a few months before.

What would happen if she didn't try to turn herself into an eccentric loner? If she let herself be open to a relationship. To love.

To Wyatt.

Huh. The future seemed to open into a world that shone bright.

"Well, I do think my work here is done." Gin pushed up to her feet and held out her hand for Erin to grab.

Once Erin was on her feet, Gin started walking toward the auto shop. "Are you going to the Mastersons' Fourth of July party?"

It sounded as if the entire town was going. "No, I don't think so."

"Because you're avoiding Wyatt?" At Erin's grimace and nod, Gin snorted. "I'm surprised he's not come after you. The man is nothing if not persistent."

"I doubt he's still interested." The thought was like a stab to the heart.

"Which means you have nothing to worry about at the party, hmm?"

The truth was unpalatable. He'd probably be with a date... and the thought hurt even worse.

"Either way, you shouldn't go alone." Gin's smile was pure sneakiness. "Since it's a potluck, come on over to my place on the fourth and help me cook. Afterward, you'll join me and Atticus."

Erin stopped. She wouldn't have to go to the party alone? The offer was...generous. "You know you don't have to be nice to me just because I stepped in to shoo away those jerks."

Gin's eyes lit, and she laughed. "I did start talking to you because I was grateful. But you're also very likable. Come over and cook—we'll have fun."

"I...okay." Erin pulled in a breath and realized she was smiling. "What are we making and what supplies should I bring?"

CHAPTER TWENTY-THREE

Out on her deck, Erin was enjoying her first coffee of the day before she had to go to work. She could hear the light buzzing from the bees that apparently adored the blooming lavender in the planters. The herb's clean scent filled the warming air.

Down below in the valley, she could see a lot of activity around the Masterson ranch, especially in the back. Preparations for their party, she guessed.

Tomorrow was the Fourth of July. Gin expected her to show up at her and Atticus' house to do their potluck cooking. Afterward, they'd all go to what sounded like a crazy-fun afternoon and evening at the Mastersons'.

Wyatt would be there.

Would he still be interested? He didn't lack for women. Yet what they'd had was special, at least it felt like that to Erin. It sounded as if he'd thought the same way.

Was Gin right? Could moving on to a new man be as simple as letting go of the old one? She wasn't mourning Troy. Their marriage hadn't been a good one. Her feelings for him had died... a long time ago.

Maybe she *could* move on.

Sipping her coffee, she watched the valley floor. A man on a horse was driving cattle to a pasture farther away. Was that Wyatt's horse? The brown shaded to black on its legs, mane, and tail. Yes, Wyatt was in the saddle. From a distance, he and Morgan rode alike, perfectly balanced, but somehow, she could tell this one was her cowboy.

Wait, no, not mine.

But...okay, maybe it was how she felt.

He stared at the text he'd just received on the burner phone.

Troy Palmer is dead, and I won't lend my influence to such a questionable bill unless you prove you have the evidence he had.

"Son of a *bitch*." He slammed the cheap cell phone down on his desk. That was the third politician who'd demanded proof. Troy had never hidden he was the one blackmailing them. He'd been paid good money to be the front man for the scheme.

Liked to live the good life, had Troy? Wasn't it a shame his fun times had been cut short?

He'd sure screamed a lot at the end.

Unfortunately, it'd been easier—and less risky—to let him keep all the incriminating evidence like the videos of politicians fucking minors or indulging in perverted kinks.

He grinned. One flabby, balding asshole's right-wing constituents would go ballistic if they saw the photos of him, naked, on his knees, kissing a whore's toes. Pedophilia and kinky behavior were a guaranteed way to lose votes.

And a great way for the possessor of the evidence to gain power.

Until now. Because the clock where Troy had hidden the jump drives with all the damning videos was *missing*.

In mid-June, the ex-con he'd hired had called from Erin's house to say he hadn't found the clock. It must be elsewhere. The convict was competent, even if he'd gotten himself killed. *Moron.*

Too many problems, not enough time, but the urgency to get the evidence back was increasing.

Where the hell could Troy's wife have put the damn clock? Could someone have already found it?

What was his next step?

CHAPTER TWENTY-FOUR

Erin jumped out of her car and stared. Cars were parked everywhere—in front of the Mastersons' ranch house, around the barn, and even down in the nearest pasture. No wonder Wyatt had been moving cattle yesterday.

She joined Gin and Atticus who'd parked beside her. "This is crazy. I think everyone from Bear Flat must be here."

"Seems like it, doesn't it? But a whole bunch of people have already come and gone by now, like the ones who have small children." Gin picked up her impressive six-layer, red velvet cake.

"We should have come early." Atticus slung a backpack with spare clothing over his shoulder.

"No way." Gin grinned at him. "I love watching the Masterson's version of the Revolutionary War."

The evening's entertainment—a massive water battle—sounded like so much fun. Thus the spare clothing Gin recommended she bring. With her backpack over her shoulder, she lifted the storage container with her own potluck offering. Hopefully, it would be acceptable.

Several signs directed them around the side of the house. At the back, Erin stopped. *So many people*. A long lawn ran down to a creek where children were splashing. Trees shaded guests playing cards and board games on folding tables.

Stacks of straw bales separated areas in an interesting maze-like arrangement.

The obvious kiddie area held a wading pool, bubbles, and balloons.

Past it was a horseshoe pit with a mix of seniors and youngsters. *So cool.*

A bigger area had teens playing soccer. A long waterslide thing down the center of the lawn appeared very popular.

More straw bales fenced off the edge of the lawn. What in the world? Like old-time mountain men, people in fringed leather outfits were throwing hatchets and knives at various targets.

She remembered the photos in Wyatt's rooms of his historic re-enactment group. They'd been shooting muzzleloader firearms and indulging in other activities from those days.

But hatchets?

When she didn't spot Wyatt, disappointment swept through her. Even if she didn't know what to say to him, didn't know exactly what she wanted, the need to see him was intense.

A shout went up as a hatchet hit the bullseye. One of the mountain men—only it was a woman—did a victory dance.

No Wyatt. Move on, Erin. She grinned at Gin. "This is like no party I've ever seen. The Mastersons are insane."

"True enough. We can all agree on that." Gin was laughing at her. "Let's drop off our food and have some fun."

Erin followed her up the steps to the back deck that ran the length of the house.

Here, it totally felt like an Independence Day celebration. Red, white, and blue bunting decorated the railing. Food-laden picnic tables were covered in white tablecloths with sparkly red pinwheels down the center. The paper plates and cups were again, red, white, and blue.

"Welcome to the revolution." Kallie waved them forward.

Erin was still staring. "Most people only decorate like this for Christmas."

"We don't decorate the outside for Christmas; no one would see it. So we go overboard for the Fourth." Kallie led the way to a long table filled with desserts. "Anywhere is fine."

"You'll like my creation, Kallie." Gin took the dark blue frosted cake out of her carrier and tipped it slightly. The top held a multitude of white stars like on the US flag. "Wait, though. I need to cut a piece for you to get the full effect."

"There's more?" Kallie handed over a paper dessert plate.

Cutting a big wedge, Gin revealed the layers where red velvet cake alternated with white, cream cheese frosting. "Voila! Behold the stars and stripes cake."

Everyone nearby applauded, and Gin bowed.

"Aren't you just the epitome of patriotism." Laughing, Mallory joined them, putting an arm around Gin's waist. Slicing a piece off the wedge, she popped it in her mouth. "Mmm. It's as good as it looks."

"Thank you." Gin beamed. "Here we have my dessert for the grown-ups. Now see what Erin brought."

When all eyes turned to Erin, she flushed. "Since I'm helping Kallie with her STEM group, I made a dessert they might like." She pulled the plastic cover off her carrier and displayed rice crispy treats. She'd used food coloring to make bright red, white, and blue layers.

A round of applause made her flush even as she smiled.

Her dessert did look striking—and it felt wonderful to contribute something she'd made.

"Whoa, rice crispy treats." Jake reached over her shoulder and snagged one. "Damn, I haven't had one of these in forever. Becca should make these when our lodge guests have children."

"Uh-huh. I can guess who'd eat them all." Becca joined them, hugged Gin—and to Erin's happiness, her too. "Your cake is spectacular, Gin. Erin, the kids, including the truly big ones, are going to go nuts for those."

Laughing, Atticus grabbed one as if to prove she was right. "Jake, want to go throw knives?"

After the men disappeared, Becca frowned at Gin. "You promised a story about why you and Erin are besties now."

"And it's a great story." Gin grinned and pointed to Erin. "Miss Humbleness is blushing already. It begins with me heading for Pierre's to pick up my car, and a couple of drunks decided they wanted female company."

To gasps and cheers, Gin continued the story—and Erin had to interject the details of how Gin had stepped right up to the fight.

As Erin collected more hugs, she couldn't stop smiling. *I have friends here in Bear Flat.*

Chatting, the women sampled the appetizers. After a while, Gin, Mallory, and Becca got involved in a discussion of the neighborhood watch, and Erin slipped away to explore.

She wasn't looking for Wyatt. *No, absolutely not.* Besides, a party wasn't the place to get into serious discussions.

At the stream's edge, children were trying to catch tadpoles, and she grinned. Hadn't she done the same thing when she was young?

She skirted the soccer area and grinned as a teen scored a goal with a shriek of happiness and cheering from her team.

Greetings came from parents of her library groups and customers of the auto shop. From Friede who was in an older group with her gray-haired husband. Getting warm, Erin headed for the deck and the drink area.

As she got herself a beer, she heard whispers and felt the cold chill of being the subject of gossip.

"Skanky bitch."

"And look at what she's wearing. Talk about no sense of fashion."

Unable to help herself, Erin glanced down. She'd thought her spaghetti-strapped tank with red, white, and blue stripes looked nice paired with denim shorts and bright red sneakers. Colorfully patriotic. Normally, she'd have worn sandals, but she'd need to be able to run if there was a water fight.

She glanced at the two women throwing shade in loud enough voices to garner attention. *Ah, right.* As usual, she'd drawn the attention of the salon's beauticians, and it seemed her avoiding confrontation had spurred them on to even greater rudeness.

Only now, Candy had chosen a new target—Barbara from the Mother Lode Restaurant. Making fun of her colored hair.

No, I'm not going to stand for this. Erin raised her voice to match the women's volume. "Oh wow, it's the mean girls' barbershop duo."

"*Excuse* me?" Candy scowled.

"Mmmhmm, you two sing the same tune all the time. And dress the same too." Not the same colors, but the same style—low cut tops, extremely short shorts, fancy sandals. Nails and toenails painted. Makeup and hair almost identical. Her mother would have told her to pity them, since they were obviously too insecure to break away from the group.

But they shouldn't have picked on Barbara, who was a kind and thoughtful person. Erin shook her head. "It's like you two got stuck in high school. Grow up already."

Laughter came from the people on the deck, probably increased by the shock in the women's faces. Had they gotten too used to their targets simply taking the abuse?

Bullies. I hate bullies.

Sipping her beer, Erin trotted down the steps and back out onto the lawn. *Whew. Bad Erin.*

Rude or not, her response still felt kinda good. *I'll never be a diplomatic politician type person like Mom.* But now, she didn't have to hold back her words to keep Troy happy. *I can be myself.* Honest and maybe a bit impolite when needed, but mostly striving for kindness. *I can do kind.*

She watched the kids—and several adults—playing on the waterslide and considered joining them. Only she hadn't brought a suit and didn't want to get wet. Not before the water pistol fight.

"Hey, Erin, are you having fun?" Sunny came up from behind her, Virgil at her side.

"I am." She smiled at Virgil, who wasn't in his police uniform. "You guys throw a great party."

"Thank you." He swept his gaze over the area. "It's a great way to see everyone in town...only I remember when some of those kids came here as babies in their mothers' arms."

"Oh, the trauma of seeing the years pass." Sunny poked him in the ribs. "Poor old man."

"Insults. Now you're going to pay, sweetheart." Bending, he hefted her, belly down over his shoulder. A sharp smack on her butt won a yelp before he secured her with an arm around her thighs.

"Erin, excuse us, please. It's been a hot summer, and this Summer needs a cool down—like maybe on the waterslide."

"Wait, no, Virgil Masterson, don't you dare. Virgil, I'll kill you. I will kill you dead and—"

As he sauntered toward the waterslide, Sunny's threats turned to pleading. Considering the man's hard face, she had a feeling Sunny was doomed.

The splash and shriek of outrage a minute later had Erin busting up laughing.

"Dammit, I didn't think she'd have the gall to show up here." The man's voice was loud, and she half-turned to see two men. One was the older police officer.

The other was a big man with a receding hairline and ruddy face. The one who'd yelled at her when she first got to town. "She's the reason we have to have a neighborhood watch, the reason—"

"Simmons, back off." Officer Lambert chided the man.

Erin's heart sank. Maybe she shouldn't have come. She'd hate to cause a problem for Kallie and the rest of the Mastersons. For

Wyatt. This man didn't seem the type to quit once he took a stance.

"Ms. Erin, you came!"

The sound of the high voice made her jump.

Heath, from the library STEM group, ran up to her and grabbed her hand. "Come and meet my Pa." To Erin's dismay, he pulled her toward the man with the loud voice. The one who hated her.

"Pa!" Heath called.

When the man looked away from Officer Lambert, his mouth dropped open. "Heath, what are you doing?"

"This is Ms. Erin. She helps with our library projects."

"No, son. Ms. Kallie oversees your class."

"Yeah, but Ms. Kallie doesn't know anything about mechanic stuff. Ms. Erin shows us how to build *everything*."

"Hey, it's Ms. Erin!" Nevaeh spotted her and ran over for a hug. "I got the paint from Mommy. So we can make flames on the sides."

"Ms. Erin, I forgot the name of what I was supposed to get." Kayden grabbed her free hand and looked as if he thought she was going to yell at him. The stout, ginger-haired boy wasn't good with words but had excellent skills with tools.

"It's called a kill switch." But forgetting again would make him feel more like a loser. She glanced at Heath's father, who was frowning ferociously. "Excuse me, sir, but do you happen to have a pen and paper?"

He did; she could see them in his shirt pocket. With open reluctance, he handed her the tiny notepad and pen.

"Thank you." She wrote *kill switch* on the paper and made a tiny drawing of it, ripped off the paper, and handed it to Kayden. "There you go. So the person you ask knows what we're hoping for."

"Cool." He looked at the paper. "It kills the kart?"

"Not dead forever. It'll stop the engine." When he frowned, she elaborated. "Sometimes throttles get stuck open or a pedal gets stuck. Pushing the kill switch shuts off the engine right away."

She could see the light go on in his head. "Oh, even if the gas is still getting to it."

"You got it." She ruffled his hair. "You, my boy, have a talent with mechanical things."

The way he lit up at the compliment gave her a smile—and hurt her heart. Children who struggled with academics were often made to feel worthless. Why didn't teachers and parents realize there were many paths to wisdom and success?

Nevaeh ran to join Kayden as he trotted off.

With a polite smile, she handed the notepad and pen to Heath's father. "Thank you, Mr. Simmons."

"It's Roger." His brows pulled together. "You really are helping the children build the go-karts."

"I am." She tried to keep her tone amiable. "It's rewarding to see them figure out how things work and troubleshoot problems when they don't. You can almost see the gears in their brains turning."

He rubbed a hand over his balding pate. "Aren't you Troy Palmer's wife?"

Here we go again. "I was, yes."

"Now, she's a mechanic." Walker strolled up with their boss, Pierre. "A damn good one."

Pierre smirked. "*My* mechanic."

"Yeah," Heath nodded vigorously. "'At's why we're building the carts at the auto shop. They gave us lots of stuff too. You should see Ms. Erin's tool chest. It's bigger'n yours."

Oh, dear God. Her brain immediately provided the sexual innuendo.

Walker put a hand over his mouth, his cough not nearly hiding his laugh.

Roger Simmons just grinned, shoved Walker back a pace, and nodded to her. "Thank you for helping teach the kids. I look forward to seeing the go-karts in action."

She could only smile.

"Hey, Sparks, how'd you get so good at fixing things anyway?" Walker asked. "I mean, not just cars, but you're helping Pierre with the small engine repairs. And I saw messed-up antique clocks in your car."

"My grandfather owned an auto shop, and it did great. But he grew up poor and just couldn't throw anything away if he could fix it. Everyone brought him stuff to repair. He taught me all of it, including fixing old clocks. He used them for Christmas presents."

Understanding filled Roger's face. "My father was the same way. I get it."

Walker snorted. "Not mine. He couldn't wrench his way out of a paper sack."

"Great rice crispy treats, Erin," Morgan called as he and Sawyer walked past. He waved the bar at her and stuffed the rest in his mouth.

"Oh honestly," she muttered and yelled back, "I made those for the children!"

"I want one." Heath grabbed her hand again. "We gotta get one for me and for Nevaeh and Kayden before they get all eaten."

As the boy dragged her away, she heard his father grumble, "You would think I'd've learned not to judge someone on rumors. I'm a dumbass. Stop laughing, Pierre."

"*Oui*, you're a dumbass."

Straw bales fenced off Wyatt's muzzleloader club from the rest of the party. With no gun range on the property, there'd be no shooting, but the group was having fun teaching the party guests knife and hatchet throwing.

Waving at the target downrange, Wyatt handed Atticus a throwing hatchet. "Take your shot."

Grinning, Atticus threw. With a muted *thunk*, the hatchet hit not too far outside the bullseye.

"Not bad for a law enforcer!" Wyatt clapped his hands. "You might need a tad more practice to down a bad guy, though."

The police detective rubbed his jaw thoughtfully. "You know, you're right. I'm sure Lieutenant Masterson will get right on ordering tomahawk targets for the station's gun range. Oh, and adding a hatchet loop on our duty belts."

Wyatt grinned in appreciation of the sarcasm. Like him, Att didn't rile up worth a damn.

"Sugar, I cain't believe you missed." Gin's slow southern drawl always made Wyatt smile.

"With an archaic tool. As it happens, I prefer my firearm." Atticus tucked his arm around Gin. "Throwing a weapon leaves you defenseless."

"Not if you hit what you aim at." Wyatt's response got only a grin and a wave of Atticus' hand toward the target.

Put up or shut up, hmm?

Wyatt unsheathed his throwing tomahawk, checked the range and area, and let fly. The blade struck with a solid *whap* in the center of the bullseye.

"Oh, I do think he won your contest." Gin's statement earned her a swat on the ass that made her giggle.

"Behave, you two." Wyatt shook his head in mock disapproval. "Save your hand for Serenity's party." Near the end of July, the SF Dark Haven club planned to visit Serenity Lodge, and as usual, Jake and Logan would host a BDSM party.

"We going to see you there?" Atticus asked.

Wyatt shrugged. *Without Erin? Probably not.*

"Are you talking about the party in three weeks?" Katelyn joined them. Grabbing Wyatt's hand in both of hers, she leaned against him. "It'll be so much fun. Like being back in Dark Haven. Remember, Wyatt?"

· · ·

Erin had stopped to chat with Becca over at the toddler area where water was running over a plastic tarp. Sitting right in the flow, Ansel was splashing away.

"He is so cute."

"Mmm." Becca sighed as her son sent a stream of water at another toddler—and received cheers and laughter. "But what is he learning? The next time I give him a bath, I'm going to get drenched. How am I going to explain that bathtub water fights aren't allowed?"

Erin snorted. "Good luck."

Walking past, Morgan slowed. "Yo, Erin, have you seen the 'hawk and knife throwing?"

She narrowed her eyes. "Hawks? You throw birds?"

His laughter stopped her before she went on an angry rampage. "No—tomahawks. Throwing hatchets. We cordoned off a space for the mountain men and women enthusiasts. Want to see?"

Would Wyatt be there? A thrill shot through her. "I...yes, I'd love to."

Becca smiled and gave her a quick squeeze. "Have fun."

As Erin joined Morgan, she confided, "I've always wanted to learn to throw a knife. Have you done it? Is it difficult?"

When he grinned, he looked so much like his brother it gave her a pang right in the chest.

And then she spotted Wyatt...and her breathing went all funny.

No wonder she hadn't spotted him earlier. He wore mountain man stuff—buckskin pants with fringe at the seams, a loose cotton shirt to mid-thigh, and a heavy leather belt holding a knife on one side and a hatchet on the other.

He was drop-dead sexy.

"I didn't even recognize him."

"Eh, he didn't used to wear the gear at our party, but his black powder buddies asked him to costume up today. They're trying to attract new members. Turns out kids are wary around the other guys...but not Wyatt."

Because everyone loved the cowboy.

Not me. Absolutely not.

Even as she denied herself, the beautician named Katelyn latched onto Wyatt's arm, batting her long dark lashes. Flirting with him.

Pure, unadulterated jealousy sliced through Erin's heart like a hot knife through butter.

She came to a halt as her feet stopped moving. *No way I am going to watch him getting hit on.* "Sorry, Morgan. I just remembered, I need to go check on—"

"No, you don't." Morgan's expression, usually so calm, held the same authoritarian edge Wyatt's often had. "You were the one to back off. Means you should be the one to move forward."

"I...what?"

Morgan grinned. "We're brothers, little bit. We talk."

Wyatt had told him what had happened? "But—"

Morgan put his hands on top of her shoulders. "He's a good man, Erin. And the two of you fit well together. Are you sure you want to just walk away?"

His blue-gray eyes were serious. Soul-searching.

She swallowed. "I came today because... I hoped, maybe—"

"There we go, excellent." With an arm behind her back, Morgan started her moving—and raised his voice. "Yo, Wyatt."

Wyatt started to turn.

Spotting Erin, Katelyn glared and pulled on Wyatt's arm to re-capture his attention. "Listen, Wyatt, I—"

"Got a lady who needs a knife to throw," Morgan called, "or maybe to knife you. She wasn't real clear."

"You jerk." Erin backhanded his stomach—and winced. His abs were as hard as Wyatt's. "Ow!"

"Erin." Wyatt pulled his arm from Katelyn's grasp. "Are you all right?"

Laughing, Morgan kept moving her toward Wyatt. "She *hit* me, bro. She's obviously lacking in discipline."

"I don't know. I usually feel like hitting you too." Wyatt took Erin's hand and drew her away from Morgan. "But being as you're my brother, I suppose I could punish her for such violent behavior. Just to keep the peace in the family, of course."

"I knew you'd step up for the team." Chuckling, Morgan glanced at the brunette. "Come on, Katelyn, these two need to talk."

Katelyn shook her head. "No. Wyatt and I were talking."

"*Now*." Morgan swept his arm in front of her in a *move out* gesture, and after a pleading look at Wyatt, she left.

Erin bit her lip, glanced at Wyatt, and tried to think of what to say. *This isn't awkward, no, not at all.* "Um." *Oh, brilliant start, Erin.*

He looked down at her, smiling slightly. "Everyone thinks Morgan's the easy-going one, and he is, right up until he decides he needs to act. Then we all give in—partly from shock, but mostly because he's the most stubborn bastard ever born."

"I get it," she murmured. "I felt like I stepped in front of an avalanche."

"Yep. Unexpected and unstoppable. But he's gone now. If you'd rather be somewhere else..."

"No." She blurted out the words she'd been practicing in her head for days, "Wyatt, I'm sorry. About what I said. At breakfast. I-I panicked."

His gaze softened as he studied her face. "The thought of a relationship with me is so terrifying?"

"Any relationship. It just seemed too soon after Troy. I was so wrong about him, and it's scary knowing my judgment was so poor. But saying I planned to return to Sacramento...it's not true." She puffed out a breath. She'd hated how Troy's politician friends were so dishonest. Yet look at what she'd done. "I told you a lie; it's been nagging at me ever since I said it."

He touched her cheek, his hand warm on her skin. "I like that you feel guilty about lying to me."

She tried to smile at him, but her emotions felt like they'd boil over, like she'd burst into tears.

Instead of pressing, he turned his hand over and ran his knuckles down her cheek, then stepped back. "Did you want to learn to throw a knife?"

"I...yes."

"You're in the right place." He turned her toward the target and pulled several knives from a bag under a table. "This set of lighter knives might work better for you."

Step-by-step, he went through how to throw, from the grip and stance, to the swing and release. He demonstrated a couple of times before handing her a knife. "Give it a shot."

She walked through it and, finally, threw the knife toward the target.

It totally missed.

She sighed. "I guess I'm—"

"You had it almost right, but you were throwing the blade like a ball." He handed her another knife, then pulled her against his body, her back against his chest, his arm around her waist. "The trick is to keep your arm pointing toward the target even as you let go."

He gripped her wrist and lifted, then swung both their arms down. "*Release.*"

She let go. The knife flew across the space—and hit the target with a gratifying *thunk*.

"It stuck!" She grinned, turning in his arms, tilting her head back and—

Her smile died. The laughter usually dancing in his dark eyes had been replaced by sadness.

"Wyatt?" Her hands flattened on his muscular chest.

"Erin." He put his hands over hers, holding her there. "Now you've apologized, do you want to pick up where we left off?"

After the years of hearing lies and evasions, his plain-spoken question and sincere gaze were like fresh air blowing away throat-clogging smoke. "I... Can you forgive me?"

"Of course." He pulled her closer and simply hugged her, so warm and giving that tears stung her eyes. He wasn't going to yell at her and subject her to days of cold treatment the way Troy had when they argued.

Squirming closer, she breathed in his scent, made even headier by the fragrance of leather. "Do you ever get angry? Why aren't you mad at me?"

"Oh, I get mad, and I'm sure we'll have some interesting battles. Because we're looking at being together, am I right?"

She sagged against him and whispered, "Yes."

"Well, now, my day is definitely looking up."

Wait, why did he sound so amused? She pulled away so she could see his face. The laughter was back in his eyes. "You're finding something funny?"

"In a way." He ran his knuckles over her cheek. "You *do* remember I'm a Dominant when it comes to sex, yeah?"

She felt her cheeks heat. "Mmmhmm."

"As it happens, makeup sex with a Dominant and submissive can get...interesting. Especially when the little subbie has been bad."

"I...what?" Oh my God, was he talking like *punishment*? Along with the wave of heat, her heart hitched like a fuel line with moisture in it.

The crease in his cheek deepened, and the look in his eyes was purely wicked.

"Who you got there, Masterson?" A man's gruff voice made her jump.

Wyatt turned, dropping his arm to around her waist, keeping her beside him. "Erin, this is one of the black powder men, Maddox Rasmussen. Maddox, my woman, Erin Lockwood."

"Good to meet you, miss." Burly as a logger, Maddox had graying black hair and a bushy beard. He shot a look at Wyatt.

"Yours, hmm? First time I've heard you lassoing yourself a woman."

"Might need a few extra knots for this one," Wyatt muttered.

Grinning, Maddox wandered off—apparently to spread the news since suddenly there was a steady stream of bearded, buckskin-wearing men coming to meet her.

To Erin's delight, there were quite a few women too. When the latest one left, she turned to Wyatt. "I thought a black powder club would have only men—or mostly men."

He smoothed his mustache. "The first clubs might have started with no women allowed, but rendezvous became family friendly." He smiled. "Fur trappers might have blazed the way into the west, but the frontier was settled by families."

"Is your group camping here?"

"A batch are spending the night in one of the area campgrounds, but this isn't a rendezvous. It's just a fun side-activity for our annual party." He kissed the top of her head. "I'll find you period clothing and take you to a real rendezvous one weekend. I think you'll enjoy it, especially since you have a talent for throwing a knife. We'll have you competing in no time."

Knife throwing. She laughed. "It wasn't on my bucket list, but it's seriously fun."

"Seriously?" Drawing near enough to hear, Morgan shook his head. "Please, no."

Wyatt smirked at his brother. "See? I'm not the only one who loves tossing a knife."

"Tell you what, Erin." Eyeing Wyatt's arm around her waist, Morgan smiled at her. "I'll show you how much fun archery is, and you'll dump the knives for the better sport."

"Archery might be fun."

"Hah, see, Wyatt?" Morgan grinned at his brother.

"You're a pain in the ass, bro." Grumbling under his breath, Wyatt pulled her closer. "Are you going to fight with me in the big battle later on?"

"Yes, yes, I will." Happiness swept through Erin. This, right here, was where she belonged.

A while later, after Erin had thrown both knives and hatchets, Wyatt grinned down at the flushed blonde. "Forget the 'hawks; knives are where your talent lies. We'll keep practicing so at the rendezvous you'll blow your competitors out of the water."

He bent and brushed a kiss over her lips. Because she was beaming.

Fuck, he loved her enthusiasm. She didn't like all activities—that would be annoying—but when she did enjoy something, she gave it her whole heart.

Including with sex. He pulled her closer. "Can I convince you to spend the night? Or to invite me over to your place?" He studied her face, searching for any hesitation.

There was none.

"Either is fine." Her smile faded slightly. "You look so...concerned."

"I've heard a rumor I can be pushy. I don't want you to feel that way. Ever."

She grinned. "No rumor, Mr. Masterson. You *are* pushy. But I like it."

If she liked it...

"The way you were talking about the future is what scared me. It's not long since my bad marriage with Troy and..."

He could be an idiot. "And I overwhelmed you. I'm sorry, Erin."

"Me too. I should have explained rather than lying and running."

Now that he could agree with. As a Dom, he needed her to be honest. And he fucking needed to be aware of when he was high-handed. "We both have things to work on."

"Especially you, Mr. PushyMcPushiness."

"Brat." He could see spankings in her near future.

"Not me; I'm an angel. Oh, speaking of angels, where's the kitty today? I've missed him." She frowned. "Do you have him in a safe place where he can't get hurt during the party?"

"Oh yeah. He's up in my apartment, and I locked the cat door so he can't come downstairs."

She snorted. "He's probably sacked out on your bed."

"Yeah, probably." Wyatt took her hand and laced their fingers together. It made him happy she missed the cat. Even better, she wasn't concerned in the least at Bat being on the bed or the couch.

Because animals on the furniture didn't bother him. As long as a pet moved when told. There were times a bed was restricted to humans only.

Tonight would be one of those nights.

Standing on the deck after night had fallen, Gin watched the Mastersons' version of a battle in the American Revolution. The epic water fight was nearing the end.

Although many soldiers had met their end, her man was still fighting bravely. However, she might not forgive him for signing on to be a British redcoat. The traitor.

A movement near him caught her attention.

Obviously targeting a group of patriots, Atticus had sneaked past a line of straw bales. The spaces between the heavy bales were too narrow for adults, but a girl, probably ten years old, was hiding there. As he passed, she poked her head out, took aim with her water pistol, and shot Atticus right in the back.

He spun—but she'd gotten him good. Playing it up to the hilt, he shouted and toppled over in a dramatic death scene.

The girl was giggling so hard she dropped her pistol as she ran over and jumped on him. He hugged her and gave her a high five before pointing to her pistol and motioning her toward the next British soldier.

Even as she laughed, Gin felt her heart melt. Her man was so wonderful.

Flopping back down, he looked toward the deck. His rueful smile held nary a trace of anger. Being bested by a child didn't bother him in the least.

And he didn't mind that Gin wasn't interested in getting soaked to the skin in a war game.

Dear heavens, but she loved him. He would be an amazing father...and maybe next year, they'd talk about expanding the family.

Since her honey was out of the game, she checked to see how the others were doing, especially the ones who might have problems.

Sawyer's PTSD had diminished enough he wanted to play—although he refused to be in charge. Instead, Mallory was captain of a full dozen "soldiers" and snapping out orders as if she was directing her construction crew.

Also ex-military, Logan hadn't joined the skirmishers but took Wyatt's usual place as commander of the artillery—the soldiers throwing water balloons from the deck. Becca had joined them too.

She saw his smile when Becca whooped at hitting her target. Yes, Logan was enjoying himself.

Okay, Gin, remove your counselor hat. This is all fun and games.

Kallie and Jake and Morgan were colonials, but Virgil, Sunny, Wyatt, and Erin had joined the redcoats, distinguished by the red vests they wore. Rather than joining the large-scale engagements commanded by Mallory on one side and Terry Breton on the other, Morgan chose to be a patriot sniper, whereas Wyatt—with Erin—were British guerillas, shooting from cover.

Wasn't it great how quickly Erin caught on to the game. "Go, girl!" Gin yelled when her new friend nailed a too-cocky man.

Erin grinned, but even better, Wyatt gave her a fist-bump in obvious approval.

Someone was quite secure in his masculinity.

And Erin had obviously taken Gin's careful suggestion and was risking her heart.

After exchanging a few words with Wyatt, Erin stepped out of hiding, shooting in a steady stream toward a hay bale. Morgan was forced to stay around the corner even as Wyatt sprinted forward. Wyatt flattened himself up against the hay bale.

Erin stopped firing, swearing as if her gun had run out of water. Grinning, Morgan jumped out to shoot her.

And Wyatt shot his brother.

Gin giggled as she watched Morgan's heartrending death. Who would have thought the quiet Masterson could be such a drama queen?

As Wyatt ran back to Erin and gave her a kiss, Gin nodded in satisfaction. The two made an excellent team. "Yes, he's a keeper, Erin."

Wyatt climbed the stairs to his apartment. An hour ago, the last of the townsfolk had headed home. Most of the food went home with guests, but enough remained to keep his family busy putting it away. With wild animals around, leaving food scraps outside was a bad idea. At least, the rest of the clean-up could wait until tomorrow.

Bending, he opened the cat door so Bat could join the family downstairs. With a snooty nose in the air and no greeting, the cat conveyed that Wyatt was going straight to hell for imprisoning a feline.

"Sorry, buddy. I'll make it up to you with a tasty treat."

Bat rewarded the adequately penitent apology by rubbing his cheek on Wyatt's ankle and accepting a chin rub.

Once back in the living room, he saw Virgil, Sunny, Morgan,

and Erin had brought in snacks. Everyone settled in to rehash the highlights of the day.

Wyatt joined Erin on the couch. With Erin leaning against him on his left, and Bat curled up on his right, Wyatt was a contented man.

"I know my favorite moment of the battle." Virgil tossed Patches a piece of bread. "Did any of you see Atticus die? It was great."

"Laughing at the death of your detective? Cold, bro, cold." Morgan shook his head.

Virgil smirked. "It takes talent to get the drop on him...and a tiny girl did the deed. Nailed him square in the back."

"Oh damn, wish I'd seen it," Wyatt said. Erin didn't make any noise, but he could feel her body shake with her laughter.

"After you killed your favorite brother"—Morgan slapped himself in case anyone was confused as to who was favorite—"who took you out?"

Wyatt heaved a pitiful sigh. "Tobias killed me dead." And he'd never admit that he'd deliberately left himself open for the trans boy's shot. The teen had endured a lot on his way to living openly in his affirmed gender. Thank fuck his attempt at suicide had failed, and his parents had seen the light.

"I saw. You died quite nobly—and loudly." Sunny snickered. "And Tobias' dad cheered louder than anyone. What about you, Erin? You were still alive after Wyatt went down."

"I circled the big battle and picked off some guerillas. I couldn't allow uppity colonials to kill you and Virgil." Erin wrinkled her nose at Morgan.

Because the cop and nurse liked rules, Virg and Sunny had gone army—the British one.

Erin's smile turned smug. "I killed Jake Hunt."

"You did?" Sunny bounced up and down. "You did! Good for you."

Erin grinned. "It was great. Only...his brother must have seen me shoot him."

"Logan?" Virgil frowned. "Wasn't he on the deck, commanding the artillery?"

"Mmmhmm." Erin sighed. "Not one, not two, but *three* balloon bombs hit me before I could get back under cover. Talk about getting drenched."

Wyatt laughed. "No wonder you looked like you'd gone swimming."

Everyone laughed at her grimace.

"The Hunts are as protective of each other as these guys are." Sunny shook her head and added, "The Mastersons also excel at being meddling nosy parkers."

Wyatt grinned and shrugged. It was true.

"Such insults from our beloved sis-in-law." Morgan tried to look pitiful. At Erin's sputtering laugh, he winked at her.

Smiling, Wyatt kissed the top of her head, happiness filling him. His brothers were easy to read. Morgan liked Erin right from the beginning. Virgil had been warier, but now? They were both pleased she was here.

Sunny thought she was great. And...hey, was probably hoping to even up the male-female ratio in the house.

Couldn't blame her for that.

Realizing the soft body against him was sagging, he tugged a lock of blue hair. "You're fading, sugar. Ready to go upstairs?"

She tried to hide a yawn. "Uh-huh."

"Night, people." Wyatt rose, pulling her up, and picked up the cat.

Upstairs, he set Bat down and smiled at Erin. "Go on and take a shower if you want. I need to feed Bat."

"After almost drowning in battle, you'd think I'd avoid more water—but I totally want a shower." She grinned.

He watched her head into the bathroom. She surely did have a fantastic ass.

CHAPTER TWENTY-FIVE

"...Friends in low places."

Erin snickered. Wyatt's rough baritone drifted out of the shower as he sang the old country tune...maybe even better than Garth Brooks.

She was curled under the covers, clean, happily exhausted, warm—and so very contented.

What a great day. Wyatt and Morgan had mad skills at ambushing people. She'd tried to imitate the way they moved and how they hid and fired from cover.

They'd told her their Independence Day battles had started off on the bare lawn, then Wyatt's mountain man group requested more opportunities to be sneaky. The field of battle gradually expanded into the forest as well as adding the straw bales. Considering their howls of success, the mountain men had enjoyed stalking their opponents.

And she'd let out a whoop or two of her own.

Heaving a satisfied sigh, she reached out to pet the cat. But... oh, right, Wyatt had told Bat he was on his own tonight and closed the cat out of the bedroom. Smiling at the memory of the cat's displeased expression, she let herself slide into sleep.

And woke to calloused hands massaging her breasts and tugging on her nipples.

Wyatt's growling voice sounded in her ear. "Ready for punishment and makeup sex, woman?"

"Um..."

"Good. Brace yourself."

"Brace?" She sputtered a laugh. "Seriously? Is this a cowboy's idea of foreplay?"

Not that she could do any bracing—he'd flattened her on the mattress.

"You bet. Now how should I punish you...before taking my pleasure in other ways?" His mouth came down on hers, and he kissed her, slow and deep and wet.

Oh wow. Her hormonal engine revved as if injected with a rich air-fuel mix. Lacing her hands behind his neck, she sank in, and the kiss turned demanding.

Propping himself up on an elbow, he ran a hand over her bare body. "Sleeping commando? Did you want a T-shirt or boxers?"

"Actually, I don't usually wear anything." At least, not when sleeping alone.

His lips curved in a slow smile. "Damn, you really are my kind of woman."

The offhand compliment shouldn't make her feel so happy.

But it did.

And so did the feeling of his bare chest against hers. He wore only a pair of loose cotton drawstring pants. His skin was warm from the shower, and he smelled incredible with a clean, spicy-citrus scent. She touched his smooth jaw. "You shaved."

"Mmmhmm. You got sunburned, sugar." He rubbed his cheek against hers, and she could feel the mild pain of burned skin. "I'll have other times to give you a good beard-burn."

Other times. The words gave her another hit of happiness. "So, what's my punishment, oh Lord and Master?"

On the dresser, micro lights studded an arrangement of birch branches in a rustic woven basket and gave off enough light she could see his firm lips quirk. "Lord and Master. That works."

She'd said it teasingly, but the confidence in his voice turned her joke into truth. He intended to take command in here—and he knew she would yield. Would *submit*.

She swallowed past a suddenly dry throat.

"It's time you learned the ropes. Your safeword is red. If you use it, we quit what we're doing. Everything stops. Use yellow if you don't want to totally quit but need to halt long enough to fix a problem. Green means keep going." He smiled slightly. "What's your safeword?"

"Red to make everything stop."

"Good. What does *no* mean?"

"Um." Safewords were mentioned in the BDSM books, but the ones she read hadn't talked about how "no" was handled. "Stop?"

" 'Fraid not. It means I'm having a great time, and you're not sure if you are. Or you want to pretend you're uncertain. But, sweetheart, it *doesn't* mean stop."

The controlled warning in his rough voice sent a frisson of excitement through her.

His hand covered her breast. "Did I mention I like playing with lady bits? Playing hard and rough and even painfully."

The word *painfully* gave her an anxious quiver, yet her nipples tightened as if eager to participate.

Surely not. "How...how much pain?"

A dimple appeared in his cheek as he rubbed his knuckles over her blatantly jutting peaks. "Never more than you can take, Erin." The crease deepened. "Probably more than you'd volunteer for."

Oh. She could feel the heat beneath her skin, the way she'd gone damp down below.

"You always have a safeword. Do you trust me to honor it?"

"Of course." She blinked in surprise at how much she meant her answer. She genuinely did trust him.

"Tonight, I won't gag you or restrain you...physically." He stroked her hair, still smiling into her eyes. "If I ask you not to move, you'll do your best to please me, won't you, Erin?"

She *would*, and the knowledge was disconcerting. "Oh no, does this mean I need to turn in my feminist card?"

"Only if you believe the bullshit that all women should be submissive to men. Truth is, any gender can be submissive—or dominant." He grinned. "Or several of my BDSM-loving, gay and lesbian friends might have a problem."

She laughed, imagining the arguments in a man/man relationship. *I'm the male, so I'm dominant* wouldn't exactly work. "So it's not a male/female thing."

"No, this is a you and me thing. Because I get off on being in charge of sex—and pushing you to your limits in pleasure. Something we'll both enjoy." He took her mouth again, firmly exploring with lips and tongue, teasing until all her attention was focused on kissing him back.

When he lifted his head, she was totally on-board with whatever he had planned. "So what's my punishment to be?"

Below the dark mustache, his smile was wicked. Rolling out of bed, he opened the bedstand drawer, put a pair of medical scissors on the top, and pulled out a roll of—

Horror widened her eyes. "Is that duct tape?"

"No, sugar. Bondage tape. PVC Vinyl. It won't stick to your skin." He pulled her up to sit on the edge of the mattress. "Hold your breasts up for me." He put her hands on her breasts, pulling upward.

Standing beside the bed, he wrapped the black shiny stuff around her torso just below her breasts and continued halfway up to her nipples until it acted like a push-up bra. When he cut the tape and smoothed it down, it stuck there.

"Huh."

He chuckled. "It's faster than rope; no knots required."

"Convenient." Naked except for the bondage tape, she felt a flush rising as he stood looking at her. Studying her breasts.

"Very nice. Hands behind your head, please."

As she raised her arms, her breasts lifted.

Again, he circled her torso with the bondage tape, this time, starting a few inches below her collarbones and moving downward. Like a merciless but gentle vise, her breasts were squeezed from the top and bottom, swelling and tight.

"Look at me, blue girl."

His eyes were so brown, so dark. So hot. "Pain?"

"No?"

He chuckled. "If you were hurting, you'd know." He put his hands on her breasts, holding her gaze. His touch was deliberately rough, making her all too aware of the way her breasts protruded, as if asking for his attention.

And oh, her skin grew more sensitive by the moment. When he tugged on her nipples, the jolt of painful pleasure had her sucking in air.

A dimple showed in his cheek. "Now, let's see about punishing you properly. Have you ever tried nipple clamps?"

Her voice came out a whisper. "No."

"Is seems it's time to broaden your horizons." He pinched a nipple, tugging until it elongated, and fastened on a rubber-tipped clamp. Slowly, he tightened the screw until she sucked in a gasp.

Then did the other.

Her nipples *hurt*.

He caught her wrists before she could yank the nasty things off. "Breathe, Erin. Slow and deep." His voice deepened. "Feel the throb—like I'm pinching your nipples. My hands are needed elsewhere, but these will give you the same sensation."

Her heart was pounding, her breathing fast. Her breasts were swollen, tight, the clamps like relentless bites on her nipples, yet every word he uttered sent heat shimmering through her veins. The way he held her wrists with such casual strength made her sex ache for anything he wanted to do.

As if he could feel the yielding deep in her center, he

tossed the covers away and pushed her back on the bed. The bottom sheet was smooth and cool against her overheated skin.

He lifted her hands upward, past her head. "Hang onto the headboard spokes. Don't let go."

The movement of her arms made her breasts jiggle—and hurt in the most sensual of ways. Carefully, she closed her fingers around the carved spindles.

Beside the bed, Wyatt looked down at her. He was so tall and broad-shouldered, with muscles upon muscles. Chest hair darkened his pectorals and arrowed down his abdomen. "Open your legs for me. Slowly, please."

His eyes held sinful amusement. He knew full well that exposing herself to him was far more difficult than having her legs pushed apart.

Wyatt waited, watching the captivatingly conflicted expressions on Erin's face. What Dominant wouldn't savor her appalled awareness of participating in her own submission.

"Farther," he murmured when she stopped. "I need room to work."

When she shivered, he had to suppress his smile.

When her legs were wide apart, he nodded. "Such a good girl."

She probably didn't hear her own tiny sigh of happiness at his approval, but he did.

Cupping her beautifully swollen breasts, he toyed with the clamps. Now so in tune with her, he could almost feel her pain turning into a heavy, liquid heat. Feel her arousal increase as he kissed her and teased her.

Removing his pants, he sheathed himself with a condom and knelt between her soft thighs. "Now, how much punishment have you earned?"

Her worried squeak was delightful.

It was tempting to push her... *No.* Not with a new subbie. He'd give her a taste and leave her wanting to explore more.

If he had his way, there'd be a lifetime to explore sensations with her.

He slid his fingers over her mound and lower to slicken his fingers. "So fucking wet." His cock was rock hard, heavy with the need to penetrate all that heat.

But first...

He played with her, learning her tells. Massaging the beautifully plump mound, rolling her inner pussy lips between his fingers—increasing the pressure slowly until he could hear her breathing change.

A detour to tease the hood above her clit made her thighs tighten on his body. "Legs apart, sweetheart. Far apart."

Her whine was adorable.

Inserting two fingers in her cunt made his dick throb with its own demand. Sliding his fingers in and out with one hand—*pleasure*—he used the other hand to mercilessly knead her labia—*pain*.

Her thighs quivered, her muscles tensed, her cunt clenched around him.

"Ah, that hurts a bit, does it?" He studied her flushed face, enjoying the conflict as the edgy pain deepened her arousal.

Oh God, what is he doing?

She could feel his sinewy fingers on her most intimate parts, rolling, pinching, pulling. When what he was doing grew painful, a heavy heat rolled through her, changing the sensation to... something almost more than pleasure. And his slowly thrusting fingers turned it all into a seething cauldron of need.

Her clit—he hadn't even touched it—throbbed with urgency.

Pulling out two fingers, he added another and penetrated her with three. "Now, I think it's time for your punishment."

Her eyes flew open. "What?"

His hand came down on top of her mound in a stinging slap.

"Aaaah!" Shocked, she put her hands over the burning spot. Only the pain was turning into a ferocious hum of need.

"Erin."

She realized she'd closed her eyes again and with an effort opened them and looked at him.

His jaw was stern, his gaze dangerous. "Where do your hands belong?"

What? Oh, *oh*. But... His eyes held hers, utterly self-confident as he waited for her to obey.

The feeling as she lifted her arms and grasped the headboard spindles again was the pure sensation of letting go. Of surrender.

"There's a good girl." His voice was like a rough velvet, darker than night. "Two more, Erin. Are you going to take them nicely?"

Shivers ran through her, only...his fingers were still sliding in and out of her, each steady thrust increasing the mind-bending pleasure. The relentless need grew and grew. "Y-yes."

"Look at me now."

His hand came down, once, in a hard smack, then his fingers teased, sliding over her clit, shocking her with the stunning sensation.

Again, the quick stinging slap, followed by the stroking over her clit that turned the hot sting to the most exquisite pleasure. His fingertips inside her were firmly rubbing over an area that made her whole body tense.

His eyes held hers as the pressure within her pelvis grew, coiling tight, and... The sensations engulfed her in a blaze of pleasure, searing across every nerve. "*Ooooob*." Her hips bucked as her body vibrated with the unstoppable waves.

"Mmm, nice." He ran both hands up her pussy, over her mound, making her clench inside.

She opened her eyes. When had she closed them?

His gaze trapped hers as she felt his cock at her entrance. With one deep thrust, he filled her completely.

"Oh god." Her back arched as she came again so violently the world whited out.

When she could focus again, he was thrusting slowly, watching her face. The creases beside his eyes crinkled. "You feel so fucking good."

The happiness of pleasing him was another sweet jolt, much like the tiny aftershocks that were still coming. She realized she'd wrapped her arms around his neck and hoped he wouldn't notice. "Am I done being punished, oh Lord and Master?"

His dark laugh sent more quivers through her. "Almost. And little subbie, this isn't punishment; just...how things work."

She frowned, trying to understand what he meant.

Pulling out, he rolled her over, setting her onto her hands and knees. Even as she got her balance, he took her from behind.

She gasped. In this position, he seemed even bigger, longer. She was stretching inside, trying to accommodate him.

"Hold still now, Erin." Reaching out, he picked up the scissors on the bedstand. The cold steel slid along her back under the bondage tape. He snipped twice. The lower and upper tape sprang loose, and her harnessed, swollen breasts dangled free. Blood surged into the tissues, and she sucked in a shocked breath, freezing in place at the sensation.

He chuckled, reached around, and removed the clamps from her nipples.

"Aaaah!" The pain was a rushing, burning wave, from her nipples through her breasts.

"Breathe through it, sweetheart." He'd stopped thrusting, and his cock was thick inside her. Balancing on one hand, he used the other to ruthlessly massage the aching mounds of flesh.

"Owwww." Her voice came out a husky whine. "You *sadist*."

He laughed. "Name calling, my girl?" His hands moved over her breasts, his thumbs circling her tenderized nipples, almost gently, almost not. Inexplicable need rolled up and over her again, until all she could feel was his fingers on her breasts and the thickness of his shaft within her.

When he started to thrust again, her breathing caught at the irresistible pleasure. At how her need grew and grew, climbing to an impossible urgency. She was caught there on the pinnacle, unable to go over, and she whimpered, trying to balance on one hand so she could—

He chuckled. "Not tonight. This is my job." His voice was a rumbling murmur. His hand slid from her breasts, down her stomach, to her mound.

He paused there.

She panted in anticipation, in need. Her breasts still tingled and ached. His cock filled her almost unbearably full as he slid in and out. Her clit throbbed, impossibly sensitive from the spanking.

And then finally... One finger slid over her clit, the touch light, slick. Over, around, brushing over and over, right at the junction of the hood and the nubbin.

It was too, too *much*. Everything in her depths exploded into toe-curling, uncontrollable ecstasy. More unstoppable pleasure poured through her with each pulsating wave of release.

Laughing, he hammered into her, forcing the orgasm to continue on and on. Her arms gave out, and she went down to her elbows, her ass high in the air.

He gripped her hips firmly as he took her with deep, driving thrusts until he plunged deep, pulsing as he found his own release.

Satisfaction still hummed through her even as she slid into a hot, sweet limp state.

Wow.

His arms closed around her as he tipped them onto their sides, staying deep inside her. He nuzzled her hair. "Do you feel adequately punished, sugar?"

"Mmm." Dear God, she'd never come so hard, never felt like this at all. "I'm not sure. You might need to do it again."

His hearty laugh made her shiver in happiness.

Wyatt had missed her in his life. In his bed. And now she was back. *Thank fuck.*

After cleaning them both up, he joined her in bed. Propped on an elbow, he looked down at her.

Her hair was tangled, her cheeks still flushed, and her mouth swollen from his kisses. She looked used—and well satisfied.

Pulling her closer, he enjoyed the feel of her—so soft and fragrant. And more... He liked all of her—her spirit, her personality. Her quirky sense of humor, her honesty, the way she cared about others. Her patience and enthusiasm with children. The happy, focused expression when she was working on an engine.

Her brows drew together. "What's wrong?"

"More like what's right." He smoothed her hair back from her face. "I know hearing this might scare you, Erin, but I'm well on my way to falling in love with you."

As he watched carefully, he could see the joy in her eyes before anxiety drove it away. Pretty much what he figured would happen.

But it was the joy he figured would win.

When the sun came up, hours later, he had a morning woodie. Seemed a shame to not share the wealth.

After rolling on a condom, he used his hands and mouth to rouse the sleepy little subbie in his bed. Erin, the prettiest mechanic in the world. *Mine.*

Teasing her sensitive nipples made her tremble in the most adorable of ways. Her gasp when he played with her clit was damn gratifying. Fuck, she was fun.

She came once, but he didn't stop, and when he took her with deliberate force, with unyielding hands, he could feel her arousal soaring. She climaxed again, even harder. And damn, her yielding response drove *him* higher.

After he came, he hugged her, kissed her, and left the bed to dispose of the condom.

Once back under the covers, he settled his adorably limp and satisfied submissive on top of him. Her face was pressed against his neck, her breathing still fast. He ran his hand up and down her smooth back and ass, enjoying the curves.

"Do we have to get up now?" She squirmed slightly, fitting herself more comfortably on top of him.

"No, no hurry." He rolled a strand of her hair around his finger. Such fascinating waves. So soft. "We've got cleaning up to do, but no one's going to get up early today."

"Oh good." Her breath was warm against his neck. "I'm going to be walking bow-legged today, you brute."

He chuckled. "I'd take offense if it wasn't real clear you get off on rough handling. And like pain on your sexy bits." He gave her a second and prompted. "Am I wrong?"

"Do you know how difficult it is to admit that?"

Stroking a hand down her soft hair, he nodded. "I do, yes. About as difficult as it is to admit to enjoying torturing those bits." Although he said it lightly, he wasn't lying. It'd taken him time to understand and accept this part of his nature.

"Huh." She rubbed her cheek against him like a kitten seeking solace. "I'm confused. I know it'll hurt—and I don't like being hurt—only then it doesn't and made everything more intense." Her voice dropped to a whisper. "I've never gotten off so hard in my life."

"Thank you. It's what I hoped to hear." He couldn't see her face, but his fingers could feel the heat. Modest Erin had the courage to discuss a topic that obviously embarrassed her.

However... Seemed like he should warn her there would be more embarrassing moments in her future. "Did you know that Serenity Lodge hosts parties for people who enjoy kink?"

Erin loved listening to Wyatt; his voice in the morning was deeper, gruffer, and incredibly sexy.

A moment later, what he had said registered.

Her mouth went dry. Her new friends had alluded to kinky parties. But at Serenity? "I'm not into swinging."

"No, sugar. Not swinging." He ran his fingers through her hair. "We're in a committed relationship, right?"

Oh. *Oh*. Her heart jolted with her happiness. "Yes."

"Well then. As it happens, commitment means I don't share."

She lifted up, bracing her forearms against his chest so she could see his face. "I don't share either."

"Good." He curved his hand around her throat and murmured, "However, I don't mind playing with you where others can see. As it happens, the Hunts have a great dungeon."

A dungeon? Oh. My. God.

"You have quite the fast pulse going there." His grin flashed and disappeared. "There's better equipment for restraining submissives." His voice deepened. "It means when I hurt you, you won't be able to move away."

Like gasoline over a sparking, red-hot engine, her body went up in flames. Even though they'd just had sex, her clit tingled, asking to start all over again. "When is this...party?"

Her heart rate had picked up...and he knew, dammit. His expression filled with evil amusement. "The end of July—about three weeks away."

Whew, not too soon. There'd be time to get used to the idea. Surely she could try one night. A few romance books were centered around BDSM clubs, and face it, she'd been intrigued. Turned on. "I might be awfully inhibited, but I...I'll try it. Okay?"

"Brave girl." He pulled her down for a long, tender kiss. When she lifted her head, his eyes were dancing with laughter. "No need to worry about the other people. After you've screamed your way through your third or fourth orgasm, you won't even realize anyone else is there."

She could only stare at him in horror.

CHAPTER TWENTY-SIX

Working beneath an ancient VW Beetle, Erin was loosening a nut when her phone rang. She jumped—and banged her knuckles on the steel shaft. *Frickity-frick-frick-frick.*

The shop policy was phones were kept at the toolbox to prevent chatting while working. She managed to make it over there by the third ring.

The cell's display showed it was Troy's brother. "Hi, Emmett. What's up?" She sucked on her knuckle, tasting blood. *Stupid phone.*

"Erin, it's good to hear your voice. I'm in the area to see a friend and hoped you'd have lunch with me."

A friend? The bigshot CEO had a friend in Bear Flat? Well, who knew, maybe he'd met someone while on his hunting trips with Troy.

Erin sighed. Lunch with Emmett? He'd undoubtedly want to talk about his brother. Her heart sank a little.

But Emmett was her brother-in-law. If he needed to grieve, she could be kind and listen. "Sure, lunch would be good. I have an hour lunch break. Maybe at the Mother Lode on Main Street?"

"Perfect. I can pick you up at noon."

She shook her head. It was better to be able to leave when she wanted. "Thank you, no. The restaurant is just down the street from the shop. I'll meet you there at noon."

After a moment's pause, he said smoothly, "Of course. I look forward to seeing you. How about if I order for you so you'll have time to finish."

"Oh, nice. A club sandwich and the soup of the day would be great."

At noon, Erin smelled the tantalizing aroma of grilled meat in the Mother Lode, and her stomach growled like a vicious dog.

Stopping by the hostess desk, she tried to see if Emmett had arrived, but the restaurant was packed full.

"Hi, Erin." The head server hurried over. In her fifties, Barbara was rarely frazzled, but today, a lock of her vibrant red hair was out of place, and a splotch of grease dotted her normally impeccable white apron.

"Busy day?" Erin asked.

Barbara rolled her eyes. "A whole busload of tourists decided they wanted lunch."

"Talk about too much of a good thing. I hope they tip very generously."

"You're so sweet. Me too." Laughing, Barbara gestured toward a back corner table. "Your friend is over there; I just dropped off your food."

"Thanks, Barbara. Can you, please, make sure the checks are separate?"

Barbara flashed her an understanding nod. "You got it."

Erin crossed the room and spotted her brother-in-law. *Huh.* When had she grown so used to jeans, T-shirts, and boots that his button-up shirt, tailored pants, and oxfords looked wrong?

"Erin, you look beautiful." Emmett rose and startled her when he bent and kissed her cheek.

Um, no. They'd never been that friendly. "Thank you." She sat across from him and unfolded the napkin. "How have you been?"

"It's been...difficult. I know Troy broke the law, but he was my brother." He shook his head, his eyes sad. "I'm pleased to see you though. How are you doing here in this pint-sized town? I'm surprised you're still here."

She chuckled. "Me too. I'd planned to sell the house here and go live in San Diego or San Francisco. But the real estate market here is dead."

"It is?" His sandy brows rose. "Is there a reason?"

"Due to the prison, unfortunately—the one Troy was instrumental in putting here."

His expression hardened, and she had a moment of guilt for what she'd said.

Turning his attention to his food, he cut a piece of chicken breast. "I believe the prison closed last year. Why would it still affect the market?"

"The prison held a lot of gang members." She picked up her spoon and sampled the soup. Broccoli-cheese and excellent. "Their fellow gang members had moved here, and the crime rate skyrocketed. They apparently turned Bear Flat into part of their pipeline for drugs and whatever else they were into, so even when the prison closed, the gangs remained."

"Ah, I see. No one wants a vacation home in a dangerous location."

"Exactly."

"I didn't see any questionable characters on the street." He glanced out the window.

"The town got together to discourage criminal behavior and effectively drove them out. But not before things got violent. It seems one gang lost several members during the prison breakout and were after revenge. They torched a resident's home and shot several police officers."

Emmett's brows arched. "Exciting times for a small town."

"Not what most people want in a small town." Erin shook

her head. "At least the citizens won their battle. A lot of the gang members either died or went to prison."

"Interesting. It must have been a rather small gang." Emmett raised his eyebrows. "What was their name?"

"The Aryan Hammers." She remembered it because the stupid gang had used a wonderfully functional tool in their name. So annoying. "I'm sure there are still gang members in the cities since the police here are worried they might try again for revenge."

She remembered Virgil's face when he talked about last summer.

"Quite possible. Violence is a gang's way of life, after all." Emmett took a sip of his coffee.

"Returning would be short-sighted of them considering what happened to the last bunch." Erin grinned. "I rather like how the townsfolk came together to make neighborhood watches."

"Because you like order." As they ate, he asked questions about her job and listened and shared a few of his own stories. Much like Troy, Emmett was a skilled socializer.

She started to relax. But the discussion veered to Troy.

Emmett leaned forward. "When I talked to Troy about the bribery charges, he said he planned to fight them. But he ran instead. Left the country, no less. I still don't understand why he was murdered. The ambassador said he'd been tortured."

Erin's stomach went tight, and she set her fork down, appetite gone. Why hadn't the FBI talked to him about the blackmail stuff? Should she tell him? Would it help him...or make things worse?

How would she feel if Mom had fled the country and been tortured and killed?

The confused pain in her brother-in-law's expression decided her. She'd want to know why. Even if the truth was upsetting.

"Emmett, what I have to say will be difficult to hear, but..."

"You know something, don't you?" His jaw set. "Tell me."

"Before Troy left, I was... I was going to his office to talk to him about the divorce, and I overheard him talking to a man on the phone."

Piece by piece, she laid out what she'd heard and what she'd done.

He stared at her in obvious outrage. "You went to the FBI? But you're his wife."

Guilt twisted in her chest. "I know. But he was—all of them were sexually abusing children. I had to put a stop to it to protect the children."

"I...see." Expression tight, he turned his head and stared out the window for a long minute. "I suppose he paid the price for what he did."

"No." She shook her head. "Prison should have been the price, not torture."

His smile didn't reach his eyes. "You have a good heart—and a strong sense of justice." When he turned his attention to his food, it was a relief.

Appetite gone, Erin pushed her plate away.

"Oh, ew, look who's here." A woman's loud voice cut through the background noise in the restaurant.

Erin glanced over her shoulder and stiffened.

Katelyn and her fellow beautician, Candy, were staring straight at her. When their gazes went past to Emmett, they were all flirtatious smiles.

Erin blinked, remembering Candy saying that Troy talked about Erin to the two women, calling her a boringly sweet wifey. "Do you know them?"

"Oh, slightly. Our hunting group would come into town occasionally to get drinks and eat food we hadn't cooked." Turning his attention from the women, he smiled at her. "I've never been in Bear Flat except in fall. What goes on here during the summer?"

"Mostly tourist activities spilling over from Yosemite park. And outdoor stuff like fishing and hiking. They had a big all-town event for the Fourth." She tilted her head. "What did you do on Independence Day?"

"Not much this year. In previous years..." His smile reappeared as he talked about summer vacations at Lake Tahoe or being in Europe where the Fourth, naturally, wasn't even a thing.

As he finished, he made a request.

She stared at him in shock. "You want to stay and spend a few days with me?"

"I do." He reached forward to touch her hand lightly. "I was always a bit envious Troy saw you first. I'd like to get to know you better."

She pulled her hand back. "I don't think—"

"I know the hotels are full. Could you see fit to let me use the spare room while I'm here? Or...maybe the guest room is over-crowded with furniture from the Sacramento house?"

"No, I donated and disposed of everything from there. I'm sorry, Emmett, but I have to say no. You're a very nice person but being married to Troy showed me I'm not suited for your type of life."

His mouth tightened for a moment. He obviously wasn't accustomed to being turned down, which made sense. Although he was quieter than Troy, they shared the same blond, blue-eyed, handsome looks. And being rich probably didn't hurt his appeal.

"I think you fit into our lifestyles quite nicely, but as you wish, my dear. Are you planning to stay in Bear Flat? With selling the Sacramento house, you should soon have the funds to return to the city."

"No, I'm finding I like the small-town life."

"Who would have thought?" He wiped his mouth with the napkin and set it to one side. "If you've left goods in storage in Sacramento, I can arrange to have everything transported here for you. I'll even oversee the movers to ensure nothing gets left behind."

"Thank you, but there's no need." She glanced at her bill, dropped a twenty on it, and rose. This was so awkward. "I do need to be going. Emmett, it was great to see you again. Have a wonderful summer."

Moving back before he could touch her, she escaped. Or would it be called *fled?*

She felt like such a dork.

CHAPTER TWENTY-SEVEN

I*'m going on a date.* As Erin stepped out of her shower in a billow of steam, she had to smile. Wyatt was home after being in the back country for three days.

In the week since the Fourth, they'd been together whenever Wyatt wasn't away guiding groups, and she wasn't working. They'd had several amazing nights together...

She grinned—and started applying her favorite lotion, remembering how one night he'd said she smelled like his favorite pastries and had nibbled his way down her body.

He was just so...easy...to be with. They cooked together, mock bickering over ingredients. He could make several scrumptious dishes, especially Mexican, but the haphazard way he cooked drove her crazy. She shook her head. He'd casually toss in food and add spices until it tasted "right". She had a wider repertoire but was all about following a recipe.

When she pointed out how different they were, he laughed and said as long as there was tasty food on the table, neither one of them cared about the technique involved in getting it there.

She grinned. He did have a point.

Staying here at the ranch had been far more fun than at her quiet vacation house. Helping him do chores, she'd learned how to get eggs from under chickens and how to clean out a horse stall. He gave her riding lessons until she felt comfortable at a trot and canter.

In return, she did maintenance on their washer and dryer. Didn't they realize the small holes designed to drain water from the washing machine shouldn't be clogged?

She shook her head, because when she'd finished with the machine and started to load up the tub, he took off his shirt to add it to the dirty clothes.

Sheesh, she'd looked up from where she was kneeling by the machine, and there he was, all muscles and broad shoulders and ripped abs. He ran his finger over her lips and smiled. "If you're going to look at me like that, you'd best follow through." And he unzipped his jeans.

She hadn't realized giving a blow job could be quite so arousing. Or how vibrations from a washing machine added interesting sensations when being eaten out on top of it.

She sighed. Wyatt was like the god of sex. Everything he did turned her on. And he always noticed...and reacted no matter the location. They'd made love in the barn with the horses watching, in the pasture by the burbling creek, on the bathroom counter. When she smacked his hand for trying to sneak cake batter, he'd yanked her pants down, bent her over the table, spanked her butt with a wooden spoon...and taken her, hard and fast.

If that was punishment, she wanted more.

And great, now she was all aroused again.

No, no, Erin. You have to finish getting ready.

Earlier today, when he returned from a guide trip, he'd called her at work to ask if she wanted to go out to eat and afterward to the ClaimJumper for drinks.

Like a real date.

In the next bay over, Marco had heard her talking to Wyatt and told Walker. The two mechanics had spent the rest of the day teasing her.

She grinned. She'd been working there—what, maybe seven weeks now?—and she was finally one of the crew. It was so nice.

As she dried off and applied lotion, she felt...happy.

Until she opened her closet. What was she going to wear? Did a date sort of occasion get the same clothes as a girls' night out?

Standing bare-ass naked in her bedroom, she picked up her phone.

"Hey, Becca. What would you wear if you were on a date, going out to eat, and to the ClaimJumper afterward?"

Smiling, she listened to the artist expound on the importance of sexy comfort.

Having friends was the best.

That evening, Wyatt took a sip of his beer and smiled at the woman beside him. Erin had obviously dressed up for tonight but in a way that didn't shout *city girl*. Most of her hair fell around her shoulders, but the sides were braided back to show off dangling red earrings. The color matched her red button-up shirt—and she'd made his night by tying the ends of the shirt in front, leaving a tantalizing strip of bare skin above her low-slung jeans.

Even better, only the knot held the front of her shirt together—and she hadn't worn a bra. Nothing showed, but between the cleavage and the jiggle of her breasts beneath the cotton shirt, he had trouble looking away.

Hell, he'd been sporting a semi all fucking night.

The evening had been good though, starting with good food, then cold beer and plenty of friends, and the finest woman in the world.

The ClaimJumper was beginning to quiet down. In fact, this was the first time it was only the two of them at the table.

And...she was frowning at him. "Problem, sweetheart?"

"Not a problem, but a question?"

He took her small hand in his. So delicate yet so competent with everything from engines to cooking. "Shoot."

"It's..." She tilted her head. "People gossip about you, you know? And I keep hearing you don't get serious with anyone."

Unable to resist, he kissed her fingertips and said in a cheesy voice, "But my darlingest darling, I was waiting for *you*."

As her cheeks turned almost the color of her shirt, he managed—barely—to keep his mouth straight.

"You, cowboy, are full of shit." Her lips were quirking though.

He had to laugh, just couldn't hold it in—and she joined him.

Then she shook her head. "Seriously, though. You're spectacular...in bed...and obviously have a lot of experience, and I was wondering why you're single and not married."

Ah. He let out a breath. "Fair enough." Enough time had passed that his grief had lessened to only an ache.

"In high school, I had girlfriends—along with the usual breaking-up and drama afterward." He gave her a rueful smile. "In small-town schools, an ex is in all your classes, in the small cafeteria, at all the events."

"Ugh." She wrinkled her nose. "Having no escape must be rough."

"It is. After school, I wasn't ready to get tied down. So I dated out-of-towners and made it clear up-front I was only there for fun."

"Your...policy...sounds cold-hearted, but it makes sense." She grinned. "I bet the local women weren't happy about you avoiding them."

"They got used to it." His gut tightened. "I met Anastasia in San Francisco. We were together almost a year—and yeah, I loved her. Would've married her, but she wouldn't move here, and I couldn't see living there. I hate cities."

Erin's gaze softened. "Oh, what a dilemma. Is that why you broke up?"

His fingers tightened around her hand. "No. I think we'd eventually have compromised, but..." Yeah, there was still some grief. Dammit, she hadn't even been thirty. "She died in a boating accident out on San Francisco Bay. She and a bunch of her work friends started the weekend early. Sounded like they were all drunk."

"Oh. Oh no." Her eyes teared up...for him. She held his hand with both of hers. "I'm so sorry."

"Thank you." Soft-hearted little submissive. So giving. Anastasia had been vanilla, which had also given him second thoughts.

With a pang, he realized he'd never cared about her as deeply as he felt about Erin. "It was a bad year. We lost Pa, and later, I lost her. But the next year, Kallie found Jake and"—he shrugged —"life is full of changes, yeah?"

"It is." Lifting Wyatt's hand, Erin rubbed it against her cheek and sent warmth right to his heart. Then her eyes narrowed. "No wonder you were so unhappy when I said I planned to return to the city."

"Yep." He chuckled. "Felt like the same shit had come back to bite me in the ass." Cupping her cheek, he traced his thumb over her beautifully curved lips. "Instead, I have your beautiful ass in my bed every night."

She nipped him and grinned. "Behave yourself, cowboy."

"Yes, behave yourself, Masterson." Coming from behind, Sawyer slapped Wyatt's back. "Erin, it's good to see you."

"Fuck, he hits me—and greets you politely?" Wyatt shook his head sadly. "This is just not right."

"You poor, poor man." Holding a beer in one hand, Mallory bent to kiss his cheek. "May we join you two, or is this a bad time?"

Seeing Erin's smile and nod, Wyatt rose and held the chair for Mallory. "Have a seat, contractor. You, too, rancher."

As the two settled in, Wyatt considered Sawyer. "I was planning to call you. I started giving Erin riding lessons, but I have a long trip next week. Any chance you can take over the lessons while I'm gone? Usual rates?"

Erin huffed. "You're not going to buy me lessons. Besides, I don't need—"

"You do. Trail rides are more fun if you're easy in the saddle." Wyatt turned back to Sawyer.

"Sure." Sawyer grinned at Erin. "How about I trade lessons for you fixing my chain saw and string trimmer. They're both sounding ragged."

Her eyes lit. "Sure, I love tuning up outdoor tools." She turned to Wyatt. "How long are you going to be gone?"

"Four days. He took her hand again. "I'm sorry. I'm gone a lot during tourist season." His heart twinged. "It's not fair to you. Not what a woman would want in—"

"I like having you around, but I won't wither up and die when you're not here." She studied him for a second, undoubtedly seeing his worry. Her smile went tender. "I'm one of those semi-introverts. Being alone doesn't bother me."

The tension in his chest released. Anastasia had hated the thought of him going off for days at a time. Erin just shrugged and said it wasn't a problem.

He kissed her palm and nipped the plump mound at the base of her thumb, enjoying her tiny squeak.

"Awww." Mallory smiled at them, looking pleased as all get-out.

Sawyer was grinning.

Wyatt could only shake his head. Since Anastasia, his friends had grown far too invested in finding him a woman. Sawyer and Mallory had obviously decided Erin was the one.

Worked for him.

Finishing his beer, he glanced around the table. "I'm going to get another drink and some fries. Anyone else? Another for you, Erin?"

"Please."

Mallory shook her head no. "We're good."

When he reached the bar, Gustaf noticed him and headed over. "Gutt evening, young Masterson. What can I get you?" The owner's gray-white hair was as sparse as his beard was full. There were rumors the old Swede had done the boxing circuit in his day—and his battered face and fists bore out the rumors.

"How about a giant order of fries, a Bud draft, and a Mountain Dew."

"Coming up." Gustaf handed over the fries order to his college-age son who was home for the summer, then started drawing the beer. "Who is your pretty girl?"

Wyatt smiled. "She *is* a pretty one, isn't she? Erin Lockwood—she's Pierre's new mechanic."

Bushy gray brows rose as Gustaf studied her for a moment before giving an approving nod. "Finally, you find a contender who can go the distance."

Thinking of how she'd reacted to hearing he'd be gone a lot, Wyatt smiled. "Seems so."

"Look who's back in town." Katelyn's high giggle was like a sharp fingernail down a chalkboard.

Candy was right behind her.

He smiled politely at the two. "Candy. Katelyn." As Gustaf set the fries and Mountain Dew next to the beer, Wyatt started to pick them up.

Moving close, Katelyn put her hand over his forearm. "I had so much fun on the ride. And I'd like to go on an overnight trail ride. When are you going out again?"

"I'm not sure what Kallie has open. She gets booked fast. Give the office a call, and I'm sure she'll try to fit you in."

"Kallie, no." Katelyn grimaced. "I want to go with one of *your* groups."

He shook his head. "To avoid problems, she takes the single women."

Katelyn leaned against him and said in a husky voice, "I won't be a single woman if I'm in your bed."

For fuck's sake. "No. Rules are rules. Besides, I'm already with—"

"Wyatt." She glanced over her shoulder.

Wyatt saw Candy had moved away to flirt with a logger.

Katelyn lowered her voice anyway. "I'm really looking forward to the party at Serenity in two weeks. I miss Dark Haven...and being with you."

The naked longing in her voice made him uncomfortable.

He was always very clear about fun-times-only when dating but hadn't thought it needed to be said about pickup scenes at a club. Over the space of a few months, he'd done three scenes with her at Dark Haven. Never called her, never dated her.

Why did she persist in trying for more?

"I'm sorry, Katelyn." He shifted far enough away to avoid bodily contact but close enough to keep their conversation private. "I'm with Erin in a committed relationship. Neither of us is playing with anyone else."

"Oh."

Her stricken expression made him feel as if he'd stepped on a puppy. "I'm sure there'll be good Doms at the Serenity party to play with."

She shook her head. "No one's like you. And you live here in Bear Flat, not way off in the city."

At a loss for how to help, he suggested, "Simon or Xavier should be able to help you find a good Dominant who's right for you."

"Oh, honestly, you're so blind. *You're* right for me, and you'd know it if you weren't so blinded by the skank."

"Katelyn." He let her see the displeasure in his face. "I don't want to hear you name-calling Erin again. It stops now."

Anger twisted her face, but she nodded once before retreating quickly. "Candy, c'mon. Let's go dance."

That didn't go well. Shaking his head, Wyatt picked up the food and drinks and headed back to the table. Where his woman waited.

CHAPTER TWENTY-EIGHT

What had Troy been thinking to marry that do-gooder bitch? But Emmett knew. His brother had wanted to be a congressman and needed Senator Lockwood's help to get elected.

His plan had worked.

Right up until the snoop had overheard Troy...encouraging... Senator Silas Welser. What happened to a wife's loyalty?

Anger had been simmering in Emmett's veins like acid since his lunch with her last week.

Two more politicians had refused to cooperate unless they saw proof he had videos of their indiscretions.

Damn her. By siccing the FBI on Troy, she'd destroyed their carefully constructed operation. And his brother had run—and been too stupid to take the jump drives with him.

The wimp had screwed *everything* up.

Hoping Troy had hidden the drives in a mattress or chair cushion, Emmett searched the house, slashed everything to pieces...and found nothing.

Later, when the whiny loser tried to hold him up for money, Emmett had been forced to get a fake passport—an easy enough task, considering his numerous criminal contacts—and fly to

Buenos Aires. After sufficient...persuasion, Troy screamed out where he'd hidden the flash drives.

A damn clock.

If he'd realized Troy had left the evidence behind, Emmett could have searched the house before Erin left Sacramento. Then again, even the FBI had overlooked the antique desk clock as a hiding place.

Damn Troy anyway. Emmett shook his head. The files could have been kept in the cloud on secure overseas servers, but no, his idiot brother had been too paranoid about law enforcement hacking in. So the files were on thumb drives.

Obviously, Erin had taken Troy's "secret storage" with her. But the ex-con who'd searched the vacation house found nothing. It was just as well. The incompetent loser had died in a car crash. Saved Emmett some money.

Emmett tapped a pen on his desk. He had a trip planned and couldn't do anything for a week or so. But after he got back...

He needed to have a long *talk* with Erin, probably the same kind he'd had with Troy, to find out where the drives were.

She was an enticing thing. Once he had the location of the thumb drives, he'd enjoy taking his frustration out on her. Watching her die.

He'd thought it would be easier to get her alone. Damn woman. And during the lunch, he learned she'd made herself at home in that bumfuck town. She had a job, friends, even a lover. Her absence wouldn't go unnoticed. Even worse, a clever person might put Troy's murder together with her disappearance.

The cops always looked at relatives first.

Fine. If he couldn't obtain her quietly, he'd have her quietly abducted during a blood bath that would also serve to have law enforcement looking at the most obvious suspects. A whole gang of them.

He just needed to find out where she'd be and when.

CHAPTER TWENTY-NINE

Getting back last evening after another three-day trail ride with Morgan, it was damn fine to be back home. With family. With Erin.

Even if the day started with early morning chores. Dammit. Since Erin had the morning off in return for working late one day earlier this week, he'd planned to sleep in with her.

Instead, here he was in the garden.

Before leaving for work with Sunny, Virgil had conscripted Wyatt, Morgan, and Erin to harvest green beans.

The damn vegetables grew furiously at this time of year. Best to pick them now. No one liked them when the beans got too fat.

Erin was delighted to help. Kneeling by the bush beans, she was humming away as she worked on filling her bowl.

Morgan rolled his eyes. Having injured a knee in a rockfall, he hated any chore necessitating getting down on the ground. "Never saw anyone so happy to be kneeling."

Color rolled into Erin's face as she carefully avoided looking at Wyatt. Because she'd been on her knees last night, arms bound behind her back, blissfully sucking him off.

Morgan noticed her expression, caught on, and shot Wyatt an amused look.

To save her from getting teased, Wyatt diverted his brother by changing the subject. *This should be fun.* Tall tales were a time-honored tradition, after all. "Hey, bro, the last night in camp. You never said if you found whatever was screaming?"

Erin's head went up. "Screaming?"

He ignored her, keeping his focus on Morgan and injecting concern into his voice "Was it Quatcher?"

Back as children, they'd invented Quatcher—and many a client had fallen for the lure.

"Probably." Morgan caught on, and his lips quirked. "Found a lot of blood—and Quatcher's tracks. I'm guessing the old boy went head-on with a cougar."

Erin's eyes were wide. "One of your friends got attacked by a mountain lion?"

"Not a friend. And there's no telling which one attacked first." Wyatt gave Morgan a worried look. "You think Quatcher got hurt? If he did, we need to switch the next guide trip to a campsite a whole lot farther away."

"Yeah, he got hurt. There was black fur everywhere."

"Fuck. If he's wounded... Hell, he's over ten feet tall; nothing in the area will be safe."

"And those claws..." Morgan put two of his fingers together in a simulation of how big the creature's claws were. "Why do you think I had my rifle in hand when I was riding drag on the way out."

"Riding drag?" Erin asked.

"Last one in line keeps the herd together. Or for us, it means the rear guard. Stragglers are easy pickings, after all, especially when there's a raging wounded animal."

"Oh my God, seriously? It would go after *you*?" Beans forgotten, she was staring at him, absolutely horrified. "You said the bears here don't attack people."

"Usually don't attack, but Quatcher is a Sasquatch, not a

bear," Morgan explained—taking lead because Wyatt was having trouble not laughing.

Pick the beans. Don't laugh.

But her face...

"A Sasquatch. Like Bigfoot?"

Wyatt dared to look. When her eyes narrowed, he tried to smother his laughter and couldn't. It burst out—and he set Morgan off, and then they were both just roaring.

"You two had me terrified. Do you do this to your poor clients?" Laughing, Erin shook her head. "In time-honored tradition, might I just say, you guys are going to pay for this."

Wyatt managed to pull in a breath. "Do your worst, little mechanic. Do your worst."

A bag of small and a bag of large zip ties.

Five harmonicas she'd bought weeks ago, planning to use on the go-karts and surprise the children.

Erin smiled slowly. It was mid-morning, and Morgan and Wyatt were out riding, moving the cattle to a new pasture, checking fences, and doing whatever else cowboy types did before the sun grew too hot.

Oh and look, their pickups are sitting here all vulnerable. Such a shame.

The harmonicas fitted ever-so-nicely behind the grillwork on the front of Wyatt's vehicle. They were just waiting for him to get moving fast with a good wind flow.

Because he did love his tunes, right?

She mustn't neglect Morgan with his tall tales of blood and fur... Picking up the package of oversized zip ties, she attached five of them to the driveshaft, not cutting off the very long tails. Once the pickup headed down the drive, those tails would flutter and smack up against all the metal on each side of the shaft—and sounding like all sorts of things were loose.

Grinning, she put everything away and headed off to work.

Morgan's pickup was in the same spot when she got home.

Wyatt's though was in a new spot. A quick glance showed the harmonicas were gone.

Oh, damn, she'd wanted to watch him drive away and see how long it would take him to notice the *music*.

Come to think of it, the sound of harmonicas was subtle. He might well have reached the paved road before hearing them.

He wasn't downstairs, so she ran up to his apartment. She walked in and... "Uh-oh."

"Uh-oh, yeah. Good summation." Wyatt stood in the living room, muscular arms crossed over his chest. Face stern. "Woman, you fucked with my pickup. That's just plain wrong."

"It is?" She tried, honestly tried to keep a straight face. "But I thought you liked music, my Lord and Master. I was only trying to help."

His lips twitched.

Oh, she had him. *Don't laugh, though. Don't laugh.*

"Lord and Master? If you're thinking of me that way, you performed this sacrilege in your role as a submissive."

Wait, calling me submissive sounds like a trap. "Um, I don't think—"

"Which means my response needs to be as your Dominant. And as your Dominant, I think you need to be punished."

Seeing amusement and heat lighting his eyes, she took a hasty step back. A second later, he gripped her shirt front, pulled her forward, and was unzipping her jeans.

"Wait, I'm sorry. Seriously." She was giggling so hard the words came out tumbled together.

"You will be, subbie. You will be." He yanked her jeans down, sat on the ottoman, and had her belly-down over his knees before she could escape.

Smack.

"Ow! Hey." The stinging barely receded before he spanked her again and again. *Frickity-frick-frick-frick*, he had an appallingly hard hand.

She reached behind her to ward him off, and he pinned her wrist to her lower back. With his other hand, he massaged her burning bottom. "I love your ass. So perky and smooth."

His deliberately painful touch while mercilessly holding her in place sent a wave of heat through her. As she struggled, he tightened his grip even as he slid his hand between her thighs.

And touched her intimately.

"Pretty girl, you're wet. Does someone like being spanked?" His laugh was deeply masculine and pleased. Then the bastard continued. Spanking—and touching—and spanking.

Afterward, he flattened her on the couch and drove them both crazy.

A little while later, Morgan shouted up the stairs, "I'm heading out to the ClaimJumper. See you tomorrow."

Erin jumped up and ran to the window overlooking the drive.

Still lounging on the couch, Wyatt raised his eyebrows. "What are you doing?"

"I want to watch."

"Oh hell, you did Morgan's pickup too?" Grinning, Wyatt joined her.

The pickup made it past the barn before the brake lights came on. Morgan drove a little farther as if not believing what he heard.

The brake lights flashed red. The pickup started backing up to the house.

Erin was laughing so uncontrollably she almost choked.

CHAPTER THIRTY

"I love being out here." Four days later, Erin leaned her head against Wyatt's arm where it rested against the edge of the hot tub.

The almost-scalding water had bubbled away all the soreness in her back, butt, and thighs. Her back pain was because of a damn import car. She'd spent hours bent over the tiny engine with its miniscule parts.

After work, she'd had a riding lesson from Sawyer. "*Heels down.*" "*Use more leg.*" "*Shoulders back.*" Despite his quiet, smooth voice, he was as much a sadist as Wyatt—at least when it came to horseback riding.

The light, cool breeze from the mountains sent the rising steam swirling around them. Overhead, the night sky was pitch black with the golden circle of the moon overhead.

"This is so beautiful." She sighed and rubbed her head on Wyatt's arm. "I'm glad you're back. Did I say that?"

"Not in so many words." He gave her a squeeze. "But the enthusiastic way you bounced on my dick was a clue."

Oh god, she really had. At least with the heat, her face was already flushed. "Sorry?"

"Mmm, I'm not." He lifted her up and onto his lap, curling his hand around her hip to keep her in place. His kiss was as hot as the water around them. "You can bounce on my dick anytime your heart—or anything else—desires."

Had she ever felt so content in her life? Or so loved?

He'd shown up at her door with a handful of wild daisies and given her an ultralight daypack for when she hiked the nearby trails. It was a gorgeous bright scarlet—"*To make you easier to spot if needed*"—and already filled with emergency hiking supplies.

The message he conveyed—that he wasn't going to put walls around her, but he'd also do everything he could to keep her safe—left her feeling warm and cherished. He reminded her of Grampie who'd taught her to be a mechanic, then insisted she learn self-defense because she'd be working with a bunch of men.

They'd been officially together three weeks now. Three wonderful weeks. When Wyatt was gone on his guide trips, she kept busy with great friends, a fun job, clockwork repairs, and riding lessons. At the library, she'd read to preschoolers and build go-karts with budding mechanics.

When Wyatt was home, they spent most of their time together.

He'd take her riding, and she'd learned a horse's canter was totally like being in a rocking chair. So cool.

After presenting her with her very own throwing knives, he coached her until she could hit the bullseye every time. In September—when tourist season slowed—they'd go to a black powder rendezvous.

Wyatt made a contented rumbling sound. "I think the next ranch purchase will be a hot tub. However, we'd have to remodel the deck or put the tub farther away."

"Oh, far away sounds good." She grinned. "Sunny and I can watch through the kitchen window as you guys jump out and run naked through the snow back to the house."

"Eh, right. On the deck it is." His hands cupped her breasts, squeezing gently. "And, in case you forgot, you're staying in Bear

Flat. This winter, your bare ass will be one of those fleeing through the snow."

She bent, burying her face in his neck.

"Sweetheart, I can feel you smiling." He lifted her head so he could kiss her, a firm, way-too-brief kiss. "What are you thinking?"

"I..." Sharing was difficult. "We've been together a while now, and you're still making plans to be with me. In the future."

He stilled, his brows pulling together. "You thought I'd...lose interest?"

"I guess...yes? I'm kind of a boring person."

His shoulders moved in a shrug. "*Boring* can simply mean the other person doesn't share your interests." He chuckled. "In college, two of the most mind-numbingly boring professors got into a pushing and shouting match over identifying a *bug*. Neither of them was bored with each other."

She snorted.

"Of course, horse-people can put non-riders right to sleep; I'm sure I've done it before." His tone said it wasn't anything he worried about.

So why did she? *Dammit.* "I hadn't realized I let Troy undermine my confidence quite so far."

"Years of sneaky, critical comments'll do that."

It had. She'd have to work on her emotional health.

"Besides, a lying, lazy-ass politician and a hard-working, honest mechanic don't have much in common. You'll do far better here in Bear Flat—and with me." His voice dropped to a growling rumble as he whispered in her ear. "I find you very interesting."

The sexy sound of his voice sent tingles through her, but it was the way he met her gaze, the honesty in his eyes, that was absolutely devastating.

Her eyes filled with tears as her heart responded. Burying her face against his neck again, she whispered, "I love you."

His arms tightened around her until her next breath was in doubt. "Say it again."

"I love you. So much."

CHAPTER THIRTY-ONE

On Friday night, Erin walked into the barn, eyes widening. Wyatt hadn't been joking when he told her where the Serenity Lodge party would be held. "They're having it *here?*"

"Yep." He curved his hand over the back of her neck. "Jake and Kallie have a nice basement dungeon, but it's not big enough for both the locals and the Dark Haven folks. Besides, city people like going all country while they're here."

The wooden barn was huge with exposed rafters beneath the two-story ceiling. Stall-like structures lining the right and left walls showed the place had housed horses or cows at one time. Chains and ropes dangled from hooks embedded in various posts and beams.

One set of chains restrained a naked male with his arms secured over his head.

Erin took in a slow breath. *Okay. Wow.*

Three of the stalls had wooden X-frames between the posts to make rustic bondage crosses like the ones named for some saint. A helpful person had even attached cuffs to one.

Erin turned to Wyatt with a nervous look. There were an awful lot of restraints available.

Near the far end of the building, a huge wooden barrel lay

tipped on its side. A female submissive was stretched across it, ass high, with her wrists and ankles secured to eyebolts on each side.

Erin pursed her lips. She'd never look at a whiskey barrel the same way again.

Scattered down the center of the barn were straw bales, apparently for people to use as they wished. One Dom had draped a blanket over two stacked bales and was tying his submissive to the makeshift table.

Erin motioned toward the Dom. "Bondage, cowboy style?"

"We do love our knots." Wyatt grinned and guided her toward the corner nearest the door. "Here's the socializing area."

More straw and hay bales had been piled up to construct long couch and chair-like furniture and covered with red-and-black horse blankets. Barrels and stumps created end tables for drinks.

Closer to the wall, a long length of plywood topped a chest-high line of stacked hay bales. On the post behind the structure, "BAR" was written on a cardboard poster.

"There's alcohol?" Oh, excellent. She could use a drink now. Maybe two.

"There is." Wyatt tugged on a lock of her hair. "It's for people who've finished playing. Anyone who gets a drink has their hand marked to keep them honest."

"What a let-down." She pouted.

He laughed. "Let me introduce you to some of the Dark Haven people." He'd talked about the San Francisco BDSM club...and how he planned to take her there.

It wasn't fair he knew precisely how to make her both anxious and aroused.

Wyatt brought her to a man who was over six feet, dressed in a black western shirt and black jeans. He had eyes the color of night and a black braid down his back. "Xavier, this is Erin. Erin, the submissives address Xavier as My Liege. He owns Dark Haven."

Seriously?

The black eyes held amusement—and a sense of authority that made her think the title might be spot on.

She dipped her head slightly. "My Liege."

"It's good to meet you, Erin." His deep voice carried a hint of a European accent.

"Masterson, it's about time you showed up to a party in your own area." The raspy-sounding voice came from behind them.

Erin turned.

This Dom wore a black T-shirt, black leather pants, and black boots. He was maybe six-two, with a blond buzz-cut, and a face made for frowning. He came across as so military she wondered if his all-black attire was to conceal massive amounts of blood.

Hopefully not from submissives.

"Hey, merc. Good to see you." Wyatt shook the man's hand and slapped his shoulder. "DeVries, this is Erin."

The two Dark Haven Doms were intimidating in entirely different ways. Xavier made her feel like a beggar girl in front of royalty. DeVries—like a mouse in front of a hungry cat.

She swallowed. "I'm pleased to meet you both."

DeVries snorted. "Bullshit." He glanced at Wyatt. "You gonna beat her for lying? Be fun to watch."

She took a hasty step back.

Wyatt laughed, so open and honest it was like a warm shower after a freezing night. "He's trying to scare you, sweetheart. Social lies to strangers aren't the same as lying to your Dom."

Her sigh of relief was audible, and all three Doms grinned.

"Wyatt, is this Palmer's wife?" A strikingly handsome man strolled up—and she had to note the all-black theme was strong in this group.

With him was a blond man in a flashy red leather chest harness and a red jock strap. Short with big brown eyes, he reminded her of a puppy. Sheesh, even as a little girl, she hadn't been as cute.

"Yep." Wyatt turned to her. "This is Stan with Homeland

Security and his submissive, Dixon. I asked Stan to find out what he could about what's going on with the investigation."

He had? On second thought, she wasn't surprised. Wyatt had expressed his concerns about Troy's crimes impacting her—and that the Feds were awfully reticent about sharing.

"It's nice to meet you, Erin." The agent had a slow Texas drawl and a stunning smile. "Do you want an update now or later?"

Now meant the others in the group would hear. She had quite a few bitter memories of being stalked by reporters. But there was open interest in their expressions. She sighed in resignation. "Now is fine."

Wyatt pulled her closer and told Xavier and deVries, "In Buenos Aires, Palmer was tortured and murdered. He'd been blackmailing a senator, probably others."

"You think the senator went for revenge?" deVries asked and glanced at the Homeland Security agent.

"Possibly. The FBI thinks it's possible the murderer is searching for Palmer's blackmail material." Stan's expression was grim. "Erin's house in Sacramento was ripped apart by someone. After Palmer died, her house here might have been searched."

"Searched?" Erin stared at him. "I thought the intruder was a burglar."

"It's possible, but"—Stan shook his head—"the intruder's very long rap sheet doesn't include burglary. And nothing was taken."

"But the place wasn't trashed like the one in Sacramento." Wyatt frowned. "Perhaps the searcher knew what he was looking for?"

"How..." Erin's stomach turned over as she realized how the searcher would know. "Troy was tortured to find out where the blackmail stuff was?"

Stan nodded. "I'm sorry, Erin. But yes, it's what the agents in charge of the case believe."

The intruder hadn't stolen even the easy-to-pocket valuables.

An ugly feeling grew in her belly. "The searcher wasn't carrying anything when he left. Whatever he was looking for, he might not have found it."

"Nothing was found on his body either." Stan's gaze was level. "It might behoove you to think over where Palmer might have hidden blackmail material."

"Like..." She raised her hands, feeling helpless. "What would I look for? Files? Photos? DVDs?"

Stan's smile was kind. "Our criminals have advanced to the digital age. I would guess there are photos and MP3 files on storage devices like USB flash drives."

"Interesting," Xavier said. "Not in the cloud?"

"This year, it's not as common. Not after recent cases where the prosecutors got into the perps' online storage."

DeVries snorted. "Your government hackers at work. Good to see."

"Isn't it though?" Stan grinned. "Well, all this talk of bad guys has my blood heated up. Are you fixin' to beat on my boy here, deVries?"

What?

The military-looking man's gaze swept over the blond cutie like he was...was prey.

"Sounds good. I haven't heard any screaming recently." DeVries' harsh voice sandpapered up Erin's spine. "Some blood won't mess up this old barn. You ready to squeal, boy?

Dixon's brown eyes went wide, and he shivered.

Erin took a step forward. Surely, they wouldn't let the sadist hurt—

An arm went around her waist, pulling her back. Wyatt whispered in her ear. "Dixon's a masochist, sugar. He wants—and doesn't want—everything deVries will do to him."

Erin frowned.

Dixon *did* look almost as eager as he did scared.

"That's exactly how you looked when I said how I'm going to

hurt you tonight." Wyatt's rough voice held laughter. "You're as excited as you are terrified."

She swallowed hard. Because he was right.

DeVries gripped the submissive's hair.

When Dixon let out a pained, aroused sound, deVries' eyes lit. Then he dragged the submissive away.

"On that note"—Wyatt grinned at the other Doms—"if you'll excuse us, I want to show Erin the other scenes before I tie her down and have a mite of fun."

Xavier's mouth quirked. "I've seen what you consider fun. She's in for an interesting time."

Interesting? How can such a normal word sound so scary?

A new song came on with a refrain of "turn me on". She blinked, tilting her head to listen.

"The band is named Whip Culture." Stan grinned. "Wyatt and I think it's a shame there's a scarcity of BDSM-inspired country-western music."

Erin choked at the concept. And yet... She eyed Wyatt. Obviously, there were cowboys into kink.

"See you all later." Wyatt nodded to the men and led Erin to where he'd left what he called a toy bag. "Let's get you into a harness."

"But...why?"

He held up a finger. "One. You're overdressed for a submissive." Another finger. "Two. You have gorgeous breasts. It's a shame not to share your beauty with my fellow Doms." With the third finger, he smiled. "Three. It will get you into the right headspace. Say: *yes, Sir.*"

Was she crazy to be here? The barn wasn't quiet. The music was whispering about sex. There was the rhythmic splatting of a flogger on bare skin. Voices whimpered, cried, moaned, gave low-voiced instructions and edgier commands. Someone across the room climaxed with a high scream.

Her whole body was humming. Sensitive. Pulling in a breath, she looked up.

Wyatt's lips curved slightly beneath his mustache, yet his gaze held no impatience. He'd wait until she was ready. He had a wicked sense of humor, but was caring, responsible. Honest. So very honest.

And I love him.

"This BDSM stuff is harder to do than it sounded like in my books." She glanced around. "Especially around other people."

"True enough." He touched her face, traced a finger over her lower lip. "Your safeword is red—and you can always call a halt. Do you trust me, Erin?"

He held her gaze with his, and the barn around them seemed to disappear.

"Yes." Could she be as honest as he was? "I want you to take control." She swallowed. "To take...me."

"Then the shirt needs to go." He smiled slowly, amusement in his eyes.

"Right. Um, yes, *Sir*."

The approval in his eyes made her wish for a tail she could wag. How pitiful. With a sigh, she pulled her top off, and when he tapped her bra, she removed it too. "I thought guys wore harnesses. Not women."

"For women, it can be a kind of breast bondage." He pulled a dark brown leather contraption out of his toy bag. The collar fastened around her neck. Straps extended downward from it to an O-ring between her breasts. More straps circled each breast, almost like a leather outline of a bra, and fastened in the back. Her breasts were bare—and by the time Wyatt finished tightening the buckles around the back and beneath each bra "cup", her breasts bulged outward.

He ran a finger beneath each strap, checking the fit. "Perfect. Comfortable?"

Was he serious? "Comfortable isn't the word I'd use."

His grin flashed below the dark mustache. "Let me rephrase. Does anything hurt?"

She shook her head.

"Use your words, sweetheart."

"Nothing hurts." But she couldn't help putting her hands over her chest in involuntary concealment.

"None of that now." He pulled a set of leather cuffs from his bag. "Hands behind your back, please." He waited for her to comply.

Even as a hot thrill ran through her, she realized her breathing had gone all fast and funny. She'd be restrained. Her neck already felt odd—because *collar!*—but to remove her ability to use her hands?

Okay, okay, I can do this. She lowered her gaze and obeyed.

"What a good submissive," he said softly, and her cheeks warmed at the praise.

After fastening the fur-lined wrist cuffs together behind her back, he stood in front of her. His focused gaze swept her from top to bottom. "You look beautiful in the harness, Erin."

The honest appreciation in his eyes flustered her.

Slowly, deliberately, he fondled her breasts.

With leather around the bases, her full breasts were bulging outward, the tightened skin heightening every sensation. She gasped and tried to move away, but he put an arm behind her to keep her in place.

Instinctively, she tugged on her wrists to get free. And got nowhere.

"Sugar." His rugged face held amused sympathy. "Now you understand. Your naked breasts are available for anything I want to do. And you can't push me away."

Her anxiety mounted—even as her core turned into a needy pool of hot lava. Her nipples bunched into throbbing dagger-points of anticipation.

"Now, let's wander around so you can see what happens in a dungeon."

"I can't walk around like—like *this*." He wanted her to stroll around, half naked? With her arms restrained?

"Sweetheart, most submissives wear something similar. If

they're not naked now, they probably will be by the end of the night."

"I think I'd rather be the Dominant," she muttered, and he cracked up.

How could his laughter always make her feel better? Like everything was all right—and the universe was filled with fun.

Right beside her, he slowly guided her around the barn.

There were so many scenes going on already. Lots of mild to heavy floggings, canings, and whippings. Spankings too. Submissives sprouted clamps of all kinds, including around testicles and balls.

Poor Dixon had clothespins down there, and the sadist deVries was using a whip to flick them off.

Watching with a smile, Stan stood beside a streaky-haired brunette about Erin's age. The woman wore pink hot pants and a vinyl top.

"Is Dixon with Stan or deVries?" Erin whispered.

"He's with Stan but needs more pain than Stan is comfortable handing out. DeVries is a heavy sadist—more than Lindsey can take"—Wyatt nodded toward the brunette—"so deVries and Dixon get together for S&M before they play with their partners."

"Huh." How would she feel if Wyatt wanted to play with another woman? How was that different from what Troy did? "The idea is a bit unsettling."

"People are complex—and at times one person can't or doesn't want to participate in their partner's kink. This kind of arrangement can work well if everyone communicates honestly and is open to compromise."

"Compromise?"

"Lindsey's okay with deVries playing with men—not women —and she enjoys watching. What's between deVries and Dixon is purely pain, so Stan's comfortable."

Compromise indeed. Erin watched deVries whip another

clothespin off Dixon's balls. *Owwww.* Yeah, if she was Lindsey, she wouldn't want deVries anywhere near her with a whip.

She turned to look at Wyatt. "Are you... Is there... Will you want, need, um, compromises like that?"

He chuckled, lifting her chin with his fingers so he could kiss her. So gently. "No, Erin. People—kinky people, Dominants, submissives—come in all varieties. What I enjoy is giving only enough pain to increase your pleasure. If what we need changes for either of us, we'll talk. But honestly, I don't see it happening."

Thank heavens. The relief was enough to make her sag against him.

"Let's head toward the back. There's a convenient batch of hay bales there."

Oh, oh, oh, she was really going to do this.

She glanced at the other scenes as they went past. To her shock, the beautician, Katelyn, was gagged on a cross thing. A man was using a riding crop on her bottom.

Noticing them, Katelyn glared at Erin.

The hatred felt like being splashed with dirty water, and Erin turned her back.

Wyatt sighed. "I'm sorry she's taking her anger at me out on you." He ran his hand through his hair. "I scened with her three times at Dark Haven. Nothing other than pickup scenes in a club. Over a year ago. She won't accept that I'm not interested in more."

Erin bumped him with her shoulder. "You're too sexy for your own good."

The worry in his expression faded. "The question is, am I too sexy for *your* own good? Let's find out."

He set his toy bag on a hip-high bale arrangement.

Next to it was a "bondage table" made of hay bales and covered with a thick horse blanket. "Up you go." Hands on her waist, he lifted her to sit on it.

After unfastening her wrists, he helped her lie back. "You are so beautiful," he murmured, running his hand over her swollen breasts and kissing her. "Now, sweetheart, what's your safeword?"

"Red."

"At some point, I might gag you." He waited for a protest, one eyebrow up.

The idea of being silenced was disconcertingly exciting, and she said nothing.

His lips tilted up. "Very good. If you're gagged, you can hoot twice, and I'll also give you a squeaky ball to hold. Squeaks or hoots are your nonverbal safeword. Make sense?"

"Yes, oh Lord and Master."

"Very nice." His lips twitched. "Make sure you use my titles when you beg me to stop...or keep going."

When he said things like that in such a low-pitched, rough voice, she wasn't sure she'd remember her own name, let alone what to call him.

Those big, dark-blue eyes. Wyatt had never seen anything so beautiful, especially the way they widened as he attached her wrist cuffs to the ropes running between the hay bale layers. When he finished, her arms were secured at her sides.

"Now, let's get my playground opened up." He had to smother a smile when she realized what he meant by *playground*.

Slowly, thoroughly enjoying himself, he removed her shoes and socks, unzipped and pulled off her jeans and briefs. He traced a finger over the crease between her right thigh and groin and felt her quiver.

Bending her left knee, he roped her heel against the back of her thigh in a basic frog tie and did the same on the right. He finished by securing her knees outward with the bale ropes.

He did like a splayed open position.

Stepping back, he performed a quick check. Her breathing was fast, her color flushed. Hands were warm, fingertips and toes pink. "Any pain or tingling? Are your hips and legs comfortable for a while in this position?"

"It's good." Her voice was nicely throaty already.

"All right then." He kissed her slowly as he fondled her breasts. So pretty. "I'm going to make your nipples—and clit bigger. The better to play with."

After lubing a suction device's rim to make a better seal, he pressed the cylinder over her right nipple. Twisting the cap created a vacuum that pulled her whole areola up and into the cylinder.

Her eyes widened, and she made an adorable sound of both excitement and distress.

He stopped, giving her a chance to adjust to the sensation, while he did her left breast. Stepping back, he eyed her and increased the suction on each device until her muscles tightened, and she started tugging on her hands.

"Breathe now." He kissed her even as he ran his fingers around her breasts. Her heart was pounding a frantic beat—from anxiety or pain? "I won't leave these on very long. Just long enough to make those pink nipples nice and puffy." Meeting her eyes, he waited.

Her gaze clung to his, her vulnerability open and honest, and then she drew in a slow breath, and he saw the sweet yielding. Her trust was the finest of gifts.

"Brave, blue girl." He touched her cheek before picking up a different suction device, this one a cylinder with a hand pump.

While moving to the end of the bale, he ran his hands over her body to make sure she knew he was there and so she wouldn't feel abandoned.

Now, for the next pink, puffy goal.

Watching her face, he ran his finger around her pussy, so nice and wet. He did a circle around her small, hooded clit. Pulling her labia farther open, he fitted the suction device over the vulnerable nub.

She stared at him in pure shock.

Just wait, little subbie. He squeezed the hand pump.

As her clit got sucked up into the cylinder, her back arched. She gasped.

Oh yeah. "One more, blue girl." He waited a second and pumped again. Her legs twitched, trying to get free. Her moan made his dick harden.

"Perfect. You're such a good girl." He ran his hands up and down her wide-open thighs as blood engorged her defenseless little clit. "Only a few minutes and they'll come off."

But if she thought they'd stop here, she was in for a surprise.

He could hear people moving around the barn, but his focus was all on Erin, her breathing, her eyes, her muscles. The quivers shaking the suction devices on her chest.

Her leg muscles had relaxed under his palms. Now to ensure her body would read anything he did as pleasure.

Pulling out two vibrators, he lubed one. Opening her labia, he set one against her pussy and the lubed one against her ass. Slowly, steadily, he pushed them both in.

"No!"

They'd talked about anal sex, and she thought she'd like to try it. He was too big for taking her there tonight. But this vibe was nicely slender. He held both devices in place. "Look at me, Erin." He waited until she met his gaze.

She swallowed hard, breathing fast.

"Look at you, all tied down, with your pussy and ass stuffed full." He stroked above the suction device, running his fingers over her pelvis. Feeling her trembling. "Very soon, it'll be my dick in your pussy. But first, you'll experience a different kind of fun."

A little edging, a little pain, up and up.

As she started to relax at the sound of his voice, he turned the vibrators on.

. . .

Aaaah. It's too much, too much. There were things vibrating inside her, not only in her pussy, but in her butt too. Making her whole pelvis hum.

And her nipples and clit were…were… There were no words for the sensations. Like someone—three someones—were sucking on her girl bits unrelentingly, to the point of pain. Pulling and twisting and burning sorts of sensations.

The vibrators kept humming, and Wyatt kept touching her, running a warm hand over her legs, over her stomach. Kissing her lightly. Never leaving her alone. He was totally in control yet *with* her at the same time.

Returning to the end of the bale, he studied her pussy for a moment before gripping each vibrator. He slowly pulled them out—and pushed them back in.

The slick friction against sensitive nerve endings sent streamers of pleasure rushing through her. Her hips jerked upward, making the suction thing on her clit bounce. She froze, unmoving as he penetrated her with the dildo vibrators over and over, until…

Frickity-frick, she needed to come so bad.

She tried to close her trembling legs. The inability to move made all the sensations more intense. She moaned.

And then he stopped.

When he chuckled, she opened her eyes. He was standing beside her left shoulder, looking down. The wicked amusement in his dark eyes was purely masculine. With one finger, he stroked the undersides of her breasts, leisurely teasing her as her whole body throbbed in desperate need.

She couldn't stop herself from whining.

His lips tilted up. "All ready for more, are you? Then brace yourself." He unscrewed the nipple devices. The pulling, tugging sensations eased, and he removed them.

Lifting her head slightly, she stared at her breasts. The nipples were much darker and puffed up in the shape of the cylinder. So, so much bigger they didn't look like hers at all.

"Mmm, so rosy." Wyatt bent and closed his lips around one.

Oh god. His mouth was searingly hot. His wet tongue slid mercilessly over one impossibly sensitive nipple and the other. The pleasure was too intense.

All the sensations coalesced—the vibrators buzzing inside her, the ferocious suction on her clit, his mouth on her breast. Suddenly, she was coming violently, shaking as her insides spasmed around the dildos.

As the waves of pleasure slowly eased, he licked around her nipples, laughing under his breath with each tiny aftershock he caused. "Very nice. Let's get the clit pump off."

Moving to the end of the hay bale, he turned off the vibrators and left them in. The overly full sensation didn't ease.

Slowly, he released the suction device on her clit and removed it, ignoring her futile jerks at the jolts of sensation. "Look." He took a mirror from his bag and held it between her legs.

Raising her head, she stared at the reflection. Her aching clit was *big*, at least three times the size it should be, like a foreign, dark pink thing.

"No." Her voice came out a whisper.

"Yes. Just right in fact. I'm going to enjoy torturing it."

What? Wait...

After setting the mirror back in his bag, he ran his finger around the swollen, puffy ball of nerves.

"Ooooh." Her clit felt different, less sensitive—yet more so. Just the brush of his touch was so painfully pleasurable it stole her breath.

Bending, he ran his tongue around her clit, teasing her with the lashing pleasure. Making her wiggle uncontrollably.

Inside, the heat started to grow again. Her breathing quickened.

"No, not yet, little subbie." He attached clamps to her labia, two high and two low, in one pinching pain after another.

"Owww." Her voice came out a total whine.

He just laughed. Using rope to tie the clamps to her thighs, he tightened the lines and pulled her folds farther apart. "There now. You're spread wide open." His voice grew deeper, rougher. "Now I can do anything I want to your pretty bits."

As her anxiety rose, all her muscles tightened. Nothing had ever made her feel so vulnerable as being exposed—open—like this. *Nothing.*

"No." She shook her head. "Stop."

He held her gaze, absently rolling her mound between his fingers, indirectly teasing her clit. His dark eyes were almost tender. "Do you honestly want me to stop?"

Her breathing was fast. Her eyes filled with tears...because she didn't. He scared her and cared for her...and broke her until she couldn't keep from showing it all.

He'd stop if she needed him to—yet the little smile on his hard lips showed he enjoyed everything he was doing to her. Savored her reactions.

Her mouth opened to say something. To use the safeword.

And the yielding feeling in her chest, the melting feeling in her bones kept her silenced. She whispered *no* in answer to his question.

Because she wanted him to do...everything.

His intent gaze caught every breath she took. Her pulse pounded against his palm, which lay over the artery between her hip and thigh. He tilted his head, reading her fear, her desire.

Her surrender.

His eyes warmed. "There's a brave girl. All right, then, let's get you ready."

Slowly, mercilessly, he worked both dildos in and out, building her edgy need until it turned the pain of the clamps into something...other. Until her whole pussy was throbbing again. She could hear how wet she was.

Her eyes opened wide when he pulled the pussy vibrator out, leaving the other inside. Leaving her insides aching.

Then he tapped his fingers on her mound.

The surprising sensation jolted all the way down to her clit. Not pain, just pure heat.

He struck her with the same two fingers lower, between her wide-open labia.

She jumped, yet the sting only increased her need. Made her want...more.

He'd been watching her face, and now his gaze met hers. "I'm going to hurt you, sweetheart, until you come again and again. And then I'm going to take you."

No. She shook her head in refusal.

Dark amusement gleamed in his eyes. Because they both knew he wasn't going to stop unless she used her safeword. The shaking in her core only increased the need running through her veins.

Picking up a thin wooden ruler, he slapped it on his palm—and the harsh sound was terrifying. Before she could react, he smacked it lightly on her mound, left, right, over and over. Each blow stung like fire...and washed away in a heavy heat.

God, she needed to come. "Please, please, I need..."

"Ah, right, you need a gag." His mouth was set in a stern line, his eyes held compassion as he took a red ball gag from his bag. "Open up, subbie."

"But, but..." She stared at him. His head tilted slightly, his gaze darkening, and her mouth simply dropped open.

"Good girl." The ball went in, and he buckled the leather straps behind her head. "Too tight?"

The ball wasn't huge, not like others she'd seen, and she could breathe all right. "Mmmph."

She. Couldn't. Talk. She tried to remove it, but her arms were restrained. She could do nothing, say nothing. Her utter helplessness was terrifying. She panted—and whined.

Wyatt cupped her chin and forced her to meet his gaze. "Erin, I won't leave you. You're safe with me."

His hand was warm, his eyes level. Not concerned, not

worried. Because whatever happened, he'd handle it. His self-confidence was as comforting as it was devastating.

"Mmmph." The sound was uncertain, just like her.

"Poor subbie." Beneath the dark mustache, a corner of his mouth tilted. "Remember, your safeword is two hoots or"—he tucked a fuzzy ball in her left hand—"a squeaking ball. Show me."

She squeaked it and was totally relieved at the high, piercing sound he couldn't ignore.

"Okay?"

Her "mmmph" came out grumpy.

The fricking bastard Dom laughed. "Let's see what other sounds you can make." He curved powerful fingers around her jaw, keeping her face turned toward him while he fondled her breasts and tugged on her ultra-tenderized nipples.

"Mmmmh." Her moan widened his smile. And when he bent and sucked and tongued her nipples, her toes curled, and she moaned again.

He'd left the ruler lying on her belly. Picking it up, he lightly slapped her swollen right breast, under, over, then the left one. The sound—and feel—on her bare, tight skin was shocking.

Above, below. With each blow, the fearful anticipation of where he'd strike next—and when he'd hit her nipples—grew and grew. She held her breath, cringing away even as her nipples bunched up tight.

Smack. The wooden length slapped her right nipple, shocking through her senses.

"Mmmph, mmmph!"

Smack. The left nipple. After each explosion of pain, the burn turned to pure arousal. And when he bent and licked over each jagged point, the brutal pleasure sent tremors through her.

One more time with the ruler, he did it all again, zeroing in on her nipples, sucking until she felt nothing but his mouth on her.

Then he straightened...and walked to the end of the bale.

Blood thrummed in her veins, faster and faster, as he looked down at her *pussy*. *Oh no, oh god, oh no.*

But he started slow, tapping his horrible ruler in lightly stinging smacks up her thighs and over her mound. Circling like a jackal around its prey.

He touched the end between her gaping folds as if to warn her before his fingers slid inside her. Not filling her, but ooooh, the hot sensation in her needy pussy was heavenly. The ruler came down on her mound in a stinging slap of exquisite pleasure —and her insides clenched his fingers.

"You're getting wetter, blue girl." His voice had grown rougher, deeper. His impaling fingers wiggled. "I look forward to how you'll feel around my cock."

He slapped her mound again. Harder.

"Mmmph!"

Leaning forward, he licked over her hugely distended clit.

Intense pleasure boiled up and turned into a pulsing need to come. His fingers slid slowly in and out of her as his tongue teased over her. Closing his lips tightly around her clit, he sucked, and the sensation was so incredible, her hips tried to rise for more.

He chuckled and straightened.

Smack. Smack. Smack. The ruler struck. *Right. On. Her. Clit.*

Pain rose in a burning ball of sensation. His fingers thrust forcefully. And *everything* inside her exploded in unstoppable waves of pleasure.

"Mmm, mmm, mmm!" Her hips jolted up and down.

Smack, smack, smack. Hot pain filled her before his mouth closed on her clit, driving her into another orgasm.

So much pleasure. The world around her turned white, and all she could hear was her pulse hammering through her arteries.

Minutes later, she was still gasping and shuddering as he undid the labia clamps. The hot rush of blood to the abused flesh made her quiver. And the evil cowboy grinned and massaged her folds, making everything worse.

"Easy, there. Let's get this off." He removed her gag and gently wiped her mouth. One by one, he removed her restraints. Lifting her easily, he set her onto her hands and knees on the lower hay bale where his toy bag had been.

Her arms gave out, dropping her down to her elbows on the thick blanket. Her head sagged.

After a moment, she heard a condom wrapper tear. Then his powerful hands pulled her knees apart, and his groin pressed against her buttocks...because the hay bale was just the right height for this position.

"Here, let's add some fun." He pulled her buttocks apart. The long anal plug began to vibrate, and she squeaked in shock.

He chuckled, massaging her buttocks. "You're so adorable." A second later, he pressed his cock against her pussy—and took her in one ruthless thrust.

"*Aaaah*." He wasn't a small man. Between his cock and the anal thing, she was terrifyingly full. Her insides clamped around both so hard the vibrations felt as if they were shaking her.

He braced one hand on the blanket beside her shoulder, and his chest was against her back as he whispered in her ear. "Mmm, little blue. I can feel the vibrator—and you shivering."

After the initial thrust, he hadn't moved, had given her time to adjust. He rubbed his chin against her hair, his rough voice a dark murmur. "Now, I'm going to take you."

Her heart rate picked up. When he nipped her shoulder, adding a jolt of pain, tremors of need ran through her.

Yes, take me. Yes. All of her pushed to be possessed. Owned.

Straightening, he closed his hands on her hips, pulling out slowly, pressing in. And then he took her indeed. The deep, driving thrusts made her pussy tighten and spasm around him. The vibrator kept going, adding to all the sensations, feeding into everything until she needed to come.

Again. She pushed back against him. Wiggled.

And he laughed. "Needy little subbie." He straightened and pulled her up, fully onto her knees, keeping her back against his chest. Still deep within her, his cock shifted, adding pressure to the anal plug, making her whine.

With one hand, he covered her left breast. The other hand—oh god, the other was on her slick clit. Rubbing firmly. The sensations were overwhelming.

He drove her up and up almost to the pinnacle before easing back. With light touches and slow thrusts, he mercilessly held her there as she shuddered on the very edge of ecstasy.

"Come for me, Erin." His finger rubbed over her clit, his hand squeezed her breast, and he thrust in, strong and fast.

Too much. She came, screaming and shaking, as the vibrations and sensations swept through her, back to front, breasts to clit, shattering her world into a lake of pure liquid pleasure.

Holding her against him, he drove into her with short, hard thrusts that kept her climax roaring—until finally he pressed deep, finding his own release.

Oh, oh, oh. She felt as if her entire being had dissolved into a tingling tangled mess.

Bending his head, he rubbed his cheek against hers. "You are magnificent," he murmured, his voice like gravel.

And everything inside her went limp and happy at his words.

CHAPTER THIRTY-TWO

After being cuddled in Wyatt's lap and drinking Gatorade, Erin had been wrapped in a soft blanket to sit while the big cowboy put everything away and cleaned up. It'd felt wrong to let him do the work, but her muscles and bones had turned into overcooked noodles. When he'd removed her harness and put her in one of his big soft T-shirts and her jeans, her fingers had been so fumbly, he'd done all the buttoning and zipping. He'd even helped her into her socks and sneakers.

The scene, the sex, her surrender—it had all left her shaky inside. And then, rather than ignoring her after sex—as she'd kind of expected—he was even more tender and caring.

When she turned all teary-eyed, he held her again for a while.

Now, as they crossed the barn, she had to admit her tender bits were grateful for the softness of his shirt. He'd said she could go bare on the bottom half, but *ha*, not a chance.

And boy, she kind of wanted to curl back up into the blanket. Her whole body felt languorous with satisfaction.

"Are we leaving now?" Glancing around, she saw a lot of the equipment was now empty. Only a few scenes were still going on.

"Nope, we'll socialize for a bit."

Grateful for Wyatt's muscular arm around her waist, Erin leaned against him as he guided her to the social corner.

Over at the hay bale bar, Dixon and Stan were bartending. Around the drink area, hay bale couches and chairs made several conversational groupings.

In one, Katelyn sat on a floor cushion, talking with several people Erin didn't know.

Please, Wyatt, don't take us over there.

Instead, Wyatt chose an area with only one person—the streaky-haired brunette who'd stood with Stan and watched deVries and the cutie. Seated on the floor, she was wearing comfortable-looking, pink sweats.

But... Erin stiffened.

Tears were streaming down the woman's face. She was obviously upset—and no one was helping her. That wasn't right.

Setting her bottle of Gatorade on a stump end table, Erin pulled away from Wyatt and knelt beside her. "Are you all right? Did someone hurt you?"

Eyes still filled with tears, the woman half-chuckled. "What a question to ask at a BDSM party."

Erin grinned even as she recognized the Texas drawl. Were the Texans invading California? "Good point. Still—is there anything I can do to help?"

"Don't I wish, but 'fraid not." The woman swiped her hands over her damp face.

Erin waited.

"It's..." The woman lowered her voice to a whisper. "I'm fixin' to have a baby in another six months. And, oh my effing God, *everything* is making me bust out in tears."

Erin patted her knee and whispered back, "*Congratulations.* Not for the tears, but for the baby. Is it a secret?"

"Kind of." Lindsey was still whispering.

Erin glanced over her shoulder and was pleased to see Wyatt had moved away to give them privacy. *The cowboy has old-fashioned manners. Does that make him a gentleman cowboy?* Standing near the bar, he was turned far enough to keep an eye on her. He winked and continued talking with Dixon.

"Should I ask why it's a secret?" Erin asked the woman. "Do you need help?"

"You are an awfully nice person. I'm Lindsey, by the way. And it's just... I wanted to let Mama know before everyone else." She scowled. "I was going to tell Zander tomorrow, but he figured out I had a secret, and during our scene, the dirty weasel-dog sadist pushed until I told him."

"Ohhh. I can see how interrogation might be easy for a sadist to do." When Wyatt wielded his ruler, well, if he'd wanted her to confess to something, she would've told him anything. "You know, if he's the only person who knows, your mama will understand. Just make sure she's next. I won't tell anyone."

"Thank you." Lindsey looked up and smiled. "Lookie there, it's one of the Mastersons. Is this one your Dom?"

Wyatt had returned. Did he want to be known as her Dom? How should she answer? "Umm."

"Yes, he is," Wyatt said firmly. "Come here, li'l subbie." He lifted Erin to her feet.

Taking a blanket from a nearby stack, he folded it into a makeshift floor cushion beside the opposing couch. "Sorry, but submissives don't sit on the furniture. Serenity's barn rules."

"What?" She gave him a suspicious look before checking around.

Scantily-dressed people—no matter the gender—were seated on the floor. *Huh.* Careful of her very tender lady bits, she settled on the blanket.

"All right there?" Wyatt sat behind her on the couch and stroked her hair with a gentle hand.

"Mmmhmm." Wrapping an arm around his leg, she leaned her head against his muscular thigh and felt oddly content. She had nothing to worry about. No plans to make.

She tilted her head to look back at him. "Just checking—is Zander another name for deVries?"

"That's right."

"Okay then."

Joining them, Xavier seated a blonde woman on a blanket and took a seat on the chair next to her. "Abby, this is Erin, who came with Wyatt. Erin, my Abby."

"It's nice to meet you." Abby smiled.

"I'm pleased to meet you." Seeing Abby tugging with a frown on her red bustier, Erin cast her a sympathetic look. Big breasts were difficult to confine.

Taking a seat behind Lindsey, deVries curled her fingers around a bottle of water. "Drink up, Tex. All of it."

She heaved a loud sigh. "Here, I thought Master PushyPants was bad before."

Biting her cheek to keep from laughing, Erin waited for the whip-wielding sadist to overreact to the insult. Then she blinked.

The scary guy had a *dimple*. Completely composed, even amused, he gave Lindsey a quick kiss.

"Is Ethan here tonight?" Wyatt asked. "He mentioned he was planning to come—and hoped to bring a woman."

The Dark Haven people all smiled.

Xavier added, "He was, but we had a problem at Dark Haven with his submissive at the heart of it. She was unsettled afterward, so they're staying at home. You'll like her, Wyatt. She's sociable, tactful, and down to earth. Bring Erin to San Francisco and meet her."

They were including her as if she truly was Wyatt's. The feeling of belonging was heartwarming.

Over at the bar, she heard Dixon's distinctive laugh and looked over to see him talking to the submissives. Once their order was up, each submissive happily took the drinks back to their Dom.

One older man, naked except for nipple clamps and a cock device, got his drinks and knelt to present one to a woman in a black catsuit. He looked utterly thrilled when she accepted the drink.

It seemed submission was definitely non-sexist.

And, when in Rome... She turned and took Wyatt's hand. "Oh, Lord and Master..."

He didn't...quite...grin, but laughter lit his eyes, even as he raised his eyebrows in inquiry.

A quiver ran through her. He didn't have fine-boned, model-like looks. No, her cowboy had weathered skin, a rugged face, and his nose had been broken at least once.

And he could make her melt with just one look.

Her question came out husky. "Might I bring you a drink?"

His expression softened, and he put two fingers under her chin, running his thumb over her lower lip. Reminding her of when she'd taken him in her mouth. The taste of him.

She ducked her head enough to catch his thumb between her lips and run her tongue over it.

Chuckling, he leaned forward and said in a low voice, "We'll work on protocol later. But...just so you know, doing that is likely to get you face-fucked."

He...he wouldn't.

The glint in his eyes said he would.

Leaning back, he smiled. "A beer would go down good right now, thank you." He picked up her Gatorade from the stump end-table. "Finish this, and you can have whatever drink you'd like."

It was an order—yet she loved how he noticed and worried. Glugging down the last of the drink, she set it on the table and mouthed, "Bossy, bossy, bossy."

Because how could she not?

His lips quirked. She'd noticed quite a few Dominants didn't tolerate backtalk. Probably most of them. But... Nothing seemed to unbalance Wyatt. Maybe because he got his way no matter how much someone snarked at him.

As if to prove it, he gripped the front of her shirt, yanked her close, and kissed the disobedience right out of her.

Her head was still spinning as she headed for the bar.

"Hey, sweet cheeks, what can I get you?" Dixon asked, dancing around his big partner—and taking every opportunity to wiggle his ass against the agent.

"A beer and a hard cider." Leaning forward, she confided, "I'm not sure, but I have a feeling Wyatt would spank my butt if I teased him like that."

"Stan will too." After setting the drinks on the bar top, Dixon waggled his ass. "Which is exactly the point."

He said the words a bit too loudly, and Stan grabbed his hair, tilting his head back. "No spanking for you, boy. You like it too much. I'm fixin' to put you in a spiked chastity device and make you watch porn."

"Holy fag-fucking-doodles." Dixon's horrified expression made Erin snort with laughter.

"Excuse me?" When Stan crossed his arms over his chest, authority filled the air around him like steam from a punctured red-hot radiator.

"I'm sorry, my Master, my wonderful, forgiving, awesome-sauce Master." Dixon lifted pleading puppy-dog eyes to Stan.

Huh. Erin pouted. Why hadn't she gotten big brown eyes? Talk about effective.

"It's good you're sorry." Lifting a cane from the bar top, Stan glanced at her. "Got your drinks?"

She grabbed the bottles and backed up. "Sir, yes, Sir."

A stifled snort of laughter came from Dixon. The cane made a whishing sound—and Dixon squeaked, holding his bare balls with both hands.

Owsers. Knowing how much getting smacked on private areas hurt, she shot Dixon a sympathetic look before noticing he had a very enthusiastic erection.

Ah-huh, he really was a masochist, wasn't he?

When she got back to Wyatt, he glanced toward the bar. "Is Dixon giving Stan trouble?"

"I think he tried." She half-grinned. "From what I saw, his Master is fully capable of handling him."

Wyatt grinned and accepted his beer, taking a long slow drink. "Thank you, sweetheart. I didn't realize how much I wanted one."

Happiness at pleasing him, at his acknowledgment warmed her heart.

"Hey, Dark Havenites. It's good to have you back here."

Erin stared as Morgan dropped down on a straw bale chair. *Wyatt's...brother. Here?*

From what Sunny had let drop, she knew Virgil was into kink. But Morgan too? She eyed his black clothing.

Since he was sitting on a chair, not a blanket, he was, obviously, one of the Dominants.

From what she'd seen here, there were a lot of different kinds of Doms. Some strutted and were in-your-face bossy. With others, the authority was all on the surface with no real pool of power.

Then there were the ones like deVries who should be wearing sergeant's stripes to go with his aura of command.

Or Xavier... She had trouble even meeting his gaze, and how weird was that?

Wyatt... Hmm. He certainly had his own more-easy-going style. Yet, both here and on the trail, when he said something, even if it didn't sound like an order, it still was, and everyone did what he said. Her lips quirked.

I'm calling his style trail-boss dominance.

Now, she'd have to watch Morgan and see what kind of authority he wielded.

Wait... How long had he been in the barn? Had he seen Wyatt putting stuff on her nipples and pussy? *Frickity-frick-frick-frick.*

As heat crept into her cheeks, she buried her face against Wyatt's thigh.

Morgan saw Erin look at him. When her face turned red, he figured he knew what she was thinking. Because he'd arrived in time to catch the end of his brother's scene with the newbie.

Meeting Wyatt's gaze, Morgan glanced at her and grinned.

Wyatt looked down to see her hiding her face, and he grinned too.

Embarrassing little subbies—the joy of every Dom in all the world.

But she was a sweetheart, so he wouldn't take it any further. "Hey, deVries, I take it you're to blame for Wyatt showing up late to our summer guide season—and dinged up to boot?"

DeVries snorted. "I asked; he volunteered. Not my fault."

"Volunteered for what?" Xavier asked.

"We were"—deVries held up a cautionary finger—"*hypothetically* delivering supplies in one of those fucked-up countries where the fighting's bad enough to keep any aid from getting sent."

Xavier's brows drew together. "So you decided to help. Did Simon know?"

"Of course not." DeVries grinned. "Although *someone* arranged the plane and time off."

Morgan shook his head. Both Simon and his wife were big-hearted people, and Simon owned the global security firm where deVries worked. An ex-mercenary, deVries was the sort who'd enjoy a bit of action now and then.

Not Wyatt, though. Morgan scowled. For fuck's sake, his brother had gone to Ethiopia to find peace, not war. But if asked, of course, Wyatt would jump in. "Wyatt did say he volunteered. What about the damage he took?" That info was what Morgan had wanted. Wyatt's explanation had been...lacking.

"Not my fault your brother wants to be a fucking hero," deVries said.

"What happened?" Morgan asked.

Wyatt's *keep-your-mouth-shut* warning look at deVries was one Morgan had received all too often when they were kids and caught in a dubious undertaking. Morgan had... usually...complied.

But deVries was a hard-ass, and compliance wasn't in his vocabulary. His smirk was subtle, but there. "An armed group attacked the village where we were offloading food from the plane. The bastards were setting fires. Your brother charged into a burning house to save some kids."

Wyatt shrugged. "Nothing that anyone wouldn't do."

No, bro, not everyone would. From Erin's stunned expression, she knew it too.

Morgan wasn't done though. "What about the slashes across his face and ribs?"

"For his face, the asshole starting the fire had a machete and was in Wyatt's way. Wyatt flattened him. His side...you *did* hear me say they were armed?" DeVries obviously noticed Lindsey's frown. "No one got seriously wounded, babe. Couple of the guys got minor wounds. I sewed Wyatt's face and side up myself."

"Did a fine job too," Wyatt said.

"Why did you stay if there was shooting?" Lindsey scowled at her Dom.

"Just buying time for the villagers to escape into the jungle," deVries said.

Xavier frowned. "I'm surprised they didn't shoot up your plane."

"Nah, deVries ordered Hawk to take off without us." Wyatt shrugged. "We didn't want the plane identified as American."

"The pilot *left* you there?" Erin looked as if she wanted to hit him herself. Morgan felt the same way.

"He picked us up a few days later when we'd gotten far enough away." Wyatt stroked Erin's hair.

"We wanted to make sure the villagers got away safely," deVries added.

Morgan met Wyatt's gaze. *Fuck. Just...fuck.* The darkness in his brother's eyes said he'd had to kill again.

"Interesting hike out." DeVries grinned at Wyatt. "Thanks for the wilderness survival tricks."

From the respect in his tone, Morgan knew his brother had probably kept the mercs alive. *Damn.* Guess he had his answers. Anger rose, swift and bitter. "You asshole."

"Bro?" Wyatt frowned.

"You fucking, selfless bastard. Off risking your life without me beside you. That's just fucking wrong." Morgan had half a mind to punch him into next week.

But Wyatt just laughed. "You're right. Our stroll through the jungle would've been more fun with you there. Next time."

"Damn straight." Morgan nodded, giving his brother an unyielding look. Sure, they could both fight solo, but battles went better with a brother at your side.

Wyatt exhaled in relief at defusing Morgan's anger, but Erin—damn, her face was pale and her expression worried.

"Hey, hey, hey." He pulled her between his legs and hugged her from behind. "It's in the past. You saw me afterward; you know I wasn't badly damaged."

She touched the whiter patches on his arms from the burns. "Do they still hurt?"

So sweet. She made him damn glad he'd jumped far enough the bullet aimed at his chest had only grazed his side. "Not—" *No, wait.* "Oh yeah, *really* painful. Later on, you should kiss every spot. Make them heal up faster."

Her snort of exasperation made him grin, and Morgan winked at him.

But he could see her worry dissipate like morning fog on the mountains. Good. He wasn't a real hero or anything. He'd only done what was needed. No honorable person abandoned women or children who were in danger.

Time to change the subject. Catching Xavier's gaze, Wyatt asked, "What happened in Dark Haven to cause problems last weekend?"

The club owner scowled. "Basically, it comes down to a Master/slave philosophical question—can a slave quit if they've changed their mind."

The discussion took them nicely away from burns and bullets.

A while later, deVries stretched and raised his voice. "I'm starving. Are we returning to the lodge or eating here?"

The people still in the barn looked over.

Logan was off to one side, talking to other guests. He raised his voice so everyone could hear. "Since we have vanilla guests at the lodge, you all might prefer to hang out here so you can talk freely. We can pop a few pizzas in the oven and carry them down."

Hand on Dixon's shoulder, Stan nodded. "Good idea. All in favor of staying here for pizza?"

Hands went up all over the barn. Locals and Dark Haven people both.

Earlier, Logan and Jake had cleaned up all the various cuffs and ropes, removing anything that appeared kinky. Made sense if he had vanilla guests who'd be exploring the area during the day.

Logan grinned at deVries. "Last time I played pool with Wyatt, he promised to teach me his flashy break. Want to come and play while the pizzas bake?"

"I'm in." DeVries rose, followed by Stan.

Wyatt leaned forward and ran his fingers through Erin's silky hair. "You want to join us or stay here?"

She bit her lip.

"Erin." Lindsey patted the floor. "Here. We'll have fun talking."

"Yes, yes, yes." Dixon bounced. "Subbie-time. We can bitch about Doms."

"Chatting sounds better than playing pool." Erin looked over her shoulder and smirked at Wyatt.

He laughed. When mischief lit her expression, she was so fucking cute. He kissed the tip of her nose, then her lips. So soft and giving. "As you wish. Don't let these two get you in trouble."

"*Moi?*" Hand on chest, Dixon widened his eyes, oozing innocence.

As Wyatt stood, Morgan joined him and said in a low voice, "They'll totally corrupt your new subbie, bro."

"Good thing I like brats," Wyatt muttered back, then called, "Logan, you did a nice sneaky job of arranging people to carry all that pizza back down here."

A grunt came from deVries. "Fuck, he did, didn't he."

Hearing about how the various couples got together had been hilarious. Erin's sides still hurt from laughing.

Abby met Xavier when she first visited the club—all dressed up as a Domme. The owner of Dark Haven hadn't believed she was dominant, not for a minute.

Apparently, deVries had been a total jerk when he and Lindsey first got together.

With Dixon, he'd tried to protect Lindsey from Stan when the agent was there to investigate her.

Erin couldn't stop laughing. " '*Back off, sweet cheeks.*' You called Mr. Homeland Security *sweet cheeks?*"

Lindsey pointed her finger at Dixon. "He did. He's super brave. What about you, Kallie? How'd you meet Jake?"

A few minutes ago, Kallie and Mallory joined them while Jake and Sawyer were unbolting the posts that made the X-shaped crosses.

Kallie grinned. "I knew Jake for years—and he never even

looked at me. Not until I got knocked down during a bar fight. Face planted right in front of him. It was so embarrassing."

Everyone laughed.

Erin raised her hand like a school kid. "Question."

Kallie pointed to her. "Shoot."

"I've seen how protective your cousins are—but all three are Doms, and I guess come to the parties? Don't they..." Erin felt herself turning red. "Isn't it kind of awkward?"

Kallie rolled her eyes. "*So* awkward. Jake and I usually play early before they show up and come back late enough to ensure they've finished. None of them would deal well with seeing me tied up, let alone spanked."

Lindsey was laughing so hard she was snorting.

"So Virgil and Sunny came earlier?"

Mallory nodded. "Been and gone. Atticus and Gin left after he and Virgil were called to the station. Atticus told Sawyer there was a house fire they suspect was arson."

"Law enforcement people have sucky hours," Dixon muttered.

"What about you, Erin? How did you meet Wyatt?" Abby waved her drink in the air.

"Well, it was my first day in—"

The barn's double doors flew open with a crash, and men poured into the barn.

What the...Erin stared in shock. They had *guns*. Military-looking rifles.

One raised a rifle and fired at the roof. *Snap-snap-snap.*

Erin's heart tried to leap out of her chest.

Two of the local male Dominants stalked forward, one yelling, "What's this about?"

"Stop right there, or you die!" The biggest invader shouted, "Shut up and sit *down*. Hands on your head. All of you."

Shaking with terror, Erin laced her fingers on top of her head. Around her on the floor, Lindsey, Abby, and Dixon did the same. Mallory and Kallie, sitting on another bunch of blankets, also complied.

Stay calm. Don't panic. She stared at the eight men, all in black cargo pants and black T-shirts. They looked like hardened criminals. Most with tats. One had piercings everywhere. One was making twitchy movements like a meth user. *Oh god.*

Near one of the stalls, Mallory's Dom, Sawyer, was quietly easing toward the men. Jake followed.

The Black man with a pistol spotted him and shot. Bullets tore up the floor in front of Sawyer.

He stopped, raising his hands in a conciliatory gesture.

The huge, black-haired leader pushed the shooter's rifle down. "No, Mad Dog. First things first."

"Just let me kill him." Mad Dog had crazy eyes. Terrifying eyes.

"Hey, dumbass, get down," the leader called to Sawyer before glaring around at the rest of the people in the barn. "All of you. Try anything, and we kill the women." He aimed a handgun directly at Erin's group. At Abby.

Abby's eyes widened. She was visibly trembling.

Reluctantly, Sawyer and Jake dropped to their knees.

What can I do? Erin felt herself shaking. Her chest felt so tight she was panting to get air.

I want Wyatt. Yet thank god he wasn't here. He'd have tried to take on the whole group of...of thugs.

Why were they *here*?

The leader pulled out his phone and showed the display to the others. "Find her. Then we'll finish up."

The thugs, all holding weapons, started wandering around, looking at each woman.

Erin stared at them. Surely people at the lodge would've heard the gunfire. Only...the lodge was quite a distance, and the sounds of shooting hadn't been loud at all. More of a snap-hissing sound than earsplitting cracks.

She eyed the weapons. Each one had a fat tube at the end of the barrel. Were those silencers?

No one away from the barn probably heard anything. Her heart sank.

"Which one of you bitches is Erin Palmer?" The leader scanned the barn.

What should I do? Tell him or—

Every woman—and Dixon—frowned at her and shook their heads a tiny amount, obviously telling her to stay quiet.

"Anyone gonna tell me?" The leader was studying everyone. His gaze landed on her—and moved on.

Why?

Ohhh. Maybe because she'd changed a lot in the last two months. If his photo was from her days with Troy, well... Tonight, she wore no makeup. Her hair was shorter and blue-streaked. She was tan—and healthy.

His expression turned cruel. "Erin Palmer. Stand your ass up, or someone point her out. Or I'll shoot a person every minute."

As Erin's mind went blank with fear, he pointed his rifle at Katelyn, then at Lindsey. "I'll start with one of you dark-haired bitches, since I know you're not the blonde target."

Oh god, oh god, not Lindsey. Not anyone...but Lindsey was pregnant.

"Wait!" Fear sapped Erin's strength, but she managed to stand. "I'm Erin. What do you want with me?"

He motioned with his pistol. "Get your ass over here."

Her legs wobbled as she crossed to him.

He scowled, looking from the phone picture to her. "Yeah, guess it's you all right."

The man beside him had thick winding scars all over his face and arms, like a kind of warped decoration. When he zip tied her wrists behind her back, she shuddered.

"If we got the cunt, are we leaving, Crow?" The bald, brutal-looking man with a big gut was like a massive Ford Super Duty truck.

"Yeah, Fats, haul the bitch out. Scars, you're with us." The leader pointed to one of his men. "Give us five minutes to get off the property. Don't forget to spread the LA gang shit around before you take off."

"Yeah, yeah, got it." Mad Dog kicked at a duffel bag on the floor and grinned. "The pigs'll go straight for the Aryan Hammers."

A T-shirt with a swastika graphic had spilled out of the half-open duffel. There were more clothes. Erin frowned. They wanted the blame to fall on—weren't the Aryan Hammers the gang causing so much trouble last summer? But everyone in the barn would know the attackers weren't a white supremacist gang. Mad Dog was Black, the twitchy one looked Latino.

But if no one was alive to say different... None of them were wearing masks. She stiffened. "You plan to kill everyone here." Her voice came out hoarse.

The crazy one's grin widened. "Oh yeah. It'll be a slaughter."

Erin met Sawyer's eyes and yelled, "They're planning to ki—"

Crow punched her in the belly so powerfully she couldn't breathe. "Bitch." He dropped a huge laundry bag over her head and down her body, then knocked her down so he could tie the bottom. "Haul her out, Scars."

They lifted her and tossed her, blind and gasping for air, over a man's shoulder.

She kicked, tried to scream, and a minute later was dropped onto a hard surface that bounced beneath her. Something slammed. When an engine fired up—and vibrated beneath her, she realized she'd been thrown into the trunk of a car.

Tears flowed.

They were going to kill everyone in the barn.

The air was crisp and cool, a refreshing change from the heat of the day. Wyatt looked up at the stars, enjoying the way moonlight spilled over the land.

An owl hooted, answered by another, and farther away, a car engine deepened.

Becca had contrived boxes so they could carry the pizzas, and the aroma of pepperoni, sausage, and cheese made his stomach rumble.

Erin was probably hungry, too, so they'd stay a while and eat. After, he'd take her home and maybe enjoy some slower, quieter loving. If she was too tired, sleeping with her in his arms was the next best thing.

In the front of the group, Logan stopped. "I don't remember seeing that car when we left." He frowned at the big SUV parked in front of the closed double doors. "Who would show up this late?"

"Not a car I recognize," Morgan commented.

They all stopped.

DeVries turned, his voice low. "Didn't you leave a doorman, Hunt?"

"Yeah. Your Aussie, Mitchell, was on the door." Logan looked around.

Wyatt glanced around. Morgan was off to his left, Xavier and Stan to his right. No Mitchell.

The sounds from the barn were wrong. His gut tightened. "There are only two men talking inside. No one else. Nothing from the women." He needed to see what was going on, but the barn had no windows. The door was closed.

"Fuck." DeVries silently walked to the barn, edged close enough to peer through two looser planks, and sped back. "Looks like five tangos with fucking machine guns. Suppressed, no less."

Wyatt scowled. No wonder no one had heard anything.

DeVries continued. "Three front, one near the back, one in the middle."

"We have one more than they do," Xavier said quietly, "but we're seriously outgunned."

Stan bent and pulled a pistol from an ankle holster.

"Hold on." The locals had parked on the gravel off to the side. Wyatt ran to his pickup, grabbed his Remington 12-gauge, and after a second's pause, his and Erin's throwing knives.

Morgan returned at the same time, his Enfield .30/06 in hand.

Unfortunately, the people staying at the lodge had walked down. Logan, Xavier, and deVries had no weapons.

"We can swing the double doors open at the same time. Spread out." DeVries frowned. "Hunt, what about the back door?"

Wyatt nodded approval. A two-pronged attack would be their best bet.

"It's narrow—and held shut with a latch on the inside," Logan said. "But there's a gap between the door and frame. A knife will lift the lever."

Wyatt frowned at the knives he carried. The others were good shots, but he was the only one who could throw a knife with any accuracy. With a pang of regret, Wyatt handed deVries his shotgun.

"You sure?" deVries asked in his raspy voice.

"Yeah, buddy. I'm sure." Wyatt handed Erin's knives to Logan and Xavier and strapped his three-knife holster to his leg. "Morgan, you're with me. We'll get the guy near the back door."

Morgan half-grinned. "Hauling me into trouble again, bro?" He looked at deVries. "I'll give a barred owl hoot a second before we charge in."

DeVries nodded. "Xavier, Logan, we'll take on the three in the front. Stan, try for the guy in the middle if you have a clear shot. Otherwise, he's up for grabs."

They all nodded.

"Let's go."

With Morgan behind him, Wyatt raced to the back of the

barn as silently as possible. The light from inside glinted through the ill-fitting door. Wedging his knife between the door and the frame, he quietly raised the latch and pushed the door open far enough the latch wouldn't re-catch.

A knife in each hand, he whispered, "Ready."

Morgan tipped his head back and hooted.

A heartbeat later, Wyatt slid through the door, Morgan a step behind. Both silent—because crashing through doors was for amateurs.

Across the barn, the double doors swung wide as Logan, Xavier, deVries, and Stan charged in. The men scattered.

Wyatt scanned the area closest to the rear. There. A bulky man held an assault rifle.

Morgan snapped, "Got him," and fired twice.

The man went down.

From the front, his 12-gauge boomed followed by the crack of a pistol.

The bearded intruder in the middle of the room, still on his feet, spun around. His rifle rose.

Wyatt threw his knives, hard and fast, one hand, then the other. His first blade went deep into the man's arm, the next, his chest. Pulling his last knife, he threw again, hitting the bastard's neck.

There was blood everywhere.

The taste of bile was bitter in his mouth. Wyatt pulled in a breath, checking the rest of the barn.

"You're so fucking messy," Morgan slapped his shoulder. His tone was light, his gaze sympathetic.

"Yeah, sorry 'bout that." Wyatt's voice came out rough.

On the other side of the barn, the three remaining intruders were down and obviously dead, two with headshots.

Xavier and Logan stood next to the body of the third, having attacked him with their knives.

As deVries strode toward the submissives, Lindsey scrambled to her feet and ran to him.

Mallory was in Sawyer's arms. Xavier was wrapped around Abby. Dixon grabbed Stan for a heated kiss.

Seeing Kallie and Jake hugging in the middle of the barn, Wyatt blew out a breath. Thank fuck the little bit was all right.

Even as he turned in a circle, trying to spot Erin, Kallie pulled away from Jake. "Wyatt, they took Erin!"

"They did." Mallory thumped Sawyer in the chest. "We have to go after her."

Wyatt felt as if his heart had stopped. "Who took her? Why?"

Kallie scrubbed her hands over her face and headed for Wyatt.

Jake pulled out his phone and started talking quietly to someone.

Arm around Lindsey, deVries followed Kallie. Sawyer joined them with Mallory at his side.

"They were looking for her, just her." Kallie took Wyatt's hand. "The leader had a photo of her on his phone. He said he'd kill one of us every minute until she was found."

Sawyer gripped Wyatt's shoulder. "When they threatened the other women, Erin stood up and let them take her. Three of the assholes left with her. The rest planned to assault the women then kill everyone. We were going to rush them as soon as the women had their attention." The grim look in his eyes showed he knew that most, if not all of them, would have died. Charging a person armed with an AK-47 was suicide.

"Good thing we showed up when we did." DeVries scowled. "Bet that was the vehicle I heard leaving."

Wyatt narrowed his eyes, looking in the direction they'd heard the engine. "It went up the mountain, not back toward town."

Jake joined them. "I called the police. Ambulance is on the way too."

Cops wouldn't be able to tell where the kidnappers' vehicle had gone. Wyatt's hands fisted as frustration increased his anger.

He was a tracker without a location to start searching. There were numerous turnouts, trails, and houses farther up the mountain.

They didn't even know what the fucking vehicle looked like.

But he'd figure it out. He hadn't been able to save Anastasia or his mother. Damned if he'd lose Erin.

He'd promised he'd always come for her. Yeah, he had a promise to keep.

When the brute carrying Erin over his shoulder tossed her on the ground, she was still in the bag. With her arms restrained behind her back, she couldn't catch herself and landed hard. Pain flared through her shoulder and hip.

Fighting panic, she sucked in a breath, half suffocating in the bag. How long had she been in it?

There'd been a long drive in the car trunk. Afterward, she was yanked out and belted onto the seat of what was probably a side-by-side utility vehicle. Whatever trail they'd followed had been a rough one. Unable to see, barely able to breathe, she'd just endured.

A man spoke. "Remove the bag."

The tenor voice was…familiar. Silky smooth, refined, patronizing. So much like Troy's.

Someone untied the bag from around her feet and yanked it off, rolling her on the ground. Dirt and stones scraped her bare arms. Struggling to sit up, she squinted against the headlights of the utility vehicles parked in a clearing. Farther away were several tents. Trees surrounded a squat ancient cabin.

Three of the men who'd been at the barn stood, looking behind her.

Still sitting, she wiggled around to see one other man—Troy's brother.

Emmett smirked down at her. "It's nice to see you, Erin. I've been looking forward to this for a while now."

"Emmett." Her mouth felt as foul as if she'd chewed on a filthy shop rag.

You fucking low-life asshole. She fought for control over her temper. Finally, she managed an even tone. "What's this about? Why did you have me dragged here?"

"Oh, my dear, haven't you figured it out yet?" He tsked and motioned for the other men to pick her up and follow. "No wonder Troy said you were short on brains as well as beauty."

The words had hurt when her husband said them, but now, they didn't even make her flinch. She might not be brilliant, but she wasn't stupid. And she might not be gorgeous, but she was attractive enough.

And Wyatt loved her.

Wyatt. No, don't think about how he must be feeling right now.

Gripping her upper arms, Crow and Fats half-dragged her toward the cabin. The third man—the one who used scars as decorations—followed behind. Plastic jugs of drinking water were stacked against the front. The splintered door sagged on its hinges.

Inside, the cabin was small and dark. There was a crudely built stone fireplace, stump chairs, and a wood slab nailed to a tall stump for a table. Curtained-off openings showed lean-tos on each side. No sink. No bathroom.

It was a hunting cabin with no electricity, no water, and no frills. Just a place for a few hunters to sleep.

Her stomach sank. Wyatt would never find her here.

Emmett waved a hand at the men. "Zip tie her ankles, undo her hands, and get out."

Crow restrained her ankles and released her wrists. As she brought her arms forward, her shoulders seemed to shriek in pain.

Fats followed Crow out, closing the sagging door behind him. Leaving her alone with Emmett.

Swaying as she stood, her balance unsteady, Erin glared at Emmet. "What do you want with me?"

"I want to know where my files are."

"What files?" She blinked. "If I had anything of yours, all you had to do was ask."

"I did, you stupid woman. I asked you if there was anything in storage you wanted." He slapped her face.

"Why would I have your files?" She was totally missing something. "Besides, I don't have anything in storage; it's all at the house. I do have files from Troy's office. If there are records you need—"

"I already searched his file cabinets, damn you." His face grew redder with anger. "I searched the whole damn *house*."

"You..." Her jaw dropped. "You're the one who trashed the Sacramento house and slashed up the furniture."

"For all the good it did me." With a snarl of rage, he knocked her to the rough plank floor. Splinters dug through her jeans into her knees.

Why is he doing this? Why?

The insight stabbed into her brain. "Troy was working with *you*. You were blackmailing people together. Using children to—"

His ugly laugh cut her off. "It was my idea. I needed congress to pass a couple of bills that would increase the profits in my private prisons. The legislators weren't cooperating. Not until they saw the videos of their *fun* times. Then they were quite happy to help."

He and Troy destroyed girls' lives for money and power? "You make me *sick*."

He kicked her in the stomach. Pain ripped through her, and she curled in a ball around her stomach, crying.

"Self-righteous fool." He shook his head. "No matter. Just tell me where my jump drives are."

Tears burned her face as she struggled to make her lungs work. As she tried to think.

The Homeland Security Dom, Stan, had been right about

where a blackmailer would store his material—on portable flash drives. "I don't know where."

He made the ugly laughing sound again. "Troy said he hid the drives in that old clock you gave him. He kept it on his desk."

Rage cleared her head. Her bastard husband had put his blackmail porn into her beautiful antique clock. The one she'd labored over to give him something he'd love. Nausea twisted her stomach.

"Where is the damn clock?" Emmett's voice had grown even silkier.

Pushing up to a sitting position, she tried to remember. Everything from Troy's office was boxed and brought to Bear Flat. If Emmett had searched the house in Sacramento... Her memory caught on the burglar who'd attacked her. "Did you have my Bear Flat house searched?"

"Of course. Where is the clock?"

Why hadn't the intruder found it? It would have... She closed her eyes as horror swept through her.

She'd given the clock to Bobby. The housekeeper's grandson loved clocks. "I...I threw it away. It got broken, and I threw it away."

"You wouldn't toss out an expensive antique. You'd repair it, Miss Fix-it." Emmett bent and slapped her. "Where"—he backhanded her—"is"—he slapped her again—"it?"

She was lying on the floor again. Crying. Her face raging with pain.

When he drew his foot back, she cringed.

If she told him about Bobby, he or whoever he sent would hurt them. Kill them. "Gone. It's gone."

He kicked her. Hard. "I don't believe you."

She clamped her jaw shut...and her world filled with pain.

CHAPTER THIRTY-THREE

Wyatt was ready to kill something, someone, but he had no target. No one knew where Erin was.

The barn was still full of people. The cops had shown up, including his brother. Virgil had asked the guests not to leave until released—and they'd been cooperative. But this was taking forever.

There'd been only a few injuries.

The door guard, Mitchell, had a rifle shoved in his face and was knocked out by another asshole, probably with the butt of a rifle. When found, the Aussie was groggy but able to talk. He would spend the night in the hospital.

When an asshole shot the floor in front of Sawyer, he'd been peppered with splinters. Nothing major.

A Dark Haven member who got between his Mistress and one bastard had been pistol-whipped.

Thank fuck everything happened after the party ended, with everyone dressed and the equipment put away.

Wyatt glanced around. So far, the only cops were Virgil and Atticus who'd attended Serenity's parties before, and Officer Cliff Lambert who'd undoubtedly seen everything in his years in law enforcement. The state police and FBI would probably be arriving shortly.

Ignoring everyone, Wyatt paced across the barn, trying to think, despite the worry squeezing his brain. "Why Erin?" he muttered to himself. "It must be because she was Palmer's wife."

Atticus fell into step. "That's what I think. Her city house was searched. The one here in Bear Flat had a burglar who didn't take anything. I figure someone's looking for whatever blackmail shit Palmer had."

Wyatt stopped dead in his tracks. "If they get what they want, they'll kill her."

Gasps came from the three submissives huddled together in one sitting area.

One of them—Katelyn—rose. "I...I might know where Erin is. Maybe." She glanced at the detective and took a step away. "I think Emmett Palmer did all this."

When she stopped, Wyatt wanted to shout, to drag the answers from her. Not a good idea. She was pure white. Shaking. *Easy, Masterson, easy.*

"Emmett Palmer?" Wyatt kept his voice soft and gentle, the way he would talk to a timid foal. "We'd appreciate any guesses at this point."

When she didn't respond, he added an edge of authority, "Talk to me, Katelyn."

She darted another look at Atticus before focusing on Wyatt. "I...Candy and me...when Troy and his brother Emmett came here for hunting seasons, we, um, got to know them."

Got to know them. Right. Undoubtedly in a very intimate way.

Erin hadn't come with Troy for hunting season, Wyatt knew. The men would have had an easy time of...entertaining. He kept his voice mild. "Go on."

"Emmett called me a few times this summer. He wanted to know how I was doing. Being friendly, you know? And he'd ask about Erin—he's her brother-in-law, after all. He wanted me to call if she went back to Sacramento. And I did, and he thanked me."

Back to Sacramento. Wyatt's eyes narrowed. When Erin's house was broken into, she'd surprised the intruder by returning a day early.

Atticus' voice was quiet. "Had he ever called you before Erin came to Bear Flat?"

"No. But...but he likes me. He said so." Her eyes held tears. "He called me on Wednesday and said he needed to talk to Erin, but she was avoiding him. He wanted to know if she'd be home this weekend, and I told him about tonight."

"So he knew she'd be here," Atticus murmured.

Wyatt frowned. Could Troy have been blackmailing his brother? It was possible, although on the hunting trip Wyatt had guided, soft-spoken Emmett had bossed Troy around.

Fuck, could the two have been working together?

Wyatt eyed Katelyn. "You said you might know where Erin is now?"

"He... I told Emmett about Levi's hunting cabin and how no one would be there at this time of year."

Atticus made a sound under his breath. "Why did you do that?"

She was wringing her hands until the knuckles went white. "He said if he could talk to her alone, in a place where she couldn't avoid him, he would convince her to go back to Sacramento." Her chin rose. "Where she belongs."

Sudden tears spilled down her face. "He didn't say he'd kidnap her. With guns. If she hadn't let them take her, that man"—she pointed to one of the sheet-covered bodies—"he'd have shot me and Lindsey."

Appalled, Wyatt glanced over at deVries' woman.

Katelyn was crying quietly. "They were planning to kill us all anyway."

Of course. Whoever planned this wouldn't want witnesses to

say Erin had been kidnapped. Wyatt pulled in a breath, turning to look at his tiny cousin Kallie.

He could have lost her.

Facing Katelyn, he reined in his temper with an effort. What kind of person would set up another woman like this? Essentially coercing her to talk to Emmett. Her behavior was past self-centered and bordering on criminal.

But Erin's act of courage had broken Katelyn's blind infatuation and let her see what she'd done. Spurred her to try to set things right.

Emmett might not be behind all this...but all Wyatt's instincts said it was him. "I'm glad you told us, Katelyn. Can you give us directions to the hunting cabin?"

As she talked, Atticus beckoned to Virgil—and suddenly they were joined by just about every man in the barn and several of the women.

Morgan set a hand on Wyatt's shoulder. "Tell us the plan, bro. We're here."

Gratitude swept over Wyatt...along with increasing worry. Would they be in time?

Hang tight, Erin.

Erin woke, and second by second, nerve by nerve, the pain in her body increased. *So much pain.* Why did she hurt so bad? Her brain wasn't running, wouldn't ignite...as if its spark plugs were corroded.

Where am I? On the ground. Did I fall?

She moved her head. Splintery, gritty wood scraped her cheek. When she opened her mouth, the ache in her face flooded her brain with memories.

Her jaw and cheeks were sore from Emmett slapping her. No punches, at least. *"I don't like seeing women with black eyes or fat lips."*

But he liked to kick.

Nothing felt broken—probably—but oh god, her ribs and stomach hurt. Her legs. And her pounding head was about to explode like an overripe melon.

She huffed a silent laugh. All the torturing Wyatt had done to her sensitive girl-bits didn't even register under the pain everywhere else. As she thought of her cowboy Dom, of his careful, competent hands, of his concern, a wave of longing to be with him shook her.

He'd want her to do her best to survive.

And he'd come looking for her. Of that, she had no doubt. Her eyes burned for a second at the wonder of such surety. *Wyatt loves me, and he'll move heaven and earth to find me.*

So how was she going to survive this mess?

Not moving, barely breathing, she listened and looked through her mostly closed eyes. Darkness was all around her. She lay in one of the lean-tos, all alone, with the curtain half-pulled.

Fats sat on the stump chair in the main room, drinking from a bottle of hard liquor.

Outside the cabin, two people were talking. "...can't get a signal up here."

"My men should've been here by now. Something's wrong." The voice was Crow's, the boss guy.

"You left five of them with assault rifles. What could happen?" Emmett sounded annoyed. "You can't go into Bear Flat. There's only one road out of this area, and if there were problems at the barn, the police might set up a roadblock."

"For fuck's sake, I told you to pick a better fucking location. Now we're stuck here until things cool down."

"You're expecting to stay *here*—the three of you?" Emmett said something under his breath. "Fine."

"Do us a favor and keep the girl alive." Crow's laugh was ugly. "Give us a diversion while we wait it out."

"Whatever. She didn't know where...what I need to know. She's useless to me."

"Good, I'll—"

"She's out cold." Emmett paused. "And I'm going to get some sleep. You can have her in the morning."

"You got her tied up? Secured? Ain't nobody gonna want to stay awake to watch her."

"Her ankles were already zip tied, and I zip tied her wrists again. She's going nowhere."

Crow barked a laugh. "Good enough. Hopefully, she doesn't die before we get our use out of her."

Through her pounding headache, Erin shifted her legs and felt the plastic ties dig into her ankles. *Dammit.* She wiggled her hands the merest amount. Her wrists were secured but, this time, in front of her. A tiny hope wakened.

Breathing through her teeth, she listened as the men talked, laughed. Emmett had his way, and everyone was going to bed. It sounded as if the hired gunmen were sleeping in the tents.

"Out." Emmett's voice came from the main cabin room.

Fats grunted in answer and left.

Emmett's lighter footsteps crossed toward Erin's lean-to. Light washed over her.

She kept her eyes closed, her breathing very slow. *Don't move, don't react.* Yet when he prodded her stomach with his booted foot, it took all her effort to stay limp.

Ow, ow, ow. Don't move.

"So many stupid people in the world. My brother—and you, his insipid wife. Damn you." One more hard kick and then he left.

The relief was so strong tears burned her eyes.

His footsteps thudded to the lean-to on the other side of the cabin. A few minutes later, the crack of light went out, leaving the cabin pitch black.

Breathing silently, she struggled to sit up. *Oh god, my stomach, my ribs!*

She hunched over, panting against the pain. Wetness seared her swollen, abraded face.

After another eternal minute, she blinked hard. *Focus.*

Moving carefully, she fingered her front jeans pocket and felt the lump of her keys. *Yes!* Crow hadn't bothered to search her. Slowly, she worked the keys up and out.

Her tiny multitool was attached to the keychain. Maybe the mini-wire cutter?

Working by touch—and it seemed to take forever—she maneuvered it open.

Snip. She cut the plastic tie holding her ankles together.

The blood returning to her feet hurt. Moving her legs hurt. Everything hurt.

Seconds later, her plan fell apart. She couldn't twist her hands enough for the wire cutter to reach the zip tie on her wrists.

Fine.

She closed the cutters and opened the knife attachment. Gripping the tool between her teeth with the knife pointing out, she sawed at the zip tie on her wrists.

Ow. She was too clumsy. It was too dark. The blade sliced her skin again and again, burning like fire. Blood ran down her arms.

The plastic tie gave way.

Free.

Kind of, but not completely. Not yet.

She wiped the tears from her face with the bottom of the T-shirt. Wyatt's shirt. Breathing in the traces of his clean, citrusy scent, she could almost feel his arms around her, hear his rough voice.

Her lips tilted up. *He's probably saying, get moving, right?*

She tucked her keys and multitool into her pocket and pushed to her feet. Her head spun; her stomach turned over.

Don't throw up. He'll hear.

She swallowed. Swallowed again. Sweat beaded on her skin.

Okay, okay, I can do this.

Silently, she crossed the main room...and if she hadn't been going so slowly, she'd have tripped over one of the stump chairs. *Oh god, close call.*

Keeping track of where she was with one hand on the chair,

she touched a soft fabric. Maybe a fleece jacket lying over the back?

Thank you so much, asshole. Even better, it'd soak up any blood from her wrists. She pulled it on, savored the warmth, and tiptoed cautiously toward where the door should be.

Found it. Ever so carefully, she eased the door open, stopping with every faint squeak. Finally, there was enough room she could slip through.

Outside, the three-quarter moon cast a faint glow over the clearing. No one moved in the line of tents.

The UTVs were parked in a line. *Uh-oh.* The men would chase after her the minute they got up. With the utility vehicles, they'd travel way faster. Could run her down. Shoot her.

Cold fear made her knees wobble even as she searched for the keys.

No keys. Dammit, it'd be too noisy and take too long to hotwire one.

Immobilize them?

Maybe do-able. There were water jugs piled against the cabin. She grabbed one, drank from it, then liberally added water to each gas tank. Best case, the engines would die after a minute. Worst case, the UTVs would run so rough the men would think twice about using them.

She looked around, trying to spot a trail. Over there must be the dirt road they'd driven in on.

Oh, she wanted so much to just run down it.

But they'd figure she would run straight back to Bear Flat. Choosing the road was a surefire recipe to get caught.

In the patchy light, she spotted an ugly snag of a tree way high on the nearest mountain. She'd head toward it. If nothing else, having a target would keep her from going in circles.

Grabbing a couple of small, bottled waters, she headed across the clearing and onto the road to Bear Flat, deliberately stepping in the loose dirt.

Nice visible tracks, Erin.

As soon as she found a spot, she jumped to a rock outcropping and left no tracks as she made her way back to the clearing and across to the other side.

This would be only a delaying action. Even if she didn't leave footprints, when they didn't find her on the road, they'd search everywhere else.

As she reached the edge of the forest, a darker area showed a possible animal trail.

Right there. Moving as best she could when *everything* hurt, she went down the narrow path, doing her best to leave no tracks. Deeper into the forest, the darkness increased. She wouldn't be walking fast, not until sunrise.

Pulling in a breath, she looked up at the sky. *Please come and find me, Wyatt. Please.*

Wyatt's jaw was tight as he jogged down the rough dirt road in the dark. It led downhill into a moist ravine, and the tree canopy thickened, removing almost all the light.

He slowed his pace to allow everyone's eyes to adapt. Tripping over boulders or exposed roots wasn't an option, especially since they were all armed.

As they neared the stream, the fragrance of conifers gave way to the scent of green vegetation. Wyatt jumped the small creek, checked that the UTV tracks continued, and turned to evaluate his group.

Morgan joined him, still moving fine. No surprise there. DeVries kept up well too. He was in good shape, just not accustomed to hiking a trail.

Having insisted they needed law enforcement present, Atticus brought up the rear. He might prefer horses, but he'd kept up well.

Carrying their weapons, they'd been on the trail for an hour now, jogging in the clear patches. On their backs were packs stripped to essentials. He calculated they had about another half hour to go.

Once Katelyn provided the location, information had poured in rapidly. Virgil had called Levi and gotten more information about his hunting cabin. Apparently, he always used either ATVs or horses. There were no adequate clearings for helicopters.

An elderly woman who lived near the trailhead hadn't appreciated being woken but confirmed she'd heard buzzy-sounding vehicles heading up the mountain off and on for a day or two, including earlier in the night. On her way to town yesterday, she'd seen pickups, one with a trailer, parked at the trailhead.

A trailer to bring in utility vehicles, probably. Emmett had come prepared.

Just in case Wyatt and his group weren't successful, Virgil would make sure those vehicles wouldn't be going anywhere.

Moving into a fast walk, Wyatt led the group out of the ravine. At the top of a bluff, he checked the sky. Full moon was a few days past, so it wouldn't set until after dawn. They'd have enough light.

It sure would've been nice to use utility vehicles like the assholes had, but everyone within miles could hear the damn things.

Since the bastards had Erin for a hostage, this was the best plan. Fast and silent.

Around now, Sawyer should be reaching the trailhead with horses and another group of volunteers, including Levi and Virgil.

Jake and Logan planned to hike up an alternate trail they'd seen on the map—one no one had used in years. It might well be blocked. If not, they'd ensure the kidnappers couldn't take Erin out that way.

Despite the chill night air, Wyatt felt sweat trickling down his back, even as desperation urged him to increase his speed.

But years as a guide had taught him that speeding down a

trail inevitably led to injuries. They couldn't afford to lose anyone at this point. Grimly, he kept on going.

Hang on, Erin.

Troy's damn wife would pay for this.

A branch whipped across Emmett's face, and he flinched at the stinging pain.

In front of him, Crow and Fats walked steadily as the gradient increased.

This better be the trail she'd taken to escape. As his temper and frustration increased, Emmett cursed under his breath.

Last night, she hadn't told him where the damned clock was. Kept saying she'd thrown it away.

She'd *lied*.

When he'd explained which clock he needed to find, he saw the moment she decided to lie. With Troy as a brother, he'd had plenty of practice spotting lies.

But Erin had stuck to her story, even when screaming in pain.

He shook his head. Slapping her so hard she'd hit the floor and been knocked unconscious had been gratifying.

This morning had been less so. Unable to sleep with the sun shining through the cracks in the walls, he got up and found only cut zip ties on the floor. No Erin.

"Got a footprint here," Crow called.

"Finally." Fats looked back. "This is the way she came, boss."

Short of breath, Emmett didn't answer. But satisfaction filled him. She wouldn't escape.

The chase would have been far easier with the UTVs. But one machine died within a minute of starting, and the other two sputtered so badly they were unusable.

So they were on foot.

At least her only options for escape were two animal trails and the narrow road leading to the highway.

Crow had found her footprints on the dirt road, and they'd lost time searching for her track. Eventually there was an area where she would've had to take the road, but no tracks marred the UTV tread marks. She hadn't escaped by way of the road.

The only other choices were the two animal trails. One went downhill and crossed a creek. According to Crow, who liked to hunt, the undisturbed moist grasses eliminated the creek path.

That left this mountain trail. And now, they knew. She was ahead. Emmett promised himself she would die screaming for wasting his time.

They'd left Scars behind at the cabin in case the others in the group showed up. It was concerning they hadn't returned.

But Scars could handle any problems. He, Crow, and Fats were the first convicts Emmett had collected. A little influence on the parole boards got them released after serving the minimum time. In return, they did occasional jobs for him. Knowing he could reverse their freedom with a word, they were uniquely loyal. And all three liked to kill.

So did he.

However... Emmett narrowed his eyes. Crow always carried a knife...and liked to carve up his victims before cutting their throats. He might have better luck in getting Erin to talk.

And afterward, they'd toss her off a cliff.

"I don't see anyone." Morgan's voice was barely a whisper in the quiet air.

Wyatt nodded. Three two-person UTVs were parked in a small clearing in front of a hunting cabin. The decrepit-looking place had no windows. Several tents were to the right of the cabin.

There was no movement, no smoke, no noise. Where were they? Where was *Erin*?

"I'll check the cabin from the back." With a revolver

borrowed from Logan, deVries faded into the undergrowth to detour around the clearing.

"I'll check the tents." Morgan gripped his rifle and glanced back at Wyatt. "Spotted owl for no one, saw-whet for a bad guy."

Wyatt nodded. Crouched beside Atticus, 12-gauge at ready, he had to force himself to be patient. Moving too quickly would risk Erin's life.

But damn it was hard.

Where *was* she?

From the tent area came *hoot...hoot-hoot...hoooot*. The call of a spotted owl. Morgan hadn't found anyone.

DeVries appeared to the right of the cabin long enough to meet Wyatt's gaze and shake his head. No one was inside.

"Hell, where'd they go?" Atticus asked under his breath.

"They're not here and not on the road coming in. Didn't take their UTVs so they're on foot." Wyatt eyed the surrounding forest. "Looks like two animal paths out of here." He pointed toward the north, then south.

Police-issued weapon in his hand, Atticus moved into the clearing. "Let's try the—"

A tall man with thick scars covering his face burst out of the undergrowth, AK-47 at ready.

Atticus roared, "*Police*. Put down your—"

The bastard started shooting with the assault weapon on full auto, blindly spraying everything in a circle.

Atticus jumped behind a tree.

Wyatt dove for cover behind a thick cedar. Up on one knee, he peeked around the trunk and shot.

Jerking like a marionette, the man fell, blood spurting from numerous holes in his chest. Wyatt hadn't been the only person firing back. No way the bastard survived that much damage.

Silence fell.

Wyatt sighed. "Atticus, stay under—" Fuck, the cop was down, holding his leg.

Staying concealed from the clearing, Wyatt duck-walked over.

A chunk of wood the size of his thumb was embedded in the cop's thigh. "That looks painful."

"No. Shit." Atticus gripped the giant splinter, preparing to yank it.

"Wait." After setting down his shotgun, Wyatt pulled the emergency first aid kit from his pack. He handed it to the cop, picked up his weapon again, and scanned the forest around them. All good.

Pulling the chunk of wood from his leg, Atticus made a pained grunt and slapped gauze over the wound.

"Yo, it's me." Morgan appeared, glanced at Atticus, and took up a guard position. "Followed back to where the guy had been —appears we interrupted him taking a dump."

Wyatt snorted. "Guess nothing is sacred anymore. Anyone else around?"

"Nope."

Working quickly, Wyatt patched the cop up. "Nothing's busted, no arteries severed. You'll be limping for a while. Good thing Sawyer's bringing horses."

A minute later, deVries showed up. "I didn't spot anyone else." He frowned at Atticus. "Bullet?"

"Nah, fragment from the tree the asshole shot up." Wyatt rose and pulled Att to his feet. "We have a couple of trails to check out. Let's get moving."

Tat-tat-tat... The sound wasn't close. As it echoed off the mountains, Erin froze partway into an open slope.

Is that gunfire? So fast—like a machine gun. Like the weapons the fake-gangsters carried. The AK-45s or whatever number it was.

A faint hope rose.

Did it come from the cabin area?

She couldn't tell. Heck, she was having trouble thinking at

all. Sweat streaked her face; her hands and knees were raw from numerous falls. Hiking in the dark wasn't for wussies. Bending, she put her hands on her thighs and tried to catch her breath.

Panting made her ribs and stomach hurt worse in all the places Emmett had punched and kicked her.

"Damn you, Emmett." She still couldn't believe he'd killed Troy—his own brother. And had kidnapped her.

He was clever; she couldn't deny it.

Last night, he'd boasted about working out deals with convicts from his private prisons. He had a pool of violent criminals who'd do anything for him. Like killing off everyone at the Serenity party and leaving evidence pointing to the Aryan Hammers, the Los Angeles gang that hated Bear Flat.

Emmett seemed certain he'd get away with the slaughter.

Blinking hard, Erin tried not to cry. Tried not to think of what might have happened to the people in the barn. Kallie, Mallory, Abby, adorable Dixon, pregnant Lindsey.

Dread filled her until her throat closed.

No, no, don't think like that. They must be all right.

The Doms would have returned from getting pizza and would have done what? A little voice asked what anyone could do against automatic weapons.

Whatever happened, Wyatt would've been in the forefront.

Please, let him be safe.

And me too. That would be good.

The sun had come up not too long ago. An hour maybe? She'd been hiking for hours. No watch, no phone. She had to guess at the time.

After her first fall, she'd given up on hiding her footprints.

Starting to walk again, she frowned. Where had the trail gone...let alone the forest? Granite slabs and dry grassy patches covered the mountainside. There was no place to hide at all.

She turned around to look at the trees where the trail emerged. It'd be smart to go back into the forest and find a better place to leave the trail.

Not that it would do her much good. As the elevation increased, the trees had grown sparse with scant underbrush.

Why hadn't she taken the trail leading downward instead of this one going up?

It's too late for regrets, Erin.

Movement caught her eye. Blue, black, a glint of metal. *Men.* On her trail.

Heart sinking, she scrambled back down the slope, angling toward the dubious refuge of the forest. *It was too late for anything.*

The knowledge she'd never see Wyatt again broke something within her.

Wyatt bent to examine the tracks.

The footprints indicated there were still three men in front of them, not even trying to hide their passage. Moving quickly. The footprints weren't deep enough for them to be carrying anything...like a body.

Wyatt smiled grimly. It appeared his tricksy woman had escaped.

His smile faded.

A while back, her footprints had shown up. She'd obviously tried to hide them at first...and done a good job of it too. But increasingly, her prints showed where she'd staggered and been slow to recover. Chances were good she was hurt. Maybe badly, although he hadn't spotted any blood.

The assholes weren't hiding their tracks and were easy to follow.

Wyatt was moving fast, jogging when possible, and Morgan and deVries were keeping up.

They'd left Atticus at the cabin to keep track of anyone arriving. With luck, it would be Sawyer with horses and reinforcements. Someone had to stay behind to turn over the dead asshole and report to them. Being injured, Atticus lost the draw.

On the trail, Wyatt eyed a patch of grass. The tracks were recent enough the bent grasses were still rebounding.

He held up his hand to stop the others so he could listen.

Nothing yet. But they'd best be cautious. He glanced at Morgan and deVries and got firm nods back.

We're coming, Erin. Hold on, woman.

"Erin, stop. It's over." Emmett's voice rose above the pounding of Erin's heart.

Not. Stopping.

Erin sped up, running as fast as she could—

Several sharp cracks sounded. The granite surface in front of her sparked and chipped.

They'd *shot* at her.

She stared at the trees in front of her. She'd almost made it to the cover. Failure sagged her shoulders.

"Next shot kills you, bitch," Crow shouted.

Despair dried her mouth, weakened her legs as she turned.

Emmett's perfect hair was matted with sweat, his face and clothing dirty. His eyes were crazy mad.

Black haired and bearded, Crow held a pistol pointed directly at her. No smile. No emotion in his dead black eyes. He'd kill her without thinking twice. He glanced at Emmett. "It's too exposed here for anything messy. Let's take this into the forest."

"I agree, yes." Emmett nodded.

Moving toward Erin, Fats rubbed his crotch. "I want her after you talk to her, boss. Just for a bit."

Her stomach turned over. *Oh god.*

At the edge of the available cover, Wyatt held up his hand to halt the other two. The sparse forest opened into one of the area's glacier-scoured rock surfaces.

And there they were. Three men...and Erin. Fury surged inside him so hot and raw he couldn't see past it.

Breathe. Stay in control. His months of practice won out.

"They caught her." He spoke just loud enough for Morgan and deVries to hear.

They joined him, crouching to mimic the scrubby underbrush.

"They're moving back toward us," Morgan whispered.

Yeah, they were. Wyatt motioned to the left. "We leave the trail and approach from cover."

Nods showed their agreement.

After Emmett had slapped her, his eyes almost mad with anger, Fats dragged her down the slope. One of his hands painfully gripped her breast, the other hand curled around her neck, half-choking her.

Panic rose inside as she struggled to get air. The brightness of the sun cut off as they re-entered the forest.

"Here, boss?" Fats stopped a little ways in.

"This is fine."

Fats bent to whisper in her ear, and his breath was foul. "After the questions, it's my turn." He rubbed his erection against her, then kicked the backs of her legs, dropping her painfully to her knees. "All yours, boss."

Crow propped his rifle against a tree. "Fats, take guard duty." He waved toward the trees to the right.

"Got it." Pulling his pistol, Fats headed farther into the forest.

Crow turned to Emmett. "Let's make this quick. We heard gunfire at the cabin. We got trouble."

"Not as much trouble as Erin's got." Emmett wiped his sweating face with a handkerchief. His mouth tightened as he stared at her. "You know what I'm going to ask."

"Nope, haven't a clue."

She had a second to enjoy the way Emmett's face turned red, then Crow slapped her hard across the face. She fell sideways, tears filling her eyes as her cheek burned.

"We don't have time for your crap, bitch." Yanking her back up, he punched her in the stomach. Her sore, sore stomach. The pain was far worse today.

Sobbing, she curled around her stomach.

"I believe you enjoy using a blade," Emmett said to Crow.

"Fuck yeah." Crow drew a big buck knife from a belt sheath. "Ask your questions. I'll cut pieces off her until she answers."

Fear formed cold ice in her guts. She couldn't seem to look away from the long blade.

Going down on one knee, Emmett stuck his face almost against hers and shouted, "Where. Is. The. Clock?"

He'd kill sweet Bobby. And Delilah too. She'd guard Delilah's grandchild with her life.

Emmett will kill me no matter what. All she'd save by talking would be pain.

She shook inside. More pain. She already hurt so bad.

No choice.

She clamped her jaw shut.

Not speaking would keep her from blurting out where the clock was. She tried to summon courage, but it had disappeared completely. Her whole body was trembling now.

Nonetheless... *I will not speak.*

"Tell me," Emmett shouted.

No. Instead, she slammed her forehead against his face.

With a yelp, he fell back, holding his nose. She hadn't broken it, more was the pity.

He swiped his hand under his nose and saw the blood. With

an ugly sound of rage, Emmett rose and motioned to Crow. "Start with her fingers."

Crow stepped in front of her.

No, no, no.

Panicking, she tried to push to her feet, to run.

He caught her by the hair. "We can start with your face instead." She was still on her knees as he lifted the knife, moving it toward—

Crack!

His knife landed in the dirt. And he was falling away from her.

There was a hole in his temple.

Paralyzed for a moment, she could only stare. *Why? Did Emmett shoot him?*

But Emmett was pulling his pistol from his belt, turning...

Crack. Crack, crack. He jerked with each shot. Knees buckling, blood everywhere, he fell.

Morgan walked out from under the trees.

From another direction, Wyatt raced toward her.

Fats stepped out from behind a tree, turned toward Morgan, and his pistol rose.

"No!" Grabbing Crow's knife, she threw it at Fats. The handle hit him in the face.

"Fuck!" He turned his pistol toward her.

Gunfire echoed off the granite slopes as Wyatt, Morgan...and another man all shot at Fats.

Unable to move, to think, she stared as he fell. *Dead, he must be dead.*

Emmett sprawled on the ground, eyes open.

Crow... Her gaze winced away from him.

They were dead, all of them. Her breathing hitched.

Dropping to his knees beside her, Wyatt carefully pulled her into his arms. "Fuck, I didn't think we'd make it in time." His voice sounded like gravel. "How bad are you hurt?"

He touched her swollen, stinging face, growled, then ran his hands down her arms, her ribs...everywhere. Pushing up the fleece jacket, he found the cuts on her wrists.

Each time she winced or sucked in a breath from the pain, his expression grew tighter.

"Were there only these three with you?" A man with short blond hair and a rasping voice stood over Fats. DeVries—it was Lindsey's Dom, deVries. He was looking at Erin to answer.

"Three here." Her voice was barely a whisper. "There must be one still at the cabin."

"Only the three, deVries. Like we figured," Wyatt called back. "The man we killed at the cabin was the only one there."

"Yo, Erin, what's the damage?" Morgan went down on his haunches beside his brother, eyes worried.

"I'm okay." Still whispering. She pulled in a breath and tried again. "Maybe a little battered."

Morgan glanced at Wyatt.

"*A little* battered is bullshit." Wyatt shook his head. "But...I can't find anything broken. Stomach's still soft, so no ruptures. But she's fucking tenderized head to toe. They beat the hell out of her."

"Well, yes. That they did." From their expressions, her attempt at a smile was a failure. "The barn..." She grabbed Wyatt's hand. "Kallie, Lindsey, everyone... Are they all right?"

"Yeah. They're fine." Wyatt helped her to her feet. "Let's get you away from here."

After a moment of dizziness, she was steady, at least until she saw the bodies again. So much blood. She swallowed hard before Wyatt shifted to block the sight.

In the shade, he settled her on a soft patch of dirt.

"How'd you find me? I didn't think anyone..." She'd figured on dying. Alone.

Wyatt's mouth flattened into a thin, angry line. "Turns out the cabin belongs to Katelyn's brother. She told us Emmett had asked to use it." He pulled his first aid kit out of his backpack.

Katelyn. Had she helped Emmett? Erin tried to decide what

to think and couldn't. Whatever. At least Katelyn had spoken up. Otherwise Wyatt and the others wouldn't have known where to come.

"What did they use on your wrists to rip them up like this?" Wyatt started putting antibiotic ointment and bandages on the slices.

"Oh, most of the mess is from the knife on my keychain multitool. I had to hold it in my mouth to cut the zip tie. And it was dark." She was lucky she hadn't nicked an artery.

Even though his expression went black, his hands never lost their gentleness.

After glancing at his brother, Morgan strolled over and leaned his rifle against a tree. "Hey, Erin."

She looked up at him, grateful for the diversion.

He grinned. "Good throw with the knife. You saved my life."

It hadn't been a good throw—the point was supposed to go in first, not the handle. After a moment, she found a real smile. Because he was right. She had kept him from being shot. "That seems fair. You all saved mine."

Her eyes burned as she realized the men really had saved her —and it was over. She met Morgan's eyes. "Thank you."

She repeated it for deVries, and he shrugged as if to say *no big deal.* Then he smiled slightly. "Appreciate you keeping Lindsey from being shot."

Finally, she turned to Wyatt who had packed away the first aid kit and was still crouched beside her. "Thank you."

He touched her cheek so very gently, his dark gaze holding hers. "Anytime, anywhere."

As the men walked farther away, conferring quietly, she leaned against the tree trunk and just...was. Every minute or two, shaking would start in her center, and she'd have to breathe and tell herself she was safe.

"Erin."

She blinked, realizing Wyatt had returned. "Oh, sorry. Time to go?"

He took her hands. "Morgan and deVries will hike back to the cabin and bring the cops and horses here. So they can pack... everything...out."

Everything. The bodies. "Oh."

She tilted her head at a sound. Those were voices, more voices. Fear swept through her. The rest of the gunmen? "Who is here?"

"Shh, shh. Just Logan and Jake. They came up a back trail." Wyatt squeezed her hands. "According to them—and the map—this trail continues, crosses the granite field, goes downward, and curves to come out on Kestrel Mountain Road. The hike is shorter than the one back to the cabin."

She frowned. "What are you trying to say?"

His gaze was gentle. "If you'd rather walk than ride a horse, we can go out that way."

"Walk? The cowboy wants to walk?" She looked at him in disbelief. The man adored riding.

"You're something, slugger." His smile was slow and appreciative. Gently, he flattened his hand over her sore stomach. "Riding a horse, especially on a rough road, can be more difficult than walking. Depends on where and how bad you're hurt. It's your decision."

"Ohhh." He was right. Horses, even walking, were...jolty. "We can walk slow?"

"Absolutely. We can take our time and have someone pick us up on the road." Beneath the dark mustache, his smile was rueful. "The cops will still require us to answer a shitload of questions, but we can avoid the ruckus for a few more hours. If you wish."

Get away from the bodies, the blood. Not have to talk to anyone except Wyatt. "Just you and me?"

"That's right, sweetheart. Just you and me."

"Yes. Please."

CHAPTER THIRTY-FOUR

Wyatt led the way, listening to Erin's footsteps behind him. She'd stumbled frequently at first, but as the distance from the shooting increased, she steadied.

Strong woman.

He still had questions for her. Needed to confirm his guesses as to why Palmer had been focused on kidnapping her. And questioning her, from what he saw at the end.

Why hadn't she answered?

But he could wait.

Reaching the top of a rise, he stopped.

When she joined him, he pointed down into the small valley. "Look."

Sparkling in the sunlight, water spilled from the top of a sheer-faced granite cliff, forming several small waterfalls before splashing into a pond.

Erin's soft gasp of pleasure at the sight was all the reward he needed. "We're going there?"

"Seems like a good place for lunch, don't you think?"

Her smile lit her face like the glow of the moon in a dark sky.

. . .

A half-hour or so later they'd reached the pond. Erin breathed in the cool, moist air. She could hear the water splashing and nothing else. *So peaceful.*

Next to the small pond, Wyatt bent to dip his hand in. "The water's freezing, but how about a quick wash while we're here?"

Wash away the fear sweat and blood...and the feel of *their* hands? The need almost shook her. "Yes, yes, *please.*"

"Go ahead and strip then."

Moving slowly, she removed her clothing. Turning, she saw Wyatt uphill from the stream, holding a tiny bottle.

"You have soap?"

"My emergency supply. It's biodegradable, but still...best to keep it out of the water supply. Come over here." His collapsible pot sat at his feet, full of water.

When she stood in front of him, his dark gaze swept over her. He said something that sounded like a whole bunch of cursing under his breath, then shook his head. "You're going to be sore for a while, slugger."

He was right. Purpling bruises, welts, and scrapes covered her body. "Just call me a human calico cat." She shook her head. "It could've been worse. During Emmett's interrogation, he lost his temper. I hit the floor hard enough it knocked me out, which ended the beating."

Wyatt's growl sounded like the most feral of dogs. He pulled in a breath then frowned. "The others weren't involved?"

Seeing the grimness in his eyes, she realized what he was worried about...and shuddered. "I didn't get raped—just beat up."

"Bad enough." Wyatt frowned. "Interrogation, huh? What was he asking you about?"

"He and Troy were partners in the blackmail scheme, and like Stan thought, the files were on flash drives. Troy hid everything in an old antique clock I'd repaired." She wet her dry lips. "Emmett tortured him to get the location before killing him."

"His own brother? Fuck, that's cold." Wyatt touched her

cheek and smiled. "Speaking of cold, brace yourself, blue girl." He poured the water over her.

"Coooold!" Before she could find an appropriate name to call him, he handed her the bottle of soap. She opened it, and the fragrance of peppermint filled the air. "It smells like you."

"It's what I use in the back country."

She could ask for nothing better than to carry Wyatt's scent, so fresh and clean. As she scrubbed herself down, he fetched another potful and dumped it on her too.

Her breathless squeak made him laugh. Even worse, he ran his fingers over her skin—"still soapy"—and fetched another pot to dump on her.

She shivered as her skin made goosebumps "You're such a sadist."

"No, sugar, that's Morgan." Grinning at her look of shock, he scrubbed himself down. Picking up their clothes, he motioned toward the lake. "Let's sit on the rocks and dry off."

Helping Erin sit on a sun-warmed granite slab beside the water, Wyatt tried to hide his anger. Seeing all the bruises and cuts, the way she moved so painfully. As he rebandaged her wrists, he wanted to revive the bastards and kill them again.

No, Masterson. It's done and over.

He let out a breath and worked on filtering the icy cold water into his canteen, then set out their gourmet lunch—granola bars.

So fucking inadequate.

Erin took a long drink and let out a contented sigh. "Thank you. I..." She glanced behind her toward the mountainside. Toward where she'd almost died. "I needed space."

"I get it. Been there, done that." After she handed back his canteen, he took a few sips before offering up another ugly part of his past. "Last year, a few convicts broke out of prison. They grabbed Gin and another social worker for hostages and headed into the wilderness. Morgan and I were with Atticus at the time, and we went with him to search. We found them—saved Gin and her colleague, but—" He grimaced. He had no problem killing to eat, but to kill a human... It was such a fucking waste of life itself.

"But...?" she asked softly.

"As you can guess, there was violence. I killed one of the convicts."

She studied him before shaking her head. "You are..." Her smile appeared. "A hero. My hero, but a hero. You'd only have gone that far because you needed to save someone."

Gratitude warmed his heart. For her to think of him that way—it was a gift. "He was aiming for Atticus."

"I thought so." She gave a nod. "But I bet the police had a ton of questions."

"Exactly." He kissed her hand—the hand that'd kept the guy with the pistol from killing Morgan.

Jesus, it'd been far too fucking close. And mostly his fault. He'd lost his head when the bastard with the knife grabbed Erin.

Oddly enough, however much he regretted the deaths, he felt no guilt at all this time.

He nuzzled her palm. "The police will be all over us when we reach the road, so let's enjoy the peace while we're here."

"Yes, my Lord and Master." Her adorable smile lightened his heart.

Slowly, she drank more water and took a tentative nibble of a granola bar—before devouring it like a starving kitten.

He handed her another. Hiking—and fear—burned a lot of calories. And any experienced guide knew there was nothing as grounding as feeding the body after a bout of terror.

Finishing his bar, he lay on his back, listening to the splash of the waterfalls, watching the pine tree branches sway in the light breeze.

A minute later, she edged closer, leaned down, and kissed him.

. . .

Erin felt almost whole again. The hike had been what she needed. Oh, she still hurt—a lot—but moving and having to use her senses to stay on her feet had shut off the flashbacks. Left no space to think about what would have happened if Wyatt and the other two hadn't come in time.

She hadn't thought she'd survive. Tears stung her eyes.

"Erin?" Wyatt reached up. Those big hands were so very gentle as he cupped her cheeks.

She tried to smile. "I kind of want to thank you. To celebrate."

"Let's maybe save the celebrating until you can move without wincing." His eyes were dark with concern. For her. "Do you, maybe, want to be held instead?"

She did. She needed…just that. Her eyes were swimming as she nodded. "I'm alive. Because you came for me." A sob caught deep in her aching chest.

"Damn straight. Hey now, sweetheart." He gently drew her down so she lay on top of him. Wrapping her in his muscular arms, he stroked her back. "Let it out. You deserve a good cry."

As if his permission was what she needed, the sobs broke free, and she buried her head against him and bawled like a baby.

When she finally stopped, she felt emptied of everything. Of the fear and the despair and yes, even the anger. With a shuddering sigh, she rubbed her cheek against his chest.

"All better?" He made a soft gruff sound—a patient one. During the storm of weeping, he hadn't tried to comfort her with useless words. He simply rubbed her back and held her.

Gratitude surged inside her. "I love you," she whispered.

His arms tightened for a moment and released before they got painful. He kissed her, long and slow, and so very gently. "I love you too."

CHAPTER THIRTY-FIVE

When Wyatt went downstairs the next morning soon after sunrise, Kallie was making pancakes. Next to her, Sunny was cooking hash browns. Morgan had charge of the sausages.

Under the big table, Patches and Bat waited patiently for their humans to remember what they were due.

"Spoiled little beasts." Picking up a sausage from the platter, Wyatt pinched off a piece, tossed it to Patches. A tinier piece went to the cat. "Mornin', all. Did Virgil get dragged back to the station?"

Sunny snickered. "He's so grumpy. He said he's going to demote Atticus to patrol duty because of all the paperwork you men created."

Scowling, Morgan rubbed his shoulder. "I told him the paperwork would be worse if we'd let the assholes get away. And he hit me."

Laughing, Wyatt asked Kallie. "Are you here just for breakfast, cuz?"

"Of course not." Kallie abandoned her cooking to give him a hard hug. She stayed in his arms, just holding him. "I'm here to check on my guys. You could've died, you dumbass."

And *she* almost had. When a quiver ran through her pint-sized body, he squeezed her back to let her know he was fine, then tugged her hair. "I *knew* I was your favorite cousin."

Her snort sounded suspiciously like a sob.

Morgan winked at him. "Ha, I already collected my hug. Because *I'm* the favorite."

Laughing, she pulled back and swiped her flannel shirt sleeve over her damp eyes. "You two are at the bottom of my list. Virgil wins."

"It's because he's the best," Sunny said smugly. She turned to Wyatt, big blue eyes full of concern. "Where's Erin? Is she all right?"

Now that was a trick question. "She's..."

A soft laugh came from the living room as Erin entered. "She's clean and on her feet. However, I swear, every single bruise hurts worse today."

Wyatt held out his arm, enjoying how she snuggled against him without hesitation. Her tanned skin had color today. He kissed the top of her head and breathed in the vanilla fragrance of her still-damp hair. "You look better."

A corner of her mouth tipped up in a rueful smile. "You look kind of tired. Sorry I woke you up." Her eyelids were swollen from crying after a nightmare.

He traced his fingertips over the small areas of her face that weren't bruised or swollen. *Those fucking assholes.* Removing the anger from his voice, he murmured, "It'll take time for your body and emotions to put things in the past."

She sighed. "How much sleep can you afford to lose?"

The worry in her voice made him gather her carefully in his arms. "As much as it takes." He rubbed his chin on the top of her head. "If you're still waking me up when we're gray-haired, so be it. And if you give me grief like the last time I talked about our senior years, your ass will be bruised along with the rest of you."

A tiny laugh burst from her...but she relaxed. "Brute."

"That's me," he said agreeably.

His cell phone rang, and he pulled it out. "Yo, Virg, what's up?"

"Your reprieve is over. Atticus gave his report, but I need you and Morgan here for your statements. And the Feds in Sacramento want to talk to Erin. They also want the location of Palmer's jump drives."

Having sat in a chair to pet Patches and Bat, Erin was close enough to hear. Her eyes darkened. "I figured I'd have to talk to them. But I need to be there when they go to get the clock."

Wyatt hadn't asked her anything about the location of the drives. He raised his eyebrows in query.

Moving his hand with the phone out of hearing distance, she stood, rising on tiptoes to whisper in his ear, "I gave it to a little boy."

Ah. He whispered back, "In Sacramento?"

She nodded.

"She's willing, but..." He frowned. There was no way he could accompany Erin if he had to talk to the cops. "Morgan and I will be in shortly. For Erin, since I can't be with her, I want Stan—Special Agent Jameson Stanfeld—to accompany her to Sacramento and be with her for everything—interviews, picking up the drives, whatever. He should still be up at Serenity."

"That's quite an ask," Virgil said slowly.

Erin stared up at Wyatt, her eyes big and surprised, as if she hadn't expected him to deal with this bullshit.

"Virg, she's a woman who's been kidnapped and abused by fucking big, violent men. There's no way I'm letting her get surrounded and intimidated by more fucking big assholes, even if they do carry badges."

Virgil laughed. "You're right. I'll arrange it. Stan will enjoy being the good guy and holding her hand as needed."

"So I figured." Wyatt curled his hand around her nape, pulling her closer. "Thanks, bro."

"I'm glad you thought of it. Good job. Figure on her getting picked up in a couple of hours, and after, you get your ass to the station. Send Morgan in now, yeah?"

"Will do."

After breakfast, Wyatt took Erin on a slow hike to his sanctuary, hoping she'd find as much comfort there as he always did. At the pile of river stones, he turned off onto his smaller trail.

Avoiding a muddy spot on the path, he grinned over his shoulder. "Did I remember to compliment you on your anti-tracking skills? Morgan and I noticed it was quite a while before any of your footprints appeared. You did good."

Her face lit with the compliment, then she scowled. "They found me anyway."

"Not because you screwed up. There were only two trails you could take—and the other one had an area where you couldn't have avoided leaving tracks. Process of elimination sent them up your choice. Blue girl, the time they needed to figure out the right trail slowed them enough for us to catch up."

Her smile reappeared.

Down the slope, he walked around the final curve and stepped to one side.

She stopped.

He followed her gaze to where a small creek cascaded down a rocky bed. At the foot of the mountain, it would feed into the stream that ran through all the valley properties. He took a long breath. Despite the dry summer, the moist air here was filled with the scent of green growing plants.

She looked around with a smile. "This is beautiful."

"I thought you'd like it. Pa let his kids and Kallie pick private campsites to give us a place to conquer demons or just escape from everyone else. I used to come here to wrestle with my temper, to sulk about the unfairness of"—he rolled his eyes and grinned—"everything a boy can whine about. It's a wonder he didn't drown me and Morgan just to stop the complaining."

She bumped her shoulder against his and winced, but grinned. "I wasn't the easiest teen either. Around thirteen was when I decided I was horribly neglected, and Mom should've stayed home and tended me rather than politics."

Her poor mother. He laughed.

Moving closer to the creek, she discovered the log bench he'd built, sanded smooth, and coated with spar varnish for a glossy surface. "What beautiful work."

Now didn't that make a man feel good.

"Thank you." He muscled the bench down the bank closer to the stream. "I like putting my feet in the water."

"Yes, me too." Smiling, she settled on the seat, took her sneakers off, and plopped her feet in the gurgling water. Her sigh was delightful.

Following suit, he sat beside her.

"Your space is very peaceful."

"It is." He put an arm around her. "After I killed the convict last summer, I spent a lot of time here, especially after Mallory taught me how to meditate. It helped. I still come here most days when I'm home."

She studied him. "This is where the calm place in your personality comes from?"

"Probably, yeah." He ran his hand up and down her arm. "Since you're going to stay here with me on the ranch..." He paused, waiting for her confirmation.

"You're sure it's all right? With everyone?"

"Yes, blue girl, everyone wants you here. And if you don't want to be here, I'll join you at your place." If it took his entire life, he would teach her how much she was loved.

Her heart was in her eyes as she gave him a wavery smile. "Yes, I'll stay here with you."

"Good. I'd like you to use this spot whenever you need a peaceful place."

"But it's your spot."

"No, sweetheart." He kissed her slowly. "Now it's our spot."

Frickity-frick-frick-frick, she ached like someone had been beating on her. Oh, come to think of it...duh.

Unfortunately the ibuprofen she'd popped before leaving Wyatt's house had worn off as Special Agents Novik and Patel questioned her...and questioned her...and questioned her.

The square box of an interview room held a table, uncomfortable chairs, a camera, and, unfortunately, two special agents.

On the upside, the Homeland Security agent, Stan, who was adorable Dixon's partner, sat beside her, just as Wyatt had requested.

"When you refused to answer Mr. Palmer about where the clock was, what happened?" Special Agent Novik looked like the stereotypical FBI agent: short hair, clean-shaven, dark suit and tie, white shirt. He focused cold blue eyes on her.

As with every time he'd asked that before, her stomach did an unsettling twist. If they kept this up, she was going to puke.

"Easy, sweetheart." Stan took her hand and squeezed it.

Dixon had a surprisingly kind Dom.

His support let her breathe—and the pissed-off expression on Agent Novik's fair face at Stan's sympathy helped her find her backbone. "You know what? I have answered variations of your question at least three times already. Consult your notes if you need the answer again."

Novik sat back as if she'd slapped him.

So, so tempting.

Instead his partner took over. "Ms. Palmer, I—"

"I'm getting the impression you boys are hard of hearing. My name is Erin Lockwood. Says so right on my driver's license... which you've already looked at. Are you deliberately trying to upset me?"

Special Agent Patel had short black hair, brown skin and eyes, and facial features sharp enough to cut wood. "Of course not. Forgive me, Ms. Lockwood. I believe it's time you told us where we can retrieve Palmer's clock."

Again? She turned to Stan. "Does your department do this kind of baloney?"

His lips twitched. "At times. But we try to confine it to the perpetrators, not the victims."

"Huh." She turned her gaze back to Patel. "Am I considered to be a criminal in any way?"

"No, ma'am, you are not. But we do need to get the clock."

"I'm perfectly happy getting the clock for you. As I said before, one of you—and Stan—may *silently* accompany me. Those are the conditions."

"Ms. Lockwood, I don't feel you understand your situation here. If we need to lock you up to get the location of the clock, we will."

She set her hands on the table, turned them over, and watched them tremble. God, she was tired. Looking up, she saw the Feds exchange a satisfied look.

They thought they'd won. Because she was shaking.

"You know, I was shaking yesterday too. When Emmett asked me for the location of the clock. When he beat the hell out of me. When Crow was going to cut parts of my body off."

Patel's mouth dropped open, and Novik's expression went blank.

She almost whispered, "Do you honestly think locking me up and feeding me three times a day is scarier than pain and dying?"

"At this point, darlin', I think we'll step back and ask for a lawyer," Stan said in an icy voice.

Patel held up a hand. "Let's all take a step back here. Ms. Lockwood, I'll accompany you and Special Agent Stanfield, and I will remain silent while you retrieve the clock."

Anger flaring in his eyes, Novik opened his mouth, caught his partner's frown, and sat back.

A little while later, Patel parked the car at the curb in front of where Delilah, Erin's former housekeeper, lived with her daughter and grandson.

Erin had called ahead to be sure Delilah and Bobby were home.

The door opened as Erin walked up. Bobby ran out and grabbed her around the waist in a vigorous hug.

Ow, ow, ow. She clamped her jaw down to keep from yelping or cursing. "Hey, my boy, how are you doing? Are you having an awesome summer?"

"Yeah. I can *swim* now."

"You're taking lessons?"

He grinned, proud enough to bust.

"Good for you."

Delilah stood in the door, frowning at Stan and the Fed, obviously having pegged them as law enforcement and trouble. "Ms. Erin..."

Erin managed to smile. "You're not working for me any longer, so just Erin works."

"All right." Delilah studied Erin, frowned, and glared at the two men. "You—"

Oh, oops. Erin touched her bruised face and noticed Bobby looked upset as well. "Oh, honey, I'm all right. A really bad man hit me." She pulled in a breath and gave Delilah a grim smile. "He'll never hurt anyone again."

"Good to hear." Delilah's smile was equally grim—and approving.

Erin looked down at the boy. "Do you still have the clock I gave you, Bobby?"

When he nodded, she painfully bent to get closer to his level. "It turns out my husband hid bad things in the clock I gave you. The man there is Special Agent Patel, and he works for the FBI."

Bobby's eyes went wide. "Whoa."

"Right." Erin glanced at Delilah and saw the same cynical expression that was probably on her face. "Anyway, the FBI needs to have the clock to do all their criminal investigation stuff. It may take a while, but they'll give it back when they're done." She looked over. "Right, Special Agent Patel?"

"No wonder you..." Comprehension changed his entire expression, and even more so when he smiled at Bobby. "Yes, we will absolutely bring the clock back to you, young man."

Huh, maybe he wasn't as much of a jerk as she'd thought. "Bobby, will you fetch the—"

Stan cleared his throat, stopping her request. "I think it'd help the case if Patel can get photos of where the clock is and bag it there. If you don't mind, ma'am?"

Delilah looked startled for a moment, then tipped her head to Stan. "All right."

Bobby took Erin's hand, and Delilah motioned them in, walking beside Stan toward the back. "You sound like a misplaced Texan."

Stan laughed. "That there would be about right. I'm based out of San Francisco, and once I got past the way the streets go straight up and down, and how fog rolls right off the Bay, I decided it's about as close to heaven as a body could get."

The clock sat on the small table beside Bobby's bed. And, as Stan had said, Patel took one look and got busy taking photos of the clock and the room.

After he dropped the clock into a big bag, he handed Delilah his card. "In case your boy starts wondering when it's coming back."

Delilah laughed. "My grandson, actually."

"Ah, my daughter is expecting her first. My wife and I look forward to being the grands." His smile made him almost likable.

Delilah tapped the card. "Thank you for this. Bobby does love his clock. He says the ticking helps him sleep."

"Oh, how could I forget?" Unslinging her mini-backpack, Erin set it on the bed and unzipped it. Her fingers found what she was looking for. "Here, honey. I brought you a fun substitute."

The cherry-red, vintage clock had tiny flowers painted around the face.

Bobby's eyes widened. "Ooooh."

Erin grinned. "It even has a musical alarm—you'll love it."

A few minutes later, they got into the car, leaving a happy kid behind—and a relieved grandmother. Because the alarm was a soft, sweet tune.

Patel didn't turn on the car. "Before we leave, can we ascertain if the jump drives are in the clock?"

Erin blinked. "Sure. Not a problem. I brought my tools in case Bobby wanted to see the inside of his new clock."

Patel heaved a relieved sigh. "Thank you, Ms. Lockwood." He handed her a pair of gloves, and she donned them and pulled out her small tool kit.

In the back with her, Stan filmed the process as she opened the back. Spotting three memory sticks, she handed the entire clock to Patel.

"There they are." He pursed his lips and blew out. "Such small things to cause so much misery and murder." Shaking his head, he tucked everything back into the evidence bag. "I'll hand the drives over to our computer guys."

After Erin stowed away her tools and tossed the gloves, he turned back around. "I owe you an apology, Ms. Lockwood. I can see why you didn't share the location of the clock." He gave her a respectful nod. "And why you didn't tell Palmer. The boy is very lucky in his friends."

She nodded...and as her eyes filled with tears, she was grateful her phone rang, giving her something to do. Even better, it was Wyatt. "Hey, cowboy."

"Hey, little bit. How's it going there?"

She could hear the concern in his deep voice. No, no, she was not going to act like a watering can.

Too late. She swiped at her eyes. "Surprisingly well. Bobby gave me the clock, and the jump drives were in it. I should be heading back soon."

Stan nodded confirmation.

"Thank fuck." Her cowboy's pleased curse made her laugh.

"All right then. I'll pick up supper from the Mother Lode. And one of those desserts you like since you damn well deserve it." Wyatt's voice had a smile in it. "So if you get home first, you just kick back and take it easy."

The way he said home, like it was where she was supposed to be, like she was part of his life, part of his family...that was everything.

Huh. I guess I'm not going to be a crazy cat lady after all. Just one cat...and Wyatt.

EPILOGUE

After studying the street in front of their booth, Wyatt decided Bear Flat's Mountain Festival was a raging success. Tourists and locals filled the blocked-off downtown street. The sides were lined with booths featuring arts and crafts interspersed with food vendors.

Even better, several of the food booths were the competitors for the best BBQ cook-off. Over the past couple of hours, he'd bribed various children to bring him samples.

There were also demonstrations of frontier crafts—like the candle-maker next to the Masterson's Wilderness Guides' booth. Wyatt had been watching when he wasn't tied up in talking to prospective clients.

Erin liked candles.

As Morgan walked into their booth, Wyatt smiled at the middle-aged couple he'd been talking with and handed them a brochure. "I hope to see you next year."

"You will, for sure." As the woman hauled her partner away, Wyatt could hear her saying, "Let's ask for days off in early June so we can see the wildflowers. And deer babies. I want to see deer babies."

"You're better at this than me or Kallie. You should man the booth for all our events." Morgan handed Wyatt a Coke, more ice than fluid—which was just what he wanted right now. The mid-August day was damn hot.

"Sharing is caring. You're up next." Wyatt took a long gulp. "I'll warn you, it's been busy."

"Oh, great."

Wyatt grinned. His brother liked people but preferred them in small numbers, preferably in a quiet setting. Not in a busy street fair with tourists chattering and kids yelling loud enough to drown out the country-western music from the food-and-beer court.

"I think Becca's photos and brochure design increased the interest we're getting." Wyatt glanced at the dark blue wall behind him covered with enlarged, eye-catching photos of various guide trips. Fishermen showing off their catches, a group of women splashing each other in a stream, families with children on horseback, people riding through a meadow bright with wildflowers.

Good times.

"We're getting a lot of adds to the email list." Wyatt shook his head. "We might have to consider hiring help next summer."

His brother didn't look pleased. "Seriously?"

"Yeah." Wyatt leaned a hip against the table. "Bro, have you seen Kallie's face when she plays with Ansel?"

Admittedly, Becca and Logan's munchkin was cuter than hell.

Comprehension swept over Morgan's face. "Oh. Fuck. Our Kallie wants kids?"

"I'm guessing yes. Not only that... I want to cut back a mite on my schedule next year. Because...Erin." Wyatt shrugged. "When I didn't have anyone, working back-to-back trips was fine. Finishing out this season isn't a problem, but I'm looking ahead."

"Right." Morgan huffed out a breath. "Damn lovebirds. I should've seen this coming."

"We're getting picked off, one-by-one. You're next, bro."

"When pigs fly."

Wyatt only grinned. He'd held the same opinion right up until a little mechanic grabbed her wrench and opened up his heart.

At the end of the street, the band was winding up their set with "Good-hearted Woman." From Stockton, the older musicians had a fondness for Willie Nelson and Waylon Jennings tunes.

Worked for him. Wyatt tapped his boot in time with the music. A small group of people were swing dancing to the music.

Morgan followed his gaze. "Too damn hot."

"No shit." Wyatt drank half the Coke, enjoying the icy bite. "But after it cools off, I'm going to get Erin out there."

At the end of the street, the volunteers for the fair were pulling sawhorses away and motioning people to the sides. The parade was one of the highlights of the small-town festival.

A few antique cars led off, followed by the school's marching band. Horse-drawn floats from various organizations and businesses went by followed by carriages and wagons.

Near the end of the parade came... Damn, those were Erin's go-kart kids. Young Heath Simmons took a hand off the steering wheel to wave.

Erin was walking beside the four small vehicles. Seeing him, she came over. Her face was flushed pink, her eyes sparkling, and she turned to wave at her kids.

"Looks like they're enjoying the hell out of this." Wyatt pulled her behind the booth's table.

"So am I." Erin couldn't stop grinning. Her kids had been given a chance to show off what they could do. "Usually it's the jocks and cheerleaders who get cheered by the town, not nerds and mini mechanics."

Farther down, Marco and Walker, the mechanics from

Pierre's, spotted the go-karts and were whistling louder than the band. They'd become totally invested in the project. Heck, so many people had. Becca had added an artist's special flourishes to the paint jobs—like the flames streaking down the side of Nevaeh's kart.

Seeing the mechanics, Kayden tooted the horn that Erin had helped him rig up in his small kart. And all the people watching the parade cheered for him.

She bounced on her toes. "I love this town."

Wyatt laughed, pulling her against him. "This town loves you, blue girl." He kissed her quickly. "I love you."

Morgan made a disgusted sound. "Get a room. Better yet, go enjoy the festival. I've got the booth."

"All yours, bro." With his big, warm hand wrapped around hers, Wyatt led her out onto the street to follow the last of the parade. The festival goers soon filled the street again, talking about the floats, the band, the go-karts.

Wyatt and Erin collected nods and greetings, and even more people stopped them to ask how she was. The concern warmed her.

Although...there were sure a lot of interested glances at their joined hands.

"Wyatt." Virgil, on duty in his uniform shirt and weapons belt, motioned for them to join him.

"What's up, bro?" Wyatt asked.

"I thought Erin might like an update, and I never seem to catch you two at home." Virgil turned his attention to her, his hazel eyes warm. "Are you doing all right, little bit?"

He was such a big sweetheart. Still worried about her even though it'd been three weeks since her kidnapping.

Her first week had been rough. Wyatt had even taken her on one of his guide trips just to be sure she wouldn't be alone. And Virgil, Sunny, and Morgan had cornered her and told her anytime Wyatt wasn't home, she should come to them if she was lonely, needed company, or a hand to hold.

"I'm fine, Virgil. I am." When he didn't look convinced, she added, "Actually, just knowing you're in the house helps. And hey, I have a giant spoiled Maine Coon cat to share my bed. Bat is excellent company."

"Okay then." Virgil smiled at her. "Since we shared information with the Feds about the mess up at Levi's hunting cabin, they did us the courtesy of updating me on the blackmail issue. Special Agent Patel was revolted at how many powerful people showed up in very incriminating video recordings."

Behind Virgil, one of his officers approached. Levi was followed by his sister, Katelyn.

Virgil continued, "On a better note, the information they recovered from the jump drives led them to a rented house in New York where six children were being held. They'll receive counseling and help in recovering their lives."

"Oh, how wonderful." Erin wanted to cheer. "They're the ones I was worried about."

"You can stop now. And your part in this is over." Virgil smiled at her.

Next to him, Levi edged forward. "Erin, ma'am, I wanted to say I'm sorry for the way I acted. I thought... Well, it doesn't matter. My behavior was unprofessional, and I hope you can forgive me someday."

Beside her, Wyatt stiffened, and his jaw tightened. Her protector.

She squeezed his hand and spoke to Levi. "Honestly, it was scary when you didn't believe me after that man broke into my house." She sighed. People were people—and the prison here had caused a lot of pain. "At the same time, I can understand. You're forgiven."

He nodded. "I learned—and I'll do better if something like this happens again."

There wasn't much more a person could ask.

"Me too. I mean, wanting your forgiveness." Katelyn joined her brother.

Virgil eyed her, then slapped Levi on the shoulder. Both law enforcement officers went back into the station, leaving Erin and Wyatt facing Katelyn.

"I don't understand," Erin frowned. "Forgiveness for...what?"

"Because I told Emmett he could use Levi's hunting cabin. He said he wanted to talk you into leaving with him, to going back to the city, and I..." Katelyn's shoulders slumped. "I hoped if you left maybe Wyatt would look at me."

"Katelyn." Wyatt's voice sounded more like a growl.

"No, Wyatt. I get it." Katelyn closed her eyes for a second. "I'm getting counseling now. Gin—she set me up with Jacob Wheeler. He asked a lot of questions, made me think, and...you know, I'm not much into the BDSM stuff. I don't like pain, and I don't get off on being submissive, but I...I talk a lot. Mom called me her chatterbox, and guys, they eventually stop paying attention to me, but in the club, during a scene... Getting all that attention on me, it's what I always wanted. The counselor helped me see how I got all obsessed by you, Wyatt, only it's more I wanted the attention you gave me and not you."

She pulled in a shuddering breath. "I was a total selfish, horrible bitch to try to break you two up, and I'm sorry."

Wow, what a lot to take in. But it was an apology. Erin shook her head. "Emmett lied to you; that's not your fault. You didn't know he was going to kidnap me."

"I'm glad you figured out what you were looking for," Wyatt said. "Finding a man who'll pay attention might be easier than finding a Dom." He turned his head, looking around, and nodded toward a man across the street.

The guy was huge. Erin had seen him before in the Claim-Jumper—maybe with a bunch of the loggers? He was staring at them.

At Katelyn.

The corners of Wyatt's eyes crinkled as he tilted his head for Katelyn to look. "I think he'd happily listen to you talk as much as you like."

"Barney?" She shook her head, then stopped. Looked at the huge man again. "He's..."

"Not a teen anymore? Wiser than he used to be?" Wyatt half-smiled. "None of us are the same as we were in high school. You might give him a chance."

"Maybe...maybe so." Katelyn took a step away and paused. "Thank you."

Letting go of any hard feelings, Erin smiled at her. "Good luck."

As the woman wove her way through the crowd, Wyatt pulled Erin into his arms. "You're a damn nice person. I think you deserve ice cream."

Wyatt was thoroughly enjoying watching Erin discover the joys of a small-town festival. The first few times someone called out to her, she'd been surprised. Now she not only waved back enthusiastically but called out her own greetings.

Fuck, she was cute.

When they reached the end of the blocked-off street, Wyatt noticed sawhorses off to the right on a side street. The blockade narrowed the ingress to allow only one person through at a time. "Shutting down Gold Dust Avenue wasn't in the festival plans."

In the blocked-off area were several people. Their attention was on something in the middle of the street, but he couldn't tell what was happening. Had someone died?

Erin tilted her head. "That's Atticus in there."

Curious, Wyatt walked between the sawhorses, still holding Erin's hand. "Yo, Att. What's up?" But as he slipped between two people, he saw what was going on—and laughed.

The center of the street had been turned into a go-kart track. The children who'd built the karts were getting to play—and letting other kids have a turn.

Nerds rule.

"Erin." Mallory left Sawyer's side to give her a hug and a

quick once-over look. Her smile was warm. "You look good, all bright colors, the darkness almost completely gone."

Wyatt exchanged a pleased smile with Sawyer. Everyone knew Mallory could see auras, and her words indicated Erin was healing from the past. Damn, it made him feel good.

Leaving Jake, Kallie pulled him off to one side. "Hey, Wyatt. The trip I'm guiding next weekend is for couples, but they want to add in three more couples. I need another guide. Want to come help and bring Erin?"

"Huh." Wyatt glanced over to see her still talking to Mallory. Erin wanted to join him on more trips. "Maybe. Let me ask my woman."

Kallie bumped his arm. "Uncle Harvey used to say that all the time. *'Let me ask the missus.'* You sound just like him at times."

There was a first-rate compliment. Pa had been one of the finest men Wyatt knew. And had won himself one of the best women—another way Wyatt hoped to be like him.

And now look...

He smiled as he watched two youngsters drag Erin over to a go-kart. Saw Erin ignore the dirt and rough road to get right down on the ground, checking beneath the kart. She called out an order, and Heath Simmons ran over with a screwdriver and wrench.

A minute later, Erin sat up and motioned to the kart. The girls piled in, fired it up, and screaming their happiness, were on the track.

Forearms on her knees, Erin just sat and watched. The sun glinted off her blue and blonde hair, her hands were dirty, and grease smeared one high cheekbone.

Laughing, Heath dropped down beside her on her left, another kid took her right, both waving hands as they chattered away...and she listened with all her heart.

When one boy took a breath, Erin glanced over and smiled at Wyatt, all her love in her eyes.

And his heart turned right into a sentimental gooey puddle. Fuck, he loved her.

Yo, Mom. Look—I found her. The one for me.

ALSO BY CHERISE SINCLAIR

Masters of the Shadowlands Series

Club Shadowlands

Dark Citadel

Breaking Free

Lean on Me

Make Me, Sir

To Command and Collar

This Is Who I Am

If Only

Show Me, Baby

Servicing the Target

Protecting His Own

Mischief and the Masters

Beneath the Scars

Defiance

The Effing List

It'll Be An Adventure

Mountain Masters & Dark Haven Series

Master of the Mountain

Simon Says: Mine

Master of the Abyss

Master of the Dark Side

My Liege of Dark Haven

Edge of the Enforcer

Master of Freedom
Master of Solitude
I Will Not Beg
Master of the Wilderness

The Wild Hunt Legacy
Hour of the Lion
Winter of the Wolf
Eventide of the Bear
Leap of the Lion
Healing of the Wolf
Heart of the Wolf

Sons of the Survivalist Series
Not a Hero
Lethal Balance
What You See
Soar High

Standalone Books
The Dom's Dungeon
The Starlight Rite

ABOUT THE AUTHOR

Cherise Sinclair is a *New York Times* and *USA Today* bestselling author of emotional, suspenseful romance. She loves to match up devastatingly powerful males with heroines who can hold their own against the subtle—and not-so-subtle—alpha male pressure.

Fledglings having flown the nest, Cherise, her beloved husband, an eighty-pound lap-puppy, and one fussy feline live in the Pacific Northwest where nothing is cozier than a rainy day spent writing.